THE BELIEVERS

THE
BELIEVERS

Zoë Heller

WORCESTERSHIRE COUNTY COUNCIL
CULTURAL SERVICES

WINDSOR
PARAGON

First published 2008
by Fig Tree
This Large Print edition published 2009
by BBC Audiobooks Ltd
by arrangement with Penguin Books Ltd

Hardcover ISBN: 978 1 408 42975 4
Softcover ISBN: 978 1 408 42976 1

British Library Cataloguing in Publication Data available

Printed and bound in Great Britain by
CPI Antony Rowe, Chippenham and Eastbourne

For Mary Parvin

The challenge of modernity is to live without illusions and without becoming disillusioned.

Antonio Gramsci

PROLOGUE

LONDON, 1962

At a party in a bedsit just off Gower Street, a young woman stood alone at the window, her elbows pinned to her sides in an attempt to hide the dark flowers of perspiration blossoming at the armholes of her dress. The forecast had been for a break in the week-long heatwave, but all day the promised rain had held off. Now, the soupy air was crackling with immanent brightness and pigeons had begun to huddle peevishly on window ledges. Silhouetted against the heavy, violet sky, the Bloomsbury rooftops had the unreal, one-dimensional look of pasted-on figures in a collage.

The woman turned to survey the room, wearing the braced, defiant expression of someone trying not to feel her solitude as a disadvantage. Most of the people here were students and, aside from the man who had brought her, she knew no one. Two men had separately approached her since she had been standing at the window, but fearful of being patronized she had sent them both away. It was not a bad thing, she told herself, to remain composed on the sidelines while others grew careless and loud. Her aloofness, she fancied, made her intriguing.

For some time now, she had been observing a tall man across the room. He looked older than the other people at the party. (Casting about in the exotic territory of old age, she had placed him in his early thirties.) He had a habit of massaging his

1

own arms, as if discreetly assessing their muscularity. And from time to time, when someone else was talking, he raised one leg and swung his arm back in an extravagant mime of throwing a ball. He was either very charming or very irritating: she had not yet decided.

'He's an American,' a voice said.

Audrey turned to see a blonde woman smiling at her slyly. She was wearing a violently green dress and a lot of recklessly applied face powder that had left her nose and chin a queer orange colour quite distinct from the rest of her complexion. 'A lawyer,' she said, gesturing across the room at the tall man. 'His name's Joel Litvinoff.'

Audrey nodded warily. She had never cared for conspiratorial, female conversation of this sort. Its assumption of shared preoccupations was usually unfounded in her experience, its intimacies almost always the trapdoor to some subterranean hostility.

The woman leaned in close so that Audrey could feel the damp heat of her breath in her ear. The man was from New York, she said. He had come to London as part of a delegation, to brief the Labour Party on the American civil rights movement. 'He's frightfully clever, apparently.' She lowered her eyelids confidentially. 'A Jew, you know.'

There was a silence. A small breeze came in through the gap in the window where it had been propped open with books. 'Would you excuse me?' Audrey said.

'Oh!' the woman murmured as she watched Audrey walk away.

Pressing her way through the crowd, Audrey

2

wondered whether she had dealt with the situation correctly. There was a time when she would have lingered to hear what amusing or sinister characteristic the woman attributed to the man's Jewishness—what business acumen or frugality or neurosis or pushiness she assigned to his tribe—and then, when she had let the incriminating words be spoken, she would have gently informed the woman that she was Jewish herself. But she had tired of that party game. Embarrassing the prejudices of your countrymen was never quite as gratifying as you thought it would be; the countrymen somehow never embarrassed enough. It was safer on the whole to enjoy your moral victory in silence and leave the bastards guessing.

Audrey halted now at the sound of someone calling her name. Several yards to her left, a stout red-haired youth was standing between two taller men in an unwitting turret formation. This was Martin Sedge, her date for the evening. He was waving and beckoning, making little smoky swirls in the air with his cigarette: 'Audrey! Come over here!'

Audrey had met Martin three months before, at a conference of the Socialist Labour League in Red Lion Square. Despite being one year her junior, he was much more knowledgeable about political theory—much more experienced as an activist—than she was and this inequality had given their friendship a rather pedagogical cast. They had been out together four times, always to the same grimy pub round the corner from where Audrey worked, and on each of these occasions their conversation had swiftly lapsed into tutorial mode, with Audrey sipping demurely at her shandy, or nibbling at a pickled egg, while Martin sank pints of beer and pontificated.

She did not mind being talked at by Martin. She was keen to improve herself. (On the flyleaf of the diary she was keeping that year, she had inscribed Socrates' words: 'I know nothing except the fact of my ignorance.') There was a girlish, renunciatory streak in her that positively relished Martin's dullness. What better proof could there be of her serious-mindedness—her rejection of the trivial—than her willingness to spend the spring evenings in a saloon bar, absorbing a young man's dour thoughts on the Fourth International?

Tonight, however, Martin seemed at pains to cast off his austere instructor's persona. In deference to the weather, and to the festive nature of the occasion, he had foregone his pilled Shetland jumper in favour of a short-sleeved shirt that revealed pink, ginger-glazed forearms. Earlier in the evening, when he had met Audrey at Warren Street tube station, he had kissed her on the cheek—a gesture never hazarded before in the short history of their acquaintance.

'Audrey!' he bellowed now as she approached. 'Meet my mates! Jack, Pete, this is Audrey.'

Audrey smiled and shook Jack and Pete's wet hands. Up close, the three men were a small anthology of body odours.

'You out of drink?' Martin asked. 'Give me your glass and I'll get you another. It's bedlam in that kitchen.'

Left alone with Audrey, Jack and Pete fixed her with frankly assessing gazes. Audrey glanced away shyly. Some of the more daring girls in the room had removed their stockings, she noticed. She

4

could see their poultry-white legs flashing in and out of the party's undergrowth, like torchlight in a forest.

'So,' Jack said, 'you're Audrey. We've heard a lot about you.'

'Vice versa,' Audrey said.

'Sorry?' Pete leaned forward.

Audrey paused, wondering if she had used the phrase correctly. 'I've heard a lot about you too,' she said.

Pete lifted his chin and slowly lowered it, as if a great mystery had now been solved. 'Bloody hot, isn't it?'

'Yes!' Audrey was wondering how to proceed with the exchange when a bearded man appeared behind Jack and Pete and planted his meaty hands on their shoulders.

'You made it!' he cried. 'How are you two old bastards? Are you having a good time?'

'Tom!' Jack and Pete cried in unison.

Their host, Tom McBride, was a postgraduate student at the LSE, notorious for his rabble-rousing activities in the student union and for the inordinate length of time he had been working on his doctoral thesis. Martin had spoken of him in worshipful tones, but Audrey, examining him at close quarters for the first time, felt an instinctive hostility. He was cocky, she thought. And there was something upsettingly pubic about his beard.

'Sorry, love,' he said, glancing at her incuriously, 'I don't know your name.'

'Audrey Howard,' she replied. 'I'm a friend of Martin Sedge's.'

'Friend of—oh, Martin? Glad to have you, Audrey!' He turned back to Jack and Pete. 'Now, you two, I want you to meet someone.' He pointed to a man standing behind him. It was the man Audrey had been watching: the American. 'Joel!' Tom cried. 'Meet Jack and Pete.' Pink with pleasure at receiving the imprimatur of Tom's attention, Jack and Pete smiled eagerly at the stranger. 'Joel is an American lawyer,' Tom told them, 'but don't hold that against him. He's quite a subversive, really.'

In spite of this recommendation, a certain hardness entered Jack and Pete's expressions. Americans, it seemed, were one of the categories of person to whom they felt reliably superior.

Joel smiled and bent towards Audrey. 'Excuse my rude friend for not introducing us. Did I hear that your name was Audrey?'

Audrey nodded.

'Joel and I were just talking about Paul Robeson,' Tom went on. 'Did you see that he's been admitted to hospital again? Exhaustion, they're saying. It turns out that Joel here has met him.'

'Well, only very briefly,' Joel corrected. 'As a kid, I used to go to this summer camp called Wo-Chi-Ca—the Workers' Children's Camp—in New Jersey. One summer, when I was twelve, Paul Robeson made an overnight visit.'

He had the American trick of seeming to smile even as he was talking. And he was stooping slightly, Audrey noticed, as if attempting to minimize the height difference between himself and the Englishmen. *He wants to be liked*, she thought.

'He was a big hero of ours, obviously,' Joel was saying, 'so we were thrilled. He toured the whole

6

camp and then, in the evening, after he'd sung for us in the dining hall, he made this little speech, asking us to dedicate our lives to fighting injustice. The whole place went nuts. We were all ready to go out then and there and lay down our lives for this guy. Anyway, the next morning, I happened to wake up early, needing to pee, and instead of walking all the way to the boys' latrines, I broke camp rules and went around the back of my cabin, into the woods. Just as I'm standing there, doing my business, who comes around the corner but Robeson! He's come to take a leak too! He doesn't skip a beat when he sees me. He just smiles and says—you know, in that incredible voice—"I guess you and I are the early risers around here." Then he goes and finds himself a tree and does his thing. So, you can imagine, now I'm completely overwhelmed. I've got the hero of the American communist movement standing right in front of me and both of us have got our dicks out. "Oh, yes, sir," I say. "I love to get up early." Although, in point of fact, this was probably the earliest I'd ever been up in my life. And Robeson says—'

Martin appeared at Audrey's side, holding two paper cups of red wine. 'Sorry about the delay. Some bloody idiot went and lost the corkscrew—'

Audrey put a finger to her lips to silence him.

'Oh! Sorry!' Martin said, glancing at Joel and hunching his shoulders in exaggerated remorse. 'Didn't mean to interrupt.'

Joel smiled good-naturedly and went on. 'So Robeson says to me, "That's an excellent habit, young man, and I advise you to keep it up. Life is too short to waste it laying a-bed." And then, while I'm still thinking of something smart to say, he

7

steps away from the tree, buttons his fly and walks off.'

There was a moment's mystified silence. Somewhere in the telling—perhaps when Martin had been shushed—the expectation of a punchline had been created. Tom gave a bark of ersatz laughter. 'Ha! Just walked off, did he? Well!'

'Fascinating,' Martin commented drily.

'This camp you went to sounds very interesting,' Audrey said, eager to help the American recover.

Joel nodded. 'Yeah, it was a sweet place. A little kooky. Instead of telling ghost stories around the campfire, we used to sing songs of praise to Uncle Joe and take pledges not to tell jokes that made fun of anyone.' He laughed. Jack and Pete, suspecting something decadent in his amusement, pursed their lips. Once again, the conversation seemed to die away.

'I feel so sorry for Paul Robeson,' Audrey volunteered. 'He's suffered so much.'

'*Robeson*?' Martin said disbelievingly. He was still smarting from being silenced. 'Paul Robeson suffers in a very good coat and an excellent car. I wouldn't waste too much sympathy on him if I were you.'

'Well, we don't have to ration our sympathy, do we?' Audrey replied. 'It's not as if it's going to run out.'

Martin blinked at her, bewildered by this unexpected betrayal. 'Oh, come *on*, Audrey,' he said with an unconvincing titter. 'No one takes Robeson seriously any more. He's still defending Hungary, for God's sake!' He glanced around the group, seeking support. Jack and Pete nodded, but remained silent.

'I think you're being a little hasty, there,' Joel said.

'Really?' Martin's face had the panicky look of someone realizing that he has swum too far from shore.

'I don't share all of Robeson's positions,' Joel said, 'but I think the guy has earned our—'

'It's always seemed to *me*,' Martin interrupted, 'that Robeson is basically a minstrel figure.'

'Whoah!' Tom cried.

'You don't really mean that,' Joel said. 'Or, for your sake, I hope you don't.' All trace of the ingratiating anecdotalist had now disappeared. 'Paul Robeson has done more for humanity than you or I will ever do.'

'*Humanity*, eh?' Martin smiled at the sentimentality of the American's vocabulary. 'Well, I'm sorry! I'm obviously trampling on some very important childhood memory.'

Joel made a weary gesture, batting Martin's sarcasm away. 'Ach . . . grow up, would you?'

A redness appeared on Martin's neck and quickly spread northward, like wine filling a glass. 'Yeah?' he said. 'Well, maybe *you* should grow up, mate . . .' His Adam's apple was bobbing grotesquely. His eyes were glittering with tears. For a moment, Audrey and the other men stood motionless, caught up in the compelling spectacle of his humiliation.

Tom raised his palms in a peace-making gesture. 'Come on, everyone . . .'

But Martin would not be placated. With a disgusted shake of his head, he stalked away. Audrey hesitated a moment, searching for some loophole in the laws of etiquette that might spare

9

her from having to pursue him. Then, with a polite nod to the men, she departed also.

After Jack and Pete had slunk off, Joel turned to Tom. 'That girl,' he said, 'what was her last name?'

'Horton, I think. No . . . Howard.'

'Pretty, wasn't she? Is she one of mine?'

'What?'

'Is she Jewish?'

Tom thought that she probably was—she had had a distinctly beaky, Hebrew look about her—but not wishing to give his friend the impression that the matter of Audrey's ethnicity was significant to him, he made a show of being startled by the question. 'Christ, I don't know. I've never met her before—' He broke off, distracted by some commotion on the other side of the room. A crowd of people was gathered around the window, exclaiming loudly. 'Well, thank God for that,' he said, peering over the heads of his guests. 'It's raining at last.'

*   *   *

'This is the rude American from last night,' Joel said, when he called the next day.

'Oh,' Audrey said, 'you're not rude.'

'I would have called earlier,' Joel went on, 'but it took me a while to find your number. Do you know how many A. Howards there are in the phone directory? I've spoken to most of them this morning.'

'You didn't need—'

'I wanted to apologize for my behaviour last night. I think I upset your boyfriend.'

'He's not my boyfriend.'

10

There was a brief silence as they registered the eagerness with which she had disowned Martin.

'And you don't need to apologize,' she went on. 'He was very badly behaved.'

On the way home from the party, she and Martin had taken shelter from the rainstorm under a shop awning on Tottenham Court Road and Martin had tried to kiss her. Prompted by a hazy sense of indebtedness, she had let him at first. But the gluey sensation of his tongue in her mouth had defeated the compliant instinct and, after a few moments, she had reared away. 'I'm sorry,' she told him, 'I can't.'

'Don't be daft,' Martin had grunted, pulling her towards him.

For a while, they had struggled—lurching clumsily back and forth, like boxers locked in a hostile embrace; then one of Audrey's pumps had fallen off into the road with a clatter and Martin had released her. 'You know what you are?' he had panted as she bent down in the gutter to retrieve her shoe. 'A fucking cocktease is what you are . . .'

'Well, you're very kind,' Joel was saying now, 'but I'd still like to make it up to you. Might I take you for a coffee or a drink some time?'

'I—'

'The catch is, I have meetings all day and evening Monday and I'm leaving Tuesday morning to go back to the States, so it's really got to be today.'

'Oh dear . . .'

'You're booked up?'

'Well, yes. I'm going to visit my parents this afternoon.'

'Hmm. And I guess you're the kind of good

11

daughter who wouldn't put your parents off just to come and have a drink with a fellow you hardly know?'

Audrey considered this.

'Okay,' Joel said, mistaking her hesitation for refusal, 'I guess I'll have to come with you to your parents.'

She laughed. 'I don't think that would work. They live in Chertsey.'

'Sure it would!' he said, warming to the role of determined suitor. 'I love Chertsey! Where is it?'

'It's an hour and a half on the train.'

'Fine! I love trains! I'll be very well-behaved, I promise.'

'I'm not sure you . . . I mean, I don't think you'd find it very amusing.'

'Let me worry about that.'

She thought for a moment. And then, to her surprise, she said yes.

*   *   *

They met at two under the clock at Waterloo. The previous night's downpour had slackened off to a steady grey drizzle and Joel was wearing a pristine, cream-coloured raincoat that seemed to glow in the dim light of the station. Audrey, who at the last minute had rejected the servile implications of trying to look pretty, arrived in an anorak and an odd little rain bonnet made of transparent plastic.

'You see, I made it!' Joel exclaimed.

'Yes, you did!'

They laughed, a little stunned by the impetuousness with which they had undertaken this adventure.

12

Once aboard the train, a silence fell upon them and they took refuge in the view—pretending to be engrossed by the vignettes of rain-blurred suburbia slipping by their window: a woman standing, hands on hips, in the junk-filled backyard of a terraced house; a black dog racing across a sodden football field; a lone youth at a bus stop, dipping a spidery hand into his steaming bouquet of chips.

From Audrey's anxious host's perspective, these scenes seemed ridiculously melancholic: a parody of English drear. She blushed angrily at the dowdiness of her country—at the folly of having brought this man to survey it. And to think that she had counted on the train journey providing the picturesque portion of the trip! She glanced at Joel, still tightly wrapped in his embarrassing mackintosh, and wondered if she ought to warn him about her parents. He was looking down the corridor now, at the slow advance of a railway employee pushing a tinkling trolley of tea and buns. Turning to meet Audrey's eyes, he smiled. His teeth were as white and symmetrical as bathroom tiles.

Joel was wondering if perhaps he had been wrong to insist on this outing. Who knew what quaint rules of English etiquette he was forcing the girl to break by thrusting himself upon her like this? Perhaps she feared for her virtue. Perhaps . . . no, he wasn't going to worry about it. He wasn't going to let anything spoil the fun. This was his first trip to London—his first trip outside North America. There was nothing his gaze lit upon that did not remind him of his intrepidity. The faded red leather of the train seats. The splendid dilapidation of that station they had just left. The

13

way Audrey sat across from him so stiffly, clutching her unbecoming rain bonnet in her fist. She was, he had decided, impossibly, romantically English: a figure out of—well, out of a book about English people.

He began to tell her about himself. He described his work with the Freedom Riders in Georgia and Mississippi. 'Negroes are the most disenfranchised people in America,' he said, 'and they're up against the most powerful people in America: the white establishment.' He joked about the time he had been kicked by a police captain in the bus station in Jackson. He mentioned, with what he hoped was appropriate humbleness, that he had recently been asked by the Reverend Martin Luther King to join his legal team. He showed her a piece of paper on which he had copied out a quote from Justice Oliver Wendell Holmes: 'As life is action and passion, it is required of a man that he should share the passion and action of his time, at peril of being judged not to have lived.' 'I carry that with me everywhere I go,' he said. 'Just to remind myself.'

Audrey nodded, trying to hide her alarm. She did not know who Justice Oliver Wendell Holmes was, or what the word 'disenfranchised' meant. She had never met a Negro.

Joel looked at her, feeling baffled and bad-tempered. Why did she not say anything? Why did she not congratulate him on the valour of his deeds, or show surprise that a man of his accomplishments was paying such courtly attention to her?

'You haven't told me anything about yourself,' he said, wondering if perhaps he had missed some

14

crucial fact of her biography that would explain her self-possession.

Her reply was a little reluctant—she was not as used to treating herself as a topic of conversation as he was—but she seemed to give up the facts truthfully enough. Her parents were Polish, she told him. (The original family name was Holcman.) She had grown up in Hackney, the younger of two sisters. Her father was a tailor—now retired, owing to a heart condition. She had left school at sixteen. She worked as a typist for an import-export business in Camden Town.

'You and I are both workers then,' he said with a smile. 'Not like those kids last night.' It was as he had thought. She was without distinction. This female dignity, unsupported by status or money, was a wondrous act of levitation, to be sure. But he was anxious to have it done with now—to be told the trick of it. A girl who could *never* be talked down to would be a little exhausting in the long run.

*　　　*　　　*

Audrey's parents lived on the ground floor of a small shabby-looking house just behind Chertsey High Street. The rain had turned its red brick to a sombre shade of brown. When the front door opened, an unpleasant, complicated smell of old meals gusted out from the interior. The woman who answered the door was white-haired and drastically fat. Her vast bosom strained against the confines of her floral housecoat; her swollen feet spilled over the edges of her slippers like rising dough escaping its pan. Audrey spoke quickly in

Polish. After a moment or two, the woman's face lit up with understanding and she extended a chubby hand to Joel. 'Come,' she said in a heavy Polish accent. 'You are welcome.' Her forlorn smile acted on her face like a stone thrown in water. Flesh rippled; chins multiplied. Only now, as he entered the dank house, did it dawn on him that this must be Audrey's mother.

In the hallway, another door opened and he was thrust into a tiny, hot, ornament-choked room where an elderly man sat slumped before an electric bar heater. Audrey and the mother both began speaking to him at once in Polish. While he listened, the man gazed at Joel appraisingly. At length, he smiled, just as his wife had done, and stood up to greet the visitor.

Mr Howard was as slender and wizened as his wife was wide and pneumatic. When he and Joel shook hands, his tendons crackled like chicken bones in the young man's firm grasp. Joel was relieved of his coat and a cat was brusquely shooed from a crumbling, doily-covered chair. Audrey and Mrs Howard left the room to make tea.

'So, you like England?' Mr Howard asked as Joel sat down.

'Oh yes, very much,' Joel assured him. The room in which they were sitting faced on to the street, so he had to strain to hear Mr Howard's soft voice over the sounds of playing children and passing cars outside. Periodically, the shadow of a pedestrian would loom up against the net curtains, making him start.

'But the business opportunities are not so good as in America?' Mr Howard asked. His face, with its sunken cheeks and rheumy eyes, could have

16

been the symbol for misfortune on a tarot card.

Joel paused. 'No, I guess not.'

'America is top place for business,' Mr Howard said. 'If I had my life over again, I would go to America. But now, is too late.'

He stared at Joel, as if daring him to challenge this melancholy conclusion.

Joel nodded. He was beginning to feel slightly panicked by the heat and squalor of the room. The chair that he was sitting on smelled strongly of cat pee. Mr Howard's sweater was dotted with food stains. Whatever malaise hung over this house could not be attributed to poverty, he thought. Cleanliness cost nothing, after all. His own parents, poor as they were, had always kept a spotless home. To this day, his mother would insist on boiling the antimacassars if company was coming. No, the dirt and disorder here suggested a failure of will, a moral collapse of some kind.

'It's very kind of you to let me intrude on your Sunday afternoon like this,' he said.

Mr Howard waved the comment away. 'How much do you pay your workers? What is average wage in America?' he asked.

It occurred to Joel that Mr Howard was under some misapprehension about what he did for a living. He was talking as if Joel were a businessman. Joel decided against correcting the error. He did not want to risk contradicting whatever Audrey had chosen to tell her parents about him. And, in any case, it seemed pedantic to insist on the truth when Mr Howard was clearly so engaged by the falsehood. Remembering his traveller's worldliness, he gamely rose to the challenge of posing as an entrepreneur.

17

Presently Audrey and her mother returned with the tea things. Audrey poured. Mrs Howard dispensed biscuits and beamed at Joel as he ate one. Mr Howard said something to Audrey. 'He says you're a clever man,' Audrey translated. Heartened by the father's good opinion and the mother's feminine twitter, Joel grew expansive. He admired Mrs Howard's teaset and affected to be interested in her description of its provenance. He listened, with a subtle knitting of his brow, to Mr Howard's sorrowful account of his heart problems. He related funny stories about his time in England and complained light-heartedly about the awful weather. Mr and Mrs Howard chuckled in their muted, unhappy way, and told Audrey— Audrey was the medium for all compliments—that Mr Joel ought to be on the stage.

Later, when both parents had briefly left the room, Joel turned to Audrey. 'I'm having a great time,' he said gallantly. 'Your father is terrific.' He paused, fearing that this last remark might have stretched credibility. But Audrey did not cringe, or challenge the generosity of the judgement.

'Yes,' she agreed. 'He's a very good man.'

Her loyalty startled him. Even now, at the age of thirty-two, Joel was still prone to roll his eyes behind his parents' backs when presenting them to his friends.

After a couple of hours, Audrey said it was time to go. Mrs Howard protested, but Audrey prevailed. Coats were fetched. There were more handshakes. Mrs Howard kissed Joel on the cheek. The door clicked shut and they were back out on the street, breathing in the blessed coolness of the damp evening. Joel felt buoyant. He had handled the queer little episode very well, he thought. And now that he was freed from the greenhouse heat of that terrible front room, the visit was beginning to seem funny: a rich addition to his store of experience.

On the train journey back to London, Audrey was silent and formidably erect in her seat. Joel watched her anxiously. He would have liked to touch her, but he could think of no physical approach that would not seem brutish. As he considered how they would accomplish their goodbyes at the station, a gloomier view of the day began slowly to assert itself. Those parents had not really been amusing at all, he thought. They—and the great, unspecified sadness of their house—had been awful. What a silly adventure this had been: how pointless to have spent one of his last days in London chasing after a girl! In forty-eight hours he would be gone and they would never see each other again.

When they disembarked at Waterloo, he turned to Audrey with a resigned smile. 'That was great. Thank you for taking pity on a foreign visitor.'

'It was my pleasure,' Audrey said, ignoring his outstretched hand. 'Shall we go back to your hotel?'

*　　　*　　　*

He was staying, along with all the other Americans in his delegation, at a place in Bayswater—a tatty Greek-owned establishment, with a grandiose foyer. He wondered if there would be a fuss about taking a woman to his room, but the desk clerk barely glanced at Audrey when he handed over the

19

key.

Up in the spartan, high-ceilinged room, with its little sink, marbled green by the dripping tap, Audrey took off her damp shoes and socks and then her anorak. Joel noticed for the first time her long and elegant arms. 'What a funny place,' she was saying as he bent down to kiss her. 'Have you been lonely staying here?'

Later, as they lay in bed together, he made a joking allusion to the difference in their ages. 'I was practically in puberty when you were born,' he said. 'Is it strange to be with such an old man?'

'Don't fish.'

'Huh?'

'For compliments, I mean.' Audrey bit at her thumbnail. It was unclear to her when their conversation had taken on its bantering, facetious tone. Perhaps it was she who had introduced it. She would have liked, in any case, to dispense with it now. She was still new to sex and uncertain of its etiquette, but she had an idea that post-coital conversation ought to be franker, kinder than this.

Joel laughed uneasily. He was growing tired of being at a disadvantage. Why had she done this, he wondered? No woman had ever given herself to him so quickly and with so little protest. She had behaved like—like a slut. And even now, there was no meekness or remorse in her. He wanted to say something that would reassert his dominance, something to make her blush or stutter.

'I think I should take you back to New York with me,' he announced.

She was silent for a moment, trying to piece together her meagre impressions of that far-off, spiky city.

20

'Yup,' he said, 'that's what I should do: marry you and take you to New York. What do you think of that?'

She sat up and looked around the room, at her rain bonnet lying in the sink, at her damp skirt crumpled on the floor. To be married. To be married to this man!

'What do you think?' he repeated, grinning.

The future was rushing up at her now. They would live together in an 'apartment'. In a skyscraper, perhaps. They would be comrades in the fight against injustice, sharing the action and passion of their time. They would go on marches and hold cocktail parties attended by all their Negro friends . . .

'Take me,' she said quietly.

'What?'

'Take me,' she repeated. 'I want to go.'

Part One

NEW YORK, 2002

CHAPTER ONE

At dawn, on the top floor of a creaking house in Greenwich Village, Joel and Audrey lay in bed. Through a gap in the curtains, a finger of light extended slowly across their quilt. Audrey was still far out to sea in sleep. Joel was approaching shore—splashing about in the turbulent shallows of a doze. He flailed and crooned and slapped irritably at his sheets. Presently, when the rattling couplets of his snores reached one of their periodic crescendos, he awoke and grimaced in pain.

For two days now, he had been haunted by a headache: an icy clanking deep in his skull as if some sharp-edged metal object had come loose and were rolling about in there. Audrey had been dosing him with Tylenol and urging him to drink more water. But it wasn't liquids or pills he needed, he thought: it was a mechanic. He lay for a few moments, holding the back of his hand to his brow like a Victorian heroine with the vapours. Then he sat up bravely and fumbled for his spectacles on the crowded bedside table. In a matter of hours, he would be giving the defence's opening argument in the case of *The United States of America v. Mohammed Hassani*. Last night, before falling asleep, he had made some last-minute amendments to his prepared address and he was anxious to look them over:

Sometimes, in our earnest desire to protect

this great country of ours, we can and do make errors. Errors that threaten to undermine the very liberties we are trying to protect. I am here to tell you that the presence of Mohammed Hassani in this courtroom today is one such error.

He squinted into the middle distance, trying to gauge the effectiveness of his rhetoric. Hassani was one of the Schenectady Six—a group of Arab Americans from upstate New York who had visited an Al-Qaeda training camp in Afghanistan during the spring of 1998. Over the last two months, the five other members of the group had all made deals with the prosecutors. But Joel hated to make deals: at his urging, Hassani had held out and pled innocent to all charges.

You have been told that Mohammed Hassani is a supporter of terrorism. You have been told that he hates America and wants to aid and abet those who would destroy it. Allow me to tell you, now, who Mohammed Hassani really is. He is an American citizen with three American children and an American wife to whom he has been married for fifteen years. He is a grocer, a small businessman, the sponsor of a Little League team—a person who has lived and worked in upstate New York all his life. Does he possess strong religious beliefs? Yes. But remember, ladies and gentlemen, whatever the prosecution tries to suggest, it is not Islam that is on trial in this courtroom. Has Mr Hassani voiced criticisms of American foreign policy?

26

Certainly. Does this fact make him a traitor? No, it does honour to the constitutional freedoms upon which our country was founded.

*   *   *

The basis of Joel's argument was that his client had been taken to the training camp under false pretences. One of his acquaintances at the mosque he attended in Schenectady had deliberately misrepresented the camp as a religious centre.

That's right: Hassani traveled to Afghanistan on the understanding that he was to take part in a spiritual retreat. In the coming days, you will hear how he tried, on more than one occasion, to get out of participating in the camp's mandatory weapons training— purposefully injuring himself in one instance so that he wouldn't have to fire a rocket-propelled grenade launcher. You will hear how he categorically refused invitations from the camp leaders to become involved in violent actions back in the United States. Ladies and gentlemen, you may take issue with Hassani's political and religious views. You may feel he is guilty of making an extremely poor vacation choice. But you cannot, in good conscience, convict this man of being a terrorist or even a terrorist sympathizer.

Joel glanced at his sleeping wife. Audrey disagreed with his strategy on this case. She maintained that he ought to be defending Hassani on grounds of legitimate Arab rage. Audrey took a much harder political line than he did on most things these days. He didn't mind. In fact, he rather enjoyed the irony of being chastised for his insufficient radicalism by the woman to whom he had once had to explain the Marxist concepts of 'base' and 'superstructure'. When he complained that she had become an ultra-leftist in her old age, he did so in the indulgent tones that another man might have teased his wife for her excessive spending at the mall. It was a feminine prerogative to hold unreasonable political views, he felt. And besides, he liked having some old-fashioned extremism about the house: it made him feel young.

Joel was still reading when, at six-thirty, the radio alarm on his bedside table clicked into life. He peeled off his clammy pyjama bottoms, rolled them into a ball and lobbed them elegantly into the laundry basket. He had been a talented sportsman in his youth—the handball champion of Bensonhurst, Brooklyn—and he had never lost the jock's habit of improvising minor athletic challenges for himself. He stood up now and stretched in front of the mirror on the closet door. At seventy-two, his nakedness was still formidable. His legs were strong. His chest, carpeted in whorls of grey hair, was broad. His penis was thick and long enough to bump companionably against his thigh as he strode out to the bathroom.

On the landing, he paused. Somewhere down below, he could hear the dim roar of a vacuum cleaner and the tuneless whistling of Julie, his sister-in-law. Ever since Julie had arrived from

England two days ago, with her husband, Colin, she had been flitting up and down the groaning Perry Street staircase with buckets and dusters and antibacterial detergents in the saintly manner of Florence Nightingale bringing succour to a Crimean field hospital. Audrey was in a terrible snit about it. The implied insult to her own standards of cleanliness did not bother her, she claimed. (This was plausible: Audrey had always been rather proud of being a slob.) What bothered her was Julie's faith in the redemptive power of lemony freshness and her assumption that others shared it. 'If she wants to practise her neurotic hygiene back home, that's one thing,' Audrey had hissed the night before, as she was getting into bed. 'But I don't see why I have to put up with her powdered fucking carpet fragrances in *my* house.'

After he had finished up in the bathroom, Joel put on sweatpants and a shirt and went downstairs. He found Julie on the second-floor landing, fitting the vacuum with a special nozzle for hard-to-reach corners. 'Good morning! Good morning!' he cried as he stepped around her. In order to discourage prolonged interactions with his sister-in-law, he always addressed her as if he were calling out from the window of a fast-moving train.

Down on the first floor, Colin was sitting at the kitchen table, reading a New York travel guide. 'Good morning to you, kind sir!' he exclaimed when he saw Joel flashing by. 'Julie and I are off to Ground Zero in a bit. Is there anywhere down there that you'd recommend for lunch?'

'Nope, sorry,' Joel said as he hurried down the hall. 'Can't help you there.'

'Might I offer you a cup of tea?' Colin called

after him.

'No thanks. I'm going out to get the papers.'

Joel was just opening the front door when he felt an answering push from the other side. 'It's me,' a voice said. 'I forgot my keys.'

The door swung open to reveal Joel's adopted son, Lenny, and Lenny's girlfriend, Tanya, standing limply on the doorstep, holding paper cups of Starbucks coffee. Tanya was wearing a jacket of ragged rabbit fur over her minidress. Lenny was shivering in a T-shirt. They both had the spectral look of people who had not slept in some time.

'Ah, love's young dream!' Joel cried with a facetious bow.

'Hey,' Lenny said. He was a tall man with a boyish, delicate face. Were it not for the gap between his two front teeth and the slight droop in his left eye, he would have been pretty. As it was, his raffish imperfections had tipped the scale and made him beautiful.

'To what do I owe this rare pleasure?' Joel asked. Lenny was officially living back at home these days, but most nights he slept at Tanya's apartment.

Lenny cast a pale hand through untidy hair. 'Tanya had a party at her place,' he said. 'Somebody pissed on her bed, so—'

'Jesus!' The vehemence of Joel's tone suggested that it was his own bed that had been violated. 'What kind of friends do you have?'

Lenny made a gesture with his hands as if he were pushing down on some invisible volume control. 'It's no big deal, Dad. The guy didn't mean to . . . Can we come in? It's freezing out here.'

'What do you mean, "didn't mean to"?' Joel demanded. 'He pissed on her bed *by accident*?'

'Whatever. Just forget it.' Lenny squeezed past Joel and headed into the kitchen. Tanya followed.

'Oh, sure, go ahead,' Joel shouted after them, 'help yourselves to whatever you want. Mi casa es su casa . . .' He stood for a moment, registering the impotence of his sarcasm, and then went out, slamming the door behind him.

Walking up the street to the bodega, he twitched and muttered to himself in disgust. Was it unreasonable for a man of his age and station to expect some peace and solitude in the mornings? Was it too much to ask that he be allowed a few hours of quiet reflection at the start of a demanding day in court? He tried to calm himself down by thinking about his opening statement, but it was no good: his composure had been lost.

Joel was by and large a sanguine man. He regarded his sunny outlook not as an accident of temperament so much as a determined political stance. His favourite quotation—the one that he said he wanted carved on his gravestone—was Antonio Gramsci's line about being 'a pessimist because of intelligence and an optimist by will'. Lenny, alas, had a rare ability to penetrate the force field of his positive thinking. The very smell of the boy fucked with his internal weather: made him prey to itchy glooms and irritable regrets.

Twenty-seven years ago, when Lenny first came to live at Perry Street, Joel had been very high on the idea of subverting traditional models of family life. Adopting seven-year-old Lenny was no mere act of bourgeois philanthropy, he had maintained, but a subversive gesture—a vote for an

31

enlightened, 'tribal' system of child-rearing that would one day supercede the repressive nuclear unit altogether. Lenny, however, had proved to be an uncooperative participant in the tribal programme. As a child, he had tyrannized the household with violent tantrums. As an adolescent, he had dealt pot from the Perry Street stoop and repeatedly been caught shoplifting. At last, in adulthood, his petty delinquencies had blossomed into a range of drearily predictable and apparently irremediable dysfunctions. Joel would not have minded—or at least not have minded *so much*—had Lenny ever put his rebellious impulses to some principled use: run away to join the Sandinistas, say, or vandalized US army-recruiting offices. But the boy's waywardness had never served any cause other than his own fleeting satisfactions. 'Lenny's not doing well,' was Audrey's preferred euphemism whenever he dropped out of some new, expensive college course, or got fired from the job that she had hustled for him at Habitat for Humanity, or set his hair alight while smoking crack, or was found having sex with one of the other residents at his rehab clinic. She chose to attribute such mishaps to the traumas of Lenny's infancy. But Joel had had it with that psychological crap. The boy was a mendacious, indolent fuck-up, that was all—a mortifying reminder of a failed experiment.

*　　*　　*

Coming back from the bodega, Joel worked up several elaborately snide remarks with which to taunt Lenny and Tanya, but on re-entering the house, he found the kitchen empty. Colin and Julie had gone off on their sightseeing jaunt and Lenny and Tanya had vanished upstairs, leaving their soggy-rimmed Starbucks cups on the kitchen table. Joel picked up the cups with a murmur of irritation and threw them in the trash. Then he switched on the coffee percolator and ambled into the living room to look at the papers.

At this hour in the morning there was almost no natural light at the front of the house, and before sitting down Joel had to wander about, turning on all the table lamps. Most of the residents on this eighteenth-century street had solved the problem of their low-ceilinged, north-facing parlours by tearing down the first-floor dividing walls and creating kitchen-dining floor-throughs, but Joel and Audrey sneered at the yuppie extravagance of these renovations. Neither of them was of the generation that had been taught to regard sunlit rooms as a birthright, and in so far as they were aware of interior design as an independent category of interest, they thought it a very silly business indeed. Over the years, they had assembled various artefacts and souvenirs pertaining to their travels and political involvements—an ANC flag signed by Oliver Tambo; a framed portrait of Joel, executed in muddy oils by a veteran of the Attica riots; a kilim depicting scenes from the Palestinian struggle— but there was not a single item of furniture here that could be said to represent a considered aesthetic choice. The love-seat, upholstered in a nubby, mustard tweed, had been given to them by Joel's mother. The giant cherrywood cabinet and the collection of miniature china shoes it housed

33

were an inheritance from Joel's Aunt Marion. A silver-plated andiron set, gamely arranged around the blocked-off fireplace, had come as barter payment from one of Joel's clients.

Joel sat down now and, with practised efficiency, began to fillet the papers for items relating to himself and today's trial. *The New York Times* and the *Washington Post* had two more or less straightforward accounts of the case that mentioned his name, but without comment. In the *New York Post*, he found an editorial that made two passing references to him as 'a rent-a-radical with a long history of un-Americanism' and as 'a man whose knee-jerk leftism is thankfully now all but extinct in today's political climate'.

He stared at the pile of newspapers for a moment and then took another pass, checking to see if he had missed anything. In a long career of defending pariahs, Joel had learned to expect and to treasure hostile public attention. It was the gauge by which he measured the importance and usefulness of his work. ('Joel never feels so alive,' Audrey liked to say, 'as when someone is wishing him dead.') Back in the 1980s, when he had been defending Al-Saddawi, the accused murderer of the Chasid leader Rabbi Kosse, protestors had organized rallies against him and put up posters around New York that said 'Litvinoff: Self-Hating Jew'. They had even made death threats against the children. By these standards, the animosity generated by the Hassani case had been disappointingly tame: one bomb threat to his uptown law office (deemed 'not credible' by the police); a couple of people shouting 'Traitor!' in the street. And one lousy mention in the *Post*. He looked at the editorial again. Well, they'd called him un-American; that was something.

He heard his wife coming down the stairs. 'Come look, sweetie,' he called out. 'The *Post* is gunning for me!'

After a moment, Audrey appeared in the living-room doorway—a thin woman of fifty-eight, with steel-coloured hair and the dark, unblinking eyes of a woodland animal. She was wearing a denim skirt and a T-shirt printed with the slogan 'One Nation Under Surveillance'.

Joel rustled his papers. 'They say I'm a rent-a-radical.'

'Bully for you,' Audrey said.

'Did you know Lenny and Tanya were here?'

'I saw them.'

'Somebody urinated on Tanya's bed last night. Can you believe it? Who are these people they hang around with?'

Audrey frowned, noticing that another of the living-room's floorboards had come loose. 'Oh, do shut up, Joel,' she murmured.

Jadedness was Audrey's default pose with her husband. She used it partly in the English manner, as a way of alluding to affection by manifesting its opposite, and partly as a strategy for asserting her privileged spousal status. The wives of great men must always be jealously guarding their positions against the encroachments of acolytes, and Audrey had decided long ago that if everybody else was going to guffaw at Joel's jokes and roll over at his charm, her distinction—the mark of her unparalleled intimacy with the legend—would be a deadpan unimpressibility. 'Oh, I forgot!' she often drawled when Joel was embarking on one of his exuberant anecdotes. 'It's all about you, isn't it?'

'What do you want for breakfast?' she asked now.

'I'll have a bialy,' Joel said.

Audrey looked at him.

'*What*?' he said, glancing up after a moment. 'I have to have carbohydrates sometimes. You want me to go to court on a bowl of yoghurt?'

Audrey went into the kitchen.

'I can't find the bialys,' she called out after a moment. 'Are you sure we have any?'

Joel looked up from the papers. 'Oh, come on! I thought you were going to get some. I asked you yesterday.' He smacked his hand against his newspaper. 'Jesus!'

Audrey came back out to the living room and gazed at him archly. 'It's a tragedy, I know. How about a boiled egg?'

'I want a bialy, goddammit.'

Audrey stood and waited.

'All right, forget it,' he said sulkily. 'Gimme the egg.'

He went upstairs to shower and get dressed. In the kitchen, Audrey poured herself a coffee and put a pan of water on the stove. She was about to return to the living room to look at the *New York Post* editorial when she heard shouting from above. Putting down her cup, she went to the foot of the stairs. 'Joel?' There was no reply. With a sigh, she trekked up to the top-floor landing, where she found her husband raging over an empty can of black shoe polish.

'Does no one but me ever replace anything in this house?' he demanded. 'Would it be too much to ask that someone else bought fucking shoe

36

polish around here?'

'Lenny must have finished it,' Audrey said calmly. 'He used it the other night, when he went to that black-tie thing with Tanya.'

The black-tie detail was an unnecessary provocation, Joel thought. Audrey had an ignoble habit of dropping Lenny in it, in order that she might then rescue him.

'Jesus!' he shouted, taking the bait anyway. 'What are we running here, a hostel for the unemployed? Next time, tell him to get his own.'

'Those aren't the right shoes for that suit anyway,' Audrey said, gesturing at the brogues that Joel had been intending to polish. 'You wear the other ones with the blue suit.'

She turned away in silent triumph and went back downstairs.

Shortly afterwards, Joel followed her. With a dish-towel tied around his neck to protect his shirt and tie, he ate the egg she had made for him and drank the coffee. Then he took her in his arms and kissed her. 'I love you,' he said.

'Yeah, yeah.' Audrey helped him on with his coat and walked him out to the front step. 'Do good,' she called as he set off down the street.

Without turning around, or breaking stride, Joel raised a hand in acknowledgement. 'Buy some bialys,' he called back.

*   *   *

In the taxi over to Brooklyn, Joel's head pains grew worse. The metal object that was lodged in his skull had shifted to his frontal lobe now and seemed to be intent on boring its way out through his forehead. The cab driver was heavy on the brake and the jerky motion of the car as it stopped and started its way through the heavy traffic on the bridge made him moan out loud. By the time he got out at Cadman Plaza, he was dangerously close to throwing up.

Standing on the kerb, waiting for his nausea to subside, he felt a hand on his arm. He looked up to see his paralegal, Kate, peering at him with concern.

'Are you okay, Joel?'

'Sure.'

'You look a little pale.'

'I have a headache is all.' Through the veil of his pain he registered a smattering of acne around Kate's mouth and a smear of red lipstick on her teeth.

'You want me to get you an aspirin or something?' Kate asked.

Joel shook his head. 'I've taken about fifty Tylenol in the last twenty-four hours. They're making it worse, I think.'

'How about some water?' She brought out a plastic bottle from her bag.

Joel smiled wanly as he took the bottle. Dear, homely, reliable Kate. How well she looked after him! He had been doubtful, when he first hired her, about taking on such an unattractive girl. He had worried that it would be too dispiriting to have to confront her tree-trunk legs and her abominable complexion every morning. But Kate's devotedness and efficiency had more than made up for her aesthetic failings. And after so many years of complicated and time-consuming office imbroglios with female employees, there was, he had to admit,

38

something rather soothing about not wanting to fuck his assistant.

'Okay,' he said, handing the bottle back. 'I'm good.'

They went in through the glass doors of the Federal Courthouse and deposited their cellphones with a lady in a booth, before joining the line at the security checkpoint. One of the uniformed men standing at the X-ray machine raised his arms in greeting. 'Heeeey! Here he is! How ya doing, Mr Litvinoff?'

Joel stared at him in mock consternation. 'What happened, Lew?' He took off his watch and placed it, along with his keys, in a plastic tray on the conveyor belt. 'They didn't get rid of you yet? I thought for sure they would have fired you by now.'

Lew laughed heartily—a little more heartily than was strictly credible, it seemed to Joel. That was all right. Caring enough to fake mirth was its own sort of compliment. Joel passed through the metal detector and picked up his briefcase, keys and watch on the other side.

'A big one today, right?' Lew said.

Joel shrugged. 'They're all big, Lew, they're all big. I'll see you later.'

'All right, Mr Litvinoff, take it easy.'

In the elevator going up to the courtroom, Joel found himself pressed tightly against a young blonde. 'Well!' he chuckled. 'My lucky day.' The woman looked away disdainfully. He felt a moment's befuddlement at the failure of his gallantry and then an urge to take the woman by the scruff of her neck and give her a good slap. But he pulled himself together and went on chatting to

Kate in a loud, cheerful voice until they reached their floor.

Joel's co-counsel, Buchman, a pink-faced kid from Virginia, had already arrived in the courtroom. Joel nodded hello to the prosecution team and stopped to say a few words to the court stenographer, a nice old gargoyle called Helen. Then he sat down and chatted with Buchman. Soon, the jury filed in, emanating the usual, stagy solemnity of citizens fulfilling their civic duty. Joel put his elbows on the desk in front of him and cradled his chin in his hands. He was feeling old. The elevator-woman's rejection had bothered him. His head was throbbing. The long day's work loomed before him like a cliff-face.

Hassani was brought up now from the holding cell, accompanied by three grimly corpulent guards. Joel stood up and stretched out his arms. 'Assalmu Alaykum!' A blush crept across Hassani's solemn, bean-shaped face as he found himself enfolded in an enthusiastic bear hug. Joel, whose personal affections tended to follow his political sympathies and who rarely managed to get through a case without falling a little in love with his client, was famous for his public expressions of tenderness towards the men and women he represented.

'You're looking good, man!' he said when at last he had released Hassani. He rubbed at the circular impression that one of his suit buttons had left on Hassani's cheek. The energy that he had expended on the hug had left him slightly dizzy, he realized. He sat down and stared straight ahead, trying to regain his balance.

Now, the court clerk entered and asked the

40

people to please rise for the judge. As Joel heaved himself up, he heard a tiny noise in his head—a brittle, snapping sound like a dry branch being broken underfoot. At the same time, a blurry, dark margin appeared at the corner of his vision. He was just wondering whether he ought to sit down again when the room tipped on its side.

No one reacted immediately when he fell to the floor. Several people would later admit that they had mistaken the collapse for one of his courtroom stunts. After a moment or two, things began to happen. The stenographer went over and took Joel's pulse. Several journalists ran downstairs to put in calls to their newsrooms. Kate asked a policeman to radio for an ambulance. Hassani leaned over to Buchman and politely inquired about how he should proceed with finding a replacement lawyer.

CHAPTER TWO

Audrey was sitting in an airy, book-lined living room on Central Park West, drinking tea with her friend, Jean Himmelfarb, before setting off for her weekly stint of volunteer work at the Coalition for the Homeless. A construction crew had begun renovating Jean's kitchen that morning and the two women were having some trouble hearing one another over the tremendous banging coming from down the hall.

'Of course,' Audrey was almost shouting as she held up a copy of the *New York Post*, 'these fascists always love to characterize Joel's position as

41

outdated and irrelevant. They haven't got any decent arguments, so they just try to marginalize him.'

'Mmm.' Jean drew her feet up on to her chair and hugged her knees to her chest. She was a tall, ruddy-faced woman in her mid-sixties with a bouncy, tomboyish bearing that she tended to accentuate with jaunty hats. Today, much to Audrey's disapproval, she was wearing a floppy, orange newsboy cap that her great-niece had knitted for her. 'Still,' she said, 'you can understand why people are nervous about men like Hassani these days.'

Audrey leaned forward. 'Come again?'

'I said it's understandable that people are a bit nervous about terrorists and so on.'

'What *do* you mean?' Audrey's face took on an impatient expression. Jean was terribly unreliable when it came to politics. The first time they met, at an ANC fundraiser thirty years ago, Audrey had been obliged to tell her off for making squeamish remarks about the 'brutal tactics' of the PLO. She had been labouring ever since to correct some of Jean's more egregious misconceptions about international affairs, but with minimal success. Jean meant well—her heart was basically in the right place—but left to her own devices, she was still inclined to take everything she read in *The New York Times* op-ed pages as gospel.

'You do understand, don't you,' Audrey said now, 'that there's a bloody witch-hunt going in this country at the moment?'

'Oh yes,' Jean nodded. 'Yes, I *do* see that . . . but sometimes even witch-hunts catch real witches, don't they?'

' "Real witches"? My God, Jean! What do you want to do—start rounding up every brown-skinned man in America? Because that's basically what this government is doing right now.'

'No, well, of course that's awful. But . . . I mean, what if your man, Hassani, really was intending to come back and start planting bombs in the name of Allah?'

'Oh, don't be *daft*,' Audrey said. 'This whole Allah thing is a total red herring. Al-Qaeda is a *political* organization, not a religious one. People bang on about fundamentalist Islam and religious fanatics, but it's obvious no one is inspired by Bin Laden for *religious* reasons.'

'Aren't they?' Jean asked. 'I mean, aren't *some* of the Al-Qaeda lot motivated by religion?' She was wishing, as she often did in these talks with Audrey, that she had bothered to read more about the subject under discussion. She was quite sure that Audrey was wrong about Al-Qaeda—or, at the very least, not wholly right—but she could sense, even before she began, that her flummoxed protest was doomed. There was nothing wrong with being the one who pointed out that things were more complex than supposed: it was a perfectly honourable and even necessary job. But it wasn't what won you arguments.

'Nooo, Jean,' Audrey said, shaking her head vehemently. 'Absolutely not. The anger that motivates the suicide bombers is a political anger. A perfectly rational anger against the American hegemon.'

Jean cupped her ear with her hand. 'Against what, sorry?'

'Against the *American hegemon*, Jean.'

'Ah, yes.' Jean nodded. 'But don't they also hate us because we're infidels?'

'What?'

'I was saying—I think there must be some religion involved.'

Audrey rolled her eyes. Oh dear, oh *dear*. 'That's just what the Bush administration wants you to believe, Jean. "They hate our freedoms . . . this is a clash of civilizations . . . we're bombing Afghanistan so that the dear little Afghani girls can have a chance to go to school." It's all bollocks. They're fighting us because we support Israel and every other shitty regime in the Middle East. And we're fighting them because there's a bloody great big oil pipeline that goes across Afghanistan.'

Jean was silent. She didn't doubt that there was malfeasance and lies involved in this Afghanistan business, but all the talk of oil pipelines and conspiracies—it was just a higher level of gossip, wasn't it? How could Audrey possibly know?

'Well,' she said, 'but the Taliban *was* a pretty awful regime.'

Audrey put down her teacup and gave a languorous stretch. 'Sweetie,' she said, 'the world is *full* of awful regimes.'

Jean sighed. There were some people with a gift for conviction—a talent for cutting a line through the jumbled phenomena of world affairs and saying, 'I'm in: this is my position.' Audrey had it. All of the Litvinoffs had it, to some extent. It was a genetic thing, perhaps. Jean had seen a film once, about a troop of French soldiers in the First World War who were charged with getting a cannon to their fellow soldiers, trapped under enemy fire. For weeks, they carted the cannon around the countryside as their number slowly dwindled. Some were killed. Some deserted. Some collapsed from exhaustion. But no matter how desperate the situation became—even when it emerged that the cannon itself was probably defective—the captain of the group kept going forward, refusing to give up. Audrey's attachment to her dogma was a bit like that, Jean thought. For decades now, she had been dragging about the same unwieldy burden of a priori convictions, believing herself honour-bound to protect them against destruction at all costs. No new intelligence, no rational argument, could cause her to falter from her mission. Not even the cataclysmic events of the previous September had put her off her stride for more than a couple of hours. By lunchtime on the day that the towers fell, when the rest of New York was still stumbling about in a daze, Audrey had already been celebrating the end of the myth of American exceptionalism and comparing the event to the American bombing of a Sudanese aspirin factory in 1998. The speed with which she had processed the catastrophe and assimilated it to her worldview had been formidable in its way and, at the same time, Jean felt, a little chilling.

'Talking of religion,' she said, hoping to change the subject, 'how is Rosa? Is she still . . . ?'

Audrey's expression darkened. 'Oh yeah,' she replied drearily, 'still off dancing the hora. It's all very gruesome.'

Rosa was the Litvinoffs' younger daughter. A little less than a year and a half ago, she had returned from a four-year sojourn in Cuba, announcing that her lifelong fealty to the cause of revolutionary socialism was at an end and that she

45

no longer believed in political solutions to the world's problems. Recently, she had delivered another, infinitely more shocking, punch to the collective family jaw by informing them that she had begun attending services at an Orthodox synagogue on the Upper West Side.

'Does she talk about it a lot then?' Jean asked. 'The religion, I mean?'

'Oh no,' Audrey said. 'She's terribly smug about it all. She wouldn't waste time sharing her thoughts with us heathens.' She gazed glumly out of the window. 'Joel's taken it very hard. He really thought she had grown up at last. He was even talking about paying for her to go back to law school. Now he's convinced that she's having some sort of breakdown.'

Jean nodded sympathetically. 'Well, perhaps she is a bit depressed. It might not be a bad idea for her to get some therapy—'

'Oh bollocks!' Audrey broke in. 'Rosa's not *depressed*. She only ever went to Cuba to show everyone how special and interesting she was. Now she's tired of playing peasant and she wants to see how much attention she can get by becoming Queen of the Matzoh.'

'Well, but—'

'Depressed!' Audrey went on indignantly. 'She's as happy as Larry, poncing about with her new, Jewy friends. If she needs anything, Jean, it's not therapy, it's a good fuck.'

'Oh, *Audrey*,' Jean said, flapping her hands in embarrassment.

'I'm serious. I don't think she's been with a man since she's been back. What's that about? She's always been a bit of a prude, Rosa. I think that's

46

why this religious business appeals to her. It's all about repressing your sexual drives, isn't it?'

The last part of Audrey's remark was drowned out by a drill starting up in the kitchen.

'Oh dear,' Jean said. 'This noise is intolerable, isn't it? Perhaps you should come back next week when they've finished the demolition.'

Audrey shook her head. 'No, I'm fine,' she said firmly. 'A bit of noise doesn't bother me.'

Jean's renovation was, as it happened, the principal reason for Audrey's visit this morning. Lenny had recently been let go from his painting job in Williamsburg and Audrey was hoping that she could persuade Jean to give him some work on her kitchen.

'I wonder,' she said now, in a wondering tone of voice. 'Lenny's free at the moment. He could probably spare you a bit of time if you want to have him come and help out with your paintwork.'

Jean nodded carefully. 'That's awfully nice of you, Audrey,' she said, 'but I think Darius has it covered.'

'But you know these guys always try to save money by putting some teenager on the paintwork. You really need a professional painter if you want the job done properly.'

'Yes . . .'

'Do you remember that beautiful work Lenny did on your country house? You loved that, Jean.'

'Oh, I know, yes.' Jean blushed. The truth, as Audrey knew perfectly well, was that Lenny had never completed the job on Jean's country house. Shortly after starting the work, he had had one of his relapses. The little he had accomplished before absconding had been so shoddily executed that

Jean had had to pay to have it done over. 'The thing is,' Jean said, 'I don't think Darius can take on someone else without going over his—you know—his estimate . . .'

'Oh!' Audrey said. 'Well! If it's a question of *money* . . .' She stared moodily at Jean's coffee table.

Audrey always referred to Jean in an aggrieved tone as 'an heiress'. She did not know exactly how much money Jean had inherited from her father's pharmaceuticals fortune; she had never made any effort to find out. To have nailed down the precise sum would have meant acknowledging that there were limits to Jean's funds—that there were, in fact, some things that Jean could not afford. As it was, Audrey's cloudy notion of her friend's infinite, fairy-tale wealth allowed her to believe that everything that happened or did not happen in Jean's life was a pure expression of Jean's will, unimpeded by workaday considerations of expense. This, in turn, made possible the consoling conviction that Jean was miserly and 'uncreative' with her money.

There was a pause in the conversation. Audrey, who was quite sure that any embarrassment arising from the silence was rightly Jean's, sat back in her chair and waited.

'Well,' Jean said at length. 'Perhaps I could *talk* to Darius . . .'

Audrey nodded wisely. 'Oh, I think that's a good idea, Jean. You really would be better off—'

Somewhere, in the depths of Audrey's handbag, a cellphone began to ring. Jean took the opportunity to get up and take some of the tea things into the kitchen.

48

When she returned, Audrey was barking into the phone. 'What do you mean? How badly?'

Jean looked at her in alarm.

'All right,' Audrey said. 'Give me the address.' She scribbled something down on the back of her chequebook. 'I'm coming now.' She put the phone back in her bag. 'I have to go,' she said. 'Joel fainted in court. They've taken him to a hospital in Brooklyn.'

'Oh, Audrey!' Jean said, clutching her forehead. 'Is there anything I can do? Would you like me to come with you?'

'No, no, don't be silly.' As if to prove how unflustered she was, Audrey picked up her cup and drank back the remains of her tea before making her way out to the hall.

'Will you call me when you find out how he is?' Jean asked, following her.

'Yes, of course,' Audrey said.

'Really, call me if you need anything. I'm here all day.' Jean handed Audrey her coat and opened the door.

Halfway to the elevator, Audrey stopped and turned around. 'And you won't forget about Lenny, will you?'

Jean nodded emphatically. 'No, of course not. I'll speak to Darius about it today.'

*   *   *

By insisting that the taxi make a couple of illegal left turns, Audrey managed to get to the Long Island Hospital in Cobble Hill in less than forty minutes. She found Kate, Joel's paralegal, sitting alone in the ICU Family and Friends Lounge.

49

'So what happened?' she asked.

Kate began diligently to describe what had taken place in the courtroom.

'Yeah, all right, love,' Audrey interrupted, 'I don't need the police procedural. What do they say is wrong with him?'

Kate put her hand to her mouth. 'Oh! I thought you'd been told. They think he's had a stroke—'

'A stroke!'

'Well, that's what the ambulancemen said. I haven't spoken to anyone since. A doctor is meant to be coming to talk to us in a bit.'

Audrey sat down in an armchair. The walls of the lounge had been painted with a special sponging technique to give the impression of fresco. Hanging above the sofa where Kate was sitting was a group of nautical prints: unmanned schooners on glassy seas. A low table in the corner of the room was piled high with back issues of *American Business* and *American Baby*. 'Well, this is a real shit-hole, isn't it?' Audrey remarked as she took out her phone.

Kate made a small noise and pointed apologetically to a sign on the wall: WE THANK YOU FOR NOT USING CELLPHONES IN THE ICU.

'Oh, *fucking* hell.' Audrey paused, weighing whether to heed the prohibition, then stood up. 'All right, I'm going downstairs. Look after my handbag while I'm gone and come and get me if anything happens.'

Outside the hospital's main entrance, she took out a pack of cigarettes from her coat pocket and went over to a man standing against a pillar. 'You got a light?'

'Nope,' the man replied in the piously emphatic tones of a non-smoker.

Audrey felt a hand on her shoulder. She turned to find a tall black woman in a turban, holding out a lighter. The woman watched intently as Audrey lit her cigarette and when Audrey made to hand the lighter back, she shook her head. 'You can keep it.'

'No, love,' Audrey protested. 'It's all right, you don't need to do that.'

'Really,' the woman said, smiling. 'Have it. I've got another one in my bag.'

Audrey looked at her suspiciously. There was something in her manner—some knowingness or unwarranted intimacy—that seemed to augur impertinent questions and unasked-for confidences. It gave her the creeps. 'All right then,' she said ungraciously, slipping the lighter in her pocket. 'Thanks.'

She walked away and sat down on a bench to make her calls. Karla, her elder daughter, did not pick up. Neither did Lenny or Rosa. She left them each a purposefully oblique voicemail: 'Just to let you know, something's up with Dad. Give us a ring when you can.' Then she called the Coalition for the Homeless office to tell them that she wouldn't be coming in. There were other people she needed to inform: Joel's mother; her sister, Julie. But she did not feel up to dealing with all that feminine hysteria right now. She would get one of the kids to make the calls later. She put the phone away and sat quietly on the bench for a moment, taking in the insulting normalcy of the scene around her. A mother wandered past, pushing a stroller. Across the street, a man leaned out from the cab of an

51

idling delivery truck and hissed an obscenity at a passing woman. Frowning, Audrey put out her cigarette and went back into the hospital.

When she came out of the elevator on the fifth floor, she spotted Joel's young colleague, Daniel Leventhal, talking intently to a nurse at the other end of the corridor. His crumpled shirt-tails were hanging out of his pants and he had slung his jacket over his shoulder in the glamorously insouciant style of a TV detective. The nurse to whom he was speaking was staring at him in much the same way that Virgin Mothers contemplate their oversized Baby Jesuses in Renaissance paintings of the Adoration.

Audrey's lip curled in a sardonic smile. Daniel had a gift for eliciting undignified behaviour from women. She had never seen his appeal herself. She accepted the fact of his attractiveness as she accepted the existence of gravity—it was the most plausible explanation for various phenomena that would otherwise have remained mysterious—but by her own judgement, Daniel was a most unimpressive specimen. There was something affected and unmanly about him, something smarmy and callow and fundamentally *unserious*. If such a word had been permissible within her lexicon, she would have said that his looks were common.

Daniel glanced up in her direction as she approached, but he made no acknowledgement of having seen her and only when she was standing directly in front of him did he look up again. 'Audrey!' he exclaimed, with a feigned quiver of surprise. Audrey sighed at this gratuitous bit of theatre. Daniel was a master of furtive insult. Had

52

he ever dared to openly disrespect her, she would have had no trouble in squashing him, but he was far too wily for that. His insolence ventured out only in lightning raids, under cover of scrupulous politeness. She was about to say something tart, when he raised his hand in a restraining gesture. 'Sorry, Audrey, could you hang on? We're right in the middle of something here.' Smiling, he turned his back on her and resumed his conversation with the nurse.

Audrey stood for a moment, absorbing the shock of his impudence, before turning abruptly on her heel and walking away. The temerity of that little piss ant! She and Joel had had many fierce arguments about Daniel over the years. Joel tended to dismiss all of her complaints about Daniel's impertinence as 'paranoia'. He maintained that Daniel was a brilliant young lawyer: one of the sharpest legal minds he had ever encountered. Once or twice, he had even hinted that he would like Daniel to take over his practice when he retired. Audrey, who refused to believe that her shrewd husband had miscalculated Daniel's talents so extravagantly, accused him of keeping Daniel around only to make himself look better. He was such a vain old fucker, she claimed, that he would rather champion a mediocrity than risk being outshone by a genuinely talented young man.

In Audrey's absence, two large, teary women had taken up residence in the Family and Friends Lounge. One of them, it seemed, had just been informed that her husband had a cancerous tumour in his brain. 'They say it's the size of a golf ball,' she was boasting to Kate when Audrey entered.

'Danny's here,' Kate told Audrey. 'He's just gone to see if—'

'Yeah, I saw him.' Audrey interrupted. 'He's down the hall, being very important and in charge with one of the nurses.'

Kate smiled nervously.

'I take it no one's been in to tell us anything yet?' Audrey asked.

Kate shook her head.

Audrey made a clicking sound with her tongue. 'Bastards.'

Presently, Daniel appeared. 'Audrey. How *are* you?' he drawled. 'I'm sorry about just now. I was trying to get to the bottom of all this.'

'So I gathered.' Audrey said. 'And what did you learn on your big fact-finding mission?'

Alerted by the sarcasm in her voice, the brain-tumour woman and her friend rustled to attention.

'Well,' Daniel began, 'they're pretty certain that he's had a stroke—'

'We know that,' Audrey said.

'And they're running a bunch of tests at the moment—'

'Right,' Audrey said. 'I heard.'

Daniel smiled at her with the twinkly forbearance of a kindly uncle handling a rambunctious niece. 'They seem to think that his condition is stable now,' he went on. 'But they really can't tell us much more until they've finished the tests. A doctor will be in to talk to us as soon as they get the lay of the land.'

'I see,' Audrey said slowly. 'So, in fact, you found out nothing.'

The room was quiet for a moment. Audrey

stood up to get a magazine from the pile on the coffee table and caught Daniel rolling his eyes good-humouredly at the tumour ladies. They simpered sympathetically back at him. Audrey picked up a copy of *American Baby* and began flicking through an article on potty training, making little cracks of thunder as she turned the pages.

At length, a young Chinese American woman came into the lounge and asked to speak to the relatives of Joel Litvinoff.

'I'm his colleague,' Daniel said, standing up and extending his hand.

Audrey remained seated. 'I'm his wife.'

'Hi,' the woman said. 'I'm Dr Wu. If you'd like to step into the hallway, I can tell you how he's doing.'

Audrey took a quick survey of the doctor: her tiny, red balloon-knot mouth, the sparkly barrettes holding her floppy hair back from her face. 'Isn't there someone more senior I could talk to?' she asked.

The doctor gave a small, unnecessary cough into her fist. 'I'm afraid not. I am the most senior person dealing with this case.'

Audrey stood up and walked out of the room. In the corridor, Daniel produced a pad and pen from his breast pocket.

'So, the situation is this,' the doctor said. 'Joel was brought in this morning having suffered a transient ischemic attack, or what we sometimes refer to as a "mini-stroke". Unfortunately, he went on to suffer another more serious stroke while we were still in the process of trying to stabilize him. He remains unconscious at this point—'

'What?' Audrey interrupted. 'Is his brain going to be all right?'

'I'm afraid we can't say at this point exactly what deficits he has incurred. When we are satisfied that all his vital organs are functioning as they should, we can—'

'What do you mean, "deficits"?'

'Impairments. As I say, we're—'

'But you must have some idea of—'

'Mrs Litvinoff, we can only take this one step at a time.'

'Tell me, has he been given anticoagulants?' Daniel asked eagerly, pen and pad to the ready.

While he and the doctor spoke about the drugs that Joel was being given and the tests that he was undergoing, Audrey gazed down the corridor to where a workman was standing on a ladder, removing one of the white panels in the ceiling. As the panel came away, a tangle of tubes and wires spilled out, looking like cartoon innards. *I didn't get him his bialy*, she thought. *All he wanted was a sodding bialy and I sent him off to work with one egg inside him.*

'I believe they'll be bringing him up shortly,' the doctor was saying. 'If you could try to keep the atmosphere as calm and positive as possible, that would be a good thing.'

Audrey turned to Daniel and Kate. 'You two had better be off now.'

'But, Audrey, I'd like to see Joel,' Daniel said.

Audrey shook her head. 'Oh no, I don't think that's a good idea. It should be just close family at this point, shouldn't it, Doctor?'

Dr Wu shrugged. 'Well, strictly speaking—'

'See?' Audrey said. 'Let's not be agitating him

by having a great big gang march in there.'

Daniel seemed about to protest, but then he nodded briskly and put his pad back in his jacket pocket. 'Got it,' he said. 'I'll come back tomorrow.'

Audrey smiled sweetly, 'We'll see how he's doing first, shall we?'

Daniel came disagreeably close to her now and patted her on the shoulder.

'Okay, Audrey,' he whispered. 'Whatever you say.'

CHAPTER THREE

The buoys in New York Harbor were flopping and bouncing like vaudevillians as the Staten Island Ferry ploughed its approach to Manhattan. Out on the ferry's upper deck, ten girls in East Harlem GirlPower T-shirts were celebrating their recent liberation from the Staten Island Children's Museum.

'Renée can't swim! I'm gonna throw her over!'

'Yeah? If I go over, you going too.'

'You need to check your hair, Ren. You looking like a homeless person.'

'Chanel's spitting at the bird! Chanel, that's mean!'

One of the girls turned to a tall, white woman who was sitting on the bench behind her. 'Rosa! Are we allowed to spit?'

Rosa Litvinoff looked up from rummaging through her handbag for her cellphone. '*No,*' she said irritably. She paused and glanced around the deck. Over by the railings, one of her charges was standing alone, practising dance moves.

'You gotta shake it, shake it,' she was singing in an off-key, playground voice as she leaned back, limbo-style, and pumped her pelvis back and forth.

'Chianti!' Rosa called.

The girl did not respond.

Chianti concerned Rosa. Over the last few months she had leaped from sweet, saucer-eyed childhood into scowling, pre-adolescence. The braids and knee socks had vanished, replaced by jiggling breasts and cigarette breath. She no longer wanted to make fridge magnets and pipe-cleaner flowers; she wanted to show off her grimy, lime-green push-up bra and perform slutty dances and hang around outside the GirlPower Center with unsuitable older boys. The other girls, disguising their envy in moral alarm, reported that she gave blow jobs.

A slim, beige-skinned man in dreadlocks came out on deck now. 'You don't want to *know* what those bathrooms are like,' he muttered as he sat down next to Rosa.

'Look at that,' Rosa said, pointing. Chianti had assumed a squatting position with her palms planted on her thighs and her buttocks thrust outward.

'Don't ever fake it, fake it,' she was singing. 'Be sure and make it, make it—ahuh, ahuh—*goo-ood.*'

'Oh my Lord,' Raphael said, 'it's Lil' Kim.'

Rosa scowled. 'It's not funny, Raphael. She's out of control . . . Chianti! Stop that now!'

Chianti looked around. The wind had given her round face the misty, purplish sheen of a plum. *'What?'*

'You don't look cool when you dance like that,

58

you know,' Rosa said. 'You look dumb.'

'No I don't.'

'Yes you do.'

Chianti looked at Raphael. 'Yo, Raph, how come you don't say nothin' when she starts pickin' on me like that?'

'Uh, uh,' Raphael said, laughing. 'Don't be trying that. I ain't getting involved. This is between you girls.'

Rosa turned away to pick off some strands of hair that the wind had whipped across her face. It always irritated her when Raphael lapsed into his 'homie' persona with the girls. Given that he had been educated with Rosa at the Little Red Schoolhouse and that his Kenyan father held a tenured professorship at Rutgers, the attempt to pass himself off as 'street' was in decidedly bad taste, she thought. But then, Raphael had always had a distressing tendency to adapt his style to suit his audience. On the few occasions that Rosa had accompanied him to gay bars over the years, she had been mortified to observe how his behaviour changed in the presence of other gay men: how he rolled his eyes like Al Jolson and addressed everyone as 'Child': 'Child, that shirt is *beyond*'; 'Child, lemme tell you, that movie is *genius*.' Once or twice, she had challenged him on his opportunistic posturing, but he had never shown the slightest compunction or embarrassment. 'Rosa, honey,' he would drawl, 'I contain multitudes.'

Rosa returned to delving in her bag and presently produced her phone. There were five messages waiting for her: two from her mother, three from her sister, Karla. The tinny urgency of their voices ascended with each successive call, like a scale.

'Rosa, just to let you know, something's up with Dad.'

'Rosa, please, you must call.'

'Where are you, Rosa? Call me.'

'Rosa, hello?'

'For Christ's sake, Rosa. It's about your father. Why are you not answering?'

'Rosa!' one of the girls cried. 'Chanel's spitting again.'

'Stop it, Chanel,' Rosa said. She turned to Raphael. 'Watch them, will you? I have to call my mom.'

'Where the fuck have you been?' Audrey demanded when she answered. Her voice was bright with anger.

'I've been out with the girls. I didn't check my phone. What's going on?'

'What's that *noise*?'

Rosa stood up from the bench and walked into the cabin. The roar of engine and wind gave way immediately to an almost sepulchral hush. Tourist couples in windbreakers sat gazing placidly out of the smudged windows at the khaki water. A smell of old cooking oil drifted down from a snack booth in the rear.

'I'm on the Staten Island Ferry. Is something up with Dad?'

'"Is something up with Dad?"' her mother mimicked. 'Yes, something's up. He's had a stroke. Two strokes. He's at the Long Island Hospital in Brooklyn.'

'No!'

'He's unconscious.'

60

'Oh Christ!'

'All right, don't get dramatic. This isn't fucking *Oprah*.'

Rosa sighed. It was a matter of something like principle with her mother that bad news be handled with a minimum of fuss. The more dreadful the event under discussion, the more insistent she was on insouciance. Joel liked to tell the story of the time, early on in their marriage, when Audrey had miscarried on the 2 train and had called Joel from a payphone, blood coursing down her legs, to tell him that she was 'feeling a bit under the weather'. Joel—not yet schooled in the art of interpreting her oracular understatements—had suggested impatiently that she take an aspirin and call him back later when he wasn't so busy. And Audrey, being the plucky little Brit that she was, had neither protested nor complained: she had simply boarded another train and taken herself off to the St Vincent's Emergency Room. Rosa knew that she was meant to be impressed by this tale of her mother's true grit, but she had never quite understood why a young woman's refusal to ask for her husband's help in a crisis was so admirable. If the anecdote taught anything, she thought, it was the futility of her mother's show-off stoicism.

'I've been calling and calling,' Audrey was saying. 'I can't believe you wouldn't bother to check your messages. Your selfishness amazes me.' Rosa could tell her mother had been rehearsing this outrage. The complaint flowed like a recitation. She glanced back through the porthole at the girls on deck. Their T-shirts were billowing in the wind, like festive pennants. Chianti was doing her horrid dance again. 'Are you there, Rosa?' Audrey said.

'Yes, I'm here.'

'Because I can't be too long. I'm in the hospital. You're not meant to use phones in here.'

'When did this happen, Mom?'

'I don't have time to give you the step-by-step, Rosa. The first one was in court. The other one was, I don't know, about ten-thirty.'

'What do the doctors say?'

'What do you mean, what do they say? They say he's very sick.'

'I'll be getting in in a few minutes,' Rosa said. 'I have to take the girls back uptown, but then I'll come straight to the hospital.'

'Oh, that's good of you,' her mother said. 'No rush or anything—'

'Mom—'

'He needs a calm environment, so for Christ's sake, don't be making a scene when you get here.'

'Why would I make a scene?' Rosa asked. But her mother had already hung up.

*   *   *

Lenny was mooning about in the ICU corridor when Rosa arrived at the hospital.

'Dad's having tests,' he told her. 'We saw him for a bit, but then they took him off again.'

Rosa studied her brother's face. 'You're not *stoned*, are you?'

'No.'

'I'll take that as a yes. Where's Mom?'

Lenny led her down the hall to where Audrey was sitting with Karla in the Family and Friends

Lounge, staring forlornly at the wall. She looked like a little girl in a Lost and Found booth at the fair.

'Hello, Mom,' Rosa said.

Audrey's expression hardened. 'Oh, she's finally joined us.'

Rosa looked at her sister. 'Has there been any more news?' Karla, who was a hospital social worker, was the most likely to have absorbed and understood any medical information that had been dispensed.

'They've done a scan,' Karla said. 'It showed there was activity on both sides of his brain, which is very encouraging. He'll definitely have incurred some damage, but from what they can tell so far, it's in the motor cortex, which suggests his speech hasn't been affected—'

'Oh, none of them know what they're talking about,' Audrey burst out. 'They're all cretins—that's why they're working at this dump and not at a proper hospital in Manhattan.'

Karla took a ragged tissue from her pocket and began dabbing it at her eyes.

'Don't start blubbing, Karla, *please*,' Audrey said.

The room fell silent.

'These people don't even know who Joel *is*,' Audrey said after a moment. 'They've got a fucking *girl* taking care of him, for God's sake.'

'Not a *female*, surely?' Rosa said, with a smile. Keeping score of Audrey's anti-feminist remarks was a private hobby of hers. She had a fantasy that one day she would compile them in a book and present the volume to her mother as a Christmas gift.

63

'Don't give me that,' Audrey said. 'I'm telling you, she's a *teenager*. She doesn't look as if she's started her periods yet.'

'You mustn't worry,' Karla said. 'I'm sure she knows what she's—'

'Shit, where's my pot?' Audrey interrupted. She patted frantically at her pockets. 'Lenny, where did I put that pot you gave me?'

The sides of Lenny's mouth turned down in an expression of complacent cluelessness. 'Dunno.'

'Can you remember where you had it last?' Karla asked.

Audrey ignored her. 'Fuck, fuck, fuck,' she said, standing up.

Karla got down on her hands and knees to peer beneath the chairs. 'Could you have left it in the bathroom?'

Lenny made a desultory show of looking down the back of the sofa.

'Jesus *fucking* Christ,' Audrey murmured, peering at the floor around her feet. 'Where did I *put* it?'

Rosa watched her brother and sister creep around the room, two wary satellites to Audrey's sun.

'Oh!' Audrey cried suddenly, as she pulled a baggie from one of the side compartments of her handbag. 'Here it is! Panic over.'

'Well done, Mom!' Karla said.

'D'ya wanna go and have a smoke?' Lenny offered. 'I'll come outside with you.'

Audrey shook her head. 'Don't be daft, Lenny. What if they bring your dad up while I'm gone?' She sat back down on the sofa and closed her eyes.

Her children watched her.

'Another thing about that girl doctor,' she said presently. 'She's got this horrible little mouth on her. It looks just like an arsehole.'

Lenny and Karla giggled. Rosa studied the floor with distaste. Her mother was always congratulating herself on her audacious honesty, her willingness to express what everyone else was thinking. But no one, Rosa thought, actually *shared* Audrey's ugly view of the world. It was not the truth of her observations that made people laugh, but their unfairness, their surreal cruelty.

'You should eat something, Mom,' Karla said. 'I could get you something from the cafeteria.'

'God, no.' Audrey made a face. 'I couldn't keep anything down.'

'You'd feel better if you ate,' Karla said. 'You need to keep your strength up.'

Audrey opened her eyes now. 'Would you stop going on about food, Karla?'

Karla stared at her hands.

'Actually, Karl,' Lenny said, 'I wouldn't mind an Almond Joy or something.'

Rosa looked at her brother disapprovingly. 'Go get your own Almond Joy, Lenny.'

'It's all right,' Karla said. 'I don't mind.'

Lenny shrugged. 'If she wants to go . . .'

'Don't be so lazy,' Rosa insisted.

'I really don't mind,' Karla repeated.

'For God's sake, let her go, Rosa,' Audrey put in sharply.

'Would you get me a coffee too, while you're down there?' Lenny asked. 'Black, two sugars?'

Rosa stood up. 'I'll come with you, Karla.'

*　　　*　　　*

65

In the elevator, the two sisters smiled awkwardly at one another.

'How's Mike?' Rosa asked.

'He's good.' Karla's face took on a defensive expression. 'He's coming as soon as he can get away. He's in a very important union meeting this afternoon. They're announcing the state election endorsements tomorrow.'

'Oh yes?' Rosa said politely. Karla always spoke of Mike's job as a union organizer with the reverence of a missionary wife describing her husband's evangelical work in Borneo.

'I see Mom's being her usual charming self,' Rosa said after a moment.

'Well, she's under a lot of strain, Rosa.'

Rosa sighed. It was hard graft trying to work up any sororal intimacy with Karla. Most siblings—however estranged from one another—could find common cause in being exasperated by their parents. But Karla refused to countenance the mildest criticism of Joel and Audrey. There was something rather tragic, Rosa thought, about this intransigent filial loyalty. Karla had always been the least noticed of the Litvinoff offspring, the one who had had to work hardest to elicit the palest ray of her parents' approval or interest. But by some strange process, her lowly status within the family had only inflamed her ardour for the institution. She reminded Rosa of one of those people who spend four utterly miserable, unfriended years at college and then turn up years later as president of the alumni club.

Down in the strip-lit melancholia of the cafeteria, they each took a tray and shuffled along

66

the winding counter, inspecting the contents of the plastic display cabinets. Karla hovered for a while over a group of elderly cheese Danishes. 'I wouldn't,' Rosa said. 'They look as if they've been there a week.' She stole a sidelong glance at her sister. Karla had put on more weight lately. The cowl of extra flesh around her jaw was slowly expanding and she was beginning to walk with a fat person's arduous, backwards-leaning swagger. Rosa did not like to think of herself as being overly concerned with appearances. She disapproved of physical beauty, in fact. The reckless good will that her own looks inspired in total strangers had always been an embarrassment to her; she tended to regard other conspicuously attractive people as participants in a con game that she was doing her best to renounce. But Karla's weight was not an aesthetic issue, it was an ethical one. It bespoke a repugnant level of greed: a fundamental lack of self-respect.

Rosa moved over to the fruit island, hoping to lead by example. After examining a basket of wrinkled apples and blackened bananas, she settled, reluctantly, on a pinched-looking orange. Karla was already at the cash register, purchasing the Danish. She put it hurriedly away in her handbag as Rosa approached.

'My God!' Rosa said, glancing into the crowded interior of Karla's bag. 'You've got a whole life-support system in there.' She pointed at a tin of medicated talcum powder. 'What do you carry *that* around for?'

Karla blushed and snapped her bag shut. 'It . . . it's for my legs, actually. When I'm on my feet too long, the inside of my thighs get, you know, chafed . . .'

'Oh, right,' Rosa said, trying not to sound aghast. 'Bummer.'

Upstairs, Joel had been brought back from his tests and Audrey and Lenny were standing at his bedside in one of the ICU rooms. 'You're not going to stay here, love,' Audrey was saying when Rosa and Karla came in. 'I'm going to phone Dr Sussman tonight and see about getting you moved to NYU.'

Joel lay motionless on the bed, his white hair pressed flat against his skull in damp, yellowish strands, his knobbly wrists sticking out from the wide sleeves of his hospital gown like clappers in a bell. In some childish part of Rosa's mind, she had been expecting the largeness of her father's personality to have survived this physical catastrophe. She had pictured him sitting up, making jokes, imposing himself on his new environment with all his usual, commanding ebullience. But whatever remained of that man in this frail, speckled creature had gone into hiding. In the frayed, faded blue of hospital issue, her father had become just another enlistee in the vast army of the sick and dying.

'You sure you need all these, love?' Audrey was asking him in a teasing tone, pointing to the profusion of tubes sprouting from his scalp and mouth and wrists. 'I think you're showing off with all this stuff—' She broke off suddenly. 'What are *you* grinning at?' she demanded of Karla.

Rosa glanced at her sister. One of the unfortunate by-products of Karla's obliging personality was an unconscious tendency to take on the facial expressions and, in some cases, the speech patterns and accents of people around her. Just now, she had been so immersed in her mother's laboured performance of good cheer that she had allowed her face to become frozen in a rictus of foolish, sympathetic gaiety.

'I'm sorry,' Karla said, wringing her hands. 'I wasn't—'

'Oh, for God's *sake*,' Audrey hissed, 'don't stand there looking like a smacked arse. *You're* the one who's meant to have the bedside manner.'

'Give her a break, Mom,' Rosa said quietly.

Audrey continued to glare at Karla. 'Go on then. Talk to him!'

'Leave her alone, would you, Mom?' Rosa said.

'*Excuse* me?' Audrey turned to her slowly.

'You keep picking on her,' Rosa said. 'It's not fair.'

'It's all right,' Karla said. 'Honestly . . .'

Audrey folded her arms. 'Oh, I see. Now that you've finally graced us with your presence, you want to instruct me on how to behave, is that it?'

'I just don't think you need to be such a bitch to Karla, that's all,' Rosa said.

'Don't fight,' Karla pleaded.

Audrey took a step towards Rosa. 'Did you call me a *bitch*?'

A tiny tremor started up in Rosa's lower lip. 'I was just saying—'

'Get the fuck out of here!' Audrey screeched.

Rosa hesitated.

'Go on!' her mother shouted. 'Piss off!'

Rosa walked slowly over to the door. 'That's right!' her mother called after her as she left the room. 'Good fucking riddance!'

69

It had rained briefly while Rosa was in the hospital and as she walked to the subway station, fizzing with adrenaline and indignation, the trees along Henry Street wept icy droplets of water on her head. Her mother was intolerable. *Intolerable*. She was becoming, in her old age, like one of those paranoid despots who see in every minor disobedience the seeds of a full-scale insurgency. You threw a pebble; she brought out a Howitzer. Rosa would never forgive her for this.

As she turned on to Clark Street, her phone rang. It was Raphael, calling from the GirlPower Center.

'Are you okay?' he asked. 'What's happening?'

'I don't know. He's still unconscious.'

'Fuck. Do want me to come to the hospital?'

'No. I'm on my way home now. I had an argument with Mom. She threw me out.'

'*What?*'

'She was giving Karla a hard time, so I told her to stop it and she freaked.'

'She threw you *out?*'

'Uh-huh.'

'Jesus, Ro. Do you want me to meet you at your apartment?'

'Nah. I think I'm just going to go to bed.'

'Are you sure?'

'Yeah, really. Look, I'm at the station now. I'll speak to you tomorrow.'

Rosa got off the phone, feeling obscurely dissatisfied. Raphael's unquestioning faith in her version of events had only aroused her self-doubt. Already, as she passed through the ticket barriers and entered the blackened station elevator, she could feel her pleasurable anger beginning to surrender to remorse. She should not have picked a fight—not when her father was so ill. She had flattered herself that she was defending her sister, but Karla had not wanted to be defended. And she had called her own mother a bitch! She, who prided herself on *never* using that ugly, sexist word. Now, as a result of her own childish petulance, she had been exiled from her father's hospital room in his hour of need.

The train was just coming in when she reached the platform. The subway car she boarded was plastered with advertisements for a sinister-looking Manhattan dermatologist called Dr Z. Beneath the multiplied gaze of the sad-eyed, translucent-skinned doctor, she contemplated her sins.

Guilt—genuine, personal guilt, as opposed to some abstract, mandatory sense of shame about being a rich white American—was a very recent addition to Rosa's emotional repertoire. For most of her life, she had been immunized against self-reproach by the certitudes of her socialist faith. All her moral disappointment had been reserved for others—schoolmates who failed to resist the temptation of South African fruit, college acquaintances who were insufficiently concerned about the fate of the Angolan freedom fighters, bourgeois parents who pretended to socialist virtue. As a teenager, she had often been urged by her father to temper her revolutionary zeal with some sympathy for human frailty. 'Only ideas are perfect. People never are,' Joel would tell her. 'When you've lived a bit longer, you'll be more

71

forgiving.' But Rosa had scorned these attempts to modify her wrath. For a person as deeply offended by injustice and inequity as she was—as committed to changing the world—a degree of ruthlessness was imperative, she felt. Her usual response to her father had been to quote Lenin's defence of Bolshevik tactics: 'Is regard for humanity possible in such an unheard-of ferocious struggle? By what measure do you measure the quantity of necessary and unnecessary blows in a fight?'

Now, though, this paradisiacal era of righteousness had come to an end. After a long and valiant battle against doubt, she had finally surrendered her political faith and with it the densely woven screen of doctrinal abstraction through which she was accustomed to viewing the world. For the first time, she was charting her course without the guiding stars of revolutionary principles. To say that this was a humbling business did not begin to convey her desolation. All her adult life, she had imagined herself striding along in history's vanguard, like one of those muscular heroines in a Soviet constructivist poster. Now she had been thrown back into the ignominious ranks of bourgeois liberalism. She had become just another do-gooder, hoping to 'make a difference' by taking underprivileged girls on museum trips. She did not—could not—wish to have her old delusions back, but how she yearned for the self-assurance she had experienced while in their thrall!

At 110th Street, Rosa got off the train and, after pausing for a moment on Broadway to check her watch, she walked quickly over to the Ahavat Israel Shul on Amsterdam Avenue. Evening prayers had already begun when she entered the building. In the reception area, a man was standing beneath two giant Israeli and American flags, handing out chumashes and siddurim. Rosa walked past him down a dim corridor. At the rear of the building, she climbed a flight of stairs and entered the women's balcony section. There was only one other woman present this evening—an elderly lady with a frilly, doily-like chapel cap on her head. Rosa leaned over the balcony railing and gazed down into the sanctuary where a handful of old men was rocking back and forth in prayer.

She had visited Ahavat Israel for the first time three months ago. One Saturday morning in December, as she had been passing the building, she had glimpsed two men in black hats slipping in the front door of the building and had decided to follow them in. The impulse was born of a mild, touristic curiosity rather than any spiritual longing: she had never been inside an Orthodox synagogue before and she thought it would be entertaining to see what serious Jews got up to when they prayed.

Almost immediately upon entering the building, she had committed a serious faux pass by seating herself in the section of the synagogue reserved for male congregants. An embarrassing kerfuffle had ensued, culminating in her being removed from the sanctuary by two red-faced men and marched upstairs to the women's gallery. At this point, having had her expectations of antique taboos and cultic strangeness so promptly met, she would have happily departed. But up in the gallery, she had found herself hemmed in on all sides by davening women. Reluctant to draw further attention to herself by climbing over them to get out, she had resigned herself to remaining in her seat until the service was over.

She had understood almost nothing of what was going on, of course. The Hebrew siddur she had been given had no English translation, and her ignorance of Jewish observance was such that she could not even be sure of having correctly identified the rabbi. The synagogue itself was a disappointment. With its plastic stacking chairs and frayed green carpet runner and sad vases of dusty silk flowers, it reminded her of the down-at-heel dental practice that she had been taken to as a child. Even the mosaic on the eastern wall—a mid-century devotional abstract executed in mustard yellow and gold—had the dowdy, third-rate quality of dentist art. Still, she enjoyed the odd mixture of formality and casualness with which the congregants conducted themselves—the way they kept breaking off from the head-banging fervour of their praying to wander about the sanctuary and chat. And there was something sweet, she thought, about the way they handled the Torah—undressing it and dandling it and parading it about as if it were an adored infant. The whole thing had a faintly preposterous, Masonic quality, but it was not, she conceded, without its anthropological charm.

At the end of the Torah service, just as the scroll was being replaced in the ark, the congregation began to sing a slow, mournful prayer. Rosa, who rarely, if ever, responded to music without knowing and approving of what it was *about*, was surprised to find herself moved. Something in the prayer's austere melody was making the hairs on her arms stand up. A thought came to her, as clearly as if it had been spoken in her ear. *You are*

74

connected to this. This song is your song. When next she glanced down at the siddur lying open in her hands, she was amazed to see the little ragged suns of her own teardrops turning the wafer-thin pages transparent.

For days after this incident, Rosa tried to reassure herself that her response had been an insignificant somatic reflex. She had been tired. She had been feeling vulnerable. Music, together with certain sorts of majestic landscape, had a well-known tendency to induce such faux-sublime moments: artificial intimations of transcendent truths, grandiose hunches about the nature of the universe. It was all nonsense. Her tears had been no different to the ones people cried at sentimental television commercials. They represented nothing but a momentary and regrettable submission to kitsch.

The next week, however, she found herself drawn back to the synagogue. She was going only, she told herself, in order to prove her previous response an aberration. But the second visit turned out to be no less bizarre and agitating than the first. Once again, she was filled with a mysterious, euphoric sense of belonging; once again, she was borne along on an irresistible current towards foolish weeping. The week after that, she attended two evening services in addition to the Sabbath service. Each time she entered the synagogue, she vowed to remain detached and rational. And each time, her composure was conquered by the same disembodied voice whispering gnomically in her ear. She was part of this. She had always been part of this.

She approached her parents with the news of

her inexplicable, quasi-revelation, knowing full well what their reaction was likely to be. Joel and Audrey had a keen contempt for all religions, but Judaism, being the only variety of theistic mumbo-jumbo in which they were themselves ancestrally implicated, had always inspired their most vehement scorn. They snarled at the sight of menorahs. They curled their lips at the mention of Seder. They refused to attend any ceremony that took place in a synagogue. Even the bar mitzvahs of their friends' children—loosey-goosey, Reform affairs, at which nothing more solemnly religious occurred than the unveiling of the chocolate fountain at the after-party—were verboten. (Joel made it a point to send back all invitations to such events with the words 'THERE IS NO GOD' scrawled rudely across their engraved lettering.) Still, it never occurred to Rosa *not* to tell her parents. She had no talent for subterfuge—especially the sort that offered to make her own life easier. As a general rule, the stronger the pragmatic arguments for discretion, the more keenly did she feel the moral obligation for full disclosure.

Audrey's initial response had been one of derision. She sang snatches of 'Hava Nagila' and asked Rosa if she intended to marry one of those smelly old men with the payess. It was Joel who was nakedly enraged. That Rosa had succumbed, however temporarily, to the idiocy of faith was terrible enough, he told her. That she should have chosen Judaism in which to dabble could be construed only as an act of parricidal malice. 'This is bullshit!' he yelled at one point. 'I know you! You're constitutionally incapable of buying into

76

this kind of fairy tale. You never even believed in the tooth fairy, for Christ's sake!'

Rosa had to smile at that. She was not so swept away that she could not see the high comedy of this spiritual seduction: a Litvinoff daughter, a third-generation atheist, an enemy of all forms of magical thinking, wandering into a synagogue one day and finding her inner Jew. But there it was. Something had happened to her, something she could not ignore nor deny. And there was a sense in which its unlikelihood, its horrible *inconvenience*, was precisely what made it so compelling.

In the synagogue now, the service had come to an end. From her seat in the balcony, Rosa watched an old man hobbling out of the sanctuary. He was so bent over with age that he looked as if he were searching for lost coins on the floor. She thought of her father in his hospital bed, still as an effigy on a tomb. After a moment, she lowered her head and began to pray.

CHAPTER FOUR

For an hour or so, Lenny and Karla had been urging Audrey to let them take her home so that she could get some rest. Audrey refused to countenance the idea of leaving Joel at the hospital overnight, so at last it was agreed that Karla would accompany her mother back to Manhattan to collect some clothes and that Lenny would hold the fort until Audrey returned.

When Karla and Audrey drew up at Perry

Street, Julie was out on the doorstep, beating a rug. 'Look at her,' Audrey muttered. 'I wish someone would put *her* in a coma.'

'Hello, Aud,' Julie called as they got out of the car. 'What's the news?'

Audrey ignored the question. 'Got everything disinfected, have you?' she snarled as she swept past.

'Oh, don't mind me,' Julie said. 'I like to do it!'

Inside the house, Audrey and Karla met Colin emerging from the downstairs bathroom, where he had been affixing a floral-scented flush device to the toilet bowl. He was wearing rubber gloves and one of Audrey's old aprons emblazoned with an image of a black fist and the word 'Amandla!'.

'Aud,' he said, lurching towards Audrey with his arms outstretched. 'How *is* he?'

'Hello, Col.' Audrey swerved deftly past him, leaving Karla to pretend that his proffered embrace had been for her.

'Oh, she looks terrible,' Colin whispered in Karla's ear as Audrey proceeded downstairs to the basement.

'What's going on then?' Julie hissed, coming up behind them.

Karla gave her aunt and uncle a brief account of Joel's condition. They dropped their jaws and pressed their hands to their mouths in kabuki mimes of horror and dismay.

'I just can't believe it,' Julie said. 'He was as right as rain this morning, wasn't he, Col?'

Colin nodded.

'We had a lovely long chat with him, didn't we?'

Colin nodded again, with less conviction this time.

'He's been doing too much,' Julie went on. 'I said to Colin just yesterday, it's not right, the way he rushes around. My friend's husband got cancer last year.' She lowered her voice to a whisper. *Cancer of the bottom.* And the doctors told my friend it was one hundred per cent stress-related. *One hundred per cent—*'

'I think,' Karla interrupted in a quiet voice, 'I should go down and see if Mom's all right.'

The basement of Perry Street was given over to Joel's chaotic office. Dirty coffee mugs and tottering ziggurats of books and papers covered most of the desk and a good part of the floor around it. A large framed photograph of Joel shaking hands with Martin Luther King, Jr, hung above the desk but, otherwise, the grubby walls were bare. Audrey was sitting cross-legged on the floor rolling a joint when Karla came down. Her overcoat, which she had not yet taken off, was puddled around her, like a melted candle.

Karla drew up one of the spindly, revolving office chairs. 'Do you want me to go up and pack a bag for you?' she asked.

'I think I can pick out my own knickers, Karla,' Audrey replied.

'Oh, I know,' Karla said, 'I just thought . . .' She stood up. 'I should probably call Rosa and tell her what's going on.'

Audrey shook her head. 'She can call herself if she wants to know.'

Karla bit her lip anxiously. She felt awful about the fight at the hospital. If it hadn't been for her grinning like an idiot, Rosa would not have felt obliged to speak up for her. Still—she glanced at Audrey—there was no point in agitating her mother any further. She would just have to wait and call Rosa later on. She began wandering about the room, gathering up dirty coffee cups.

'Don't do that,' Audrey said.

'I might as well, Mom—'

'*Leave it.*'

Karla sat down again.

Audrey studied her with dissatisfaction. 'You look like you've put on weight.'

'Thank you.'

'Don't get the hump. No one else is going to say it.'

'Okay,' Karla said evenly.

'What kind of a response is that?'

'I don't know. Just . . . okay.'

Rosa often berated Karla for her passivity in the face of Audrey's remarks about her weight. 'Why do you put up with it?' she asked. 'Why don't you just tell her to fuck off?' But Karla never did. She could not have explained it to Rosa, but there was something in the brutal candour of her mother's sallies that pleased her. Her mother was right: no one else would say such things to her. No one else would ever speak the dread word 'fat' in her presence. It was not for want of courage so much as lack of interest. It would simply never occur to anyone else that Karla's figure was worthy of comment.

Her problems with size were not, after all, a recent phenomenon. She had been sent to her first summer fat-camp in the Berkshires when she was twelve. And, while the matter of her girth was an intense and ongoing saga for *her*—a daily drama of doughnuts nobly forsworn and later feverishly salvaged from the garbage; of non-fat-yoghurt

80

lunches cancelled out by furtive French-fry snacks; of painfully tiny losses and appallingly sudden gains—for most people, she could see, her weight did not register as any sort of narrative at all. It was a static fact, an eternal and therefore unremarkable feature of the landscape. Only her mother, it seemed, was still sufficiently invested to notice when she grew infinitesimally smaller or bigger. Only her mother retained faith in the possibility of a non-enormous Karla. Although Audrey didn't like to speak of it as a rule, she too had had weight problems when she was young. Once, long ago, she had shown Karla a picture of herself, aged nine—a furious, balloon-faced child, busting out from her frilly nylon party dress like a sausage from its casing. 'You get it from me, love,' she had said sadly. 'And I got it from my mum. The only answer is discipline. Constant discipline.'

'Are you going to do something about it?' Audrey asked now. 'The weight?'

'Yes.'

'It's important, you know. Mike might not say it but, believe me, he'd be over the moon if you lost forty or fifty pounds.'

Karla was silent, wondering if her husband had actually been so disloyal as to discuss her weight with her mother.

'And,' Audrey went on, 'apart from anything else, it'd probably help you with getting pregnant. It can't help. The extra flab, I mean.'

Karla nodded. 'Uh-huh.'

'And how is all that?'

'What?'

'The trying to get pregnant.'

'Mom!'

'What's the big deal?'

Upstairs, the doorbell rang.

'That'll be Mike,' Karla said, getting up. 'I told him to meet me here.'

'Stay,' Audrey ordered. 'Julie'll get it. What were you going to say about trying to get pregnant?'

'I wasn't. There's nothing to say.'

'Oh, fine. Be a woman of mystery.'

There was a pause and Karla allowed herself to hope that her mother had now exhausted the subject of her fertility.

'So.' Audrey took a long, hungry drag on her joint. 'How much *do* you weigh at the moment?'

'*Mom* . . .'

Her mother smirked. 'All right, buzz off then. You don't need to babysit me.'

Karla found Mike and Colin and Julie in the front room, emanating the slightly affronted gloom of relatives who have been consigned to the sidelines of a family drama. At the sight of Karla, they all set their teacups down and stood up. Mike approached Karla and pressed his cheek against hers. 'Where's Ma?' he asked. 'Can I go see her?'

Karla shook her head. 'I'd hold on for a bit. She'll be up soon.'

'I told him he should wait,' Julie said crossly. Clearly, she thought Mike's behaviour very pushy for someone who wasn't even a blood relation.

'I think I should go down,' Mike said.

Karla laid a restraining hand on his arm. 'No, Mike, really, I wouldn't.'

Mike's presence in her parents' house always made Karla tense. In private with her, he often spoke unkindly of Joel and Audrey. He accused them of being self-satisfied champagne socialists and claimed—not entirely unjustly—that they thought he was boring. Yet, whenever he came to Perry Street, all trace of this animosity disappeared and he became feverishly anxious to please and impress. He flirted with Audrey and sucked up to Joel. He pontificated about politics and used lots of gratuitously fancy words incorrectly. (Once, after Karla had gently pointed out to Mike that the phrase 'mute point', which he had been using all evening with her parents, was correctly pronounced 'moot point', he had refused to speak to her for three days.) It never occurred to Karla to give the disparity between Mike's private pronouncements and his public behaviour the name of hypocrisy. She thought it touching that in spite of all his understandable class resentment, he should still crave her parents' good opinion. She only wished, for his sake, that he could relax a little and not try so hard. Rosa and Lenny were always sniggering at his obsequious manners behind his back. And even Audrey and Joel, who were by no means averse to the subtler forms of flattery, seemed embarrassed at times by the brazenness of their son-in-law's fawning. 'He's a good kid,' Joel had once remarked after Mike had left the house, 'but, Christ Almighty, I wish he'd stop kissing my ass.'

'Do you think Aud's hungry?' Colin asked now. 'She should probably have a bite to eat.'

Karla, who had consumed nothing since the hospital Danish, stood up quickly. 'I'll go and see what's in the fridge.'

'No, no,' Julie protested. 'Let me. You've had a long day.'

Karla felt a mild panic at the thought of being

hostage to someone else's culinary choices. She liked to prepare her own food. 'Honestly, Julie— it's no trouble.'

'But I'd *like* to do it.'

The polite but intense struggle over who would get to author the refreshments was still going on when Audrey appeared.

'Ma!' Mike said, advancing quickly across the living room. He hugged his mother-in-law tightly and then held her at arm's length, to study her face. 'You look tired. Come, sit down.'

Karla glanced over at her aunt and uncle. Colin was watching Mike much as a circus audience watches a lion tamer placing his head in the lioness's jaw: half admiring of the courage, half desirous of witnessing a bloody calamity. Julie, taking advantage of the distraction, was attempting to scuttle out to the kitchen, unnoticed. Unwilling to accept defeat, Karla pursued her.

When the two women returned to the living room fifteen minutes later with a tray of sandwiches, they found Audrey standing in front of the fireplace. 'It's an absolute disgrace,' she was saying. 'It's a fucking travesty!' Colin was sitting pinkly in an armchair, pretending to read a magazine. Mike was pacing.

'What's wrong?' Karla asked. 'What's going on?'

'Honestly, Karla,' Audrey said, 'I don't know how you could put up with this. I couldn't show my face if I were you.'

'What are you talking about, Mom?'

'The endorsement!' Audrey shouted. 'Did your husband not tell you? Your shitty fucking union is planning to endorse the governor for re-election.'

Karla's mouth opened and closed. She looked at

Mike. 'Is it true?'

Earlier in the year, the Republican governor had pledged two billion dollars to raising salaries for the union's employees and there had been widespread speculation that he was buying the union's support for his re-election bid. Karla had refused to believe it. The governor had reinstated the death penalty in New York. He had vetoed an increase in the minimum wage. Her union, she had insisted, would never stoop to doing deals with a man like that.

Mike squared his shoulders defiantly. 'It's nothing to be ashamed of,' he said. 'The governor has been a good friend to the union.'

'Shame!' Audrey cried.

Julie set the tray of sandwiches down on the coffee table. 'Food's up!'

Audrey shook her head. 'I haven't got time for food. I have to get back to the hospital.'

'Oh, Audrey,' Julie protested, 'you must eat something. Look, I made cheese and mayonnaise just the way you like it.'

'I'm going to get my clothes,' Audrey said, walking out of the room.

A moment later, she called to Karla from the staircase. Karla hurried over to the door. 'Yes, Mom?'

'Just remember, Karl,' Audrey shouted, 'no more than two of those sandwiches, all right?'

*   *   *

Karla and Mike were quiet most of the long subway-ride home to the Bronx. Mike groomed his hair with the special military hairbrush that he

85

kept in his briefcase and read the paper. Karla examined advertisements for technology institutes—'Are you ready for a rewarding career in database management?'—and gazed out at the tunnel.

'I'm worried,' she said eventually. 'I think Dad might die.'

'Don't talk like that,' Mike said. His tone was gruff, irritated.

Karla glanced at him. 'I'm sorry you got a hard time from Mom tonight.'

Mike turned his head to the side, considering his profile in the train window. 'It's no more than I expected. She doesn't understand union politics. She thinks she knows better than the leadership how to best serve the members.'

Karla nodded. He was right, of course. The leaders knew what they were doing. If they judged that supporting the governor was the best thing for the union, it wasn't Audrey's place—or Karla's—to second-guess the decision. 'Do we . . . will we have to vote for him then?' she asked.

Mike bristled. 'What do you think? There's no point in an endorsement if the members don't follow the directive.'

'Right, no, of course. I just wondered.'

Mike looked up as the train pulled into the 242nd station. 'This is us.'

Karla and Mike lived in a dark, pre-war block just down the street from the Botanical Gardens. The hallways of their building were permeated by the fumes of a vicious, Mexican cleaning agent called Fabuloso that the super used to sluice the floors twice a week. Upon entering the lobby, Karla always took care to breathe through her

86

mouth for the first five seconds or so in order to offset the initial olfactory shock.

This evening, as she stood greenly by the elevators, waiting for Mike to check the mailbox, the elevator doors opened and a middle-aged Filipina woman in knee socks and plastic sandals stepped out. 'Hello, Mrs Mee,' Karla said. 'How are you?'

The woman looked at her with a bloodhound's expression of jowly suffering. 'Terrible,' she said, shaking her head slowly. 'Terr-i-bul.'

'Oh dear.' Karla cocked her head in concern. 'I'm sorry.'

Mrs Mee, who lived with her three grown-up children and her husband in the apartment next door to Karla's, was a woman of baroque sorrows—a martyr not only to her ingrate family and her poorly paid job at a Manhattan nail salon, but also to a host of chronic ailments, including back pain, asthma and angina.

'At work today, the air conditioning was off,' Mrs Mee said, 'and the nail polish got in my throat so bad I couldn't breathe. I said to them—'

Mike appeared now. He stepped in front of Karla, as if to physically shield her from Mrs Mee's complaint. 'Hey, Mrs Mee,' he said, 'I'm sorry, but Karla can't stop to chat. Her dad had a stroke this morning. She's been at the hospital all afternoon. She needs to get inside and rest.'

'Oh!' Mrs Mee said, excited by the bad news and, at the same time, a little offended at having her own misery bested. 'Sure, sure. Go on then.' She patted Karla on the wrist. 'I talk to you tomorrow.'

Karla and Mike rode the elevator to the fourth

floor and walked down the echoing corridor to their apartment in silence. Once they were inside, Mike sat down at the kitchen table to examine the mail and Karla went into the living room to check the answering machine. There were no messages. She stood for a moment, in the darkness, looking around the room. Even in soft, evening light, there was something off-puttingly austere and hygienic about her apartment. She had made considerable efforts over the years to cosy the place up and to give it, as they said on the home-improvement shows, 'personality', but no matter how many interesting objects she scattered and how many colourful throws she draped, she had never succeeded in banishing its sad, dorm-room ambience.

Mike came in and turned on the lights. He was holding the ovulation test that she had taken that morning. The result had been positive, indicating that at some point in the next twenty-four hours she was liable to release an egg.

'You want to try tonight?' he asked. His tone was exquisitely reasonable. 'I mean, if you're too upset and everything, it's okay. But we probably shouldn't waste—'

'No, no,' Karla agreed. 'I think we should.'

Mike nodded approvingly and sat down in an armchair to watch the end of a PBS documentary about Robert Oppenheimer. Karla went into the bathroom to make herself ready.

Two years ago, Mike had persuaded Karla to see a gynaecologist about her incapacitating menstrual pain. Karla had suffered unusually heavy and painful periods since late adolescence, but until Mike had begun nagging, it had never occurred to her to seek medical help. She had simply accepted that it was her lot in life to spend five days of every month in mute agony, medicating herself with handfuls of Extra Strength Advil. To have made a fuss about something as petty as her periods would have struck her as unseemly. But Mike had been insistent. And when Karla wouldn't make an appointment herself, he went ahead and made one for her.

The gynaecologist was a kind, elderly man with cool hands and a soothing way of discussing baseball scores while he probed. After giving her an internal exam, he ordered a laparoscopy. Within a few days, it was established that Karla was suffering from a combination of uterine cysts, fibroids and Stage 2 endometriosis. 'You hit the trifecta!' the gynaecologist announced cheerfully. He went on to explain that her various conditions were almost certainly responsible for her failure to get pregnant during the three years that she and Mike had been married. Her reproductive health was 'impaired' and if she was serious about wanting a baby she would need to start on a programme of fertility drugs.

Mike had taken this very badly. He came from a large, extended Irish family—there were twenty-three cousins in the New York area alone—and his expectation had been that he would sire four children at least. 'I don't understand,' he had told Karla. 'The women in our family have never had this sort of problem.'

For her part, Karla had responded to the news with curious calm, prompting Mike to accuse her one evening of having known that she was 'barren' all along. He later regretted the remark, of course, and apologized profusely. Karla did not hold a grudge. It was natural, she thought, that he should feel angry and cheated. And, in a way, he was correct: she *had* always known—not that her reproductive organs were defective, but that her body was, in some mysterious and profound way, against her. She had always been fat. She had never been able to dance or catch a ball. Her hair fell the wrong way and her skin was the troublesome 'combination' sort. When she saw a photograph in a book of what advanced endometriosis looked like—what a gruesome, jungly mess it made of a woman's ovaries—she found herself nodding, as if in recognition. Of course, she thought to herself, *of course*: I am as ugly inside as I am out.

After the initial trauma of the diagnosis, Mike had recovered quickly. One evening, Karla returned from work to find that he had drawn up a plan of action. She would start taking the ovulation drug that her doctor had recommended. If, in two years' time, they had not conceived, they would adopt. (He had already ruled out the idea of using a surrogate, he said, on the basis that it was exploitative of poor women and, in any case, 'weird'.)

Mike quickly became an expert on fertility science and involved himself in every aspect of Karla's reproductive health. No detail was too mundane or recondite for him to overlook. He bought and prepared fertility-enhancing foods for her. He doled out fish-oil supplements and outlawed Diet Coke. He frequented online chat rooms to glean advice from other reproductively challenged couples. He spent hours researching

90

ovulation testers on consumer websites and broke with his customary frugality to purchase the most expensive and complex model on the market. Thereafter, he insisted on coming into the bathroom with Karla every month, to hover gravely while she conducted her early-morning ovulation experiments with strips of litmus paper and test tubes of her pee. (Karla had once gently suggested that she might be left to carry out these procedures on her own, but Mike had stared at her with such astonished, uncomprehending hurt that she had immediately let the matter drop.)

A few months ago, there had been a false alarm when Karla's period had been a day late. She had kept it to herself, wanting to wait at least forty-eight hours before raising Mike's hopes, but when she had returned home from work that evening, she found that Mike had already made the calculation himself and purchased a pregnancy test. She had begun bleeding while he was still studying the test instructions.

In spite of such episodes, Karla was surprised to find that she enjoyed the baby-making project. She liked the suspense of it. Several of the books about fertility that Mike had borrowed from the library contained warnings about letting the desire to conceive become paramount. 'When one or both of you become obsessed with the reproductive "goal",' Selena and Kenneth Daniels wrote in their book *Making Love, Making Babies*, 'difficulties can arise in sustaining the spontaneous, joyful aspects of sex.' But since neither spontaneity nor joy had ever been prominent features of Karla and Mike's sex life, they had been spared the demoralizing effects of a slow abatement in these areas. If anything, it seemed to Karla, the quest to make a child had slightly improved things between them sexually. Now, at least, their terse bedroom encounters had a dignifying purpose.

But time was running out. Twenty-two months of efficient 'trying' had already elapsed. Just the other day, Karla had found a scrap of paper in Mike's jeans with the address of a Manhattan adoption agency scribbled on it.

In the shower, Karla sniffed the air suspiciously. Lately, she had begun to detect the smell of Fabuloso infiltrating the apartment. Once or twice, she had had to get up in the middle of the night and brush her teeth a second time, just to get the ghostly, lavatorial tang out of her mouth. She turned off the shower now and applied a small amount of scented body lotion to her damp body, before putting on her nightgown and hurrying out across the hall, into the icy bedroom. The heating was very poor in their building. Mike often complained to the landlord, but there was nothing, apparently, short of replacing the entire heating system, that could be done. At night the two of them uttered little cries of anguish as they skittered across the chill floor into their frigid cave of blankets, and in the mornings they awoke to find themselves slippery-skinned and dry-mouthed, stewing in their own tropical biosphere.

Karla heard the mournful cello solo accompanying the closing credits of Mike's programme and, soon after, the whine of his electric toothbrush from the bathroom. She curled up like a prawn, trying to generate some heat.

Prior to marrying Mike, Karla's sexual experience had been limited to three partners and precisely seven acts of intercourse. Compared to the hectic bedroom chronicles of most of her peers, this was a demure record, indeed, but Karla had never considered herself deprived. Her life as a single person had given her a perfectly adequate purview of the erotic fundamentals, she felt. Sometimes, when the conversation among her female colleagues at the hospital grew bawdy, allusions were made to practices or positions with which she was not familiar. But even then her incuriosity was resolute. Whatever specialized pursuits they were talking about, she was quite sure they had nothing to do with *real* sex. Real sex she knew about. It had a simple, teleological order: kissing, then petting—both of which could be reasonably pleasant—followed by penetration, which rarely was. In some rare and regrettable instances, a tense oral episode might be interpolated somewhere in the routine. (She didn't mind administering, but she could not bear to be administered to.) And that was it—the universal coital formula.

Mike came in now and began to undress. After he had folded his dirty clothes in a neat pile and placed them in the laundry basket, he went over to the closet and began to select his outfit for the next day. Karla watched him as he moved about the room, his hard, white body gleaming like a silverfish in the darkness: *Jack Sprat could eat no fat*. When he was finally done, he climbed into bed, set the alarm and lay back on his pillow with a sigh.

Even on nights such as this, when there had been an explicit agreement that intercourse was to take place, Mike always came at Karla tentatively—crab-wise—with creeping, uncertain

93

hands. At the beginning of their marriage, Karla had found this hesitancy charming. She had attributed it to a kind of gallantry on Mike's part—a reluctance to trouble her with his base, male needs. But then one night, a few years ago, when she had turned to receive Mike's advances a little more readily than usual, she had caught him off guard, wearing a look of such intense unhappiness that she had almost cried out in sympathy. The expression had been equal parts repulsion and resignation—a sort of stoic anguish, like a child squaring up to the task of eating his spinach. It had lasted for only a fraction of a second and then it had disappeared, replaced by a watery smile. But the import of that fleeting grimace was not to be denied. Her husband, she had understood, performed his connubial duties with as little relish—possibly less—than she did.

Pressing himself close now, Mike licked the fingers of his right hand and thrust them between her legs. Karla closed her eyes and tried to concentrate on what was happening. (A study that Mike had read about in one of his chat rooms suggested that women were more likely to conceive when they had orgasms.) But her mind refused. She thought about her father's stroke. She thought about the Danish she had bought at the hospital cafeteria—the soggy weight of it in her hand, the garish yellow ooze that had emerged when she bit into it . . .

A memory came to her now of sitting around the kitchen table back in Perry Street with her brother and sister, watching her father make French toast. It had been a tradition, when they were young, for Joel to get up early on Sunday mornings and make them breakfast while Audrey slept in. He considered these occasions a vital opportunity to catch up with his children and to teach them about the philosophical and political ideas that were important to him. Since he was frequently away from home during the week, he had always been very particular about observing this Sunday ritual, and long after the children had all become teenagers he continued to insist that they come down for Sunday breakfast, no matter how late they had been out the night before.

On this Sunday, the subject of his lecture was the ethics of armed struggle. It was a topic with special significance for the household because Lenny's biological parents had both been founding members of an underground revolutionary outfit called the New York Cong (Lenny's father had died when Lenny was still an infant, attempting to construct a bomb. His mother was serving a life sentence for killing a police officer during an abortive bank robbery.) Joel strode about the kitchen, messily breaking and beating eggs. He was wearing his standard breakfast attire: a pair of leather slippers, flattened down at the back by his giant, grey heels, and a balding, terry-towelling bathrobe. From time to time, the two sides of the robe would flap open like theatre curtains, revealing the proscenium arch of his groin and a terrifying glimpse of pubic froth.

'In certain situations,' Joel was saying, 'some people feel that non-violence is no longer effective and that they must take the next step into violent action.' He was dipping slices of white bread into the bowl of eggs and laying them in a hot frying pan. Lenny was paying only fitful attention,

95

prowling around the table in a bored, feral way, occasionally pausing to stroke Rosa's hair.

Rosa and Karla were rapt.

'Killing people, you mean, Daddy?' Karla asked.

'Sometimes, yes, even killing people . . .'

Lenny began to make machine-gun noises, pretending to mow down Joel.

'Stop that,' Joel said coldly.

Lenny shot him a doleful glance from beneath his long, girlish lashes and desisted.

'Now,' Joel said, resuming his tone of jovial didacticism, 'the idea of armed insurgency is a legitimate idea that has occurred to people many times throughout history and all over the world.' He brought a plate of French toast to the table and the children began to eat. 'In fact, our own country, the United States, came into being through armed struggle. People got tired of living under the yoke of the English king . . .'

'Yolk,' Lenny said dreamily.

Joel ignored him.

'George III,' Rosa said.

'That's right, honey,' Joel smiled. 'George III. So they started shooting down British soldiers between Lexington and Concord . . .'

Karla, who had been groping for something to contribute, blurted now, 'No taxation without representation!'

But Joel wasn't listening. He was looking at Lenny, who was pretending to be a wounded British soldier and sinking in theatrical agony to the floor. 'For Chrissakes!' Joel shouted. 'Sit down, Lenny! Try not to act like a moron for ten minutes!'

The room was silent. Sullenly, Lenny got up and

took his place at the table.

Joel stared at him furiously. 'Why do you always have to play the fool?'

Karla, who dreaded these confrontations between Joel and Lenny, tried to distract her father by pretending to seek clarification. 'So . . . so . . . it's okay sometimes to kill people, Daddy?'

Joel winced. 'No, it's never "okay", Karla. It's always a very terrible and serious thing to do. But in some circumstances it may be justified. If you look at history, you see that people who fight for their rights are often called terrorists, guerrillas, or whatever. But if they succeed—if they win their fight against oppression—they become national heroes. They become the new government.'

'Like the Zionists who founded Israel,' Rosa said.

Joel nodded. 'Exactly, sweetie. That's a very good example.'

Lenny slipped out of the room. He was going, as he often did on these Sunday mornings, in search of Audrey. Karla pictured him easing open the door to their parents' room, clambering on to the tall bed and nestling in the warm hollow left by Joel's body. How she envied Lenny's indifference to Joel—his refusal to participate in the battle for paternal approbation!

'*Karla!*' Joel said suddenly. 'What're you doing?' Karla jumped. Joel pointed at her hand, which was reaching out to take the last piece of French toast on the serving platter. He smiled, trying to lighten the admonition. 'Don't you think you've had enough, sweetie?' Karla put her fork down and stared at her lap in remorse.

97

Mike appeared to be in the final furlong. His teeth were gritted, his nostrils flared. Even as Karla opened her mouth to utter some encouraging groans, he froze and, with an angry little 'Yuh!', slumped, done. She lay still, registering the familiar aftermath—the sense of warm things growing cold, of tumescence shrivelling; the tiny, wet sound as Mike slipped out of her.

In the days before the fertility drugs, this would have been Karla's cue to get up and fetch a warm washcloth. (Mike liked to be wiped down and made fresh before he slept.) But for a while now, she had been excused from this duty. Mike went to get his own washcloth, so that Karla might remain recumbent, her legs straight up in the air, for twenty minutes, with the aim of abetting the conception process with gravity. Mike had suggested that they adopt this method, after reading about it in one of the fertility books. Karla was not particularly hopeful of its efficacy, but as the deficient partner in the reproductive process, she did not feel in a position to contest any of her husband's increasingly desperate ideas. In the darkness, she arranged a pillow beneath her haunches, and raised her legs. Another technique recommended by Selena and Kenneth Daniels was positive visualization:

Here's one for the ladies: try sending out positive thoughts to your mate's sperm as they set out on the journey to your egg. We have no scientific evidence that this kind of cheerleading works, but hey—it can't hurt!

98

Karla had tried this once or twice—scrunching her eyes shut, and picturing the silent struggle for life that was beginning somewhere within: the clamorous tadpole horde racing through the darkness of the cervical canal; the egg in its pink fallopian boudoir, languorously awaiting its courtiers. But at some point, the positive images always got hijacked by negative ones. The sperm who had set out so boisterously would grow languid and start to dawdle. Or vast mushroom-like fibroids would billow out from her womb, barring their way. Or the egg would turn out to be ensnared, like a fairy-tale princess, within an impassable thicket of endometrial scar tissue.

She didn't really believe in the possibility of making good things happen with the sheer strength of your desire for them. If anything, it seemed to her, the opposite was true. The moment you wanted anything too fervently, the moment you yearned, the universe gazed with disgust upon your mewling and withheld. To get things, you had to be careless about them, the way that Rosa was. Rosa, who tied her blonde hair back in an untidy ponytail and wore cheap sneakers until they fell apart on her feet, and washed her face with soap and water, but still looked like a French film actress . . .

Mike was hissing something in her ear. 'Up! Up!' he seemed to be saying.

'What?' Karla said sleepily. She opened her eyes to see Mike's face scowling at her in the darkness.

'Put your legs up!' he said. She felt the angry jab of his foot against her thigh. 'The twenty minutes aren't done yet.'

Part Two

CHAPTER FIVE

'Mrs Audre-ey!'

Audrey woke from a doze on her living-room sofa to find Sylvia, her cleaning lady, standing over her.

'I gotta vacuum in here,' Sylvia said in a teasing singsong. 'Don't you got a bed upstairs?'

Audrey groaned. When she had sat down to read the paper, the living room had been chilly and dark. Now, sunlight was filtering in through the dirty windows, striping her shirt and gently broiling the fusty velvet of the sofa. It was upsetting to have Sylvia discover her recumbent and snoring in the middle of the day. To offset some of the embarrassment of having an elderly Latina scrub her toilets, she usually made sure to be elaborately, importantly busy whenever Sylvia was in the house. 'I'll get up,' she said. 'Just give me a minute.'

'Okay.' Sylvia wagged her finger. 'Don't be too long!'

Audrey watched her as she left the room. Maintaining the fiction of chummy equality with your help could be very wearing at times. Privately, she thought her socialist conscience could have survived a *tiny* bit more deference from Sylvia. She closed her eyes and tried to recollect the dream she had just been having. But the few stray images that had survived Sylvia's intrusion were already escaping—slipping away from her grasp, like the prizes in a fairground machine falling from the clumsy mechanical claw. After a while, she gave up and opened her eyes again. She looked at her

103

watch. She was supposed to be meeting Rosa in Brooklyn in an hour to take Joel's mother, Hannah, to see Joel. She hadn't even put gas in the car. She got up and began hunting in her handbag for her keys.

Audrey hated napping in the daytime. It was demoralizing. It made her feel like an old lady. She wasn't getting enough night-time sleep, that was the problem; she wasn't *scheduling* things efficiently. By day, she sat at Joel's bedside in a narcoleptic stupor; by night she rattled around the Perry Street house, a lone pea in an oversized pod. Her domestic life, which for forty years had been framed by Joel's clamorous, demanding presence, had become a shambolic, unpunctuated affair. She frittered her evenings away, gazing listlessly at the television, smoking joints, wandering in and out of the kitchen to open and close the fridge—always putting off the moment when she would have to clomp up the stairs to bed. The procrastination had nothing to do with fear of the dark, or of the bogeyman: it was simply that without Joel she didn't have the gumption, the discipline, to call a halt to the day by herself.

The keys were not in her bag. She went into the kitchen and began searching through the piles of newspaper and mail on the kitchen table.

She felt a sort of guilty nostalgia now for the early, hectic days of Joel's illness. In the first week after the stroke, the crisis had formed a cocoon into which nothing resembling normalcy had been allowed to intrude. Joel had had two emergency surgeries to stop bleeding in his brain. His heart had stopped beating twice. She had set up camp in the ICU—sleeping in the chair next to Joel's bed at

104

night and showering in the maternity ward in the morning. Rosa and Karla had taken compassionate leave from their jobs. And every day a procession of Joel's friends and colleagues and former clients had passed through the Family and Friends Lounge. Sometimes, there had been as many as twenty people gathered in the little room, telling sentimental stories about Joel and ordering in bagels and lox from the deli across the road. One night, Judy Collins had come by and they'd all sung 'We Shall Overcome'.

Six weeks on, that first, exhilarating spike of catastrophe had subsided. Joel, still languishing in the no man's land of his coma, had been demoted to 'sub-acute' status and moved to a rehab centre in NYU. His law office had been closed and his small staff—with what seemed to Audrey rather heartless efficiency—had found themselves new jobs. Rosa and Karla were back at work. Audrey had come home.

Everyone had assured her that coming home was the sensible thing to do. Joel would likely be in the rehab place for months to come and it would be silly, they said, to wear herself out at this stage in hysterical displays of saintliness. She needed to conserve her energy for the long haul. The nurses had been instructed to phone her immediately if Joel's condition changed in her absence and in the case of an emergency she could get from the house to the hospital in under half an hour.

Still, there was a part of Audrey that was appalled by her decision. Six weeks Joel had been in a coma—just six weeks—and already she was making choices based on what was practical and convenient? As a child she had often fantasized

105

that her failure to perform certain tasks—to stay off cracks in the pavement all the way home from school, or to touch the stair banister before her bedroom door swung shut—would result in cosmic disasters. Now, when she lay on the sofa late at night, listening to the familiar creaks of her gently subsiding house, she was visited by similar superstitious forebodings. What if staying with Joel had been a test of her devotion? What if her presence at his bedside had been the one thing keeping him alive and, by coming home, she had condemned him to death?

A few nights ago, Jean had persuaded Audrey to accompany her to an anti-war meeting in Chelsea. Audrey needed to get out in the world and recharge her batteries, she said. She needed a change of scene. It had seemed a reasonable enough idea at the time. But the outing had proven to be a terrible mistake. Audrey was not ready yet to put her personal calamity in the perspective that social life required. It did not reassure her to know that life in the great world was going on as before: it offended her.

The meeting, which had been convened to strategize protest actions against a US invasion of Iraq, was largely taken up with a debate about whether to make a pro-Palestinian stance part of the official anti-war platform. Towards the end, it had digressed into a not very productive squabble over whether or not actors were appropriate speakers at anti-war rallies.

'Everybody always wants to have Susan Sarandon at these things because she's good-looking,' one man said, 'but how well-informed is she, really?' Half the meeting nodded. The other half hissed. The Sarandon defenders accused the anti-Sarandon man of being sexist. ('What about Tim Robbins?' a woman cried angrily. 'You're going to let Tim Robbins speak and not Susan Sarandon?') The anti-Sarandon faction indignantly demanded a retraction of this slander. ('But I don't like Tim Robbins either,' the man insisted.) And so it went on. Audrey had listened with tears of rage blurring her vision. Joel was lying unconscious in a hospital bed—and these people were fretting over the bona fides of Susan Sa-fucking-randon?

At the bar afterwards, several people had approached her to ask after Joel's health. She had been waiting impatiently for some acknowledgement of her troubles, but as soon as it came she found she didn't want it after all. Some of the well-wishers offered medical advice: inspirational coma-recovery stories gleaned from NPR, internet apocrypha about the miraculous properties of hyperbaric chambers. Some bragged about how 'blown away' they had been by the news of Joel's misfortune—what scary thoughts of their own mortality it had conjured. Others, having mumbled their condolences, lapsed into discomfited silence and simply stared at Audrey, waiting to be rescued from their ineptitude. Audrey tried to perform, tried to be brave and breezy. But she misjudged her tone, apparently— overdid it somehow. A few people were visibly shocked by what they took to be her inappropriate levity. The rest seemed to be persuaded that Joel was not in such bad shape after all. One man she spoke to concluded their exchange by asking her to give Joel his best. *His best.* As if Joel were laid up at home with a bad case of gout!

Audrey was still going through the crap on the kitchen table. Beneath a wodge of unopened, coffee-stained mail, she came across a copy of Noam Chomsky's 9/11 book. She sat down and stared disconsolately at its cover. A few nights before Joel's collapse, she had declined to make love to him because she wanted to read this book. (Joel, who had a passing acquaintance with Chomsky, had jokingly threatened to write to him, complaining that his critique of the American imperium was interfering with his sex life.) Now look. The book remained unread. She had never made it past the first three pages. How terrible to have missed what might have been her last chance to make love to Joel—for Chomsky! She shook her head. Remorse of this sort was useless; it was sentimental. In the great Icelandic saga of a marriage, such minor spousal failings were nothing. Footnotes at most. Married life was like good health: there was no bloody point to it if you could not occasionally abuse it or take it for granted.

Sylvia was coming back downstairs now, making the house tremble with her stomping tread. 'Mrs Aud-rey,' she called.

Audrey got up and went out into the hallway.

'I found these in the bathroom sink,' Sylvia said, dangling Audrey's keys over the banister. 'You want them?'

*   *   *

'You're late,' Rosa said when Audrey arrived at Hannah's apartment.

108

Audrey wiped her feet carefully on the doormat. 'And good afternoon to you too, dear.'

'I'm not going to be able to come to the hospital with you,' Rosa said, closing the door and following her mother down the hallway. 'It's too late. I have to be somewhere at three.'

'Don't be daft,' Audrey replied airily. 'You know I can't manage Nana and the wheelchair on my own.'

The air in Hannah's dark sitting room was thick with the thriftstore scent of old person's dwelling. Hannah lay asleep in her electric recliner with the scissors and magnifying glass that she had been using to clip articles of interest from *The New York Times* still resting in her lap.

'I have an appointment,' Rosa said.

Audrey walked over to turn off the radio, which had got stuck between stations and was now emitting a faint contrapuntal roar of Bartok symphony and KISS FM. 'Call up and tell them you're going to be late,' she said.

Arranged in a semicircle on the mantelpiece, was a group of framed family photographs: Hannah, aged three, in a Brooklyn photographer's studio, shortly after arriving in America from Odessa in 1912. Joel's father, Irving, making his maiden speech at a meeting of the Trade Union Unity League in 1924. Hannah's brother, Lou, in the uniform of the Abraham Lincoln Battalion, boarding a boat to Spain in 1933. Joel, aged seven, marching down Fifth Avenue with his parents in the 1937 May Day parade. Audrey turned away with a grimace. She had never liked old photographs. All those dead relatives staring out reproachfully from the past, humming their vanityof-human-wishes dirge. You might as well decorate your house with skulls, she thought.

'What is this thing you have to go to?' she asked, turning back to Rosa.

'I'm going to Monsey for the weekend.'

'Muncie? What, in Idaho?'

'No, Monsey upstate.'

Audrey looked at Rosa's calf-length navy skirt and high-necked black blouse. Her eyes narrowed. 'Is this something Jewy?'

'Actually, I'm attending a Shabbaton.'

'And what the fuck is *that* when it's had its hair washed?'

'It's an extended Sabbath, with extra lectures and things.' Rosa paused. 'I'm staying with a rabbi and his family.'

'Oh for God's sake—'

'I'm not going to argue about this, Mom.'

Hannah woke up now and peered about her indignantly. 'Where's Magda?'

'I think she just popped out for a second,' Audrey said. Magda was the morose Polish lady who came in five days a week to cook and clean for Hannah. Audrey had passed her on her way in, sneaking a cigarette in front of the building.

Audrey went over and crouched down next to Hannah's recliner. 'How are you doing, Nana?'

'Fine,' Hannah said curtly. She began to fumble through the ranks of yellow plastic prescription bottles on her side table. In the buttery light of the table lamp, her face, with all its intricate whorls and cross-hatchings, looked like the surface of the ocean seen from a plane.

'Do you need something, Nana?' Audrey asked.

'I can't find the . . . oh, there it is.' Hannah

110

picked up the keypad that controlled her chair and began jabbing at the buttons. There was a loud, promising hum of hydraulics, but the chair remained stationary.

'Can I help with that?'

'No,' Hannah snapped. 'You don't know how it works.'

Hannah's fiendishly expensive and complicated recliner had been a gift from Joel on the occasion of her ninetieth birthday. It was equipped with five angles of repose and three modes of massage, none of which Hannah knew how to operate. Consequently, a substantial portion of her waking hours was spent riding helplessly back and forth in its rigid velveteen clutches, furiously refusing all offers of assistance.

'Come on, Nana,' Audrey said. 'Let me have a look.'

'No!' Hannah hugged the keypad jealously to her chest. The recliner gave a sudden, violent judder and lurched backwards, sending the scissors and magnifying glass on her lap clattering to the floor. As Audrey stepped forward, preparing to wrestle the keypad from Hannah's grasp, the recliner came zooming forward again, abruptly delivering Hannah into an upright position.

'There you go!' Audrey said. 'Good for you, Nana!'

Hannah, sitting as straight-backed now as an Egyptian queen, lowered her eyelids witheringly. 'No need to congratulate me, dear. I am not a halfwit.' She looked over at her granddaughter. 'Rosa! What was it we were talking about just now?'

'We were discussing the piece in *The Times*,

Nana.'

'Ah, yes.'

'What piece?' Audrey asked.

Hannah pointed to the pile of newspapers at the foot of her chair. 'There's an interview today with the head of Karla's union.'

Audrey nodded. She had been meaning to read the article that morning but had fallen asleep before she had a chance. 'Oh *that*. I couldn't be bothered. I don't need to hear Judas trying to justify himself.'

Hannah's face took on a pained expression. 'No, no, dear,' she said, 'you are blaming the wrong people. If the Democrats had done anything in the last twenty years to support the labour movement, the union wouldn't have been forced to strike this sort of deal.'

'Well, but isn't the labour movement supposed to advocate for *all* working people?' Audrey said.

Hannah closed her eyes. 'Perhaps, Audrey, if you had ever been in a union . . .'

Audrey gave a tinkling little laugh. 'I'm not sure we can really call the health-workers a union any more, can we, Nana? It looks to me like they've turned themselves into a special-interests group.'

Hannah declined to acknowledge this remark. 'It's just as Joel's father used to say,' she observed. 'The labour movement requires solidarity and solidarity requires discipline and discipline—'

'Bugger discipline!' Audrey interrupted. 'If Karla had any gumption, she'd hand in her membership.'

Hannah smiled a private smile and began to hum to herself.

Rosa stood up. 'I should go.'

'What's that?' Hannah said.

'I have to go now, Nana.'

'Didn't Rosa tell you?' Audrey said. 'She's not coming to the hospital. She has a very important appointment with a rabbi.'

Hannah made a guttural sound of disapproval.

'Now, now,' Audrey said. 'We mustn't be mean about Rosa's religious friends. She'll get angry with us.'

Rosa exhaled noisily. 'Mother, could you not—'

'Let me tell you something, Rosa,' Hannah said. 'My parents came thousands of miles on a boat to get to this country . . .'

Rosa gazed at the floor with studied patience.

'Three weeks they were at sea,' Hannah continued. 'In steerage. With two small children. And what do you think my mother did the day the boat came into New York Harbor and she saw the Statue of Liberty for the first time?'

Rosa waited.

'She took off her headscarf and threw it in the water! And, you understand, this was an extremely scandalous thing—a shanda—for a Jewish woman to show her hair in public. People were shouting at her, telling her she was going to bring God's wrath on them, but my mother didn't care. "I am in America now," she said. "From now on, I am going to be a free woman. I am not going to listen to the rabbis who tell me what to eat and how to dress. You all can do what you like, but this is my decision." Can you imagine what courage that took? They nearly threw her overboard! And why did she do this? So that her children and her children's children would not have to grow up under the tyranny of religion as she did. What do

113

you think she would say today if she could see her great-granddaughter futzing around with all the hocus-pocus and pie in the sky that she rejected a century ago?'

'Well, I hope, Nana, that she would respect my freedom to make up my own mind about these things.'

'Come on,' Audrey said, clapping her hands. 'Don't be wasting your breath on Rosa. Let's get this show on the road, shall we?'

Hannah sighed. Talking about her mother had put her in a melancholy frame of mind. 'What a dreadful thing, to be visiting your own child in the hospital!' she said. 'You can't imagine what it is for a mother to see her son like this.'

'Well, it's not easy for any of us, Nana,' Audrey said sharply.

'When I think of him lying there all alone—'

'He's not alone. I'm with him almost all the time. And he has a lot of other visitors too.'

Hannah brightened. 'Yes, Karla told me that Jesse Jackson was in the other day. He stayed for over an hour, she said. Wasn't that nice of him?'

Audrey yawned. 'Jesse's all right,' she conceded. 'He does bang on a bit, though.'

Hannah's expression suggested some impatience with this refusal to be impressed by famous politicians. 'Still,' she said, reverting to her previous subject, 'it's not right for Joel to be sick when I am well. *I'm* the one who should be in a hospital bed. I've had my time.'

'Oh, *Nana*,' Rosa protested.

Audrey, who rather thought her mother-in-law had a point, remained silent.

One of the patients at Joel's rehab clinic was celebrating a birthday this afternoon. Several forlorn bouquets of helium balloons had been taped to the walls of the main ward and a frayed plastic HAPPY BIRTHDAY banner was hanging in a limp crescent from the ceiling above the nurses' station. As Audrey and Hannah passed the ward recreation room, they caught a glimpse of the glassy-eyed birthday boy propped up in a chair with a paper crown planted tipsily on his lolling head. Three nurses were standing over him, trying vainly to interest him in his cake. Audrey grimmaced and picked up her pace.

Just as they arrived at the door to Joel's room, she spotted Joel's neurologist, Dr Krauss, standing at the water cooler at the end of the hall. She hastily deposited Hannah at Joel's bedside, then went back out. 'Hello!' she shouted. 'Could you hang on a minute?'

Krauss, pallid and lanky in a double-breasted brown suit, turned and peered at her as she trotted towards him. 'Ah! Hello, Mrs Litvinoff.'

'I've been trying to get a meeting with you for the last ten days,' Audrey said.

'Really?' Dr Krauss drank back his water and bent down to get some more. 'That's not good. You can always phone my office and make an appointment, you know.'

'I wanted to talk to you about what's going on with my husband.'

'Of course.' Dr Krauss had overfilled his little paper cone. He held it at arm's length to avoid spilling water on his shoes. 'I'm afraid this is not a good time, though—'

'I'm concerned about the care Joel's getting.'

'The thing to do is to make an appointment.'

'He's been here for two weeks and nothing's happening.'

'My secretary's name is Pam. If you give her a call—'

'I want to talk to you *now*.'

Dr Krauss laughed like a department-store Santa. *Ho Ho Ho*. 'Well. What exactly is your concern, Mrs Litvinoff?'

'I don't think Joel's getting enough treatment. I'm in here all the time and mostly he's just lying there like a lox.'

'I believe that Joel is on a pretty rigorous schedule of physical therapy—'

'Yeah, but it's not enough. What about the treatments I've been reading about on the internet—sensory stimulation, G-therapy? How come he's not getting any of that?'

Dr Krauss closed his eyes, as if weary at the thought of trying to bridge the vast gap of knowledge that lay between him and Audrey. 'Well, you know, Mrs Litvinoff, a great many of the so-called therapies out there have little or no basis in science.'

'I saw this article the other day about some doctor—not a quack, a real doctor—who's been getting coma patients to start communicating by implanting electrodes in their brain—'

'Yes, that is fascinating stuff, isn't it? But I think you'll find that those patients were at least minimally responsive prior to treatment.'

Audrey shook her head impatiently. 'It just doesn't seem to me that you're trying as hard as

116

you could with Joel.'

'I can assure you,' Dr Krauss said, growing pink, 'that is not the case. In fact, I challenge you to find a facility in America that would be willing to offer Joel a more aggressive course of therapy than the one we are pursuing.' He made a jutting, chicken-like movement with his neck as he loosened his tie. 'It's important,' he went on, 'that we place appropriate parameters around our expectations.'

'How do you mean?'

'Well, Joel is not a young man. He has suffered a very major insult to his brain—'

'I'm aware of that,' Audrey interrupted. 'Dr Sussman says no one knows for sure what Joel's progress is going to be. He says the window for improvement is at least a year and, until that window closes, the sky's the limit.'

'Ye-e-s . . .' Dr Krauss seemed to be considering how to contradict a colleague without appearing to contradict a colleague. 'Strictly speaking, what Dr Sussman says is correct. We can't be absolutely sure what is going to happen to Joel, but we can make some intelligent guesses based on precedent.' He paused. 'You know, this really isn't an appropriate setting for this conversation. I would much prefer to discuss Joel's situation in my office when I have more time.'

'What are you saying?'

Dr Krauss gave a heavy sigh. 'Joel is in a vegetative state. Every day he remains in this condition, the chances of his ever regaining an acceptable quality of life grow slimmer. I know that you have expressed strong resistance to signing a DNR order for your husband, but most families in cases like Joel's do see the wisdom of—'

117

Throughout this small speech, Audrey's eyes had been growing steadily more protuberant. Now, they threatened to depart their sockets altogether. 'What's the matter with you?' she shouted. 'Were you not in medical school the day they took the Hippocratic oath?'

'Mrs Litvinoff, I must—'

'Oh—' Audrey made an awkward flailing gesture, 'go fuck yourself, would you?'

As she walked back up the corridor, she rubbed at her smarting eyes with her knuckles, like a child. She was going to report that creep to the medical council. She was going to have his bony arse fired. She clenched her fists, making angry, crescent-shaped impressions on her palms with her fingernails.

In Joel's room, Hannah was leaning against the plastic rails of the bed, talking to her son. Audrey paused on the threshold, watching motes of dust drift lazily through the room's muted grey light, listening to the pacific murmur of her mother-in-law's one-sided conversation. Presently she went over and joined her. Every day, it seemed to Audrey, the essence of her husband—the Joelness of him—was receding a little further. In addition to the EKG wires attached to his chest and the catheter line in his bladder, he was now sporting a trach line in his neck, a PEG line in his gut and an intracranial pressure monitor embedded in his skull. Soon, she thought, he would disappear altogether beneath this welter of life-preserving gadgetry.

At the edges of her fury with the doctor, there was an embarrassed awareness of her own hypocrisy. She and Joel had never been

118

sentimentalists about death. Over the years, their discussions about their own mortality had always been showily phlegmatic. 'When the day comes that I can't take a piss on my own,' Joel had told her a few years back when he started having trouble with his prostate, 'I want you to have me chopped up for horsemeat, okay?' How often had they shaken their heads ruefully at the dotty sanctity-of-life types who insisted on keeping their loved ones alive when they were no more sensate than parsnips? How often had they congratulated themselves on the fact that, as atheists, they were uniquely well-equipped to face the end of life with dignity? 'We've got nothing to be scared about,' Joel always said. 'We *know* there's nothing else.'

Yet now that the discussion had departed the comfortable realm of dinner-table posturing—now that she was confronting the possibility of actually presiding over her husband's death—she understood how cowardly their former bravado had been. All those jokes about not wasting public-health resources and suffocating one another with plastic bags—what had they really been but avoidance? Refusal to confront the horror of extinction?

She reached over now and tried to stroke his hand through its awkward anticontracture brace. She had always loved Joel's hands: the dry, fleshy palms, the long, knotted fingers. His touch, she used to joke, was his secret weapon, the balm for all marital resentments.

She remembered the day, thirty-four years ago, that he had come to see her in the Mount Sinai maternity ward after she had given birth to Karla. The baby had been delivered by emergency

C-section the night before, while Joel was still trying frantically to get back from fog-bound Boston. By the time he finally came bursting through the doors, she had been lying alone in her hospital bed for twelve hours. She watched resentfully as he danced about the ward, setting the nurses a-twitter with his charm, serenading the baby with 'Soliloquy' from *Carousel*.

> My little girl,
> Pink and white
> As peaches and cream is she.
> My little girl
> Is half again as bright
> As girls are meant to be!

'Thanks for showing up,' she had muttered, when at last he handed the baby back to the nurses and they were left alone.

'Aww, my poor honey.' Joel pulled the curtains around the bed and climbed in next to her.

'You're such a bastard, leaving me to do this alone.'

'I tried to get back, sweetie—'

'You shouldn't have gone in the first place! You're not meant to bugger off to Boston when your wife is nine months pregnant.'

'Sweetie . . .' Beneath the sheets his hands roamed over her swollen, fizzing breasts, across her bandaged belly wound, down to the swampy mess between her legs.

'Oh, I'm disgusting right now,' she muttered. 'Everything's oozing.'

Joel didn't care. He had none of the usual male queasiness about female biology. He loved all of her body, even its secretions.

'I'm sorry, baby. I really am. Did it hurt *very* much when they cut you?'

'Not really,' she admitted. 'It felt like someone rummaging around in my sock drawer.'

He laughed. 'Brave girl.'

He began to sing the song from *Carousel* again, but softly this time, just for her.

Dozens of boys pursue her,
Many a likely lad
Does what he can to woo her
From her faithful dad.
She has a few
Pink and white young fellers of two or three—
But my little girl
Gets hungry ev'ry night
And she comes home to me . . .

'Jesus,' he whispered after a while. He put her hand on his groin. 'How long before we can fuck again?'

*   *   *

Later that afternoon, as Audrey was parking the car back at home, she spotted Jean crossing the street towards her. 'Hello, dear!' Jean called. 'What excellent timing!'

Audrey had quite forgotten that Jean was meant to be coming by. She glanced unhappily at her friend's high-waisted, schoolteacher jeans and red beret. She often felt self-conscious in public with Jean. The contrast between their two figures—Jean, towering and wide-hipped, she, short and skinny—made them a comical couple, she feared. And then—thanks to Jean's odd, mannish get-ups—there was always the discomfiting possibility that people would mistake them for *lesbians*.

'Isn't it a gorgeous evening?' Jean said. She was pointing west towards the Hudson River. The sun, swaddled in luminous, orange-and-pink cloud banks, had begun to set over Jersey City, and all along the divider of the West Side Highway, spindly young trees in metal calipers were wagging their frothy blossoms at the passing traffic. Audrey smiled. Long ago, when she had first come to New York, she had been too absorbed by the city's dark melodrama to notice pockets of prettiness like this. Back then, the allure of the city had lain entirely in its capacity to intimidate her—in its steaming, black streets and dank subways. But the noirish metropolis of her youth had softened and shrunk with use: now, forty years on, it had become a place of sunsets and magnolia trees.

The two women began to walk, holding their heads up to catch the last tepid rays of sun on their faces.

'How were things at the hospital?' Jean asked.

'Fine. Rosa buggered off so I had to get Hannah to the hospital and back on my own.' Audrey did not want to tell Jean about her run-in with Dr Krauss. If Jean did not share her outrage—if Jean thought that the doctor had a point—she wouldn't be able to bear it.

From the other end of the street, a tall, middle-aged black woman was approaching. Her long, greying dreadlocks were gathered in a ponytail and she was carrying a backpack that thudded up and down in time with her steps. Audrey had a sense that she knew her from somewhere, but they passed one another without any greeting being spoken.

Outside her house, Audrey took her keys from her bag, wondering idly if she had any milk in the house for tea. As she and Jean climbed the stairs, she glimpsed the dreadlocked woman returning down the street. Perhaps she was lost, Audrey thought.

'Excuse me,' a voice said. 'Audrey?'

Audrey turned around.

The woman was standing at the foot of the steps, wriggling clumsily out of her backpack. 'My name is Berenice Mason. I wondered if I might have a word.'

'What about?'

The woman hesitated. 'About your husband. About Joel.'

'Yes?' Audrey spotted a menu flyer stuck between the front door and the hall mat. She squatted down to remove it.

'I'd prefer not to go into it out here,' the woman said. 'It's a little delicate. Could I come in for a minute?'

Audrey cast Jean a sardonic glance. *A little delicate*. The woman had surely rehearsed that prissy phrase.

'Are you a reporter?' Jean asked.

The woman shook her head. 'Oh no.'

Audrey stood up and studied her. She was a big woman with heavy breasts, dressed a little inappropriately for her age, Audrey thought, in a long, purple skirt and running shoes. 'So how do you know Joel then?' she asked.

The woman smiled. 'I'm a friend. A good

123

friend.'

'Really?' Audrey said. She had identified the woman now. She was a fan. A camp-follower. One or two such lost souls turned up at Perry Street every year, hoping to establish—or imagining that there already existed—some special relationship with Joel, their radical hero. They were pitiful creatures for the most part, but it never did to indulge them. Beneath their cringing manner, there usually lurked a steely resolve. 'Well, it's nice to meet you,' she said briskly, 'but I don't have time to talk at the moment. Joel's not here and I'm very busy.' She turned to go into the house. 'Come on, Jean.'

The woman began walking up the steps.

'Excuse me,' Audrey said, turning around again. 'I just told you, Joel isn't here.'

'I know that,' the woman said. 'It's you I need to talk to.'

'Right. Well, another time—'

The woman reached into her backpack and pulled out a photograph.

'Really,' Audrey said, 'I'm not—'

'Look!' The woman thrust the photograph at her.

Audrey gave in and took it.

The picture showed the woman sitting on a blanket in a park, with a baby on her lap. Squatting behind her, with his hands on her shoulders, was Joel. His hair was standing in vertical white wisps on his head like a cirrus cloud. It must have been taken at a rally of some sort, Audrey thought. People often asked Joel to pose for photographs at such events and Joel, not a man who had ever felt unduly burdened by his celebrity, always obliged.

'Look, Jean,' Audrey said. 'Isn't this nice?'

Jean smiled. 'Lovely.'

'Thanks for letting me see this,' Audrey said, turning back to the woman. 'I'm afraid I really do have to go in now.' She held out the photograph.

'Wait,' the woman said, 'you don't understand—'

'*That's enough.*' Audrey pressed the photograph into the woman's chest. 'Take this. You need to leave me alone.'

The photograph fluttered to the ground. Audrey opened the door and went into the house, pulling Jean after her.

'Please!' the woman cried as the door slammed.

Audrey drew the bolt. 'That's it! I'm calling the police! Jean, get me the phone.'

Jean ran into the kitchen.

'If you don't leave immediately,' Audrey shouted through the door, 'I'm going to start dialling!'

There was no answer. Audrey went into the front room and peered out of the window. There was no sign of the woman. Across the street, a tortoiseshell cat lay on a stoop, taking a sunbath. Two men walked past the house, holding hands and laughing about something. Audrey stared after them for a moment, listening as the hoots of their laughter faded.

'It's all right,' she said when Jean appeared holding the cordless phone. 'She's gone.'

'Well,' Jean said, following Audrey into the kitchen, 'that was *most* unpleasant.'

'Wasn't it?' Audrey said. She was feeling sheepish now about having threatened to call 911. She and Joel had always maintained that privileged white people should not seek the assistance of the police, except in cases of direst emergency.

'What do you think she was after?' Jean asked.

'Oh, who knows? *She* probably doesn't know. She's a nutcase, isn't she—' Audrey broke off suddenly. 'Oh God.'

Jean looked at her. 'What, dear?'

'I've seen her before.'

'No!'

'Yes! She was at the hospital the day Joel had his stroke. She was hanging around outside.'

'Oh, Audrey, are you sure?'

'I swear! She gave me a light.'

'How extraordinary.'

'How fucking *creepy*,' Audrey corrected. 'What was she doing there? How the fuck did she know Joel was there?'

'She could have been in the courtroom when he collapsed,' Jean said. 'I mean, if she's really some sort of stalker, she probably goes to all his cases.'

'Don't say that. What if she's one of those freaks like the one who shot John Lennon?'

Jean made a face. 'Perhaps you *should* let the police know about this, Audrey. I mean, I'm sure she's perfectly harmless, but it doesn't hurt to be on the safe—'

From the hallway there came the sound of the letter box snapping.

Audrey stared at Jean. 'Oh, *Jesus*,' she whispered, 'do you think that's her again?'

Jean cocked her head, listening. 'I don't know. Do you want me to go and look?'

'*No*,' Audrey hissed. 'Stay here. What if she's staring through the letter box or something?'

Emboldened by Audrey's fear, Jean stood up. 'I'll just take a peek.'

A few moments later, she returned, holding a piece of folded paper in her hand. 'This was lying on the mat.'

Audrey took the note and placed it on the table in front of her. It was addressed to 'Ms Audrey Litvinoff'.

'It must be from her, right?'

Jean nodded. 'I would imagine so.'

'What do you think it says?'

'Why don't you read it, dear?'

Audrey reached out her hand and then pulled it back. 'Oh, I can't. You read it to me.'

Jean unfolded the piece of paper and began to read aloud:

Dear Audrey,
Since you have refused to speak to me in person, I feel I have no choice but to communicate with you by letter. I know that what I have to tell you will cause you a lot of pain, and I am sincerely sorry for that. But I believe that the truth is important and that, sooner or later, we must all confront life not as we would like it to be, but as it really is. Now that Joel is sick, it is time for the truth to be known. For a period of three years, between 1996 and 1999, Joel and I were lovers. In 1998, I gave birth to Joel's child—a beautiful boy whom we named Jamil.

'Good God!' Jean said, looking up. 'She really *is* mad.'

'Go on,' Audrey said.

Jean resumed reading:

Even though Joel and I are no longer romantically involved, our friendship has endured and the bond we share as Jamil's parents can never be broken. Joel has a very special love for his son and he has always supported him both financially and emotionally.

Audrey—I am so sad to think of the shock and sadness you must be feeling as you read this. I know there is nothing that will take away your unhappiness right now. But please believe me when I say Joel and I never intended to hurt you. In time, I hope you can come to terms with what has taken place and honor the important connection that we have—for our children's sake, at least. I am including my phone number, as well as my email address, and I ask you, please, Audrey, to contact me as soon as you feel able.

In peace,

Berenice Mason

'What a thing!' Jean said. 'Has Joel ever mentioned a Berenice?'

'Of *course* he hasn't,' Audrey snapped. 'There's nothing in that letter that's *true*.'

'No, of course not,' Jean said. 'I was just asking.'

Audrey went over to the fridge and got out two greying carrots from the bottom drawer. To be fair to Jean, it wasn't *inconceivable* that something had happened between Joel and that woman. Not the child business, obviously—that was rubbish—but it was possible that Joel had slept with her. She wasn't really Joel's type, of course: too large, too odd-looking. But Joel's sexual choices had surprised Audrey before. Perhaps he'd been feeling frisky one night and mad, chubby Berenice had been the only thing available.

Jean held out the letter. 'What do you want me to do with this?'

'Throw it in the bin.'

Audrey watched as Jean tore the paper carefully in two and thrust the pieces deep in the garbage can. 'I told you she was a crazy, didn't I?' She took one of the carrots and cracked it loudly between her teeth. 'Totally fucking tonto.'

CHAPTER SIX

Standing at the corner of Forty-seventh Street and Fifth Avenue, waiting for the bus to Monsey, Rosa quietly celebrated her escape from her mother and grandmother's low-level hostilities. Audrey and Hannah had been at war with one another for as long as Rosa could remember. The ostensible subject of their bickering varied, but the underlying source of conflict was always the same: who understood Joel better, who loved him more passionately, who had the superior claim on his affections. There had been a time when Rosa and Karla also participated in this degrading competition, but Rosa had long ago recused herself from the fight, and Karla—well, Karla had never been that serious a contestant to begin with: she was happy just to be able to touch the hem of Joel's garment from time to time. Audrey and Nana, however, were never going to give up the ghost. They would go on jostling with one another

129

like groupies at a stage door until the bitter end. In fact, now that Joel was sick, the battle between them had only intensified. In his silence Joel had become a perfectly passive prize, an infinitely interpretable symbol: a sphinx whose meanings and ownership they could squabble over for ever, without fear of decisive contradiction.

Rosa looked around at the crowd of Orthodox Jews who were waiting with her for the bus. Almost all of the men were wearing dark suits and oversized black fedoras. The female portion of the group had a slightly looser but no less distinctive dress code that involved long skirts, wigs and an aggressively frumpy layering of shirts and sweaters and cardigans. Rosa felt exposed and a little flustered to be consorting in broad daylight with such ostentatiously Jewish Jews. She wondered anxiously if any of the pedestrians walking by on Fifth Avenue mistook her for one of this clan. She turned and considered her reflection in a shop window. The outfit she had cobbled together for this occasion was modest enough to daunt the most lascivious gaze. But, she could see now, she was in little danger of passing for an authentic, Orthodox woman. She looked like nothing so much as a mad Victorian governess trying to hide a skin disease.

'Rosa?'

She looked around and saw a man in shorts and a tank top staring at her with an irritating expression of round-eyed, drop-jawed surprise. '*Rosa?* Is that you?'

Not now, she thought. *Please, not now.*

'It's Chris,' the man cried. 'Chris Jackson? From Bard?'

Rosa lightly smacked her forehead. 'Oh! Of

course! Sorry, Chris, I was miles away. How *are* you?'

'I'm good, I'm good.' He cast a quick, curious glance at her attire. 'What's up? Someone told me you were living in Cuba these days.'

'Yeah, I was, but I've been back for more than a year now.' She spoke softly in the hope that Chris might follow suit.

'Wow, that must have been awesome!' he exclaimed. 'I hear Cuba is amazing.'

'Yeah.' Rosa wondered what upset her more: being observed by the Jews chatting with a loud, half-naked Gentile, or being discovered by Chris hanging out with the characters from an Isaac Bashevis Singer story.

'So,' he said, 'what're you up to now?'

'I'm working at an after-school programme for girls in East Harlem.'

'Oh yeah? That's cool.'

With a great hissing and steaming, the big, white Monsey bus now pulled up at the kerb. It had smoked-glass windows and the words MONSEY TRAILS plastered along its side.

'How about you?' she asked. 'You're living in New York now?'

'Yeah. I'm making documentaries. I have my own company, actually.'

'Great!'

'Uh-huh. We've got a movie coming out next fall.'

'That's really wonderful, Chris. Good for you.'

The doors to the bus had wheezed open and people were now boarding.

'I mean, it's not going to be a blockbuster or anything, believe me,' Chris said, 'but, yeah, we're

131

pretty psyched about it . . .'

Rosa gestured at the bus. 'I'm sorry, Chris, I'm going to have to go.'

Chris looked around. 'You're getting on this?'

'I'm going upstate for the weekend.'

'*Ohhh.*'

'It was great running into you,' Rosa said.

'Have you got a card or something? We should get together some time.'

'A card? No.'

'What's your phone number then?' He took out his cellphone, preparing to add her to his contacts list. After a moment's hesitation, Rosa surrendered her number.

'Okay then!' Chris said. 'I'll give you a call.' He pointed at her suitcase. 'Here, let me help you with that.'

Before Rosa could stop him, he had lifted the case and was carrying it up the bus steps.

'Wow, this is pretty interesting,' he said loudly, peering into the bus's dim interior. Coming up behind him, Rosa saw a black curtain hanging down the middle of the aisle with male passengers on one side and female passengers on the other.

She turned to Chris and gently pushed against his chest. 'Off you go now,' she said firmly. 'I can take it from here.'

*   *   *

The rabbi with whom Rosa was staying had emailed her detailed directions to his house from the bus stop, but she still managed to get lost. What should have been a ten-minute walk from the bus stop ended up being a bewildering forty-minute ramble through the suburban streets of Monsey. She stopped at one point to ask a man who was walking past if he could help her, but he reared away from her, as if from a wild animal, and hurried away, his hand pressed to his big black hat, without a word.

The rabbi's house, when she finally found it, was grander than she had been expecting: a large 1930s villa of red brick, with a big swathe of lawn in front of it and what looked like a larger yard behind. A middle-aged woman in a beige dress and stockinged feet answered the door.

'You must be Rosa,' she said. 'I'm Mrs Reinman. You're late! You missed the candlelighting!'

'I'm so sorry,' Rosa said, 'I got a little lost . . .'

Mrs Reinman beckoned her in and took her coat. 'It's *such* a pity you didn't get here in time. We waited as long as we could . . .' She pointed at Rosa's feet. 'Would you mind?'

Rosa looked at her, mystified.

'Your shoes,' Mrs Reinman said.

Rosa bent down to slip off her black flats. She was wondering what Jewish edict it was that required shoelessness on the Sabbath, when Mrs Reinman gestured at the pale green carpet. 'I'm sorry, it's new and I've found it shows up every mark.'

In the Reinmans' elaborately damasked and furbelowed living room, a small group of women and girls were drinking lemonade. 'Well, she's here at last!' Mrs Reinman said. She held up her arm in Rosa's direction and let it flop. 'Better late than never!'

Rosa, who thought it churlish of her host to harp on so about her tardiness, waved apologetically.

133

'Hi, everybody.'

Mrs Reinman pointed around the room, identifying people. There were two daughters, twelve-year-old Rebecca and six-year-old Esther, a pregnant niece, Leah, who was visiting from Dallas, and a young friend of the family, Karen. The men were still at shul. Once she had completed the introductions, Mrs Reinman returned to the kitchen, instructing Karen to show Rosa where she would be sleeping.

'You and I will be sharing a room,' Karen said as she led the way out into the hall. She glanced around, challengingly. 'I hope you're okay with that.'

'Oh, yes, of course,' Rosa replied. As they trudged upstairs together, she caught a glimpse of frilled white ankle sock beneath the swishing folds of Karen's long skirt.

The guest room, on the third floor of the house, had two alarmingly narrow beds on one of which Karen had laid out her nightdress and a couple of religious-looking books. 'Those things are mine,' Karen said, pointing.

'Right.' Rosa nodded.

Karen gazed at her with pale, red-rimmed eyes. 'I know you are unfamiliar with the Jewish observances. If you have any questions about what to do or how to behave while you're here, you should feel free to ask me.'

'Thank you.'

Karen pointed out the way to the bathroom and alerted Rosa to the timer device that was set to automatically extinguish the lights in the room at eleven o'clock. 'You understand about not turning lights on and off during Shabbos?' she asked.

Rosa nodded. She was curious to know what people did if they wanted to turn the lights out *before* eleven o'clock, but, unwilling to encourage Karen in her self-appointed role as religious docent, she kept quiet.

They went back downstairs to the living room. Leah poured a glass of lemonade for Rosa and invited her to sit down on the sofa. 'This is a special room, isn't it?' she said. 'My aunt has such an eye.' She gestured at a set of ruched, royal blue curtains behind Rosa. 'Aren't the window treatments lovely?'

Rosa made a non-committal noise. 'What do you do in Dallas?' she asked.

Leah seemed puzzled by the question. 'Well, I'm recently married.' She looked down at her belly. 'And I will have a baby in October, baruch Hashem.'

'Ah, yes. Congratulations. Boy or girl?'

Leah shook her head reprovingly. 'We don't try to find these things out,' she said. 'We will be happy with whatever Hashem gives us.'

Rosa was unclear whether Leah was referring to her and her husband's preference in 'these things', or to some more general community prohibition. In any case, she could think of nothing more to say on the subject of pregnancy. She looked down at the Reinman sisters, who were sitting cross-legged on the floor, examining a sheaf of computer printouts.

'What grade are you in, Rebecca?' she asked.

'Sixth.'

'I thought so. You know, I work in an after-school programme with girls your age.'

Rebecca did not seem very interested in this

135

information. She nodded and looked down at her papers with an air of embarrassment.

'What's that you're reading?' Rosa persevered.

The younger sister, Esther, turned around. 'Commentaries on this week's parsha,' she told Rosa. She was a pretty, grave-faced little girl who had recently lost both of her front teeth. Two new ones, their edges serrated like postage stamps, were just beginning to poke through the gum.

'She means commentaries on the Torah portion,' Rebecca said. 'We read a portion of the Torah every week.' She nudged her sister. 'Goyim don't know what parsha is, silly!'

'I'm *not* a Goy,' Rosa said indignantly.

Karen sniggered.

Rosa stood up. 'Where would I find the bathroom?'

The Reinmans' guest facilities were just down the hall, signposted with a porcelain POWDER ROOM plaque. Once she had safely locked herself inside, Rosa sank down on the toilet seat and took a deep inhalation of pot-pourri-scented air. She was horribly disappointed. She had imagined Rabbi Reinman's house as a humble, cosy, *Fiddler on the Roof* sort of place, filled with boisterous children and plates of kugel and at least one feisty old grandma telling stories from the shtetl: instead, she found herself in a harem of suburban prisses analysing soft furnishings.

She considered her escape options. Coming down with food poisoning was a possibility. She doubted that she had the acting chops, though. The simplest ruse—the one that her hosts would be least likely to challenge—would be to pretend to call her mother and hear of some fresh medical crisis involving her father. But she was not brave enough to risk the karmic repercussions of such a dastardly lie. And, besides, she was pretty sure she wasn't allowed to use her cellphone on the Sabbath. No, there was nothing for it but to stay and endure. She got up and batted vaguely at her hair in the mirror. She was being babyish, she told herself. It was silly to reject this experience simply because it failed to deliver the anticipated clichés. Where was her sense of adventure? Her curiosity?

When she opened the door, she was startled to find Karen standing outside.

'Don't turn the light off!' Karen cried. But Rosa's finger was already flicking the switch. Karen let out a yelp as the bathroom went dark. 'I thought you might forget,' Karen said. 'That's why I came to remind you.'

Rosa clenched her teeth. 'Oh *God*. Sorry. I didn't . . . Shall I turn it back on again?'

'No!' Karen said. 'You can't.'

There were voices in the entrance hall signalling the return of the shul party.

Karen folded her arms. 'Oh, well,' she said, 'we shall have to keep it dark now until the end of Shabbos.'

In the living room, Rosa was introduced to the men: Rabbi Reinman and the three teenaged Reinman sons, Leah's husband, Michael, and Mrs Reinman's ancient, bald father, Mr Riskin.

'Ah, yes!' Mr Riskin cried when Rosa was presented to him by Leah. 'The naughty girl who missed lichts-bentschen!'

Rosa observed him warily. His bare scalp had the mottled, fragile look of a quail's egg. At its centre, there was a shallow depression that seemed to pulse, like an infant's fontanelle.

'What held you up?' he asked, leering at her with doddery aggression. 'Too busy talking to your boyfriends?'

'Grandpa!' Leah exclaimed indulgently.

Mr Riskin's mouth began to twitch, heralding the approach of another witticism. 'I hear you turned off the light in the bathroom,' he said. 'You wanted to make us do our pee-pees in the dark this evening?'

Leah covered her mouth with her hands, pretending to be scandalized by her old scoundrel of a grandfather.

'Your family does not keep Shabbos?' Mr Riskin asked.

Rosa's lips grew thin. 'No.'

Mr Riskin looked at Leah and raised his arms in a gesture of hopelessness.

People were beginning to file out of the living room now. In the small, formal dining room across the hall, the table settings promised a long and complicated meal. Rosa took a quick survey of the place cards and discovered, to her dismay, that she had been seated between Karen and Rebecca, directly opposite Mr Riskin. She was about to pull out her chair, when Karen grasped her roughly by the arm. 'Not yet!' she said. 'First we welcome the Shabbos angels!' A moment later, everyone around the table linked hands and began to sing.

> Shalom aleichem malachei ha-shareis
> malachei elyon
> mi-melech malchei ha-melachim
> Ha-Kadosh Baruch Hu

After the song had ended, the adults sat down and the Reinman children approached their father one by one, to receive his blessings. Then the rabbi rose to sing by himself. He was a short, delicately built man with little white hands and a tiny scarlet mouth that blazed out from his thick beard like a campfire in the woods. His singing voice was startlingly strong and resonant. Karen explained to Rosa in a loud whisper that he was singing Ayshet Chayil from Proverbs, 'a song of praise for a wife'. And when Rosa glanced down at the other end of the table, she saw that Mrs Reinman's eyes were demurely lowered. There was something ludicrous, she thought, about this elfin man yodelling a uxorious hymn to his matronly wife at the dinner table: ludicrous, yet touching also. Her own childhood mealtimes at Perry Street had been napkinless, slapdash affairs, presided over by a fuming mother for whom food preparation was the focal point of all housewifely resentments. When she tried to picture Audrey sitting in Mrs Reinman's place, being serenaded by Joel, the image was so dissonant that she very nearly laughed aloud.

Some time later, after kiddush had been said and everyone had ceremonially washed their hands and the challah had been blessed, dinner was served.

'So, young lady . . .' Mr Riskin said to Rosa as a bowl of matzoh ball soup was set before her. Rosa gazed at him, waiting impatiently for the rest of the sentence to hobble its way down the rickety neural pathway. 'How did you like my son-in-law's singing?'

Rabbi Reinman made shushing gestures. 'Leon,

please . . .'

'I enjoyed it very much,' Rosa said. 'Rabbi Reinman sings very nicely.'

The rabbi raised a hand to fend off praise. 'Ah, you are kind. But I am no singer. You should hear Michael.' He pointed at Leah's husband. 'Michael is a great singer.'

Michael shook his head. 'No, no, Marty. I am only a fair singer. I grew up in a family of musicians, so I have a good idea of how limited my gifts are.'

'Michael comes from a long line of cantors,' the rabbi explained to Rosa. 'His father, blessed be his memory, was Shlomo Lamm, one of the finest and most famous cantors in all of Canada.'

Michael chuckled in modest acknowledgement of his prestigious ancestry.

The rabbi was distracted by one of his sons further down the table, announcing his marks in a recent maths test. Karen leaned across the table to Mr Riskin. 'Rosa works with children, you know, Mr Riskin.'

'You're a teacher?' Mr Riskin said.

'No,' Rosa said, 'I help run a programme that provides after-school and vacation activities.'

'Oh yes?' Mr Riskin said. 'Where is this?'

'It has two branches in Manhattan, downtown and uptown. I work at the East Harlem branch.'

Mr Riskin considered this. 'You're looking after, what, black children?'

'Most of the children are African American, yes.'

'I see! And . . . you like this work?'

'Yes, I do.'

Mr Riskin shrugged. 'For me, a person should

140

look to help his own community before he starts helping others.'

'Well, these girls *are* my community,' Rosa said. 'They're New Yorkers just like I am.'

Mr Riskin pressed his hand to his chest and swallowed a burp. 'Just like you, huh?'

Rosa smiled coolly and turned to Rebecca, sitting on her other side. 'You must be having your bat mitzvah soon,' she said.

Rebecca shook her head. 'No, we—'

'We don't do that,' Mr Riskin intervened. 'Bat mitzvah celebrations are not Orthodox.'

'Oh, I see,' Rosa said, not seeing at all.

'The bat mitzvah is just something the Reconstructionist Jews cooked up so that girls would not feel "left out",' Mr Riskin explained. 'Then the Reform got in on the idea and now it's big business.'

'Ah.'

Mr Riskin patted his napkin against his flabby, lower lip. 'I suppose,' he said, 'you are the sort of woman's libber who thinks our girls are deprived because they don't do bat mitzvah.'

'Well, I don't know much about it, Mr Riskin,' Rosa replied, 'but I can see how some girls might want—'

'Yes,' Mr Riskin cut her off, 'I suspected as much! You are one of these women who wants to be a man. The women's libbers think it is degrading to be female, but you see, in the Jewish religion, we prize our women. They are the high priestesses of their homes.'

Rosa stared at her soup spoon and fantasized about smashing it against Mr Riskin's horrid, pulsing skull. Why was she obliged to be solicitous

141

of his tender religious sensibilities? He was not worried about offending *her*. 'Well,' she said, after a moment, 'I dare say a woman could be a high priestess *and* have a bat mitzvah. Couldn't she?'

Mr Riskin made a shooing gesture with his hands. 'You are talking nonsense, young lady!'

Their altercation had now drawn the attention of the other family members.

'Leon, please,' Rabbi Reinman said from the end of the table. 'You mustn't bully our guest . . .'

'You think you are talking about religion,' Mr Riskin said, wagging an arthritic finger at Rosa, 'but you're not. You have a chip on your shoulder.'

* * *

After dinner, Rabbi Reinman took Rosa to one side and beckoned her into his study.

'I am afraid that my father-in-law was a little hard on you this evening,' he said, when they had sat down.

'Oh no,' Rosa protested, 'it was my fault. I'm sorry that I offended him.'

'Don't worry about that. He's pretty tough. I hope you were still able to enjoy yourself this evening. I want you to feel at home here.'

'I'm having a very nice time. I loved all the singing at dinner.'

'Good.' The rabbi nodded. 'So now, Rosa . . . I would like to know a little more about you. How is it that you have become interested in Jewish observance?'

Rosa looked at the floor. 'I don't know, really. I come from a family that has never taken any interest in religion.'

142

'I see. Forgive my asking, but are you by any chance related to Joel Litvinoff, the lawyer?'

'Yes, he's my father.'

'I thought there might be a connection. I know a little bit about him. He is a socialist, no?'

Rosa smiled, remembering all the arguments she had had with Joel over the authenticity of his socialism. 'Of a kind, yes,' she said.

'And an atheist?'

'Oh yes. An atheist certainly. An anti-theist, in fact.'

The rabbi leaned forward. 'An anti-theist? What does that mean?'

'Well . . . I guess it means that he thinks religion is a bad thing.'

'I see.' The rabbi smiled. 'So he *disapproves* of the God in whom he doesn't believe.'

'He's a good man,' Rosa said, feeling suddenly protective. 'He's very sick at the moment.'

'I'm sorry to hear that. What is wrong with him?'

'He had a stroke six weeks ago. He's in a coma now.'

The rabbi winced in sympathy. 'That's terrible. It must be very hard for your family.'

There was a pause. Rosa looked up at the ceiling.

'So,' the rabbi went on gently, 'you were going to tell me about your interest in Judaism. You, I take it, are *not* an anti-theist.'

'Well, for a long time I was. Until a while ago, I would have described myself as a Marxist.'

The rabbi's eyebrows rose. 'Marx, eh? You know, I suppose, what Marx wrote about the Jews?'

Rosa shook her head.

The rabbi got up from his chair and began looking through his bookshelf. After a moment, he took out a thick volume and began to read from it. ' "Emancipation from haggling and money, from practical real Judaism, would be the self-emancipation of our time," ' he quoted. ' "Money is the jealous God of Israel beside which no other God may stand." '

Rosa made a sceptical face. 'Marx wrote that?'

'Yes,' the rabbi said, 'I'm afraid your Mr Marx was one of the more ferocious anti-Semites. His parents converted to Christianity when he was a boy, you know . . .' He broke off with a sudden grin. 'Excuse me, I am talking too much. It is a bad habit that many rabbis have. Our "deformation professionelle", as they say in France. Go on. For a long time you were a Marxist. And how were you cured of that?'

'Well, I lived in Cuba for four years and—'

'My goodness! How did that come about?'

'I went in the summer of my second year at law school. It was a working vacation organized by a Cuban-American Solidarity group. We were meant to be refurbishing health centres. While I was there, I met a man—'

'Aha! You fell in love!'

Rosa laughed. 'In love with Cuba, yes, maybe. When the other brigadistas went back to the States, I decided I was going to stay behind and live with this man and his family. They had a pig farm in a place called Vinales. It was very primitive, just a couple of shacks. No indoor bathroom, no running water—'

'My goodness!'

'But the family were very warm, generous

144

people. The first year I was with them, I was really happy.'

'And after the first year?'

'Well, I guess I began to see a lot of problems with the system. A lot of repression and injustice.'

'But you stayed?'

'Well . . .' Rosa hesitated. People always seemed to think that you stopped believing things in a single, lightning-bolt moment, an instantaneous revelation of loss. For her, at least, the process of disenchantment had been achingly slow. Her faith in Cuba had come with an elaborate system of defences for coping with evidence injurious to itself, and for a long time there had been almost no contradiction within the regime, no embarrassing truth about the deprivations of the Cuban people, that she could not defuse with her stockpile of ready-made rationales. *You can't appreciate facts in a static way: facts have to be understood dynamically. To cavil about 'human rights' shows that you have not yet freed yourself from bourgeois attitudes. What society has achieved perfect democracy? The revolution is still in process. Propaganda is a perfectly legitimate tool for maintaining revolutionary discipline. The success of the revolution is more important than the free speech of the revolution's enemies.* 'I guess . . .' she told the rabbi, 'I guess I didn't want to leave.'

'Well,' he replied, 'you certainly learned your lesson the hard way!'

Rosa smiled uneasily. However discredited her former faith, there was a part of her that cherished its memory, that still felt pain when it was mocked. She was not ready to have her story co-opted as a conservative fable.

'And Judaism?' the rabbi asked. 'How did you come to that?'

'By accident, really.' She told him the story of walking into Ahavat Israel for the first time. 'It felt as if there was this huge part of my heritage that I'd been ignoring all these years. There was something . . .'

The rabbi nodded encouragingly. 'Yes?'

'There was something very powerful to me about being among my fellow Jews, about realizing that I was part of something bigger . . .' She stopped, embarrassed by her own banality.

'That's wonderful, Rosa,' the rabbi said. 'Wonderful! I believe it was no accident that you walked into that shul that morning. It was what we call in Hebrew "bashert"—intended.' He paused. 'Now tell me, how do you plan to proceed?'

Rosa squinted. 'I don't . . . what do you mean by "proceed", exactly?'

'Well. Something has happened to you, Rosa. You are from a non-religious family. Nothing in your life, so far, has encouraged you to take an interest in religious matters. In fact, you have been firmly discouraged. And yet, you have felt a pintele yid, a little spark of Jewishness within yourself, which has led you to shul, which has led you here to Monsey. I am wondering, what are you going to do with that spark?'

'Oh . . . Do you mean, am I going to start being observant?'

The rabbi gave her a twinkly look.

'I don't think I'm really ready for that,' Rosa said.

'I see. And what do you think needs to happen for you to be ready?'

Rosa thought for a moment. 'Can I be completely honest with you, Rabbi?'

'I expect nothing less.'

'Well, it's true that going to shul has been an important experience for me. And I can see now that a lot of the negative ideas about religion that I grew up with were based on ignorance. But I'm not sure I'd ever be ready to—you know—live as you and your family do.'

The rabbi nodded calmly. 'Tell me, Rosa, do you believe that the Torah is God's word?'

Rosa hesitated, trying to gauge just how much frankness this conversation could bear. 'I guess . . .' she said slowly, 'I guess I would have a hard time accepting that it was *literally* His word,' she said.

'May I ask how much of Torah you have read, Rosa?'

'Not much.'

'Have you read the Prophecies?'

'No.'

'I strongly advise you to take a look at them. They contain things that will astound you—things that it is impossible that men two thousand years ago could have predicted themselves. "Ye will be torn away from the land whither thou goest . . . and God will scatter you among the nations . . . thou wilt find no ease and there will be no resting place for the sole of thy foot . . . And then God, thy God, will return . . . and gather thee together . . ." This is the story of our people, the story of Israel, you understand?'

Rosa ground her teeth nervously. She did not want to have an argument about Zionism. 'But it's a circular argument, isn't it?' she said. 'I mean, the Jews wouldn't have thought about creating a homeland in Israel if they hadn't got the idea from reading the Bible in the first place.'

'And did the Jews also get the idea of the Diaspora from the Bible? Did they deliberately scatter themselves, in order to prove the Prophecies right? Did they invent the Nazis? Go and look, Rosa! "So shall I provoke them with a non-people, with a vile nation shall I anger them." Does that not make you wonder just a little?'

Rosa looked down at her lap. Why was it so important for her to dismiss these prophecies as hokum, she wondered? Surely, if she prided herself on her rational mind, it behooved her to *consider* the possibility that they came from God?

'Don't intellectualize it,' the rabbi urged. 'What does your intuition tell you?'

Rosa smiled apologetically. 'My intuition tells me that the world was not built by God in six days.'

'You know, Rosa, Orthodox teaching isn't necessarily inconsistent with evolutionary theory. Maimonides said that "what the Torah writes about the Account of Creation is not all to be taken literally, as believed by the masses". There are many respected Orthodox scholars who believe that the Hebrew word "yom", which is usually translated as "day", can also refer to an undefined period of time.'

'So there are Orthodox Darwinists?'

'As in all things there is a broad spectrum of opinion. Obviously, an Orthodox Jew does not believe the processes of evolution are random.' He stood up and began looking through his bookshelf again. 'There's an Israeli physicist who's done a lot of very interesting work on reconciling Jewish theology with modern science. I have one of his

148

books here, somewhere. He claims that carbon dating is much less reliable a method than is generally understood. He also argues that the fossil evidence shows mutation to be a very minor phenomenon.'

'So he's basically trying to discredit Darwin.'

'Well, now, why are you so certain that Darwin was right? Have you yourself studied fossils and carbon dating and so on? Or have you simply taken your convictions from other people—your father for instance?'

Rosa's face darkened. This was unfair. No one could claim to have been more challenging of parental authority than she. Was it possible that the rabbi was interested in her only because of who her father was? Converting the daughter of the famously godless Joel Litvinoff would no doubt be considered a major coup in rabbinical circles . . .

'Found it!' The rabbi handed her the book he had been looking for. 'I hope you don't feel that I'm browbeating you, Rosa, but this is important. You say you used to be a Marxist. Were there not occasionally concepts you came across in your study of Marxist texts that were puzzling or obscure to you? And did you then immediately throw up your hands and say, "Enough! I can't subscribe to this!"? No, you persevered. You applied yourself and hoped that things would become clearer to you. Well, here we are, talking about Hashem, a power and an intelligence that passes all human understanding. Don't you think He deserves at least the same courtesy that you extended to Mr Marx?'

Rosa smiled, suddenly ashamed to have imputed cynical motives to this sweet man. She studied the

149

cover of the book. Perhaps he was right. Perhaps she *had* taken evolutionary theory too much on trust.

'There is a place in New York City that I would like to recommend to you,' the rabbi said. 'It's an educational institute for Jewish women who want to learn more about their religion. The head of the centre is the wife of a friend of mine and the teachers there are good. You would find it very stimulating, I think.'

Rosa nodded politely. 'Thank you. Maybe I'll look into it.'

The rabbi looked at her searchingly. 'I understand how you're feeling, Rosa. You have taken a huge step outside your secular comfort zone and now you find yourself in a world in which much is alien and even disturbing to you. All I ask is that you live with that discomfort for a while. Don't run away. Stay. Explore it and see what happens.'

Later, when Rosa went up to bed, she found Karen tucked in and reading a book called *Journey to Jerusalem*. 'Did you enjoy your talk with Rabbi Reinman?' Karen asked. She sounded aggrieved.

'Yes, it was very interesting.'

Karen gazed at her, waiting for some elaboration. 'Rabbi Reinman is an extremely learned man. It's a great honour, you know, to have him take such an interest in you.'

'I'm sure.' Rosa took her toothbrush from her overnight bag.

'You mustn't brush your teeth!' Karen said, sitting up suddenly. 'It's not allowed on Shabbos. It counts as work.'

Rosa's shoulders slumped in dismay. 'No one

150

brushes their teeth from Friday night to Saturday evening?'

Karen shook her head. 'We don't shower or bathe either. You may,' she added, 'have a mint in the morning if you want to freshen your breath.'

Rosa looked at the toothbrush in her hand and then back at Karen. Did her obligations to her hosts extend so far as abstaining from oral hygiene? She was still debating this tricky point of etiquette when the timer on the lights clicked, plunging the room into darkness. She sighed, laid her toothbrush back in her overnight bag, and groped her way to bed.

CHAPTER SEVEN

Somewhere in the Columbia Presbyterian geriatric ward a woman was crying. Her staccato sobs rang out like a car alarm: *AY ay! AY ay! AY ay!* Karla, who was standing in the corridor waiting for a nurse to finish changing the bandages on her next patient, listened with interest. In all the years that she had been working in a hospital, she had never ceased to be impressed by the aural variety of human suffering. There was a uniformity to the way people looked and smelled when they were ill, but the *sounds* that they made were always deeply personal. Some snivelled. Some boomed. Some screamed like infants. There were drama queens who wailed actual words and sentences—'Oh Go-od, oh, no-o'—and stoics who emitted only muffled sneezes of sorrow. There were even old-school boo-hooers who cried as if they had learned how from reading comics. The ways to express misery were infinite.

The door at which Karla was waiting opened now and a nurse barged out, holding her latex-sheathed hands in front of her, like puppets. 'You'd better come back later,' she said, glancing bad-temperedly at Karla. 'She's just had an accident with her bag. It's going to take a while to clean up.'

Karla went upstairs to the fifth floor. Her next patient was a new intake and before entering his room she checked over her notes.

Jameson, Nicholas, b. 5.4.85. Paraplegic since birth. Parents deceased. Living until recently with relative at above address. Currently homeless. No wheelchair. Uses a skateboard for transportation. Admitted to ER 5.19.02, complaining of 'pains in his back'. Prelim exam showed severe knife wound in his lower back. Patient claimed not to know how he incurred the injury, but speculated that he had been attacked by unknown assailants while sleeping in the street. Aggressive and uncooperative behavior.

The boy appeared to be sleeping when Karla opened the door. His face was densely covered in acne and from a distance he looked as if he were wearing a mask. The nurses had propped him up in bed so that his legless torso lay on the pillows at a 45-degree angle. Karla had a guilty sense that she was examining a natural-history exhibit.

'Nicholas?' she said.

The boy opened his eyes at once. 'Tha's not my

152

name.'

Karla looked doubtfully at the nurse's childish handwriting at the top of the chart. 'It says—'

'My name is Monster,' he interrupted. 'Tha's what everybody know me by.'

Karla paused. 'I see.'

He grinned, revealing rotten teeth, and raised his thick, muscular arms in a gesture of monstrousness. Years of bearing his weight on his hands had turned them into something like hooves. His palms were the translucent yellow of Parmesan rind.

'My name is Karla O'Connor,' Karla said, pulling up a chair. 'I'm a social worker. I wanted to see if I could help you with a few things. First off, I understand you don't have a working wheelchair at the moment?'

The boy looked at her. 'I ain't used a wheelchair since I was six. I jus want the skateboard they took off me when I came in.'

Karla nodded. Nicholas had created such a fuss when the ER nurses first attempted to part him from his skateboard that he had very nearly been sectioned in the psych ward. He was meant to be using a wheelchair while he was in the hospital but the nurses said that whenever he was left unattended, he hoisted himself off the chair and went swinging down the hospital corridors on his hands.

'Well, you can't use a skateboard in the hospital,' Karla said. 'It isn't safe. I can promise you your skateboard will be returned to you when you leave.'

'Fucking safe!' the boy exploded. 'It's a lot safer than the fucking wheelchair.'

153

Karla smiled. 'I'm sure you're right about that. Wheelchairs can be pretty awkward. Still, I think it might be useful for you to own one—for, you know, places where they don't allow you to use your skateboard.'

The boy was silent. While Karla waited for him to respond, she made a mental inventory of the lunch she had brought from home: a container of cottage cheese; one small apple; a diet mint. She had already been bad today and consumed two almond croissants on her way to work. In order to stay within the 1,500-calorie allotment prescribed by her current diet, she would have to throw away half the cottage cheese and skip dinner.

Nicholas made a sudden, sputtering noise. 'Fuck off!' he shouted. 'I don't want you in here!'

Karla nodded. 'I understand. I won't be long, Nicholas. But I do need to talk to you about your living situation. If you give me the go-ahead, I'd like to make some calls this afternoon to see about—'

'You gonna put me in a shelter?'

'Well, I would hope we could come up with something better than that.'

'I ain't going in no facility!'

'You don't want to go on sleeping on the street, do you?'

'There's only retards and spazzes living in them facilities. They don't even keep them clean.'

'But, Nicholas—'

'I've *got* a place to live.'

'Your aunt's, you mean?' Karla had spoken to the furious aunt on the phone that morning. *No! I don't care what happens to him any more. The little bastard took my money and when I told him to give it*

154

back, he come at me with a knife! He can stay on the streets for all I care . . . 'I've called your aunt, Nicholas,' Karla said. 'She's not willing to have you back just now.'

Nicholas closed his eyes. 'She's fucking about.'

'Well, maybe, but . . .'

'She'll take me back.'

'She says you stole from her.'

'Fuck off!' he roared. 'Amount of times she's taken my disability money!'

'All right—'

'Fuck off!'

Karla folded her arms tightly against her navel. 'Please don't shout, Nicholas—'

'You fucking come in here and accuse me of thieving!'

'I'm not accusing you of anything, Nicholas. Your aunt—'

'Fuck off! Fuck off!'

In his distress, Nicholas began to heave his trunk from side to side. As he did so, his nightgown rode up to reveal two glossy, tapered stumps poking out from his adult diaper. Pointing at the diaper, he began to cry. 'Why . . . why'd they gotta put me in *this*?'

'I don't know,' Karla said quietly. 'Have you been having problems in that—?'

'I ain't gonna shit myself!' he sobbed. 'I ain't a baby!'

'Nicholas . . .' Karla placed a hand on his shoulder.

In a flash, he reared up, grasping her neck in his great yellow hands, and tipping her off her chair on to the bed. Her face was now pressed into his truncated lap and her legs were hanging off the

155

side of the bed, kicking helplessly in the air. She tried to scream, but the only sound that emerged was a muffled squawk. His grip grew tighter. She could feel him twisting at her neck as if it were a recalcitrant bottle top. *He is going to kill me*, she thought.

For many reasons (not least among them that her corpse would be found wearing a skirt clearly labelled XL) Karla did not want to be killed. But she was a practical woman, accustomed to managing her expectations, and she had already gone a considerable way towards accepting the fact of her own demise when she felt a sudden, intense pressure on her back. Someone had clambered on top of her and was attempting to prise Nicholas's fingers from her neck.

There was a sound of running footsteps, followed by cries and shouts in assorted registers. The struggle to free her seemed to go on for a very long time but at last Nicholas's hold relaxed and the person who had been sitting on her back dismounted. She rolled over. A crowd of nurses and porters was now surrounding Nicholas. Through the tangle of their arms, she glimpsed the boy's terrified face. His eyes were rolling wildly. His teeth were bared in a snarl. 'Please don't hurt him . . .' she cried.

A nurse appeared with a hypodermic needle and squeezed herself into the scrum. 'There!' she exclaimed a moment later, brandishing the needle triumphantly. Nicholas went limp.

All the shouting ceased. For a moment, the only sound in the room was the panting of the nurses and porters.

'Are you all right, miss?' a voice said.

A middle-aged, brown-skinned man with a large, crumpled face and a prodigious crag of nose was standing over Karla. His heavy-lidded, slow-blinking eyes seemed to bespeak great gentleness of purpose.

'Are you all right?' he repeated. 'I'm afraid I may have hurt you when I got up on your back.'

All around the edge of his lips there ran a thin line of pale, slightly raised skin, like the thread of pith on a tangerine segment. Karla had a crazy urge to test its softness with her finger.

'Miss? Can you hear me?' he said.

She sat up slowly and raised a hand to her throbbing neck.

'Would you like some water?' he asked. He passed her a plastic beaker.

He was a large man, she saw now, with hands and ears built to the same monumental scale as his nose. She estimated that he was a good thirty pounds overweight. (It was often assumed that Karla, being a fat person, had more forgiving aesthetic standards than other, slimmer people, but this was untrue. Years of attending to her own physical failings had made her, if anything, more closely attuned to the nuances of bodily imperfection than most. Her girlfriends, many of whom took guilty reassurance from the fact that they were Not-as-Fat-as-Karla, would have been shocked to discover how unsparing she was in her assessments of their figures.)

The porters were trooping from the room now, casting deferential glances at her as they went. A nurse approached Karla. 'You all right?' she asked. She was a blonde, pert-faced woman, very tidy and clean. Her pastel pink scrubs had little teddy bears printed on them.

'I'm fine,' Karla said.

'Don't get up right away,' the man urged. 'Take it slow.'

The nurse looked at him. 'And you are?'

'I work downstairs,' the man said. 'In the newspaper shop.' He pointed through the open door to a trolley of newspapers and magazines standing in the corridor. 'I was just doing some deliveries,' he said, 'and then I heard shouting—'

'I see.' The nurse touched her cheek, her hair, as if reassuring herself of her own fragrant neatness. 'Well, I think we have the situation under control now, thank you.'

The man looked at Karla. 'Will you be all right if I go?'

Karla was reluctant to appear to be endorsing the nurse's rudeness, but she did very much want to be left alone. She nodded.

'Okay,' the man said. 'Take care.'

'Thank you for helping,' she called out after he had left the room. But she could not be sure that he had heard her.

The nurse turned to Karla and rolled her eyes conspiratorially. '*Arab*,' she mouthed silently.

*   *   *

An hour or so later, as Karla was passing through the hospital lobby on her way to eat lunch in the hospital garden, she spotted the man who had assisted her through the glass front of his newspaper shop. He gestured for her to wait. A moment later, he came out.

'Shouldn't you be lying down?' he asked.

158

'No, no, I'm fine. I didn't thank you properly before. I'm very grateful to you for coming in like that.'

He waved his hand. 'Please. Anyone would have done the same.'

'I'm sorry that that nurse was so . . . unpleasant to you.'

'Oh, her. She didn't like me, did she?' He pursed his lips in an imitation of the nurse's prudish expression. ' "*I think we have the situation under control now.*" '

Karla laughed, surprised by the accuracy of his mimicry. And then, because she did not want him to think that she regarded the racism of hospital staff as a laughing matter, she shook her head sternly. 'She's not a nice woman, I'm afraid.'

The man gestured at the brown paper bag in her hand. 'Are you having your lunch outside?'

'Yes.'

'Would it be okay if I ate with you?'

Karla hesitated. She was shy of eating in front of strangers. She pointed at the shop. 'Don't you have to . . . ?'

'No, I can close it. I just put a sign on the door.'

'Oh, okay.'

'Are you sure?'

'Sure!'

He held out his hand. 'I haven't introduced myself. My name is Khaled.'

Karla, keenly aware of the dampness of her palm, grasped his fingertips loosely. 'I'm Karla.'

He went back into the store to get his lunch and to lock up. When he returned, they walked out to the garden.

'Let's sit where there's shade,' he said, pointing

at a tree on the far side of the lawn. Karla nodded, although she would have preferred to sit on a bench. She always felt ungainly sitting on grass. And she was wearing a skirt, so there would be modesty issues.

When they got to the tree, Khaled took off his jacket and laid it on the grass.

'Please. Sit on this. You will get your clothes dirty otherwise.'

'Oh no,' Karla protested. 'I don't need that.' Standing over him, she could see the place at the back of his head where he was beginning to go bald: a small spot, round and brown, like a penny.

'You must,' he urged.

'What about you, though?'

'Oh,' Khaled gestured at his jeans. 'It doesn't matter for me. Please. Sit.'

There seemed no way to go on politely resisting. Karla knelt down carefully on the jacket.

Khaled produced from his nylon backpack a spoon, a fork, a napkin and some Tupperware bowls filled with rice and some sort of vegetable stew. 'My brother's wife makes it for me,' he said with an apologetic smile. 'It is Egyptian food. I hope you don't mind the smell.'

'Not at all!' Karla said quickly. 'I like it.'

It was true. Whatever he had in his little bowls smelled delicious. Sheepishly, she reached into her bag and brought out her cottage cheese.

'So . . . are you from Egypt?' she asked.

'Yes, from Alexandria.'

'And how long have you worked in the newspaper store?'

'It is my store,' Khaled corrected her. 'I have had it for two years.'

160

'Oh, really? That's great.' Karla's kneeling position had begun to cut off feeling in her calves and feet. She set about the tricky task of extending her legs in front of her without revealing too much pantyhose.

'Tell me, what will happen to that cripple boy now?' Khaled asked. 'Have the police been informed?'

'Oh no!' Karla said. 'No, no . . . I wouldn't press charges.' She paused. 'We don't actually refer to people like Nicholas as cripples any more . . .'

Khaled seemed not to register this gentle reproof. 'I don't think it's fair for the hospital to let ladies deal with people like that,' he said. 'It's too dangerous. He was a wild animal! What if I had not been outside the room when he attacked you?'

'Well, I'm very glad you were there, obviously,' she said. 'But, you know, Nicholas isn't really a *bad* kid. He's just very angry and unhappy.'

'I must disagree with you. I saw him. He was trying to strangle you! You can't say someone like this is good.'

Karla shook her head. 'You have to think of what someone like Nicholas deals with every day. I dare say we wouldn't be very nice if we had his life.'

Khaled gazed at her admiringly. 'You are a very good person. Have you ever done an enneagram test?'

'I don't know what that is.'

'It's a personality test. You fill out a very detailed questionnaire and then it tells you which one of eight personality types you are. It's amazingly accurate.'

'Oh.' Karla's face took on the polite expression

161

that she reserved for hearing about other people's implausible beliefs.

'I am sure you'd be a type 2. The 2 is the Helper. Very kind and giving. That's why you do the job you do.'

Karla frowned down at the bulky outline of her thighs and carefully placed her handbag across her lap. People were always telling her that she was a 'born social worker'. In truth, though, her earliest inclination had been towards a career in law. As a child she had loved going to see her father perform in court and had spent many happy hours in her bedroom re-enacting important historical trials with her Barbies and her gerbil. It was only in late adolescence that her legal ambitions had faded. Picking up on certain familial hints—the mood of rueful scepticism that arose whenever she spoke of law school, her mother's breezy speculations as to whether she might not be 'a bit dyslexic'—she came to understand that she had been horribly overestimating her potential. Having realized her mistake, she quickly set about correcting herself and by the time she graduated high school her aspirations had been lowered to a level with which everyone could feel comfortable. Before applying to college, she even took the precaution of asking her parents if they thought college was worthwhile for her. 'Of course,' her mother said. 'Why not? Perhaps you could do a vocational course somewhere.'

'You should train for one of the caring professions,' her father told her. 'Nursing or something like that. You're a nurturer.'

It had not escaped Karla that being a nurturer occupied a very low rung on her parents' hierarchy of valuable life pursuits. And she had doubted in any case that she deserved the designation. Beneath her placid exterior, it seemed to her, she harboured a lot of distinctly unnurturing emotions. Rage. Frustration. The not infrequent desire to smack her mother in the face. The argument, such as it was, for her compassionate nature rested on nothing more substantial than a childhood incident in which she had brought home an injured bird. (The bird had later died of starvation while in her care.)

Still, she had been at an age when to be crisply summed up in any manner was vaguely flattering and whatever misgivings she had about her father's account of her were outweighed by the potent pleasure of finding herself the object of his scrutiny. Now, sixteen years on, the idea of her caring instinct had become so fixed a component of family lore—so central to the world's understanding of who she was—that she had long since ceased to question its accuracy. Only very occasionally—when some well-meaning person like Khaled was confidently assuring her of her kind and gentle disposition—did she experience a twinge of long-forgotten doubt and a dim resurgence of anger at her vocational doom.

'Wait,' Khaled said, 'is that all you are having for your lunch?'

Karla looked up to see him pointing at her tub of cottage cheese. 'Yes,' she said. 'There's a lot in here.'

'Nooo. It isn't enough! You will be hungry again in an hour.'

'Honestly, I'm good.'

He shook his head. 'You must have some of

mine. I have too much for one person.'

Karla's refusal grew slightly desperate. 'Thank you, but, really, I don't like a big meal at lunchtime.' She resumed eating, spooning the cottage cheese into her mouth in a rapid, anxious motion, as if she were expecting at any moment to be struck.

Khaled took a forkful of his rice and chewed it slowly. 'May I ask you . . . are you on a diet?'

'Me?' Karla gestured comically at her own bulk. 'Does it look like it?'

He looked at her with concern. 'I'm sorry,' he said. 'I think I have offended you.'

Karla tried to give herself some time by pretending that her mouth was full. 'No, not at all,' she said, after a moment. But as she spoke, a large, hot tear plopped into her cottage cheese.

'Oh my God,' Khaled cried. 'I am a stupid person. I didn't mean to—'

'*Please*,' Karla said. 'It's *all right*.' She wanted to hit him.

'But I have upset you.' Khaled put his food down and pressed his fingers against his shining temples.

'It's not your fault,' Karla said. 'It's nothing to do with you. It's . . . it's something else. Something private. I'm sorry to have spoiled your lunch.'

Tears were coursing down her cheeks now. She put the lid back on her cottage cheese, placed the container in her handbag and stood up. Glancing down, she saw that her buttocks had left two large oval depressions in the lining of Khaled's jacket.

'Don't go,' he said.

She could no longer speak. Shaking her head, she walked quickly away across the grass.

164

In the restroom off the hospital lobby, she took a long, punitive look at her reflection in the mirror. Her nose was swollen and glowing, a joke-store accessory. Her blouse had ridden up, revealing several intersecting lines of pink-and-white crenellation where her waistband cut into her belly. She let out a small groan of despair. She had cried—cried *about being fat*—in front of a stranger. Two women came in now and broke off from their chatter to register her distraught appearance. She walked quickly into one of the stalls and stayed there, listening to the slam of stall doors and the roar of hand-dryers until the women had left. Then she came out again, splashed her face with cold water and went back upstairs to her office.

She was intending to get some work done, but as soon as she sat down at her desk, she discovered that her computer screen had frozen. She jabbed at various keys for a while and then began to whack the side of the computer with her fist.

'Temper, temper,' a voice drawled behind her.

She turned to see one of the hospital porters standing in the doorway. 'Oh! Hi, Ray.'

He gave a lugubrious chuckle. 'Busy, are you?'

'A bit.'

Ray was a squat, indolent man in his early sixties. His heavy style of campy, knowing pessimism made him deeply unpopular among his colleagues at the hospital. Karla, attuned to the high, mosquito whine of his neediness, always felt obliged to be especially nice to him.

'I heard you got in a spot of trouble this morning,' Ray said. 'Some fella on the fifth floor tried to rape you.'

'No, no, it was—'

165

'Ooh, how awful. They should pay you danger money.'

Karla disliked receiving visitors in her office. The cubicle was hardly large enough to accommodate one person; two people within its doll-size confines were forced into a physical intimacy bordering on the indecent. Ray was so near to Karla now that she could see the rheum in the corners of his eyes and the scurf in his ear. Subtly, so as not to offend him, she leaned away, pressing her head against a filing cabinet.

'Must be a full moon,' Ray went on. 'They've all been acting up lately. Some nutter on the third floor threw his lunch down the toilet and caused a flood yesterday . . . it was like a Third World country in there. I told them, it'll be a miracle if we don't all get dysentery.'

'Oh dear,' Karla said.

'Yeah, well, same old same old . . . What's wrong with your computer then?'

'Frozen. I should call IT.'

'Oof.' He rolled his eyes. 'Good luck. You'll be waiting a while before any of that lot get down here. They're all too busy sitting up there playing poker . . .'

Through the triangular space between Ray's torso and his bent arm, Khaled's face suddenly appeared. 'Sorry,' he said, 'am I interrupting?'

Ray turned to him with a sardonic stare. 'You want to talk to Karla, do you?'

'Only if it's convenient . . .'

'Don't mind me. I should be off, anyway.' He gave Karla an arch look. 'I'll leave the two of you alone then. See you later, Karla.'

'Bye, Ray.' Karla watched helplessly as Ray

lumbered off down the corridor.

'I hope I didn't intrude,' Khaled said. 'I came to apologize for upsetting you just now.'

'You didn't have to,' she replied curtly. 'I'm fine.' There was something almost sadistic in this man's pursuit of her, she thought. What was *wrong* with him?

'I feel very bad,' Khaled said. 'You just had this terrible thing happen with the boy and now I said something stupid to hurt your feelings—'

'Honestly, it was nothing. I'm just in a weird mood today. It wasn't anything you did.'

He bent down and took out a packet of M&Ms from his briefcase. 'I brought you these.'

'Oh no!' Karla said. 'Really . . .' The tactlessness of the offering astonished her. Was this the only gesture of propitiation he could think of? Did gluttony so override all her other discernible qualities?

'*Please*,' Khaled said. 'If you don't take them, I'll know you are still angry.'

He sounded so sincerely unhappy that for a moment Karla forgot her dignity and the tragedy of her fatness. 'Okay,' she said, taking the bag of candy from him and setting it down on her desk. 'Thank you very much.'

'We are friends again?'

Karla nodded. 'Of course. We were never *not* friends.'

'And you accept my apology?'

'Sure.'

Khaled glanced around the cubicle. 'So. This is where you work.' He pointed to a photograph of Mike and Karla on her corkboard. 'Is that your boyfriend?'

'Husband,' Karla corrected. She looked at the photograph. It had been taken at a union party seven years ago, shortly after she and Mike had begun dating. Mike was squinting coolly at the camera with a can of beer in his hands. She—fresh off a diet of cabbage soup and laxatives—was wearing size 10 jeans and flashing a peace sign. She could still remember the excitement of that night: the dazed elation she had felt at being out in public on Mike's arm. Mike had been one of the union's most eligible bachelors in those days. The nurses used to grow flustered and giggly at the sight of him swaggering down the hospital corridors with a toothpick clenched between his teeth. Women in the union offices would stare at his butt and exchange significant looks when he passed their desks.

Everyone had been astonished when he decided to take a romantic interest in Karla—Karla perhaps most of all. She had spent much of their early courtship half-expecting to discover that she had been made the victim of an elaborate practical joke. Mike had always been very sweet and reassuring about her lack of obvious qualifications to be his girlfriend. There might be prettier women, he told her—prettier women and wittier women and women with better bodies—but he didn't care about superficial things like that. He was looking for someone he could talk to, someone who understood his values and commitments. Someone he could *respect*. And Karla, caught up in the delirium of her unsought-for, undreamed-of privilege, had believed this to be the sweetest thing any man had ever said to her.

'Is he a fun person?' Khaled asked.

'Yes,' Karla said quickly. 'Very.'

'You have children?'

She stiffened. 'No . . . not yet. We're . . . trying.'

'Ah. That's nice. Children are nice. I spend a lot of time with my nephews. My brother and his family live near me, so I often take the boys out to McDonald's and whatever.' He pointed at her messy desk. 'You work very hard, I can see.'

Karla shook her head in modest demurral. 'Not so hard.'

'Yes you do. I see what time people leave this place and you are always working late.'

Karla gave a nervous laugh, unsure whether to be flattered or spooked that he had observed her comings and goings. 'Well, I'm not working very hard now,' she said. 'My computer's frozen. I was about to call IT.'

'I know a bit about computers. Would you like me to take a look?'

'No thanks. I really should—'

'But it may be something quite simple. Let me try.'

Reluctantly, Karla got up and squeezed herself against the wall to let Khaled sit down.

'I think we have to restart it,' he said.

Karla gazed at his bald spot dubiously. 'Have you studied computers then?'

'No, I just spend a lot of time on mine. The internet and all that. I am single, you see. It's a good way for me to make friends.'

Karla felt a little oppressed by this unsolicited glimpse into his lonely, private life. Did he use the internet dating services, she wondered? Or the pornography sites?

Khaled turned to her suddenly. 'I don't look at

169

dirty pictures or anything like that. I wouldn't want you to think . . .'

Karla blushed. 'No, of course not.'

After a few moments, he sat back. 'Well, that was easy.'

'Really? Is it working again?'

'All I did was restart it. Sometimes that's all it needs.'

Karla came and peered at the screen. 'Wow. Thanks.'

He stood up. 'I guess I should leave you in peace now.'

'Well, I should be getting on.'

'Do you think we could have our lunch together again some time? I promise not to upset you again.'

Karla smiled. 'Okay.'

'Great!' He picked up his briefcase. 'We will talk next week.'

As soon as he had closed the door, Karla reached for the packet of M&Ms and tore it open. What an odd man he was! What questions he asked! She tipped back her head to receive the rattling candy into her mouth. He was kind, in his clumsy way. And clearly not a dummy. You could tell just by the way he had mimicked that nurse that he *got* things. She probed with her tongue at a little piece of M&M that had become stuck in one of her molars. Had he meant it, about their having lunch again? Half of her hoped that he hadn't. It would be a relief not to have to endure the tension of another encounter. The other half wanted him to have been in earnest—if only, she told herself, so she might correct the awful first impression she had made.

CHAPTER EIGHT

'Lenny, have you seen my bag?'

Audrey stood at the foot of the stairs, waiting for a response. A few seconds later, she shouted again. 'Lenny?'

'Yeah?' a groggy voice came back.

'Have you seen my bag?'

'No.'

'Well, get a move on. We have to be off in a minute.'

Audrey and Lenny were going this morning to see Lenny's mother at the Bedford Correctional Facility in Westchester. Visiting Susan was a chore that Audrey generally tried to avoid but Lenny had been without a licence since his last DUI conviction and if she didn't drive him today he would be forced to take the nasty prison bus. As she wandered into the kitchen, the phone rang.

'Hiya, Audrey,' Daniel chirruped.

'Oh, it's you,' Audrey replied. 'I'd forgotten you existed.'

Daniel was now working at a downtown law firm specializing in environmental law. He had not been to see Joel in several weeks.

'Well, I'm still here,' he said.

'Saved any whales lately?'

He made a desultory sound of amusement. 'No, not yet. How are you, Audrey?'

'Tickety-boo, thank you. Is there any reason for this call?'

'I was wondering if I could arrange a time to come and see you, actually.'

171

'What for?'

'I need to talk to you about something.'

'What?'

'I'd rather not mention it on the phone.'

Audrey gave a mocking laugh. Daniel was always being gratuitously mysterious about utterly unimportant things. It was one of the many ways in which he tried to make himself seem important.

'Don't be an idiot, Daniel,' she said. 'Just tell me.'

Lenny entered the kitchen, holding her bag. She made an astounded, where-on-earth-did-you-find-it face and blew him a kiss.

'It really wouldn't be appropriate, Audrey,' Daniel was saying. 'It's something that needs to be discussed in person. It is quite urgent, though, so if you could make time to see me today . . .'

'I can't,' Audrey said. 'I'm going up to Bedford to take Lenny to see his mother.'

'What time do you expect to be back?'

'Bloody hell, Daniel, can't it wait until tomorrow?'

'Today really would be better.'

Audrey grunted in irritation. 'All right. I'll meet you here at five.'

She hung up and turned to Lenny. 'You clever boy! Where was it?'

'On the landing.'

'Really? How weird! Are you ready to go then?'

'Yeah.'

She looked him up and down. 'I don't suppose you want to shave?'

Lenny gave his chin an exploratory rub. 'Nah.'

On their way out of the city, they stopped to get gas. Audrey sent Lenny in to pay while she pumped. When he returned, she found that he had used her change to purchase a Gatorade and a large hot dog the colour of doll flesh.

'Why didn't you wait?' she asked as they got back into the car. 'I would have stopped somewhere decent if I'd known you were hungry.'

'Yeah, but I was starving,' Lenny said. 'I didn't have anything for dinner last night.'

Audrey glanced at him as she steered the car back on to Houston Street. 'Why not, you silly?'

Lenny bit into his hot dog. 'No money.'

'Oh, *Lenny*.' For the last three months Audrey had been giving Lenny an allowance of a hundred dollars a week. This, together with some odd jobs that he was doing for Jean and other friends, was meant to tide him over until he could find full-time work.

'I feel really shitty about it, Mom,' Lenny said. 'But I had to give Tanya back the money I owed her. And then I've been having to pay all these taxi fares to go and see Dad and—'

'Taxis!' Audrey exclaimed. 'Lenny, there's something called the subway.'

'I asked Jean for an advance,' Lenny said. 'But she doesn't want to pay me till I've finished the work.'

'She wouldn't give you anything?' Audrey exclaimed. 'Not twenty bucks?'

Lenny shook his head dolefully. 'The thing is, I don't want to borrow any more money from Tanya—'

'All right, all right,' Audrey interrupted. 'I hear you. My bag's on the backseat. Take fifty bucks.'

There was a silence. Lenny went on chewing his hot dog.

173

Audrey smiled the complicated smile of someone knowingly submitting to a con. 'A hundred then, but no more.'

'Are you sure?'

'Don't give me that. Just take the money.'

Joel had been telling Audrey for years that Lenny was a wastrel, that he did not deserve her indulgence. He had once accused her of treating Lenny as if he were her 'gigolo'. But none of these reproaches had ever come close to making her change her ways. Audrey was rather proud of her reckless devotion to her son. To hear Lenny attacked only excited her heroic sense of being for him contra mundum.

Twenty-seven years ago, on the night that Lenny's mother had been arrested for bank robbery, it was Audrey who had been delegated to drive uptown and retrieve seven-year-old Lenny from his babysitter. There had been a snowstorm in the city that day and it had taken her an hour to drive up the hushed, white island to Harlem. She had spent another hour going around in circles, trying to locate the address, and by the time she finally entered the tiny apartment above a barber shop on St Nicholas Avenue, it was long past midnight. She had found Lenny curled up on the sitting-room floor watching cartoons, with a giant, panting bull-mastiff at his side. 'Am I going to get paid?' the babysitter had demanded. She had just finished painting her nails and was shaking her flexed hands in a slow up-and-down motion, as if she were casting off water or making an incantation. 'Because the extra hours is time and half, you know.'

'When's Mommy coming?' Lenny had asked,

174

without taking his eyes from the television.

Up to this moment in her life, Audrey had never evinced the slightest sentimentality about children. In so far as she had recognized them as an independent category of personhood, she had tended to think of them as trainee humans. Inadequate adults. She loved her own daughters well enough—wanted them to be happy and so forth—but they had failed to inspire in her that mad, lioness passion to which other mothers so preeningly testified. She was still in some shock regarding the servility of motherhood—the sheer, thankless drudgery of it. All the cleaning up messes she had not made and preparing meals she did not want to eat. She fed her girls regularly, and diligently brushed their teeth twice a day, and made sure they were more or less appropriately dressed for the weather, but beyond a dull sense of satisfaction at having fulfilled her maternal duties, she received no pleasure from performing these tasks. Try as she might, she could not feel her daughters' happinesses and sorrows as her own. The miniature dramas of their daily lives bored her, to tell the truth. When Karla or Rosa woke in the night, complaining of bad dreams, she irritably instructed them to think of pleasant things and sent them briskly back to bed. When they came home complaining of school friends who were being unkind, she shrugged and told them to buck up. 'What do you care what those ninnies think of you, anyway?' she would demand, exhaling dragon-clouds of cigarette smoke as she rustled through her newspaper.

She had never felt guilty about her lack of maternal zeal. Hers was the sane response to motherhood, she thought. The shiny-eyed parenting maniacs she encountered when she dropped her daughters off at school—the grinning Super-moms and -dads who hung around after the bell rang, hankering for 'more access' to their children's classrooms and fretting over the PTA's efforts to fund a language lab for the kindergarteners—*they* were the crazy ones. There was something infantile, it seemed to her, about their passionate identification with their children. Clearly, they were compensating for a terrible lack or inadequacy elsewhere in their lives.

But something had changed on the night that she found Lenny in the Harlem apartment. Gazing down at his owl-eyed face—noticing the chalky moustache of Yoohoo on his upper lip, the glistening scribble of dog drool on his pants—she felt a tiny aperture clicking open, a pilot light being lit somewhere deep within. Her temples throbbed. She had a panicked sense of onrush, of internal torrent. She wanted to pick the boy up and—she didn't know what—squeeze him, kiss him, swallow him whole.

The next morning, she had tried to describe this bizarre physiological drama to Joel.

'It was like I was having an anxiety attack or something,' she told him.

'Yeah, well, it's a big thing, taking on another person's kid,' Joel had muttered. He was pulling on his pants at the time, hurrying to get to the police station to see Susan. He glanced at Lenny, who was lying next to Audrey in their bed, still asleep. 'Don't worry. It'll only be for a couple of days.'

But he had misunderstood. It was not the

burden of responsibility for Lenny that had threatened to overwhelm her; it was the long-awaited appearance of maternal instinct.

In the years since then, Audrey's attachment to Lenny had been a frequent source of tension in their marriage. Joel, for all his talk of communal child-rearing and tribes, deeply resented the idea that Lenny should have succeeded in evoking Audrey's passion where her 'real' children had failed. 'Karla and Rosa are your flesh and blood,' he would chide her. But these appeals to sanguinary loyalty missed the point, she felt. If anything, the fact that Lenny was not hers made it easier to love him. As the co-author of Karla and Rosa, she could not help but look upon them with the dissatisfied eye of an artist assessing her own flawed handiwork. Lenny, on the other hand, was an unsolicited donation: she was free to enjoy the gift of him without any burden of genetic responsibility for his imperfections. She had *chosen* to love him. The disparity in her feelings towards her daughters and her son was regrettable but it was not something that was in her gift to correct.

*　　　*　　　*

The gates were still closed when Audrey and Lenny arrived at the correctional facility. After Lenny had stuffed the contents of his pockets in the car door, they joined the visitors who were milling around outside the bunker-like building. At the bottom of the driveway, a bus drew up and a group of passengers, mostly women and children, got off. A little boy had just thrown up, it seemed, and his grandmother—a weary-looking woman in hot-pink stretch pants—was wiping his face roughly with paper towel. 'Be still!' she shouted at him as he squirmed. 'You want to smell bad when you see your mommy?'

Audrey glanced at Lenny. As a boy, he had always been carsick on the journey to Bedford. At least once and often twice she would have to pull into a rest stop, swab him down and change him into a new set of clothes. He had never been ill on other car journeys; it was the stress of visiting his mother that had made him puke. Later on, in the visiting room, he would crouch in his chair, smelling of bile, asking Susan to explain, one more time, how she had got caught, what crucial planning error had led to her capture. When the bell sounded at the end of the hour, he would cling to her, sobbing for her to come home with him. 'Why don't you escape?' he had asked once. 'You could climb out a window. If you ran fast enough, they wouldn't be able to catch you.'

Audrey had found these visits almost unbearably wounding. It had enraged her that Susan should enjoy the privilege of Lenny's devotion when it was she, Audrey, who was down in the maternal salt mines, reading him stories and singing him lullabies and cleaning up his vomit. What had Susan ever done for the boy, except abandon him to inadequate childcare while she buggered off to play urban guerillas?

The gates were open now and the line had begun to shuffle into the visitors' processing area. There was a window with a counter where you could drop off food and clothes for the prisoners. A handwritten sign stuck on the glass instructed, 'No thong, fishnet, g-string or bikini panties. No

178

lace or sheer bras.' Audrey and Lenny passed through the metal detectors and walked down a corridor into a large cafeteria-like room with vending machines along one wall. Susan was sitting at one of the tables. Her face broke into a wide smile when she saw them enter. 'Hey,' she said softly, elongating the syllable. She stood up and wrapped Lenny in a tight embrace, rocking him back and forth for several long seconds. Lenny, Audrey was pleased to note, looked mortified.

They sat down now, with Susan on one side of the table and Lenny and Audrey on the other.

'It's good to see you, man,' Susan said, taking Lenny's hand and gazing solemnly into his eyes.

During her days in the Underground, Susan had been a notoriously intimidating figure. She had worn men's overalls and styled her hair in a fearsome Plantaganet bob. She had carried a knife 'for killing pigs' in the sole of her shoe. Shortly after the arrest of Charles Manson and his followers, she had composed an infamous Cong communiqué, praising Manson as 'a brother in the struggle against bourgeois America'. But incarceration, or age—or both—had had an emollient effect on her. Her hair was long and white now, and she wore it loose about her shoulders in the prophetess style favoured by veteran women folk singers. The pig-killing rhetoric of yore had long since subsided into a dreamy singsong of healing and conciliation. Over the years at Bedford, she had founded several educational programmes for her fellow inmates, including one on AIDS awareness and another— much to Audrey's secret derision—on 'parenting skills'. Her literacy programme, in which inmates

179

were encouraged to write and perform plays about their lives, was so well-regarded that pilot programmes based on her blueprint had now been set up in several prisons around the country.

'So, what's up, man?' she asked. 'What's going on with your band, Lenny? You been playing recently?'

Lenny shook his head. 'Not much.'

'Hey, Lenny, man, don't neglect your music.'

Audrey turned away to hide her smile. Lenny's band wasn't really a *band*: it was a couple of stoner guys with guitars who got together once a month or so to ad lib tuneless, ironic songs on miniature domestic themes. Their signature number—their anthem, more or less—was a mock-heroic tribute to the drummer's cat:

You eat tuna and Cap'n Crunch.
You got a face like Alice in the Brady Bunch.

Susan was always trying, in her earnest way, to lend Lenny's half-hearted pursuits a serious, progressive inflection. If Lenny got a job in a restaurant, he was 'getting into food', which was great, because it was such a special thing to nourish people. If Lenny took a free trip to Morocco with one of his rich, druggy friends, he was 'exploring Arab culture', which was fantastic, because it was so important for young people to fight American parochialism and bigotry. Audrey treasured these misreadings as proof of Susan's inanity.

'So what else you been up to?' Susan asked now. 'What's going on in the world?'

'Well, a bunch of things have happened with Joel,' Lenny said. 'But Audrey should really tell

180

you about all that.' (Out of respect for Susan's feelings, he did not refer to Audrey and Joel as Mom and Dad in her presence.)

Susan turned to Audrey. 'Audrey, how's it going?'

Audrey looked at her sourly. She never felt quite respected by Susan. There was a laboured politeness in the way that Susan spoke to her—an awkward condescension—that seemed to imply some difficulty in relating to a woman of Audrey's thoroughgoing conventionality. *You are a very straight housewife*, her tone said, *and I am a fearless renegade but I am doing my best to find a connection here*. It drove Audrey nuts. 'The cheek of that woman!' she had often complained to Joel. 'She fucked up a bank robbery, she made a couple of dud bombs and she didn't use deodorant for ten years. For this she thinks she can lord it over me like she's fucking Alexandra Kollontai?'

'Joel's not doing badly,' she said now. 'He's had a couple of infections but he's come through them very well—'

'Yeah, Joel's a tough old fucker,' Susan remarked.

Audrey flared her nostrils like a rocking horse. Speaking irreverently of Joel was a right she reserved for herself and very few others—certainly not for Susan. Besides which, she had not yet finished her account of Joel's medical status.

'And how about *you*, Audrey?' Susan asked. 'You keeping strong?'

'Yup.' Audrey thrust her hands in her pockets as a preventive measure against Susan trying to hold one of them. 'We're all doing fine, aren't we, Len?'

Susan smiled at Lenny. 'Is that right? You doing

181

okay?'

Lenny nodded.

There was a brief pause. Susan looked around the canteen. 'I got a letter from Cheryl this week,' she said. Cheryl was a young Puerto Rican inmate with whom Susan had become romantically involved some years earlier. She had been released now and was back living with her boyfriend, but she and Susan continued to correspond. Susan wrote her a lot of love poems, some of which she had been known to read aloud to Lenny.

'She's training to be an AIDS counsellor,' Susan went on. 'I'm so proud of her.'

Audrey shut her eyes. The woman was shameless, she thought. Having dealt with Joel in three sentences, she was now going to revert to discussing herself and her sordid lesbian romance. Joel always said it was unfair to criticize long-term inmates for being self-absorbed. It was inevitable, he said, that the outside world should become abstract and somewhat unreal to them. But Audrey disagreed: Susan had always been a narcissist in altruist's clothing.

Towards the end of the visit, Susan asked Lenny to get a soda for her from one of the machines. Once he had left the table, she turned to Audrey.

'Is he okay?'

'He's fine,' Audrey said.

'He's not doing drugs again, right?'

Audrey bristled. 'No. Why would you say that?'

'I don't know. He's kind of vague today. He doesn't look good . . .'

'He didn't shave, that's all. He's fine.'

'Are you sure?'

Audrey folded her arms and smiled tightly. 'I

182

think I would know, Susan.'

*   *   *

Lenny was morose on the drive home. Audrey tried to cheer him up, but her chatter seemed only to agitate him. After a while, she accepted defeat and drove in silence. Halfway back to the city, Lenny said he needed to pee, so they pulled over at a rest stop. It was a place they had often visited on their trips back and forth to Bedford: a tatty strip-mall with a newspaper shop, a McDonald's and a cinnamon-roll franchise called Snack Attack. While Lenny was in the bathroom, Audrey stood in the parking lot and smoked a cigarette. The day had grown warm and the air smelled of burger and car exhaust. She watched as a group of obese senior citizens in 'One Nation Under God' T-shirts descended from a bus and came barrelling across the macadam towards her. Joel had always hated places like this: malls, big-box stores, leisure parks—anywhere he was forced to confront his suburban countrymen en masse—but Audrey rather relished her encounters with lumpen America. Even after all these years in her adoptive country, she was still enough of a foreigner to be gratified by real-life sightings of under-dressed Americans grazing on trans-fats while they shopped.

She finished her cigarette and went into the mall to buy some coffee. When Lenny finally reappeared they sat and drank their lattes outside on a bench overlooking the McDonald's mini-playground.

'Look at him,' Lenny said, pointing at a boy who

183

was sitting at the top of the slide. 'He just bit the girl in front of him, little bastard!' He laughed with admiring incredulity.

'You've brightened up a bit,' Audrey remarked. She glanced covetously at the cinnamon roll that she had bought for him. It lay, coiled and gleaming, in its little polystyrene case, like the spiral flourish at the bottom of the Perry Street stair banister.

'You not eating that?' she asked.

'I'm not hungry.'

'Go on, eat it.'

'You eat it. I don't want it.'

'Go on, Len. You've had nothing since that hot dog.'

'*Jesus*, Mom—'

'All right, all right.' Audrey picked up the roll and put it in the trash. She gazed at him. 'Len . . .'

'Yeah?'

'You'd tell me if you were using again, wouldn't you?'

Lenny sat back on the bench and raised his eyes skywards. 'Come *on*.'

'Don't be like that,' Audrey protested. 'I'm just asking. You would tell me, wouldn't you?'

'*Yes*. But I'm not.'

'Honestly?'

'For real. A bit of spliff now and then and that's it, I swear.'

Audrey smiled. 'That's what I thought. It was Susan who wanted to know. She said you were behaving funny. I wouldn't have asked otherwise.'

He leaned over and kissed her cheek. 'Well,' he said with a sigh, 'I'm glad *you* trust me, anyway.'

Audrey dropped Lenny off at Tanya's apartment in the East Village before going back to Perry Street. The traffic was terrible getting over to the West Side and she arrived home to find Daniel waiting for her on the front stoop. He was wearing skinny green pants the same lurid shade as Babar's suit and he had some sort of gel in his hair that made it stand up in stiff little peaks like a frozen sea.

'Do they make you dress like that at your new firm?' Audrey asked as she opened the front door. 'Or is this a look you came up with by yourself?'

Daniel smiled tolerantly. 'I was about to leave. I thought you weren't coming.'

'I'm ten minutes late, Daniel. Don't get your knickers in a twist.' She led the way into the kitchen.

'Now look,' Daniel said as they sat down, 'I'm not going to beat around the bush. I know that Berenice Mason came to see you a few weeks ago—'

'Oh *her*,' Audrey gave a little hoot of laughter. 'She's started stalking *you* now, has she? Has she told you all about her romance of the century with Joel?'

Daniel was silent.

'Oh, *Daniel*. What is it? You think Joel fucked her, do you?'

He lowered his eyes. 'More than that, I'm afraid. She and Joel have a child together.'

Audrey lit a cigarette and exhaled a plume of smoke in the direction of the ceiling. 'Yeah, she gave me that one too. The woman is barking.'

'Audrey, this isn't a joke. I've spoken with Joel's

assistant. She's known about this woman for some time, apparently.'

Something swayed and lurched in Audrey's gut. 'Kate?' she said. 'She's just a little girl. She'd believe anything.'

'The woman has evidence, Audrey.'

'Like what?'

'She has an Acknowledgement of Paternity form with Joel's signature on it.'

'Well, anyone can fake one of those—'

'It's not fake. I've seen it. And there's other stuff too—'

'Oh, *please*,' Audrey said. But even as she spoke she could feel her disbelief lifting like a mist. She turned and looked out of the kitchen window. In a bathroom on the third floor of the house opposite, a naked man was stepping carefully out of the shower. 'How old?' she asked.

'Sorry?'

'How old is this child supposed to be?'

'Oh, four, I think. Yes, four.'

'And what's the other stuff?'

'What?'

'You said there was other stuff. Other proof.'

'She has records of monthly payments that Joel made into her account—'

'*Payments?*'

'You know, for child support.'

'Oh.' Audrey squeezed the bridge of her nose between her finger and thumb.

'She also has a lot of correspondence,' Daniel said. 'Poems, cards—'

'Poems!' Audrey spat. 'See, now I *know* she's full of shit. Joel never wrote a poem in his life.'

'I don't know what to tell you, Audrey.'

186

'Why is she coming out with this now? What does she want?'

'I'm not entirely sure. I think she wants to, you know, get things out in the open. And she's mentioned that she'd like the child to have a relationship with his half-brother and -sisters—'

'Pfah!'

'She needs money as well. Joel's payments have stopped since he's been in the hospital.'

'Wait. She thinks she can come up with some cockamamie story about shtupping my husband and I'm going to pay her *pocket money*? Doesn't she have a job?'

'She's an artist.'

'*Ohhh*. An artist!'

'Well, a photographer.'

'*Super.*'

'I think you have to take this seriously, Audrey. It's not something you'd want to end up in court.'

'Is she threatening that?'

'No, no, she's not threatening anything. But it's the logical next step for her. She does have a legal right to support for the child.'

'What does she say Joel was paying her?'

'Uh, it varied, I think. But for the last two years, about twelve hundred dollars a month.'

Audrey squinted. Her maths had never been very good. 'What's that a year?'

'Fourteen thousand four hundred.'

'Fourteen thousand?' Audrey was torn between rage at the significance of the sum and embarrassment at its inadequacy. She turned back to the window. The man across the way had wrapped a towel around his waist and was examining his face in the mirror above his sink. For

187

years to come, she thought, her memory of this conversation would be bound to an image of pink flesh and white terrycloth glimpsed through a fogged-up window.

'If you give me the go-ahead,' Daniel said, 'I'd be happy to try to work out a deal with her.'

Audrey shook her head. 'No thanks.'

'Audrey—'

'If there are any deals to be made, I'll make them, Daniel.'

'Are you sure that's a good idea?'

She glanced at him. 'I think you can go now.'

'I'm sorry, Audrey. I know this must be—'

She turned away. 'Goodbye, Daniel.'

*　　　*　　　*

For a long time after he had gone, Audrey remained at the table, absently tracing one of the jagged channels that Lenny had carved in its wooden surface with a pen. A part of her seemed to be hovering overhead, disinterestedly observing her reactions. *You're a bit dizzy. Are you going to cry? Doesn't this feel unreal?* She remembered now the amazement—the affront—she had felt years ago when, as a little girl out shopping with her mother, she had come upon her second-grade teacher, Miss Vale, buying apples with her fiancé. Up until then, Audrey had tended, like most small children, to regard the world as a frozen parade of people and scenes that only came truly alive in her presence. It had never occurred to her that Miss Vale might have an independent, civilian existence outside the classroom, complete with male companions and fruit preferences. The assault to her illusion of omniscience had been devastating. Reality, she had suddenly understood, was not a series of discrete tableaux staged solely for her benefit, but vast and chaotic and unmasterable. Even people she saw every day— even her *family*—contained worlds that she would never fully fathom.

But she had forgotten that childhood lesson, it seemed. For forty years now, she had been confusing proximity with intimacy—believing that she had plumbed her husband's mysteries—when all the while she had been making love to his shadow. God knows, it wasn't the infidelity that shocked her: she had always prided herself on her realism about that part of married life. The first time she had caught Joel cheating on her, they had been married less than four months. For a week, she had rent her garments and torn at her hair. And then, with solemn, nineteen-year-old munificence, having extracted all the appropriate promises about its never happening again, she had forgiven him. But six months later, a friend of Audrey's had spotted Joel in Washington Square holding hands with a girl from Students for a Democratic Society. And not long after that, Audrey had found a love note in his pants pocket—a patchouli-scented scrawl from a teenaged folk singer called Spanish Wells. So it had gone on.

There had been phases in their marriage when Joel had been faithful—at least she thought there had been—but they had never lasted very long. 'It's the great female mistake to take sex personally,' Joel had once told her. 'Fucking is just a reflex, you know. Like scratching an itch.' Slowly,

189

painfully, over the years, she had come to accept this rationale. It wasn't that she had ever stopped minding about the affairs. She had always minded. But with considerable psychic effort, she had learned to put her unhappiness in perspective. What did it matter if a few little tarts got to boast about sleeping with Joel Litvinoff? Infidelity was short, married life was long. She was going to remain Joel's wife and the mother of his children long after all the tawdry, loveless fucking had been forgotten. From time to time, when a dalliance had seemed in danger of developing into something more serious, she had been forced to take discreet action—to call up the woman in question and warn her to stay away. (Joel, she sensed, was often grateful for these interventions.) Mostly, though, she had sat back and waited for the affairs to wither of their own accord.

How pathetic it seemed now—how *tragic*—to have worked so hard, for so long, at making allowances and adjusting her expectations, only to discover at the eleventh hour that she had been a dupe, after all. That even Joel's pipsqueak *assistant* had known more about her marriage than she did.

She stood up suddenly and went to the kitchen drawer. After a moment or two of searching, she pulled out the family phone book and leafed through its grease-spotted, doodled-filled pages until she found Kate's number.

'It's Audrey,' she said when Kate answered. 'I've just had a visit from Daniel—'

Kate's voice was small and frightened. 'I think I know why you're calling, Audrey. I just want to say—'

'No, no, I don't want to hear what you have to say. I just want an answer to something. On the day that Joel had his stroke, did you phone that woman and tell her to go to the hospital?'

There was a pause on the other end of the phone. 'I didn't *tell* her to go,' Kate said at last. 'I just—you know—told her what was happening. I thought she had a right to know.'

'That's all,' Audrey said, and hung up.

Mechanically, she began to make a cup of tea. As she filled the kettle, her gaze lit on a row of glasses that Sylvia had left drying on the draining board. She put the kettle on the stove and then slowly, in an almost experimental fashion, she encircled the glasses with her forearm and swept them on to the floor. She stood for a moment, inspecting the glittering mess she had made. Then she opened the cabinet and started taking out more glasses: tumblers, wineglasses, brandy snifters, liqueur cups. One by one she dashed them on to the linoleum. The destruction grew boring after a while, but having started on the project, she felt a dim sense of obligation to see it through. She delved into the back of the cupboard and retrieved the remaining breakables: three champagne flutes that Lenny had stolen from the Plaza Hotel. A Martini glass imprinted with the legend 'It's Cocktail Time!'. A Murano goblet that someone had given them for their twentieth wedding anniversary.

When everything had been reduced to shards, she removed the singing kettle from the burner and crunched back to the kitchen table. She sat down and looked out of the window at the house opposite, searching for the shower man. But he

191

was gone now and the bathroom in which he had been standing was dark.

Part Three

CHAPTER NINE

The Jewish Women's Learning Center was located on the ground floor of a residential building on West End Avenue, in an apartment that had been bequeathed to the organization a decade earlier by a pious widow named Rivka Danziger. Almost no alteration had been made to the original layout and decor of the place since the old lady's death: the kitchenette had its pre-war faucets and tiles, the bathrooms had baths. The carpet of the former master bedroom, which now served as a seminar room, still bore four round marks where the posts of Mrs Danziger's double bed had once stood. It was into one of these blackened depressions that Rosa was absently poking the toe of her flip-flop one hot June evening as she listened to her instructor, Mrs Greenberg, discuss the 'poroh adumah' or 'red heifer' commandment in that week's Torah portion. According to the commandment, a perfectly red heifer was to be slaughtered and burned so that its ashes might be used in a purification ceremony for those who had come in contact with the dead. The paradox was that while the ashes purified those who had become contaminated, they also contaminated the people who performed the purification.

'The commandments in the Torah are divided into three general categories,' Mrs Greenberg was saying. 'There are eidos—commandments that testify to past events, such as the observance of Shabbos and the High Holy Days. There are mishpatim—commandments that we understand instinctively, such as not stealing, not killing and so on. And then there are the chukim—commandments that cannot be explained in logical terms, that defy human reason. The "red heifer" belongs in this category. King Solomon himself declared, "I have said I am wise but this matter is remote from me." '

Rosa had initially approached the centre in a sceptical spirit, with the assumption that any instruction aimed specifically at women was bound to be a low-grade affair. She had pictured the parsha class as a sort of religious coffee klatsch: a group of giggly women sitting around eating crumb cake while they discussed what God meant to them. But Torah study, she had discovered—even at this most elementary level—was a rigorous, challenging endeavour. There were no light-hearted digressions or jokes in Mrs Greenberg's class and certainly no tolerance of idle, personal opinion. Mrs Greenberg began each week by outlining the general significance of the events described in the parsha and subsequently delivered a minute, sentence-by-sentence, phrase-by-phrase analysis of a particular section within it—referring, where appropriate, to the rabbinical commentaries. At the very end, she offered a brief interpretation of the text's spiritual import.

Rosa loved the methodical process of unwrapping the layers of meaning in the Torah. She loved the modesty that the process demanded. Above all, she loved the atmosphere of scholarly comradeship—of shared commitment to deciphering a complex, intricate text. It seemed to her that in excavating the wisdom of the rabbinical sages, she was discovering something distinctively

Jewish about her own way of thinking.

'Now the Torah specifies that the red heifer is "the decree of the Torah",' Mrs Greenberg went on. 'Why is this? Why should this most mysterious of chukim—this commandment that baffled even King Solomon—be singled out thus? Because the "red heifer" represents the willing suspension of logic in deference to the divine will and it is this humility before Hashem that is the central lesson, the very foundation of Torah. When we truly follow in Hashem's path, we do not demand explanations. We are motivated not by logic, but by our acceptance of the heavenly yoke.' Mrs Greenberg laid her hands flat against the lectern. 'That, I'm afraid, ladies, must be all for today. I hope to see you all next week.'

The students began to disperse. Rosa put away her Chumash and went out into the hall. One of the centre's volunteer workers, a pretty woman in a long, denim skirt and a headscarf, was standing on a chair, pinning a flyer to the noticeboard.

'Hey!' she called out.

Rosa waved. 'Hi, Carol.'

'How is your father? I've been praying for him.'

'Oh, he's pretty much the same . . . Thanks, though.'

Carol got down from her chair. 'Good class?'

'Great.'

'I hear you are quite the scholar. Mrs Greenberg was saying the other day that the angel must have touched you very lightly on the lip.'

Rosa looked at her blankly.

'The Talmud says that every child in his mother's womb is taught the entire Torah by an angel. When it's time to be born, another angel touches the baby on the lip and all the knowledge is forgotten. So, if a person has a natural gift for Torah learning, we say the angel touched him lightly on the lip.'

'Ah.' Rosa smiled uncertainly. Was Carol offering this as a charming bit of folklore, or did she really believe in angels paying in utero visits? It was hard to tell. Rosa liked Carol. She was intelligent and serious. But the intensity of her religious commitment made conversing with her a slightly exhausting business. Unlike most of the other young women at the centre, Carol had been raised in a non-observant family. As a teenager, she had been allowed to attend late-night parties and to date Gentile boys, and even to dabble briefly in Wicca. It was only during her freshman year at Boston University, after she had fallen in with a group of Orthodox Union students on campus, that she had begun to wonder if there might be a God-shaped hole in her life. Over the course of many earnest late-night conversations with her OU friends, she had come to see that her parents' lack of interest in shul was not, as she had supposed, a logical extension of their affable agnosticism, but a symptom of their Jewish self-hatred. She had also learned, with infinite sadness, that her brother, who had recently become engaged to a young Indian woman, was contributing to 'the silent genocide of the Jewish nation'. Within three months, she had become a ba'alat teshuvah, a repentant Jew. Within six months, she had abandoned her anthropology major in order to study at a yeshiva in Jerusalem.

Now, five years on, she was married with three kids and living in an Orthodox community in

Washington Heights. She kept her hair covered in public. She did not carry keys or push a stroller on a Saturday unless she was within the boundaries of her community eruv. When she bought new clothes, she sent them to a special shatnez lab to make sure that they did not violate the biblical injunction against mixing wool with linen. And every time she defecated she said a prayer, thanking God for creating her 'ducts and openings'.

The story of Carol's transformation evoked complicated feelings in Rosa. It appalled her, of course—the idea of an educated, metropolitan woman voluntarily casting off every vestige of modernity in order to make herself over as a medieval ghetto-dweller, was unconscionable—but it also inspired a sneaking envy. By submitting to the restraints of Orthodoxy Carol had not only performed an impressive act of self-denial—an act guaranteed to appeal to Rosa's ascetic sensibility— she had also freed herself from the burden of trying to improvise her own moral code. These days, she always knew what the right thing to do was and, if she didn't, she knew a rabbi who did. Every aspect of her daily life was consonant with her convictions. How did Rosa's half-assed experiments with religiosity compare? She professed some woolly spiritual allegiance to Judaism but refused to observe a single tenet of Jewish life. She studied Torah, yet dismissed out of hand the possibility that any of its injunctions might apply to her.

Rosa glanced up at the flyer that Carol had posted on the noticeboard.

199

THE JEWISH WAY OF LIFE

Starting in July, JWLC volunteer Carol Baumbach will be leading a series of field trips designed to explore various aspects of Jewish culture. Our explorations will include a guided tour of Crown Heights, a visit to a mikvah, an outing to a kosher bakery and much more! Participation is free of charge and all are welcome! Please see Carol for more details.

'What do you think?' Carol said, following Rosa's gaze. 'It's the first time I've ever done something like this. I'm excited.'

'It sounds fun,' Rosa said.

'Really? Would you be interested in coming along on some of the tours?'

'Sure.' Rosa shrugged. 'I mean, if I can make time, I'd love to.'

'Listen, I've been meaning to ask,' Carol said. 'Do you want to have lunch at my house this Shabbat?'

Rosa blushed. 'That's really kind of you, but I'm afraid I can't.'

'No problem. You'll come another time.'

'Well, actually, Carol, I usually work on Saturdays in the summer.'

'Oh!'

Rosa's blush deepened. 'I'm sorry. It's my job, you know—'

Carol waved her hand. 'No, no, I understand. Everyone has to go at his own pace.'

Rosa hesitated. 'Well, I'm not sure I—'

'It's always really hard when you start out,' Carol said. 'You look at all the mitzvot and they seem like this unscalable mountain. Believe me, I've been there. But you have to keep in mind, Rosa, God doesn't expect you to do everything all at once.'

Rosa glanced at her watch. 'I'm going to have to dash. I've got an interview with a parent at work.'

Carol patted her hand. 'Go. Just remember, Rosa—as long as you're moving in the right direction, it's okay to say to God, "I know I'm supposed to do this, but I can't just yet." '

The heat that awaited Rosa on West End Avenue was so thick and confining that, for the first minute or two after leaving the lobby, she could think of nothing else but trying to stave off her panic. Slowly, though, as she made her way uptown to the GirlPower Center, she began to settle into her discomfort, and her thoughts returned to the conversation she had just had with Carol. She reviewed Carol's little pep talk with increasing indignation. She wished now that she had not apologized for working on the Sabbath. What a prig Carol was! She seemed unable to conceive of a person having rational objections to Orthodox observance that were not rooted in fear or denial; she spoke as if the only thing stopping Rosa from being frum was a lack of moxie. Rosa was not *scared*: she was unconvinced. Over the last six months, she had discovered a powerful affinity with Judaism and, thanks to certain ineffable intimations she had experienced at Ahavat Israel, she would even go so far as to say that her lack of faith in God had been shaken. But none of this made her remotely inclined to give up oysters and bacon, or to thank God every time she took a shit. She would never want to live the way Carol did—

201

she would never see *the point* of living the way Carol did—and it was maddening of Carol to insist that she would.

*   *   *

In a large, echoing room above a Methodist church on 113th Street, the GirlPower girls were making collages on the theme of 'What Makes Me Angry'. High on a shelf cluttered with Mancala boards and art supplies, a boom box was playing Mariah Carey. 'Hi, Rosa,' the girls called out in a singsong. 'What you doing here?' Tuesday was Rosa's day off. She had been called in this evening for an emergency meeting about Chianti, whose poor attendance and bad behaviour were now threatening to get her expelled from the programme.

Rosa found Laura, the head of the GirlPower programme, sitting with Raphael, Chianti and Chianti's mother in the tiny office off the main room. Laura and Raphael greeted her in tones of rather phony good spirits. Chianti's mother acknowledged her presence with a barely perceptible lowering of her eyelids.

'Raphael was just bringing Mrs Gates up to speed on some of the issues we've been having with Chianti lately,' Laura said. 'Do you want to go on, Raphael?'

'Sure.' Raphael leaned forward, resting his hands on his knees. 'As I was saying, Chianti's attendance has really deteriorated over the last couple of months. She has been out five days over the last two weeks—'

'It's not fair,' Mrs Gates interrupted. 'Other girls

202

miss days. I don't see them made to pay for it.' She was a handsome woman with a long, arrow-shaped nose and a hair weave of shiny black ringlets. Her eyebrows had been plucked and redrawn in thin black slanted lines, like a child's rendering of crow's wings.

'That's really not true, Mrs Gates,' Laura said. 'The same rules apply to all the girls in this programme.'

'And, if I may, Mrs Gates,' Raphael added, 'it's not *just* a question of attendance. A lot of the time when Chianti's here, she's been behaving in a really inappropriate and uncooperative way.'

'Like?' Mrs Gates demanded.

'Well, the last time she was in was Thursday and she spent most of that afternoon outside the building, smoking and talking with friends who are not in the programme.'

Mrs Gates made a sucking noise with her teeth. 'That true?' she asked her daughter.

'I was only outside one time.'

'No, Chianti,' Rosa said, 'that's not accurate—'

'You was smoking?' Mrs Gates demanded.

Chianti shrugged.

Calmly—almost casually—Mrs Gates leaned across and slapped her daughter's face. 'Why you be like that?'

Rosa and Raphael half rose from their seats.

'Mrs Gates!' Laura cried.

Mrs Gates continued to address herself to her daughter. 'I told you if I catched you smoking, I was going to beat you—' She slapped Chianti again.

Laura stood up. 'Mrs Gates, if you keep hitting Chianti, I'm going to have to ask you to leave.'

Mrs Gates pressed her tongue into the side of her cheek and stared off into the middle distance.

'The question at this point,' Laura said, sitting down again, 'is how to proceed? We are all anxious to keep Chianti in the programme. But for that to happen, she has to start showing some respect for the rules.' She turned to Rosa. 'Do you have any thoughts?'

Rosa had not yet recovered from the shock of seeing Mrs Gates strike her child. She shook her head. 'I don't really know . . .'

'Tell me something, Chianti,' Raphael intervened, 'do *you* want to be in the programme?'

Chianti shrugged.

'Is that a yes or a no?'

'It's all stupid stuff you doing here.'

Laura looked stern. 'That's not a very useful attitude, Chianti. We're all trying our best to help you—'

Raphael raised a hand. 'May I, Laura?' He smiled at Chianti. 'I want to ask you a question. Can you tell me what sort of things you would *like* to be doing at GirlPower?'

Chianti picked at the seam of her jeans. 'I dunno.'

'Well, think about it. What wouldn't be stupid stuff?'

Chianti was silent.

'This isn't a trick question,' Raphael said. 'I'm just trying to figure out what activities you would enjoy. I know you like dancing, right?'

'Yeah.'

Raphael turned to Laura. 'How would it be if we organized a dancing session a couple of times a week? Would that be okay?'

'I don't see why not.'

'What do you think about that, Chianti?' Raphael asked. 'Maybe you could be in charge of the choreography.'

Chianti raised her head warily. 'For real?'

'Hold on,' Laura said. 'For any of this to happen, you'd have to do a lot of work to clean up your act. We'd need to see perfect attendance and punctuality from you. We'd need a new, positive attitude. No sass, no smoking, no nothing. Do you think you could give us that?'

Chianti nodded her head.

'Are you sure?'

'Yeah.'

'You understand, we're putting a lot of trust in you, Chianti. The first time we see you messing up—not coming in when you're meant to, back-chatting the counsellors, whatever—the whole dance thing goes away, right?'

'Right.'

'How does this sound to you, Mrs Gates?'

The corners of Mrs Gates's lips turned down in an expression of grudging acquiescence. 'So long as she's not messing in the street with boys.'

'Well, okay!' Laura said, clapping her hands. 'I think we have a plan. I want to see you here tomorrow morning, Chianti, at nine o'clock. Not ten past or quarter past. Nine on the dot. And then we can start brain-storming about how to put a dance group together.'

Walking to the subway, Raphael was in a buoyant mood. 'That worked out pretty good, huh?'

'Sure,' Rosa replied, 'if you don't count the fact that Mrs Gates nearly fractured her daughter's skull.'

Raphael giggled. 'Man! She's a piece of work, isn't she?'

'She's a monster,' Rosa said passionately. 'If she's prepared to smack her daughter around like that in public, can you imagine what she's like at home?'

'Well, she cared enough to turn up. That's something.'

Rosa widened her eyes in mock amazement. 'My God, Raph, you're right! Let's notify the Mother of the Year Awards immediately.'

'What bug got up *your* ass?' Raphael asked.

Rosa shook her head. 'I don't know.'

They had turned on to 110th Street now. On the north side of the street, a group of men was lolling sweatily on the steps of a single-occupancy-room hotel, muttering lazy hostilities at one another. On the south side, behind the boundary railings of Central Park, two little boys were fishing in the Harlem Meer.

'I'm just not sure I see the point,' Rosa said suddenly. 'It's like we're all sitting around, killing ourselves trying to figure out ways to keep Chianti with us. And part of me feels that it doesn't really matter if she stays or goes.'

Raphael made a puzzled face. 'Are you kidding? Of course it matters. It matters a lot. If she stays in, she's less likely to become pregnant, less likely to start taking drugs, more likely to get decent grades—'

'Yeah, yeah,' Rosa said impatiently, 'I know. I know all that. But she's not really going to . . . I mean, there's so much about her life that is messed up and that we're never going to change.'

'What, the fact that she's got a scary mom?'

'No, not that. Well, not *just* that. I mean—'

'No, I know what you're saying. There's always more to be done. But you can't let yourself get hung up on that. You have to focus on one day at a time and the small improvements you're making. Otherwise you just get overwhelmed.'

'Yes but, Raph, the small improvements are *so* small.'

A note of exasperation entered Raphael's voice now. 'I don't know what you're getting at. We're just one little programme—'

'Exactly. We're just one little programme. Maybe we keep them off drugs for a while, and maybe we defer pregnancy for a few years, but they still have shitty parents and they still go to shitty schools and they're still going to end up with shitty jobs, or no jobs. Their . . .' she made an expansive gesture with her arms '. . . their class destiny is still going to be the same.'

Raphael stopped and leaned his head back. '"Class destiny"?' He began to laugh. *'Class destiny?* Rosa, you're buggin' out, man! Come here, you need a hug.'

Rosa shook her head, offended. But Raphael reached out and pulled her to him. 'Crazy woman,' he murmured.

Rosa breathed in the warm dampness of his polo shirt. It smelled pleasantly of spray starch and fresh sweat.

'You take things too seriously, Ro,' Raphael said, stroking her hair. 'It's not good for you, I swear.'

CHAPTER TEN

Karla was sitting in her office cubicle, examining a thick ring-bound booklet from the BabyLove Adoption Agency of New York State. On its front cover, there was a line drawing of an infant in swaddling and beneath that the slogan 'BabyLove: Bringing New York Families Together for Fourteen Years.'

Two days earlier, she and Mike had attended an orientation meeting at BabyLove. They had been shown a short film titled *Adoption: A Journey of Love*, and afterwards they had been taken into an office for a preliminary interview. Their adoption counsellor, Michelle, had been wearing tiny pearl studs in her ears and a silk scarf knotted around her neck in the air-stewardess style. She had begun by outlining the basic stages of what she promised would be 'a long and sometimes challenging process'. And then she had asked Karla and Mike to share with her their reasons for wanting to adopt a child. Karla, alert to the irony of her position—a social worker being social-worked—had been determined to acquit herself well. 'It's me, actually,' she confessed cheerfully. 'I can't have them.'

'Right—' Michelle said.

'And also we like the idea of giving a child a good home,' Mike added.

'That's wonderful. There are certainly a lot of children out there who need good homes. But I was actually hoping to hear a little more about your personal expectations of parenthood. Do you think you could both be specific about what you're hoping to get from the experience of raising a child? Karla?'

Karla cleared her throat. 'Well . . .'

She paused. She and Mike had been 'trying' for so long, that the thing for which they were trying had become a rather abstract notion. Karla had never been one of those childless women who cast covetous glances at strollers in parks and who moaned sadly over receiving blankets in layette stores. Mike's fecund female relatives were always inviting her, in honeyed tones of compassion, to hold their infants, but she rarely accepted their offers. The truth was that babies—real, drooling, oozing babies—frightened her a little.

She became aware of Mike's knee juddering with impatience next to hers. She looked at him and then at Michelle with a growing sense of doom. She could not summon up a single reason why she wanted to be a mother. 'I'm sorry,' she said, shaking her head, 'I'm having a bit of trouble with this.'

Michelle smiled. 'Don't worry. It's a very big question. These things can sometimes be hard to put into words. Take your time.'

Something about Michelle's sibilant, whispery way of talking made Karla feel injured and tearful. There was another long silence. 'I've always wanted to be a mother,' Karla said at last, 'because . . . I love kids and I think raising one would be very fulfilling. Kids,' she added, despairingly, 'are so much fun.'

'Okaay . . .' Michelle turned to Mike. 'Do you have anything you'd like to add?'

Karla glanced at him imploringly. *Please be nice.*

209

Please don't say 'mute point'.

'I guess,' Mike said, smoothing back his hair, 'my reasons for wanting to be a parent have to do with the kind of childhood my own parents gave me. I grew up in Pelham Park with two brothers and two sisters and loads of cousins living near by. Our house was very loud and busy. Very warm, you know? Always filled with people and laughter.'

Karla glanced at Michelle, who was nodding faster and faster as Mike spoke. She felt a childish pang of envy. Mike was acing the test.

'My dad was crazy about baseball and we used to have these big family games in the park on weekends. My mom was more gentle. Even when we got to be teenagers, she sang us lullabies every night. She had this amazing voice. Probably, if she hadn't been a mom, she could have been a professional singer . . . So, anyway, I guess I have very happy memories of growing up. And when I think of being a parent, I think of giving those things back to my kids.'

Going home, afterwards, Karla apologized for her poor performance. 'I don't know what happened. I totally messed up. I'm sorry. *You*, though—you were great in there! So eloquent!'

Mike stared at her reproachfully. 'I wasn't being *eloquent*, Karla,' he said, 'I was being *real.*'

Karla put away the adoption booklet now and began tidying up her desk. She and Mike were going out for dinner this evening with his cousin and his cousin's wife: she had promised Mike she would not be late.

Downstairs in the lobby, Khaled the newspaper man was in the process of closing up his shop. 'Come in for a minute,' he said, beckoning from the doorway.

Karla shook her head. 'I shouldn't. I've got to get home.'

'Go on.'

She smiled 'All right. Just a minute then.'

A month or so had passed since the fiasco of Karla and Khaled's first meeting. They had eaten lunch together in the garden several times since then and lately he had taken to stopping by her office when he was making his delivery rounds. For Karla, whose small social circle was composed almost entirely of union activists and other political progressives, this new friendship was a bemusing development. Khaled was oblivious, as far as she could tell, to current affairs, domestic or foreign. (Apart from the astrology and sports sections, he didn't really read the newspapers.) He had no interest in her union activities and did not bother to hide his indifference when she spoke of them. To the extent that he had any politics at all, she strongly suspected that they were reactionary. And yet, she liked him. She did. She enjoyed his company and always looked forward to seeing him. In spite, or perhaps because, of their lack of shared interests, they seemed to have bypassed the prescribed stages for polite, co-worker relations and advanced straight to the free-flowing, aimless talk of intimates. Often, in his company, she felt a weight lifting from her—a burden of cares, whose heaviness she had not fully realized.

Inside the store, Egyptian pop music was playing on a cassette player. Khaled pulled out a stool from behind the counter and gestured for Karla to sit down.

'Are you hungry?' he asked.

211

'No, I've eaten.'

'Wait.' He disappeared into his stockroom.

Karla sat swinging her legs. On the counter next to her there was a revolving stand filled with miniature sewing kits and eyeglass-mending kits. She gave it a little spin. 'What is this music?' she called out.

'This is a very famous Egyptian singer,' Khaled said, returning with two cans of apple juice and a brown paper bag. 'She's maybe the most famous of all.'

'Ah.'

He began to sing along in a funny, high-pitched voice, imitating a seductive female dance.

'You're in a good mood tonight,' she said.

'You've put me in a good mood.' He danced over to the plastic bucket in which he kept cellophaned bunches of flowers. 'Here, take some of these.'

She shook her head. 'I don't need flowers.'

'I know you don't *need* them,' he said. 'I just want you to have some.' He held the bouquet in his outstretched fist, like the Statue of Liberty with her torch.

She took them. 'Thanks.'

'Look at this.' He opened up the paper bag he had put on the counter and brought out a slab of halva. 'I got it from the Greek place around the corner. You want some?'

'I shouldn't really.'

He glanced at her with comic scepticism.

'All right then. Just a tiny bit.'

Khaled loved to buy treats for himself. Whenever Karla saw him, he seemed to be eating, or preparing to eat, something delicious: a

212

doughnut covered in soft, white icing; a fat Chinese dumpling shaped like a miniature sack of burglars' swag; a juicy clementine, rattling in its baggy, pocked jacket. She was slightly shocked by his guiltless public gorging. She had been surrounded all her life by people who were either indifferent or actively hostile to food and eating was for her a solitary vice. Her mother had never really cooked so much as thrust nominally edible items on to the table and demanded that they not be 'wasted'. Mike drank protein shakes for lunch and wouldn't let anything pass his lips after six o'clock, for fear that he wouldn't metabolize it before he slept. ('Some people live to eat; I eat to live,' he was always saying, as if his rejection of pleasure were a personal badge of honour.)

She watched as Khaled carved the halva. The black hair on his forearm curled around his watch strap and lapped at a glossy, bubblegum-coloured scar that was peeping out from his rolled-up sleeve.

'It's ugly, no?' he said suddenly, gesturing at the scar with his knife.

Karla reddened. 'No! Not at all. I was just wondering how you . . . How did you get it? If you don't mind saying.'

'I was playing in the kitchen one time when I was a kid. My mother had hot fat on the stove and I knocked the pan off.'

'Oh!' Karla felt a great wave of tenderness for Khaled's injured childhood self. 'That must have been terrible.'

He handed her a slice of halva. 'I guess. My mother says I cried for two days, but I don't remember it.' He looked down at a magazine that

213

was lying on the counter and began flicking through its pages. 'Look at this.' He pointed to a photographic spread of a celebrity's mansion in the Hollywood Hills. 'This is the house I want to live in some day.'

Karla examined the magazine with a small grimace of disapproval.

'See that?' he said. 'That's a fish tank with a real shark in it. Right in the guy's living room!'

'Poor shark,' she murmured.

'Wait. This guy has his own movie theatre.'

Karla glanced at a photograph of a velvet-lined screening room. 'It's a bit selfish though, isn't it?' she said. 'I mean, for one person to take up that much space.'

'It's his money. He can spend it how he wants.'

'Yes, but it would be nice if he did something more useful with it, I think.'

Khaled put the magazine down, disappointed. 'He probably gives a lot of money to charity.'

Karla looked away, suddenly disgusted with her own sententiousness. What a bore she was, spoiling his daydreams with her goody-two-shoes lectures!

'Do you want some more halva?' he asked.

'No.' She held up her hands in a gesture of satiety. 'I should go soon.'

'Are you visiting your father tonight?'

'No. I'm going out for dinner with my husband's cousin and his wife.'

'Ah,' Khaled said, nodding. 'That's nice.'

'We're going to a Mexican place.'

'Huh.' He stared gloomily at the counter.

Karla wondered at the sudden change in his mood. No doubt she had irritated him with her refusal to be excited by the celebrity's house. 'This

214

song is nice,' she said, anxious to redeem herself. 'What's it about?'

'She's singing about missing her lover.'

'Oh.'

'She's saying, "Come back, come back. Without you I am like a boat on dry land."' He began to dance again now, holding out his hand to Karla.

She shook her head. 'I'm not a dancer.'

'Oh, sure you are,' he said, grasping her hand.

For a brief moment, Karla let herself be swayed stiffly from side to side.

'See,' Khaled murmured, 'you *are* a dancer.'

In the glass front of the store's refrigerator, Karla caught a glimpse of herself: a fat woman, jiggling foolishly on a stool. 'That's enough!' she said sharply, pulling her hand away from Khaled's.

He stepped back in surprise.

'Sorry,' she said. 'I just—'

'No, no, don't apologize. I'm sorry.' He reached up and turned off the music. Out of the sudden quiet came the distant thunder of a floor-polishing machine in the hospital lobby.

'I should go.' Karla stepped down from the stool and shook out her skirt.

Khaled watched her unhappily. 'Will you come by tomorrow?'

'Maybe. I'll see.'

'Don't forget your flowers.'

'No, of course not.'

Outside, on the hospital forecourt, she stopped to stuff the flowers in a giant, green 'Keep New York Clean' trash can. It was an awful waste, but she would have felt silly walking along the street with them. And, besides, she would not have known how to explain them to Mike.

215

CHAPTER ELEVEN

'Audrey, dear, you don't have to do this,' Jean said as they walked up Central Park West together. 'You can still call it off.'

The two women were on their way back to Jean's apartment from the drugstore, where Audrey had been buying something for her upset stomach. In a little less than half an hour they were due to meet Daniel and Berenice at Jean's.

'I'm not calling it off,' Audrey said flatly. She wiped her slick forehead with the back of her hand and absently rubbed the sweat off on her T-shirt. It was one of those washed-out New York days of deadening, grey heat. All along the avenue, droning AC units were dripping condensation on to the baked sidewalk. High overhead, the pale sun wobbled and fizzed in a milky sky, seemingly too weak and soluble an entity to be a plausible source of the monstrous temperature.

'You know,' Jean said, 'you're not going to achieve anything by confronting this woman. It'll just be horribly upsetting.'

Audrey gave her a low-lidded look of contempt. '*I'm* not the one who's going to be horribly upset, believe me.'

Jean nodded. 'I think it's amazing how brave you're being, Audrey. I know that I couldn't be as strong as you in your position, but I do wish you'd be a bit gentler on yourself. Your emotions are still so raw—'

'Oh, Jean,' Audrey exclaimed, 'my emotions are *fine*.' She paused, trying to find the right tone. 'I mean, I'm *annoyed*, of course. I'm *very* annoyed. Joel's been a terrible fool. If he weren't in a coma, I'd like to give him a good smack. But'—she sighed and canted her head in a gesture of philosophical resignation—'it is what it is, Jean. There's no use crying about it, I just have to deal with it.'

'Well, you don't have to deal with it right now—not when you're still in shock about the whole thing.'

Audrey gritted her teeth. It was rude—it was *tactless*—of Jean to go on like this. A friend's job in such situations was not to poke and prod and insist on ferreting out your 'real feelings': a friend's job was to shut up and take you at your word.

'But, Jean, that's what I'm telling you, I'm *not* in shock,' she said. '*You* know how Joel's always been. I'd have to be very slow on the uptake to be surprised by his tom-catting at this stage in the game.'

Jean looked away shyly. She and Audrey had rarely spoken of Joel's infidelities, except in the most elliptical way. It felt awkward to make this sudden leap into frankness without any acknowledgement of the discretion that had preceded it.

'You don't stay married to a man like Joel for forty years if you can't cope with the odd bit of bad behaviour,' Audrey said. 'All powerful men are the same way. It's a biological thing. Look at what Jackie Kennedy had to put up with—'

'I understand, Audrey,' Jean interrupted, 'but this *isn't* just another bit of bad behaviour, is it? He's fathered a child—'

'Oh, please!' Audrey stopped walking. 'You think I care? You think I'm staying up nights

217

because that slag had Joel's baby? You're wrong! I don't give a shit.'

'I hear what you're saying,' Jean said as they resumed walking. 'I do. But I still don't understand why you have to deal with this woman personally. A lawyer could do any of the negotiating that needs—'

'*No,*' Audrey interrupted. '*Absolutely not.* I'm not having anybody else involved with this.'

'But, Audrey—'

'You tell one person and, before you know it, it's all over town. Do you have any idea what kind of a field day Joel's enemies would have with this story? The great man of the left having a secret bastard son? Reactionaries live for this kind of thing. It's like Clinton getting a blow job from that intern, or Marx fucking his maid. "See, look, Karl was a bit of a scallywag—he must have been wrong about dialectical materialism . . ." And, besides, I *want* to deal with that bitch myself. I want to tell her what I think of—Oh *shit.*'

A tall, toothy female figure was coming towards them, pushing a baby stroller.

'Oh my God, Audreeey,' she cried as she drew near. 'It's been *ages*! How *wonderful* to run into you!'

'Melinda, this is my friend Jean,' Audrey said. 'Jean, this is Melinda. Her daughter was at the Little Red Schoolhouse with Rosa and Karla. She's from England too. But much posher than me, of course.'

Melinda laughed nervously. *Ma ha ha.* In deference to their shared nationality and the vague sense that two British women living in New York *ought* to be friends, Melinda always affected great

218

chumminess with Audrey, but she never managed to look anything but terrified while doing so. 'It's so *funny* that I should see you now,' she said, 'I was just on my way to the London Market to get some chocolate digestives!'

'I've never understood why people go to shops like that,' Audrey replied. 'If you all miss your crappy English biscuits so much, why don't you go back home?'

Melinda threw her head back and opened her mouth wide in a silent show of hilarity. 'Oh, *Audrey.*' She looked down at the bovine child in her stroller. 'Have you met this member of my brood? This is my grandson, Zac. Daisy's a mother of two now—can you believe it?'

Audrey glanced at the boy without comment. Melinda was a terrible bore about children. Once, many years ago, Audrey had been persuaded to accompany Karla on a 'play-date' at Melinda's house. The ninety minutes she had spent perched on Melinda's sofa, sipping warm white wine and discussing the Suzuki method while the little girls screechingly interacted over a bucket of educational wooden blocks, had confirmed all of her worst suspicions about the child-centred life.

'Tell me,' Melinda said, 'has any of your lot reproduced yet?'

Audrey shook her head absently. She was thinking about the pleasure it would give Melinda if the story of Joel's illegitimate child were ever to get out—the gleeful faux empathy with which she would skip about the Village, retailing Audrey's humiliation to all their mutual acquaintance: *Did you hear? Isn't it awful? Poor Audrey.*

'Really?' Melinda urged. 'Not a one?'

219

'No,' Audrey replied. 'My lot are all barren, it seems.'

Melinda's face sagged. 'Oh . . .'

'Joke, Melinda.'

Melinda gave another noiseless roar of laughter. 'Well, you must jolly well get them to hurry up. Being a granny is such good fun! And how is everyone, anyway?'

'Joel's in the hospital.'

Melinda's brow corrugated. 'Oh yes, I did hear he'd been unwell. Is he doing any better now?'

'Not really,' Audrey said. 'He's in a coma.'

'Oh!' Melinda pressed her hand against her mouth. 'Oh, gosh, Audrey . . .'

Audrey had given up the information only to embarrass her. Now that the words were out, she regretted them. 'Well,' she said brusquely, 'we mustn't keep you.'

'Right.' Melinda nodded. 'Right. I should be off. Do send my love to the girls and Lenny, won't you?'

*　　　*　　　*

The housekeeper was waiting for Jean and Audrey when they arrived at the front door of Jean's apartment. 'They're *here*,' she stage-whispered. 'The visitors you was expecting, they've been sitting in the living room for quarter of an hour. The man said there wasn't so much traffic as he thought there was going to be.'

'That *bastard* Daniel,' Audrey hissed. 'He did this on purpose, I know it.'

'It's not too late,' Jean said. 'If you don't want to do this—'

220

'Don't be daft.' Audrey drew her shoulders back. 'Come on, let's get in there before she nicks all your candlesticks.'

Daniel and Berenice were examining the framed photographs on one of Jean's side tables when Audrey and Jean entered.

'Well, this is cosy,' Audrey said.

Berenice turned around. She was wearing a tight, sleeveless dress and open-toed flat sandals, decorated with shells. 'Hello,' she said calmly.

Audrey looked her up and down, silently auditing her flaws: the slack flesh on the underside of her arms, the mannish thickness of her calves. After a moment, she turned to Jean. 'Do you think we could have the air conditioning down? It's like a meat locker in here.'

'Yes, of course. Good idea!' Jean rubbed her hands together. 'Would everyone like some lemonade? I'll just go and get some . . . Audrey, perhaps you could help me?'

'The state of her!' Audrey cried as soon as they reached the kitchen. 'Did you see that dress?'

Jean, who was twiddling with the thermostat, did not reply.

'Talk about mutton dressed as lamb,' Audrey went on. 'And her legs! Ooh! She should be playing rugby for England with those things . . .' She let her sentence trail off. Crowing over Berenice's imperfections was not as satisfying an exercise as she had hoped. Had Berenice been very young, or very pretty, Audrey would have had the consolation of dismissing her as a tootsie, a plaything; she would have been able to laugh scornfully at the banality of Joel's old-man desires. As it was, Berenice's unexceptional looks hinted

221

troublingly at other, more substantive qualities. If Joel had not wanted her for her beauty, what had he wanted her for?

She glanced around disconsolately at Jean's kitchen. She had not been in here since the renovations had been completed. 'This turned out nice,' she observed.

'Mmm,' Jean said. 'I'm not sure I should have chosen stainless steel for the appliances, though. It's endless upkeep.' She took out a jug of lemonade from the fridge and began setting out bowls of nuts and olives on a tray.

'What *are* you doing?' Audrey demanded.

'Oh!' Jean stared doubtfully at her tray. 'Is this not appropriate? I just thought food might be helpful . . .'

Audrey turned away. 'Whatever. Make it a fucking cocktail party if you want.'

When they returned to the living room, Berenice and Daniel were sitting side by side on one of Jean's leather sofas. Berenice had a plastic file folder on her lap.

'What have you got in there then?' Audrey asked. 'Is that your evidence?'

'Audrey,' Daniel said, 'I think it would be helpful if we could all—'

Audrey terminated his sentence with a glacial stare. 'I suggest, Daniel, that you speak when you're spoken to.' She turned back to Berenice. 'So, come on. Show us what you've got.'

'What is it that you want to see?' Berenice asked. She leaned over the coffee table and scooped a handful of nuts into her mouth.

'Well, now, Daniel says you've been boasting about the love letters Joel's written you. Why don't

222

we start off with those?'

'I didn't bring any personal correspondence with me.'

'No, I bet you didn't.'

Berenice handed her a sheaf of papers. 'You'll find my son's birth certificate and the Acknowledgement of Paternity form that Joel signed. There are also copies of all the cheques that Joel has sent me over the years.'

At the sight of Joel's daddy-long-legs signature on the top page, Audrey felt her hands begin to tremble. She leafed through the papers quickly. 'Well done, love,' she said, looking up after a moment. 'You've got it all covered, haven't you? You're quite the expert at this sort of thing, I can see.'

Berenice shook her head. 'No, Audrey, not an expert.'

'Why don't you just go ahead and tell me how much you are looking to get out of me? I can tell you now, there's not a lot.'

Berenice shook her head. 'I need you to know, Audrey, this is not just about the money for me.'

'Oh *really*? Is that right? What is it about then?'

'Many things. I appreciate that you're feeling a lot of hostility towards me right now and I want you to know that I honour your anger. At some point in the future, though, I would like to think that you could come to an acceptance of me. For our children's sake, at least. It's important to me that Jamil have a relationship with his brothers and sisters—'

'Are you *high*?' Audrey interrupted. 'My children know all about you and, believe me, they want nothing to do with you or your bastard son.'

'Audrey!' Jean cried.

'Tell me, Berenice,' Audrey went on, 'why didn't you have an abortion when you got pregnant by another woman's husband?'

'Audrey,' Jean cut in, 'this is not a productive line of conversation.'

'No, it's okay,' Berenice said, 'I'll answer that. I did consider an abortion.'

'Ahh, what was it made you change your mind?' Audrey said. 'Did you see a little sonogram and come over all soppy about your unborn brat?'

The room fell silent. Audrey looked around at Daniel and Jean and Berenice, frozen in the headlights of her wrath. Out of the depths of childhood memory, a phrase came to her, something she had read once in a school history book: 'King Henry was much feared by his people but he was never loved.'

'Okay,' she said wearily, 'let's just get this over with.' She pointed at Berenice. 'You'll get your money. Whatever it was that Joel was giving you before. But you will have nothing to do with my family. You and your son will stay away from me, my children and Joel. Is that clear?'

Berenice looked down at her lap. 'If you insist.'

Audrey smiled bitterly. 'All right, love, you can stop the theatricals now. You've got what you wanted. Just fuck off, would you?'

She watched as Jean led Berenice and Daniel out into the hall. Then she went and lay down on the sofa with her feet up on Jean's coffee table. It was incredible, she thought. Within half an hour, she had managed to dissipate every shred of her moral advantage. She had convinced everyone in the room that *she* was the chief offender. Even

224

Jean had been horrified by her behaviour.

How had she ended up like this, imprisoned in the role of harridan? Once upon a time, her brash manner had been a mere posture—a convenient and amusing way for an insecure teenaged bride, newly arrived in America, to disguise her crippling shyness. People had actually enjoyed her vituperation back then, encouraged and celebrated it. She had carved out a minor distinction for herself as a 'character': the cute little English girl with the chutzpah and the longshoreman's mouth. 'Get Audrey in here,' they used to cry whenever someone was being an ass. 'Audrey'll take him down a peg or two.'

But somewhere along the way, when she hadn't been paying attention, her temper had ceased to be a beguiling party act that could be switched on and off at will. It had begun to express authentic resentments: boredom with motherhood, fury at her husband's philandering, despair at the pettiness of her domestic fate. She hadn't noticed the change at first. Like an old lady who persists in wearing the Jungle Red lipstick of her glory days, she had gone on for a long time fondly believing that the stratagems of her youth were just as appealing as they had ever been. By the time she woke up and discovered that people had taken to making faces at her behind her back—that she was no longer a sexy young woman with a charmingly short fuse but a middle-aged termagant—it was too late. Her anger had become a part of her. It was a knotted thicket in her gut, too dense to be cut down and too deeply entrenched in the loamy soil of her disappointments to be uprooted.

'Are you okay, dear?' Jean said, returning from

the hall. She placed a tentative hand on Audrey's shoulder.

'Oh, who cares if *I'm* okay?' Audrey snapped. 'Just as long as that cow has her fucking monthly cheque.'

'Audrey—'

'Your snacks went down well.' Audrey gestured at the near-empty bowl on the table. 'Did you see her? She couldn't keep her trotter out of those nuts.'

Jean was silent.

'Yeah, I know,' Audrey said. 'I mustn't be mean about poor old Berenice. Poor single mother Berenice. You've really warmed to her, haven't you? Perhaps you can have her back over sometime. I'm sure she'd like to have some rich friends now that's she's going to be getting fat— fatter, I should say—on my bank account.'

'You know, Audrey, I'm not sure this *is* about the money for her.'

'Oh no, you're right, it's not *just* about money. It's worse than that, isn't it? She wants a piece of him. She wants to be *part of my family*. She's a very homely woman who's lived in obscurity all her life, taking her poncey photographs, and now she sees her chance to be at the centre of things. Having Joel's baby is the most glamorous, important thing that ever happened to her.'

'Was that true, what you said about the children? About them not wanting to meet her?'

'Of course it wasn't! I haven't told them about this.'

'Perhaps you ought to, Audrey.'

'Why on earth should they know about their father's leg-over with some photographer bint? I

226

will not have their respect for Joel destroyed.'

Jean shook her head. 'These things have a way of coming out in the end, Audrey. They just do. And if the kids ever discover that you kept this from them, they'll be—' She stopped and peered at Audrey, who was bent over with her head in her hands making an odd, whooping noise. Jean was about to ask what was so funny, when it dawned on her that for the first time in their thirty-year friendship, she was seeing Audrey cry.

CHAPTER TWELVE

Raphael and Rosa sat on plastic chairs in the GirlPower Center watching Chianti and seven other girls perform a dance routine. The song playing on the boom box was a young woman's paean to her boyfriend's talent as a lover.

Ooh, when you do what you do, I . . . Ooh
It's a feeling so totally new, I never even had a
    clue

The girls rolled their heads and pressed their hands to their chests in pre-pubescent imitations of sexual ecstasy.

'This is pretty good!' Raphael whispered.

Rosa looked at him.

'Oh go on, Rosa! It is. Look how well synchronized they are!'

The girls had now lowered themselves into a prone position and were bouncing their groins up and down on the linoleum.

'They're humping the floor, Raphael.'

'Well, it's not meant to be ballet, you know.'

The song ended now, with the girls lying on their backs, arms and legs extended like starfish.

'Bravo!' Raphael shouted. 'Great job!'

The girls sat up, giggling.

'Serious?' Chianti said breathlessly. 'You liked it?'

Raphael shook his head incredulously. 'Are you kidding? That was *amazing*. I am so proud of you guys.' He patted Rosa's knee. 'Rosa liked it too.'

'You did?' Chianti asked.

Rosa paused, searching for an honest answer that would not be too discouraging. 'It was fine. A bit graphic for my taste—'

'You know what I think?' Raphael broke in. 'You guys should do a performance at the GirlPower show in September. Wouldn't that be great, Rosa?'

All the girls began to chatter and shout at the same time.

'Seriously?'

'Could we?'

'Ooh, we going to be famous!'

'You going to let us, Rosa?'

Rosa pressed her finger to her lips for silence. 'I guess you could. As long as you were prepared to tone down some of the slutty stuff—'

'Awwww,' the girls chorused in disappointment.

'What you talking about, "slutty"?' Chianti demanded petulantly. 'We wasn't slutty.'

'Yeah, we wasn't slutty,' the other girls murmured.

Raphael gave Rosa a sardonic thumbs-up. 'Nice one, Ro.'

'I have to go,' Rosa said, standing up. 'We can discuss this tomorrow, Chianti.'

'Off to synagogue, are you?' Raphael asked spitefully.

'No, Raphael. As a matter of fact, I'm going home. Lenny's coming over.'

'What's synagogue?' one of the girls asked.

'It's the place where Jews go to pray,' Raphael replied.

'What're Jews?'

'Cha!' Chianti exclaimed. 'You don't know? Jews the people who killed Jesus.'

Rosa wagged her finger reprovingly. 'That's not quite right, Chianti. Jesus *was* a Jew, you know. And, strictly speaking, it was the Romans who killed him.'

'That ain't what *I* heard,' Chianti said.

'I'll be happy to continue this conversation tomorrow, Chianti, but I really do have to go now.' Rosa walked over to the door. 'I'll see you all tomorrow, okay?'

As she left the room, Chianti muttered something under her breath and everyone, including Raphael, started to laugh. The sound of their mirth followed Rosa all the way down the stairs to the ground floor.

*   *   *

Jane, Rosa's room-mate, worked long hours in the public relations department at Tiffany & Co., and most evenings Rosa had their little apartment on 102nd Street to herself. Tonight, however, as soon as she opened the front door, Jane darted out into the hall, holding a bottle of wine and bringing with her a gust of the Shania Twain CD that was playing in her bedroom. 'Hey!' she shouted shrilly over the music. 'Do you want some vino?'

Rosa shook her head. It was best, she had learned, not to give Jane any quarter when she was in one of her strenuously festive, bon temps rouler moods.

'Are you sure? I'm all on my ownsome tonight.'

'No thanks,' Rosa said. 'Isn't Eric around?' Eric was the hulking, baby-faced young man to whom Jane had recently become engaged.

'Nah.' Jane pouted playfully. 'He's got a stag night . . . Hey! You wanna see what he got me?'

Before Rosa could reply, Jane had ducked back into her room and re-emerged with a large, white, stuffed bunny. Between its paws, there was a red heart, embroidered with the slogan 'I love you better than carrots!'

'Isn't it cute?' she cried.

Rosa considered the bunny stonily. 'It's very nice.'

Rosa had some cause to regard herself as a worldly woman. As a child, she had broken bread with Daniel Ortega, sung freedom songs with ANC activists in Soweto and played softball with Abbie Hoffman. By the age of eighteen, she had seen both her parents arrested for acts of civil disobedience and had twice been arrested herself. Yet, in truth, her worldliness applied to a very narrow band of the world and there were large areas of ordinary American life about which her impeccably progressive, internationalist upbringing had left her astonishingly ignorant. Until a year ago, when she had answered Jane's ad for a room-mate on Craig's List, her contact with bouncy, suburban-American young women for whom cuddly toys were a meaningful expression of adult love had been negligible. And even now, twelve months later, most things about Jane—from the 'Best Daughter in the World' certificate hanging on her wall and the dog-eared library of Chicken Soup books lining her Pier One bookshelf, to the holiday cookies she baked for Eric and the thrice-weekly, hour-long phone conversations she had with her concerned parents in Fort Lauderdale—posed an appalling anthropological mystery for Rosa. She approached all their interactions in the wary, squeamish manner of a schoolchild dissecting a frog.

Happily, Jane's natural obtuseness, enhanced by years of self-esteem training, had saved her from taking offence at Rosa's froideur. In so far as she registered it at all, she attributed it to social awkwardness. Rosa, she had decided, was a shy girl who needed bringing out of herself. To this end, she was always appearing at Rosa's bedroom door—goose-flesh hips spilling over the top of her low-rise jeans, a mug of Celestial Seasonings in her cupped hands, wanting to parse a celebrity interview in *In Style* magazine, or to deliver a bulletin from her hectic life in the fast lane of public relations. Not long ago, while listing the super-A-list invitees to an upcoming 'Russian Winter'-themed Tiffany party, she had placed a consoling palm on Rosa's shoulder and assured her, 'My job isn't as glamorous as this all the time, believe me!' Rosa, to whom the idea of Jane's job being glamorous had honestly never occurred, was stymied. She could not help but be irked by this idiotic girl's condescension. And she could not

231

help but be disappointed with herself for being irked.

'Are you *sure* you won't have a glass of wine?' Jane asked now.

Rosa opened the door to her room. 'Absolutely sure.'

'What are you doing tonight?'

'Not much,' Rosa said, closing the door gently behind her.

The size of Rosa's room was in keeping with the minimal rent that she paid for it. Aside from a pile of books on the floor by her bed and a bag of raw almonds lying on the table—emergency rations for when she got hungry at night and didn't want to risk being ambushed by Jane in the kitchen—it was furnished as impersonally as a Motel 6. A smudgy window looked out on a blackened airshaft; the only other source of light was a fluorescent tube on the ceiling. 'Oh my *God*, Rosa,' Raphael had cried on the one occasion that he had visited her here, 'I *love* what you've done with this place!'

Rosa sat down on her bed and ate an almond. There were two messages waiting for her on her answering machine. The first was from Chris Jackson, inviting her to the Bowery Ballroom on Thursday night to see a band whose name she did not recognize. 'The guitarist is kind of a close friend of mine,' he said, 'so we'll probably get to party with them afterwards.' The second message was also from Chris. He wanted to make clear, if he hadn't already, that the gig on Thursday was a pretty hot ticket and that if, for some reason, Rosa couldn't make it, she should let him know as soon as possible so he could ask someone else.

Rosa pressed the erase button. Chris had called

232

to ask her out at least five times since their meeting at the Monsey bus stop. In the beginning, she had taken care to sweeten her refusals with the pretence of having other plans, but he had kept on calling and now she found herself growing increasingly impatient with him. How did one explain such thick-headedness? Such presumption? Perhaps he imagined he was wearing her down. Perhaps he regarded a preliminary display of female scorn as a necessary formality in the courtship ritual. At any rate, he was a pain. Rosa leaned over and picked up a book lying by her bed entitled *How Jews Pray*. Through the papery apartment walls, she could hear the thump of the Shania CD and the baby-doll laughter of Jane, talking to someone on the phone. With an irritable sigh, she found her page and began to read.

Lenny arrived an hour late, smelling of cigarettes and unwashed clothes. 'I brought someone with me,' he told Rosa as soon as she opened the door. Behind him, lurking in the hallway shadows, Rosa glimpsed his friend Jason. She nodded a chilly greeting. She had hoped to have a private conference with Lenny this evening. He had been behaving in a worrying way of late and she wanted to ask him some forthright questions about his current drug use. (At this point in the long and miserable history of his addiction, she had no illusions about her ability to avert any relapse for which he might be headed, but it was always useful to know what was in the offing with Lenny and to let him know that you knew.) Now, however, her plot had been foiled. Lenny—who was a good deal craftier than his cultivated air of haplessness tended to suggest—had no doubt intuited her agenda for the evening and enlisted Jason's presence precisely in order to forestall it.

'Whatup, Ro?' Jason said as he stepped across the threshold. 'How's it going?' He was an unprepossessing man in his late twenties with a babyish pot-belly and a tiny patch of reddish beard, like a ketchup splash, on his chin. He spoke with the smirking defiance of a person accustomed to being unwelcome. 'Hey, do you mind if I use your bathroom?'

Rosa pointed him down the hall. As he sloped off, she turned to Lenny with hunched shoulders and pointed chin. 'What the—?'

'I'm sorry,' Lenny said, 'he just kind of tagged along.'

Rosa led the way into the kitchen. 'You shouldn't be hanging around with guys like Jason, anyway, Lenny.'

'Oh, Jason's okay.'

'No he's not.'

Lenny sat down at the kitchen table. 'He's my friend, Rosa.'

'So. Make a new one. You know you look terrible, right?'

He smiled. 'I love you too, sis.'

Jason came back from the bathroom. 'What's there to eat, man?'

Rosa had not considered food. She opened the refrigerator and gave its contents a cursory inspection. 'I could make you some spaghetti with butter and cheese, I guess.'

'My God, Rosa,' Lenny said. 'You shouldn't have gone to so much trouble.'

Rosa closed the refrigerator door smartly. 'Well,

234

I wasn't expecting to be hosting a *dinner party*, Lenny. Do you want spaghetti or not?'

'Okay, yeah.'

Rosa filled a pot with water and lit the stove.

'Have you got anything to drink?' Jason asked.

'There's some water in the fridge and some orange juice.'

'That's it?'

'Hi, guys!' Jane poked her head around the side of the kitchen door.

Rosa gave her a discouraging smile. 'This is my brother, Lenny, and this is Jason, Lenny's friend.'

'Hi!' Jane gave a little wave.

'Hi, Jane.' Lenny and Jason looked her up and down, taking in her French manicure and her pink, fluffy slippers.

'You guys want some wine?' Jane asked.

'Sure,' Lenny said.

Jane went off to her room and came back holding a bottle of Chardonnay. 'Are you making pasta?' she asked Rosa.

'Correct.'

'Would you like some?' Lenny said.

'Really?' Jane looked over at Rosa. 'Would that be okay?'

Rosa shrugged her shoulders.

'Yeaaah, no problem,' Lenny said expansively.

Jason pulled out a chair. 'Come on, join us!'

'Awesome!' Jane said. She sat down. 'I'm actually kind of starving. I only had a Cliff bar for lunch.'

'Busy day then?' Lenny spoke with a self-conscious, faintly facetious charm, as if it were an amusing novelty for him to traffic in such banalities.

'Oh my God, *yes.*' Jane stuck out her tongue to indicate her exhaustion. 'It was so hot today! I thought I was going to pass out on the subway platform.'

'Yeah? That's rough, man,' Jason said.

Rosa's expression grew rigid. Jane, it seemed, had piqued some snobbish amusement in Lenny and Jason, and now, in the guise of paying her courtly attention, they were going to entertain themselves by sniggering at her provincialism.

Lenny poured himself some wine and examined the bottle. 'This isn't going to last us. Give me some money, Ro, and I'll go to the liquor store.'

Rosa shook her head. 'If you want to drink, Lenny, pay for it yourself.'

'I've got some cash!' Jane offered.

Lenny rewarded her with his most beguiling smile. 'Great! You wanna come with me?'

'Sure!'

Left alone with Rosa, Jason stretched out on his chair. 'So, it's too bad about your dad. I guess he's not doing so good.'

Rosa nodded. 'Uh-huh.'

'That's got to be rough, man—the coma thing.'

'Mmm.'

There was a pause. 'I hear you're into religion these days,' Jason said.

Rosa, who was trying, bad-temperedly, to bend the spaghetti into a too-small pot, gave a small shudder. 'Is that how Lenny put it?'

'Judaism, right?'

'Right.'

'Yuh *mon*—getting down with the rabbis. Are you gonna start wearing a wig and all that stuff?'

'Jason—'

236

'No offence,' Jason said quickly. 'If you don't want to talk about it, that's cool.' He waited a moment. 'I've never really been into religion myself. I mean, I'm not against religion *per se*, I'm just not into organized religion, you know? I was raised Catholic and, *man*, that is the worst, most hypocritical shit. If I was going to get religious, it'd be something a little freer.'

Rosa stared grimly into the spaghetti water.

'Have you ever been to Stonehenge?' Jason asked.

She shook her head.

'Aw, man, you got to go. It's like this circle of humongous stones that these guys built in England thousands of years ago—'

'I know what it is, Jason.'

'They used to dance around these stones in the nude, or whatever, drinking potions and praising their gods. I could totally get into a religion like that, you know what I'm saying?'

She turned around from the stove. 'I know what you're saying, Jason, I'm just not that interested.'

Jason raised his hands in surrender. 'Fair enough, fair enough.'

Fifteen minutes later, when Lenny and Jane returned from the liquor store, Rosa served up the spaghetti.

'This is raw, Rosa,' Lenny complained, prodding sulkily at his serving with a fork.

'Dude,' Jason said, 'this is al dente.'

'Whatever, it tastes like sticks, man.'

Rosa, who had inherited her mother's contempt for the domestic arts, was unabashed. 'Don't eat it if you don't like it.'

'I could make some grilled cheese if you're still

hungry,' Jane suggested.

'Nah, it's okay.' Lenny pushed his plate to one side and took out his rolling papers.

Rosa cast him a minatory look. Lenny always claimed—and perhaps, at some level, genuinely believed—that smoking dope and drinking alcohol did not contravene his sobriety. It was a fantasy that his five recoveries and relapses had failed to puncture.

'Is it cool with you if we have a spliff, Jane?' he asked.

'Sure,' Jane said, with careful insouciance. 'No problem.'

'You smoke?'

Jane smiled shyly. 'I did a bit of the wacky baccy at college.'

Lenny and Jason exchanged sidelong glances of amusement.

'Hey, Jason,' Lenny said, 'did you know Jane works at Tiffany?'

'Yeah? Cool. Do you get, like, a discount on the jewellery and stuff?'

'Oh, totally!' Jane replied. 'Thirty-five per cent. But I don't actually work in the store. I'm in the PR department.'

Lenny lit his joint. 'Jane's like an executive,' he croaked as he inhaled. 'She hangs out with all the celebrity customers.'

'*Awesome!*' Jason said. 'Who have you met?'

Jane began to list the various famous people she had encountered—detailing their quirks and preferences with an unsettling combination of grovelling reverence and impudent familiarity. 'J.Lo can be kind of a diva. But you know who's really a doll? Eve. The rapper? Yeah, she's, like, the sweetest, most down-to-earth person . . .'

Lenny passed the joint to her. 'You gonna have some?'

Jane gave an exaggerated shrug. 'Whatever.'

'That's good stuff,' Lenny said, watching her put the joint tentatively to her lips. 'Lebanese. It's going to give you a good buzz.'

Jane spluttered and flapped her hands as she exhaled. 'Whoah, that's strong!' She held the joint out to Jason.

'Have a bit more,' Lenny urged. 'Try to keep it in your lungs for a while.'

Rosa made a murmuring sound of disapproval. As a teenager, she had watched Lenny presiding over his girlfriends' drug-taking in much the same way as this—teaching them how to construct joints, how to snort coke, how to conduct themselves when stoned. There was something terribly sad about seeing him, fifteen years on, still playing the wise old druggie—still delivering his know-it-all lectures on the provenance and quality of his gear.

'I'd go slow with that, Jane, if I were you,' she said.

Lenny waved the comment away. 'Don't listen to her, Jane. She's a party pooper.'

For the next hour, Rosa sat and watched them get stoned. It took Lenny longer than the other two to start displaying any real sign of intoxication, but by the time he began rolling the third joint, even he had begun to laugh at jokes several minutes longer than was strictly warranted. Jane was now coming to the end of a lengthy anecdote about the time she had met Seal's personal assistant in a bar and he had told her she looked like Samantha from *Sex in the City*. 'I was, like,

"Get out!" And he was, like, "No! For real!" And I was, like, "Oh my God!"'

The boys gazed at her, bleary-eyed.

'Yeah, it was crazy. He actually really wanted to introduce me to Seal, because evi*dently* that show is, like, one of Seal's super-favourites.'

'Wow,' Jason said solemnly. He and Lenny began to snort with laughter.

Sensing mockery, but eager to be a good sport, Jane looked back and forth between the two men. 'What's so funny, you guys? Tell me! *What?*'

'I'm baked,' Lenny announced when at last their guffaws had died away. 'You,' he added, pointing at Jane, 'are *really* baked.'

Rosa could take no more. 'Well,' she said, rising suddenly from her chair. 'It's late.'

The three of them looked up at her with naughty smirks.

'Off to bed then, Ro?' Lenny inquired.

'Yes. You should be too.'

Lenny made a comically chastened face. 'You're right.' He turned to Jason and Jane. 'She's right, you guys. We should all go to bed *very, very* soon.'

Rosa looked at Lenny. 'Well, come on then.'

'In a bit. Me and Jase are just finishing our wine. You don't have to escort us out, you know.'

'Fine.' Rosa went over to the door. 'Please try not to make too much noise when you're letting yourselves out.'

As she left, they erupted in giggles. It was, she reflected, the second time that day that she had exited to the sound of derisive laughter.

*   *   *

On her way to the bathroom the next morning, Rosa met Jane in the hall, looking gratifyingly hung-over.

'Well!' Rosa said with slightly sadistic good cheer. 'I guess you made quite a party of it last night.'

Jane nodded uneasily.

'What time did they finally go?'

'Actually—' Jane's response was interrupted by the sound of someone coughing and hawking behind her bedroom door.

Rosa froze. 'Is that . . . ?'

She turned around to see Lenny emerging from Jane's room in nothing but a pair of grubby boxer shorts. Behind him, she caught a glimpse of scattered clothes and rumpled sheets and five burned-out cigarette butts standing in a row on Jane's night-table.

'Hey,' Lenny said. He gave a sleepy, childlike wave and walked into the bathroom.

'Hey,' Rosa repeated mechanically. It was years since she had had occasion to witness her brother's near nakedness. The revelation of his bony, yellow chest and emaciated pin-legs was almost, but not quite, as distressing to her as the apparent fact that he had spent the night with her room-mate.

'*So*,' she said, looking at Jane.

Jane cringed. 'I hope you don't mind, Rosa, it was just—'

'Please! You don't need to justify yourself to *me*.' Rosa turned and walked briskly back to her bedroom. At the door, she glanced around at Jane, who was standing where she had left her, staring abjectly at the floor.

'Jane?'

'Yes?'

Rosa leaned, smiling, against the doorjamb. 'I don't want to alarm you or anything, but you might want to get yourself checked out by a doctor. My brother does have quite a history of venereal disease.' With that she disappeared into her room and closed the door.

CHAPTER THIRTEEN

Karla lay on her bed, sucking messily at a nectarine and scribbling on a yellow legal pad. In a couple of hours, she and Mike were due at Perry Street for a family celebration in honour of Audrey's fifty-ninth birthday, but Mike had not yet returned from the gym and she was taking the opportunity to do some work on a letter she was writing for her neighbour, Mrs Mee. The boss of the nail salon where Mrs Mee worked had recently introduced a new tipping policy: customers were now being asked to leave their gratuities with the cashier at the front desk instead of giving them to the manicurists directly. In theory, the tips were pooled at the end of the day and distributed equally among the workers, but the women strongly suspected that they were being scammed. Karla's letter, which was to be presented to the boss by the entire staff, demanded that the old system be reinstated and threatened recourse to the Labor Department if it were not. She paused now to read over the paragraph she had just written.

We the undersigned believe that we have a right to receive our tips from the patrons. This is the standard procedure in other nail and beauty salons throughout New York City. It ensures, among other things, that each employee is rewarded for the level of service that she provides.

She sighed. She had performed countless favours of this sort for Mrs Mee over the years: written character recommendations, made referrals, located medical specialists, organized therapy sessions, researched clinical trials. She had yet to see evidence that any of it had really helped. Somehow, Mrs Mee always found something to object to in the services that Karla rendered. The sought-after asthma doctor with whom she had arranged a rare consultation was accused of having a 'disrespectful' manner. The marriage counsellor who agreed to see Mrs Mee and her husband for no charge was judged to be inconveniently located. The training programme that Karla found for her at a high-paying Upper East Side beauty salon was dismissed as 'too boring'. Karla was not unaccustomed to dealing with people who were hard to help: she spent a good deal of her working life assisting those for whom the most elementary acts of self-preservation were a challenge. Yet even by these standards, Mrs Mee was a tough case. There was something wilful, something *defiant* in her perpetual, low-level unhappiness. It was as if suffering had become so integral to her identity that the prospect of any real, material improvement in her life would pose a threat to her deepest sense of self: she had invested her entire

243

personhood on a horse called Put Upon and she was damned if she were going to change her bet now.

Karla looked up at the sound of the front door opening. A moment later, Mike came into the bedroom. He was wearing track pants and a muscle T-shirt with a large Rorschach blot of sweat on its front.

'Hi,' Karla said. 'Good workout?'

'Fine.' He gestured at Karla's writing pad. 'Is that your essay?'

'Yes.' She drew the pad to her bosom.

The BabyLove Adoption Agency required prospective parents to compose autobiographical essays as part of their application. Mike had completed his paean to the sun-dappled days of his Bronx childhood some weeks ago, but Karla, despite persistent nagging, had yet to get beyond her first paragraph. The other day, she had called the agency to see if they had any sample autobiographical statements, but the woman on the other end had only laughed. 'We don't give out samples,' she had said. 'It wouldn't be appropriate. The autobiographical statement is a personal document. There isn't any right or wrong way to do it.'

'Is it nearly done?' Mike asked.

'Nearly.'

'Let me see what you've written so far.'

'No,' Karla said, recoiling from his outstretched hand, 'let me finish it first.'

Mike sighed irritably. 'I don't know why you're making such a meal of this. Are you using the guidelines?'

Karla nodded. 'Yes, of course.'

The guidelines provided by the agency recommended, among other things, that applicants attempt to answer the following questions:

What was your parents' style of child-rearing?

What were your past relationships with your parents and siblings?

What are your current relationships with your parents and siblings?

What level of education have you reached? Are you satisfied with this?

What is your job? Do you find it fulfilling?

What are some of the significant failures and successes you have experienced in life?

Whenever Karla considered this list, she became overwhelmed and depressed. It seemed to her that to supply all the required information accurately and honestly would take months of labour and at least ten thousand words.

'Why're you eating?' Mike said suddenly, pointing at the nectarine in her hand. 'You're going to have dinner in a bit.'

Karla wiped at her mouth guiltily and threw the nectarine down on the bedside table. 'It was just a snack,' she said. 'It'll help me not eat so much when I get there.'

'What's she giving us for dinner, anyway?' Mike asked suspiciously. He had not yet recovered from a recent Perry Street dinner at which Audrey had upended a can of spaghetti and meatballs on to a serving plate and carved the congealed cylinder into slices.

'I think she's doing take-out.'

'Oof, that's a relief.' He began to undress. 'I was thinking that we could make an announcement tonight about the adoption.'

Karla grimaced. 'Oh, I don't know, honey. It's Mom's night . . .'

'So? She'll be thrilled. What nicer present could we give her?'

Karla tried to picture her mother being thrilled by the present of grandmotherhood. 'Well . . . if you want to,' she said.

Mike went into the bathroom to take a shower.

'Honey,' she called after him, 'if Mom starts going on about the endorsement tonight, don't get into it, okay?'

'Well, if she asks me, I'm going to say what I think,' he called back.

'Oh, Mike, please don't. She *knows* what you think . . .'

Mike returned now, wearing a towel around his waist. 'I'm not going to let her lecture me on union politics.'

'But it'll get into an argument and it's her birthday . . .'

Mike shrugged. 'If she doesn't want an argument, she shouldn't bring it up.'

*   *   *

Audrey opened the front door at Perry Street, looking very much as if she had just got out of bed.

'Happy birthday!' Mike cried.

246

'Nothing happy about turning fifty-nine,' Audrey said bleakly, running her fingers through her unbrushed hair.

Mike let his mouth fall open in playful disbelief. 'Fifty-nine? Get out! You don't look a day over thirty!'

'All right, Omar Sharif,' Audrey said, 'simmer down.'

On entering the living room, Karla could not help giving a small gasp. Since her last visit to the house a few weeks earlier, the standard Perry Street disarray had degenerated into full-scale squalor. Pieces of clothing, full ashtrays and old newspapers were strewn over the floor. A half-eaten baked potato was sitting on top of the television. The whole place smelled of something sweet and rotten. 'Has Sylvia been here lately?' she asked.

Audrey looked around her, as if noticing the disorder for the first time. 'Yeah, she came on Monday but I had to send her away. I wasn't feeling well.'

There was an uncomfortable pause.

'We brought you a present, Ma!' Mike said, handing over a bottle of wine and a large, gift-wrapped package.

'Oh! Isn't that nice.' Audrey took the offerings and set them down on a chair.

'I'll go and get some glasses for the wine,' Karla volunteered.

'You don't want to open it now, do you?' Audrey said. 'Why don't you wait until people get here? I've got beer in the fridge.'

Karla glanced at Mike as she left the room. She did not mind failing to qualify as Audrey's idea of

247

'people', but he surely would.

The nasty smell was even stronger in the kitchen. And the mess was epic. A sinister brown substance was oozing from one of the three gaping trash bags on the floor. The filthy linoleum sucked at Karla's shoes. In a pot that was sitting on the stove, she discovered the source of the smell: putrefying chicken soup. She hastily replaced the lid. 'Mom, how long has this soup been sitting here?' she called out.

'What?' her mother called back.

'How long have you had this chicken soup?'

'The soup?' her mother shouted. 'Oh no, don't have any of that. Jean made it for me last week. It's probably gone off by now.'

Karla shook her head. She took three beers out of the fridge and began searching for glasses. The cupboard where they were normally kept was empty. She went through all the other cupboards and then checked the sink, but after digging around in the festering dishes for a while, she was able to locate only one cloudy tumbler with the dessicated dregs of red wine coating its bottom. She went back into the living room. Mike and her mother were sitting on the love-seat, arguing about the union endorsement.

'Mom,' Karla said, 'where are your glasses?'

Audrey turned to her. 'Mike says you're actually going to *campaign* for the governor. Is that true?'

Karla looked nervously at Mike. They had not, in fact, discussed this matter. In the past, she had always done canvassing work for union-endorsed candidates, but privately she had been hoping that she might quietly recuse herself this time around.

'Oh, Karla!' her mother cried.

'Well—' Karla began.

'She has nothing to be ashamed about,' Mike said. 'The Democrats always talk about how much they love us, but they never do anything to help us. I'd rather have the help without the love, quite frankly, than the love without the help.'

'My God,' Audrey said. 'I never thought I'd live to see the day . . .'

'About the glasses, Mom,' Karla said.

'Hmm?'

'Your glasses. I can't find them.'

'Really?' Audrey made a mystified face. 'Well, not to worry. It's only beer. We can drink from the bottles.'

'They can't all have disappeared. I'll keep looking.'

'Don't be such a fusspot,' Audrey said sharply. 'Mike won't mind drinking from a bottle, will you, Mike?'

Out in the hall, the front door banged shut. 'I'm here!' Lenny shouted. He came into the living room and threw his leather jacket on a chair. 'Hey, guys.' He had a nasty sore on his forehead and the skin around his eyes was a sickly purple colour.

'Hello, love,' Audrey said. 'You look tired—' She broke off at the sight of Tanya in the doorway, wearing a cowboy hat and a 'Jesus is My Homeboy' T-shirt. 'I didn't know Tanya was coming.'

'Really?' Lenny scratched his head. 'I thought I told you, Mom.'

'No.' Audrey's tone was firm. 'You didn't.'

Tanya glanced about the room with stagy diffidence. She seemed to be enjoying the awkwardness that her presence had caused.

'I could have sworn I did,' Lenny said.

Audrey sighed in resignation. 'Well, she's here now.'

'Listen, if it's a problem . . .' Tanya said in her reedy, little-girl's voice.

'No, dear,' Audrey said. 'It's not a problem. Sit down.'

'Seriously,' Tanya went on, reluctant to relinquish the idea of her unwantedness. 'I don't mind going.'

'Oh do shut up, Tanya,' Audrey said.

Lenny laughed and leaned over to kiss the top of his mother's head. 'Happy birthday, Mom. Sorry we're late.'

'It doesn't matter. Rosa's not here yet, anyway.'

'Is she at one of her Jewish classes tonight?' Tanya asked.

Audrey looked up at Lenny sharply. 'What classes?'

'Huh?'

Audrey smiled. 'You heard. What classes is Tanya talking about?'

Lenny shrugged. 'I dunno. I think she's studying the Talmud or something.'

'*Jesus.*' Audrey flopped back in her seat. 'I've got these two'—she pointed at Karla and Mike—'voting Republican. And now Rosa's training to be a fucking rabbi. What is *going on* with this family?'

Karla picked up the package that Audrey had left on the chair. 'Hey, Mom, why don't you open your present?'

'Yeah, go on, Ma,' Mike said. He took the package from Karla and placed it in Audrey's lap.

Still shaking her head, Audrey tore away the paper. Mike and Karla's gift was a hardcover book with the title *Schmatte: Garment Workers in*

250

London's East End. A Photographic History.

'Oh, very nice,' she said.

'Ooh, it's beautiful,' Tanya cooed. 'I *love* old black-and-white photography.'

Karla nodded, pleased. 'Yes, so do I.'

Tanya, who liked to think of even her most unremarkable enthusiasms as her patented idiosyncracies, looked irritated. 'No, but I'm, like, *obsessed*,' she said possessively.

Mike knelt down next to Audrey. 'We thought you'd find it interesting,' he said, 'with your dad being a tailor and everything.'

'I was the one who found it on the internet,' Karla added quickly.

'Mmm . . .' Audrey flicked quickly through the pages.

'I wrote something in the front,' Karla said.

Audrey turned to the page on which Karla had put her inscription. 'For Mom, with love and admiration, from Karla and Mike.' 'Very nice,' Audrey repeated. 'What a thoughtful present. Thank you.' She closed the book and laid it on the floor by her feet. 'Now, what about that beer? Or would you like some wine, Lenny?'

'Wine, please.'

'Right you are. Go on, you open it.'

'Maybe Mike should do that,' Karla suggested. She knew that her husband would resent Lenny opening the wine that he had brought.

'Whatever,' Lenny said.

'Get some mugs, Karla,' her mother commanded, 'and the Chinese menu. It's in the drawer next to the fridge.'

When Rosa arrived an hour later, the food was sitting in the oven and Karla was on her hands and

251

knees, scrubbing the kitchen floor.

'Shalom!' Karla heard Audrey drawl as Rosa entered the living room. There followed a brief exchange, most of which Karla was unable to make out. Then Rosa came into the kitchen.

'What on *earth* are you doing?' she demanded.

Karla, her round face pink from her exertions, looked up apologetically. 'It was so filthy in here. I just thought . . .'

Rosa gave a little moan of irritation. 'You're not Mom's indentured servant, you know.'

'Sorry,' Karla said, scrambling up.

'Don't say sorry,' Rosa snapped.

'Sorry . . . I mean, okay.' Karla smiled. 'How are you? How was your day?'

'Fine until I got here,' Rosa replied sulkily.

Karla laughed nervously.

While they were taking the foil containers out of the oven and setting them on the table, Lenny wandered in. 'Sup, girls?' he said, leaning unsteadily against the kitchen counter.

Rosa looked away. 'I'm not in the mood to talk to you right now, Lenny.'

'I didn't tell Mom about your classes,' Lenny said. 'It was Tanya. She didn't know it was a secret . . .'

'It's *not* a secret, you idiot.'

'So what's your problem then?'

Rosa did not reply.

'Okay then,' he sighed. 'Suit yourself.'

Rosa wheeled around suddenly. 'Tell me, does Tanya know about your little *sleepover* at my house the other night?'

'No. Why? Do you want to tell her?'

'Oh no. God forbid I should be the one to break

252

up your beautiful romance.'

Lenny yawned. 'Jesus, Ro. Chillax, would you?'

'*Don't!*' Rosa burst out. 'Don't tell me to chillax, okay? What are you, fourteen years old?'

'Guys,' Karla said. 'Remember it's Mom's birthday . . .'

'Did you know that Jane has a boyfriend?' Rosa asked. 'A fiancé, actually?'

'Sure.' Lenny smirked. 'She showed me the bunny he gave her. It was awesome.'

Rosa glared at him. 'If she's such a big joke to you, why did you sleep with her, Lenny? Does it make you feel like a big man to seduce people you don't respect?'

Lenny let his head fall to the side, in a gesture of exhaustion. 'C'mon, Ro, I respect her.'

'Sure, that's why you and that skeeve, Jason, spent the whole night laughing at her.'

'We were having *fun*, Rosa! We were nicer to her than *you* were—sitting there like it was fucking *Judgement at Nuremberg* the whole night. What's your problem? Are you against laughter as well as fucking now that you're such a big Jew?'

'That's it,' Rosa said, folding her arms. 'I can't talk to you.'

Audrey walked into the kitchen now, with her hands on her hips. 'So where's this bloody food then?'

*   *   *

Dinner was fraught, even by Perry Street standards. Rosa was haughty and distant. Lenny was monosyllabic. Audrey alternated between bouts of moony distraction and small explosions of

253

temper. The conversation at table would have lapsed entirely on more than one occasion had it not been for Tanya.

'*I'm* totally against the war in Iraq,' she informed the family soon after sitting down. 'I'm a total pacifist, aren't I, Len? I won't even let you kill cockroaches in my apartment, will I?'

Lenny grunted a reluctant corroboration.

'So you would have been against us fighting in the Second World War, would you, Tanya?' Mike asked.

'Totally!' Tanya cried. 'Totally, I would have been against it. Violence only leads to more violence, Mike.'

Karla listened, fascinated as always by Tanya's confidence in the value of her contribution. How much simpler life must be when you believed that your grade-school opinions had the status of knowledge!

'Hear that, Audrey?' Mike said. 'Tanya wishes we hadn't fought against the Nazis!'

'What?' Audrey looked up from spooning food on to her plate. 'Oh yeah, well, Tanya's got a lot of interesting ideas . . .' She studied the foil container in front of her. 'I tell you what, Rosa,' she said, 'I don't think you'll be wanting any of this. It's got *pork* in it.'

Rosa continued eating.

'By the way,' Audrey said, 'what *is* the Hebrew for "chopsticks"?'

Rosa put her chopsticks down. 'Ha ha. Very funny, Mother.'

'Lenny and I went to this hilarious party last night,' Tanya said, after a moment. 'We were walking past this place in TriBeCa and the guy on

254

the door was this old friend of Lenny's, so he let us in. It turned out to be a Doritos party—you know, the chips? They were launching a new mesquite flavour. There was this enormous room with, like, *ice sculptures* of Doritos chips everywhere. It was *amazing . . .*'

Karla listened with earnest concentration. She dimly understood that Tanya's enthusiasm for the Doritos party was facetious—a joke of sorts, like her T-shirt—but it depressed her, even so, to think of Lenny wasting his life on such foolishness.

'. . . and then, at about one o'clock in the morning,' Tanya was saying, '*Enrique Iglesias* came down these big stairs. For real! It was *fucked up.*'

'Who is Enrique Iglesias?' Audrey asked.

'He's a pop singer, Ma,' Mike explained.

'There was, like, dry ice everywhere,' Tanya went on, 'and Enrique was singing this song about how great and tasty the new chip was . . .'

Mike shook his head dourly. 'That's capitalism for you. Worshipping graven images of potato chips while Kandahar burns.'

Tanya giggled. She didn't seem bothered by how poorly her anecdote had been received. She looked pleased, as if the family's failure to be amused were flattering confirmation of her challenging, unorthodox sensibility.

'So come on, Rosa,' Audrey said, poking her with a finger. 'Why don't you tell us what you learned at Jew class tonight?'

'I already told you, Mom. I wasn't at a class tonight. I was at the hospital.'

'Oh, give her a peanut! She visited her father!'

'I saw Dr Krauss. He seems very concerned about—'

'Please! Don't talk to me about that useless fucker. I hate that pigeon-chested, flat-arsed, albino bastard.'

Everyone but Rosa laughed.

'I do, though!' Audrey went on. 'He gives me the creeps! There's something not clean about him. He looks like he's got genital herpes, I swear to God.'

There was more general, outraged amusement. Rosa stared down at her plate with a pained expression.

'Go on, smile, Rosa,' Audrey said. 'It won't crack your face.'

'I would smile, Mom, if anything funny had been said.'

'Oooh.' Audrey pretended to cower. 'Yentl's angry.'

'I was trying to tell you what Dr Krauss said about Dad—'

Audrey slammed her hand down on the table, 'Well, maybe I don't want to talk about your father on my fucking birthday!'

Mike sat forward and tapped a spoon against his mug of wine. 'If I could have everyone's attention for a moment . . .'

Karla hugged herself with embarrassment. This was it. He was going to announce their adoption plans.

'No, no, Mike.' Audrey cut him off with an irritable wave of her hand. 'Don't be a silly. We don't want any of that.'

Mike reddened and put down the spoon.

Lenny stood up. 'I need a piss.'

'Oh charming, Len,' Audrey drawled. 'Let us know when you do a number two, won't you?' She watched him leave the room and then she turned to Rosa. 'So, now, tell us, when you *do* go to class, what do you learn?'

Rosa shook her head. 'I'm not talking about this with you.'

'How to do a nice brisket?'

'Please, Mom, just drop it.'

'What's the big secret? It's not fucking Mossad, is it?'

Rosa closed her eyes primly. 'I study parshat ha-shavua,' she said, pronouncing the Hebrew words carefully. 'Each week we examine a portion of the Torah.'

'*Ohhh*. How useful!'

Rosa gave a superior smile. 'I guess it depends on how you define useful. I know very little about my religious heritage and I'd like—'

'*Excuse me*,' Audrey interrupted. 'There's a lot of things you know very little about. You know fuck all about quantum physics but I don't see you taking a class in that.'

'Come on, Mom, let's have a nice time,' Karla said. 'It's your birthday.'

'Yes,' Rosa said, 'that's true. But right now, I'm interested in finding out something about my people and where I come from.'

'Where you come from?' Audrey repeated. 'Your people? What *are* you going on about, Rosa?'

'The Jews,' Rosa said. 'I hate to break it to you, but we *are* Jewish.'

Audrey clapped her hands. 'And Mike is a Gentile. Should he be thinking about joining the Aryan Nation?'

'So do you actually believe in God now, Rosa?'

Mike asked with a smirk.

Rosa paused. When she spoke it was with great, self-conscious dignity. 'I can't really answer that, Mike. Sometimes I do.'

'Oh bloody marvellous!' Audrey exclaimed. 'Sometimes you do! What does that *mean?*'

'You know,' Rosa said, turning to her mother, 'it would be nice if once in a while you were actually supportive of something I did or said, instead of automatically shitting on it.'

Audrey looked at her with exaggerated astonishment. 'What *are* you talking about? I've never been anything but supportive of my children.'

'Sure, Mom. If you say so.'

'What? All I've ever wanted is for you to do well and be happy.'

'Really? That's not been my impression.'

'And what's your impression been then?'

'I think it would kill you if you thought I was really happy.'

All eyes turned nervously to the head of the table where Audrey sat. 'Dear oh dear,' Audrey said after a moment. 'This religion business is making you paranoid, Rosa.'

Mugs clinked and chopsticks clicked.

'*I* think it's so cool that Rosa's doing this,' Tanya said. 'I would love to develop my spiritual side.'

'I bet you would,' Audrey muttered.

'I mean it,' Tanya said. 'I think it's important to be tolerant of other people's faiths.'

'Why?' Audrey said, turning on her suddenly. '*Why* is it important? Why should I respect a point of view that I think is crap?'

'Well,' Tanya replied, undaunted, 'you want

258

other people to respect your beliefs, don't you?'

Audrey laughed. 'Yeah, well, that's a bit different, love. *My* beliefs are based on observable fact and scientific deduction. Rosa thinks there's an old man in the sky who has a fucking heart attack every time a Jew eats a prawn. When people start believing in that shit, you don't respect their point of view, you call the fucking doctor.'

'Is it just prawns you're not allowed?' Tanya asked. 'Or all seafood? Because I don't think I could give up lobster rolls . . .'

'Oh, don't worry. Giving up stuff suits Rosa down to the ground,' Audrey said. 'She loves a bit of hair shirt, doesn't she? Denial is her thing. That's how she lived in a mud hut in Cuba for four years—'

'Yes, wasn't I silly?' Rosa interrupted. 'When all that time, I could have stayed home, just like you, directing the revolution from my mansion in Greenwich Village.'

Audrey looked at her thoughtfully. 'You know what I think you need, Ro? A boyfriend. I bet Mike could introduce you to someone nice in the union, couldn't you, Mike?'

'Mom—'

'I'm serious, Rosa. A bit of sex would do you the world of—'

'*Stop it! Just stop it!*'

Audrey sat back and smiled. 'See? That's what I mean. You're very tense. You need some release.'

Again, Mike raised a spoon and tapped it lightly against his mug. 'I'm afraid I really must insist now,' he said.

'Lenny's not here,' Karla whispered, tugging at his sleeve. 'You have to wait for Lenny.'

'I'll get him!' Tanya volunteered. She stood up and left the room.

'Ma,' Mike continued, 'Karla and I have chosen today, your birthday, to announce some very special news—'

'You're pregnant!' Audrey broke in. 'Well, it's about bloody time.'

Mike opened and closed his mouth like a fish. 'No, Ma. It's not that. We have decided to adopt a child.'

'Oh!' Audrey paused. '*Oh*. I see.'

Tanya came back into the kitchen now. 'Uh, you guys . . .'

Audrey ignored her. 'Is it going to be American or foreign?' she asked Karla.

'Sorry?' Karla said. 'Oh, the baby, you mean? American, I guess. I mean, the agency deals with American children.'

'Well, *that's* a shame. Why wouldn't you get one from Africa? They're the ones most in need.'

'Guys?' It was Tanya again, louder this time.

Audrey turned around. '*What?*'

'I think Lenny might have had an accident. The bathroom door is locked and he's not answering.'

*　　　*　　　*

Lenny had not had an accident, as it turned out. Nor was he, as Mike tactlessly suggested while attempting to break down the bathroom door, dying or dead. He had simply fallen into an opiate stupor while sitting on the lavatory. By the time the door had surrendered to Mike's karate kicks and Mike had slapped him around the face with perhaps more vigour than was strictly necessary,

260

Lenny was able to stand up and walk unaided to the kitchen. Here, having vomited briefly in the sink and given himself a wash-down with a wet dish-towel, he pronounced himself quite well again.

'You silly thing,' Audrey said, ruffling his hair. 'You scared us all shitless.'

'We thought you'd done an Elvis,' Tanya giggled.

Rosa clutched her head in frustration. 'Hello? Could we stop acting like he did something cute?'

'What do you want me to do?' Audrey asked. 'Spank him?'

Mike, furious that his adoption announcement had been upstaged by Lenny's collapse, gave a nasty little laugh. 'That'd be a start.'

'He was unconscious just now,' Rosa said. 'This doesn't concern you, Mom?'

Audrey got up from the table. 'Do you want a cup of tea, Lenny?'

'Yeah, all right.'

'He should have some camomile,' Tanya said. 'Or peppermint.'

'Have you taken heroin this evening, Lenny?' Rosa asked.

Lenny shrugged. 'I just smoked a bit. I didn't inject.'

Rosa turned to Karla. 'Am I the only one who thinks there's a problem here?'

Karla studied the congealing remains of Chinese food on the table. 'It *is* a bit worrying, Lenny,' she said reluctantly.

'He hasn't injected for ages,' Tanya put in.

'Maybe you should think about going back to rehab, Lenny,' Karla suggested.

'He can't do rehab,' Audrey said quickly. 'The health insurance won't pay for another one. Do you want sugar, Len?'

'Yeah—give me lots.'

Mike sat up and slapped his thigh. 'Right. We should be off soon.'

'Not yet, Mike . . .' Karla whispered, blushing at her husband's insensitivity.

'No,' he insisted, in a voice congested with anger, 'we need to go.'

Karla looked at him. His left leg was vibrating like a jackhammer. The journey home would be grim, she thought.

'I'll go and get our jackets,' he said, getting up.

'What's *his* problem?' Audrey asked as he marched out of the room.

'Nothing,' Karla said quickly. 'He just needs to get up early tomorrow.'

Mike returned and, with officious gentlemanliness, helped Karla into her jacket. 'Goodbye all,' he said tightly. 'Thank you, Ma, for a lovely evening.'

'Yeah,' Audrey said. She smiled despondently, 'it's been a laugh riot, hasn't it?'

CHAPTER FOURTEEN

On the second Tuesday in July, Carol conducted the first of her much anticipated 'Jewish Way of Life' field trips: a tour of a mikvah. Rosa was running late that afternoon and when she arrived at the brownstone on West Seventy-eighth Street, where the tour was to take place, the rest of the group had already gone in. After pressing the button on the video entry phone and identifying herself to the fuzzy, suspicious voice on the other end, she was admitted into the basement of the building. She found Carol and fifteen other women from the Learning Center milling about in a small, windowless lounge. The room was decorated in the morbidly feminine style of a gynaecologist's office, with peach-coloured sofas and floral throw cushions and impressionist prints. On one of the walls, someone had posted a small, handwritten sign: COME JOIN A GROUP OF WOMEN WHO RECITE TEHILIM FOR THE SICK AND THE SOLDIERS IN ISRAEL. WE MEET EVERY TUESDAY P.M. Next to this was a larger printed placard. BE PROUD, it said, YOU ARE A DAUGHTER OF ISRAEL.

Rosa was still puzzling over this obscure imperative when Carol brought everyone to attention with a polite cough. 'Welcome, ladies. I believe everyone is here now. The mikvah attendant will be with us shortly, but while we are waiting, I thought it would be useful if I gave you just a little basic information about the mikvah and the role that it plays in Jewish life.' She looked down and began to read nervously from a sheaf of notes:

The mikvah is the Hebrew word for ritual bath. It has several purposes. It is used in Jewish conversion ceremonies; Orthodox men sometimes use it to prepare themselves for Sabbath or important holidays. Also, many traditional Jews immerse their new utensils in the mikvah before using them. But the primary function of the mikvah is related to taharat hamishpachah—the Jewish laws of family purity, which dictate that during a woman's menses and for seven clean days thereafter a woman is niddah, or sexually unavailable. For a minimum of twelve days, a husband and wife are prohibited from intercourse and all other forms of intimate contact. This period of abstinence is officially concluded each month with ritual immersion in the mikvah.

Rosa was puzzled. She had always liked the sound of a mikvah. She had pictured it as a sort of religiously sanctioned spa: a women-only Turkish bath. This sounded more like mandatory, once-a-month self-mortification.

Although the Reform and Conservative denominations have largely ceased to observe the laws of mikvah and niddah, the Orthodox regard them as gufei ha-torah—that is, the essential laws of the Torah. We read in Leviticus, 'And unto a woman while she is impure by her uncleanness you shall not approach to uncover her nakedness.' The Torah gives the law of taharat hamishpachah not once, but three times. It also specifies that those couples who disobey the law shall suffer the awesome punishment of karet. Their souls shall be cut off from their people—

Rosa raised her hand.
'Yes, Rosa?'
'I don't understand. Why is a woman considered

unclean when she is menstruating?'

'Good question!' Carol said gamely. 'I'm really glad you brought that up. The Hebrew word "tum'ah", or impure, is left over from Temple times. It only means ritually impure—unfit for Temple access. No one regards a menstruating woman as literally dirty.'

'Okay, but why should she be considered even ritually impure? Doesn't that suggest a fundamentally negative attitude towards the female body?' Rosa was aware of some sighing and eye rolling from the other women. Already, it seemed, she had identified herself as the obstreperous class bore.

'I can assure you,' Carol said, smiling, 'that is not how generations of Jewish women have seen it. If you ask around among Orthodox women, I think you'll find that they have many very positive things to say about mikvah.'

An old woman dressed in floral housecoat and slippers entered the room now.

'Ladies,' Carol said, 'this is Mrs Levine, who will be giving us our tour today. Mrs Levine has been an attendant at this mikvah for seventeen years!' There was a smattering of applause for the longevity of Mrs Levine's service, but Mrs Levine made no acknowledgement of the tribute. Her manner—stiff and proprietorial, bristling with anticipatory insultedness—suggested no great enthusiasm for having her inner sanctum gawped at by outsiders.

The class arranged itself in a crocodile formation and followed Mrs Levine down the hall to a small warren of tiled shower rooms and bathrooms. In this area, she explained, women

265

made themselves ready for the mikvah by removing anything—dirt, jewellery, make-up, nail polish, Band Aids, dentures—that might conceivably come between their skin and the sanctified water. They also checked themselves internally for any residual traces of menstrual blood, using special white cotton cloths that were provided. After one such cloth had been passed around so that everyone could sample its exemplary softness, the tour continued on into the mikvah room.

The stark, white-tiled chamber, which contained nothing but a small, square pool, a stool for Mrs Levine to sit on and a vaguely sinister contraption for lowering disabled women into the water, was something of an anticlimax.

Mrs Levine described how she went about inspecting naked women prior to their immersion. 'Mostly, what I am looking for at this stage is a stray hair, or perhaps a little particle of dirt somewhere,' she said. 'You'd be amazed,' she added, lapsing briefly into chummy confidentiality, 'at how many little bits and pieces I find hanging about in the belly button and in the pubic hair.'

Back in the lounge, Carol asked if there were any questions. Rosa looked around. Most of the women were placidly writing notes on their information sheets. Presently a hand went up. Rosa recognized the young woman from her parsha class. She was a Christian from Tennessee who had recently become engaged to a Jewish man and was preparing to convert. 'You know when you were talking before, about intimate contact?' she said. 'I'm a bit confused about what that means. I've heard people say different things.'

Carol nodded. 'It is true, there is a range of opinion within the Orthodox community as to how strictly the prohibition is to be observed. In some households, a husband will refrain even from passing things to his wife while she is niddah. If he wishes to give her car keys, for example, he will place them on a table and let her pick them up. In other households, husbands and wives do touch each other and even express mild forms of physical affection, such as holding hands.'

The young woman's eyes grew very wide. 'Just holding hands?'

Carol laughed. 'I will not pretend that these restrictions are always easy to observe. For loving couples with healthy sex drives, taharat hamishpachah requires enormous discipline. We live in a society that bombards us daily with pornographic images, that is constantly encouraging us to "let it all hang out" and do what feels good. But, I promise you, there are many benefits to be had from submitting to these rules. For one thing they help to keep the spiritual dimension of a marriage alive. Every month, for two weeks, a husband and wife are required to find non-sexual ways to communicate their love for one another. Conversely, the observance keeps the sexual component of a marriage strong. How often do we hear of men in the secular world who seek excitement outside the home because they have become sexually indifferent to their wives?' (Several women nodded in rueful assent: Ah, yes, such things were heard of all too often.) 'This, I can assure you,' Carol went on, 'is much less likely to occur in an Orthodox household where a husband has severe limitations on when he may take sexual pleasure in his wife.'

A young girl wearing a kippah tentatively raised her hand. 'I worry because I often have spotting between periods. How would the law apply in such cases?'

Carol smiled sympathetically. 'Good point. Many women have irregular cycles. Many women experience "spotting", as you say, and it is not always easy to ascertain exactly when their bleeding has finished. In most cases, these things can be worked out. My rabbi has sometimes written me a note in such circumstances.'

Rosa stared at a reproduction of Monet's water lilies on the wall. Was this, she wondered, what the millennia of Jewish wisdom came down to? A group of women sitting in a bathhouse parsing Iron Age blood taboos and fretting over stains in their panties? This was not about God at all: it was the expression of some schoolgirlish masochism, some hysterical need for rules and restrictions, the pettier and more arduous, the better.

After the class was over, she and Carol walked up Columbus together. It had grown windy while they were in the mikvah. Candy wrappers and plastic bags and other bits of urban tumbleweed skittered and swirled around their ankles as they pressed their way along the sidewalk.

'I could tell you were uncomfortable about what you heard this evening,' Carol said.

'Not uncomfortable,' Rosa objected. 'Upset. I find the whole idea of these laws incredibly degrading.'

'I see how they might appear that way to you, Rosa. But I promise you—'

'How can it *not* be degrading to be put into

268

quarantine and treated like Typhoid Mary every time you have your period?' Rosa demanded. 'To have to get a note from your rabbi before you can sleep with your husband? How does the rabbi make his decision, anyway? Does he inspect your underwear?'

Carol looked pained. 'I believe there are some rabbis who require physical evidence. But my rabbi has always trusted me to be honest.'

'Oh, the honour system! How liberal-minded of him!'

'The aim is not liberal-mindedness, Rosa. The aim is to obey God's commandments. In Judaism, a distinction is made between the chomer, the act, and the tzuvah, the essence of the act. You have to go beyond the limited physical reality of these duties and appreciate the dignity, the holiness of the ritual. Once you do that, you find you can achieve a kind of sanctity through the humblest of actions.'

An empty cardboard box was bumping towards them down the street. Rosa stepped to one side to get out of its path. 'I don't know what to tell you,' she said. 'It's hard for me to believe that God cares if a husband hands his menstruating wife the car keys or not. It's hard for me to believe that He's such a pedant.'

They stopped at a cross street to wait for the light.

'You don't call it pedantic,' Carol said, 'when your surgeon is concerned about giving you exactly the right dose of anaesthetic, or when a scientist concerns himself with minute differences in the measurement of a chemical reaction. Why should small actions not have large consequences in

269

matters of spirituality?'

Rosa gazed at a homeless man who was standing next to her on the sidewalk, humming companionably to himself as he delved through a trash can. There was some logical flaw in Carol's analogy, she was sure; she just could not figure out what it was.

'The thing is,' Carol said, 'you're looking at all this from a secular, feminist perspective. And you can't make Orthodoxy fit with that. They are two completely different modes of thought. Feminists say that the mikvah denigrates women. But do I look like a denigrated woman to you? Do you think I feel angry and oppressed when I go to the mikvah? Not at all! The truth is, mikvah is one of the highlights of my month. I love being a woman . . .'

'Well, yeah, so do I,' Rosa said.

'*Do* you?' Carol turned to her. 'Forgive me for saying so, but I get the feeling sometimes that you feel you have to hide your femaleness in order to be taken seriously.'

Rosa raised an eyebrow. This had the ring of some long-hoarded aperçu. 'What do you mean?'

'The way you dress, the way you do your hair— it's like you're trying to ignore the fact that you're a woman.'

'Excuse me—'

'Please, I'm not trying to be rude. It just occurs to me that one of the reasons you're so uncomfortable with these laws is that you're not really at ease with your own sexuality.'

Rosa gave an icy laugh. 'I can assure you, I have no problems whatsoever in that department.'

Carol looked at her dolefully. 'I am sorry, Rosa.

I don't mean to offend you.'

The homeless man had retrieved a chicken wing from an abandoned KFC Bonus Meal and was plodding away now, pushing his rattling cart of soda cans across the street.

'Come.' Carol pointed to the traffic light. 'We can walk.'

'No thanks,' Rosa said curtly. 'I think I'll turn off here.'

'Oh, please don't.' Carol gripped her arm. 'I don't want us to part on bad terms.'

Rosa studied Carol's hand a moment and then gently removed it. 'Goodbye, Carol.'

*   *   *

On arriving home, Rosa went straight to her bedroom, knelt down before her dresser and began rummaging through the bottom drawer. At length, she unearthed an ancient pack of Marlboro Lights. She laid the cigarettes on the bed and considered them. The mere act of smoking, evil as it was, was not yet sufficiently evil for her purpose. She stood up and went down the hall to run a bath. Here was decadence: she would smoke in the tub.

Lying with her knees protruding from the water like two pale islands, she inhaled wincingly on her stale cigarette and considered the cityscape of shampoos and conditioners that Jane had arranged around the edge of the bath. There was a wavering area of darkness hovering at the edge of her consciousness: a familiar despair, waiting to move in like a weather system. If only she had not gone to that stupid place, she thought. If only she had not had that awful conversation with Carol!

271

Perhaps Carol was right, though. Perhaps Rosa *was* hanging on too hard to the limited physical reality of things. Was it not possible that her objections to the mikvah sprang from a failure of imagination? An inability to appreciate metaphor? She was always accusing the Orthodox of being literal-minded about Torah: maybe it was *she* who was guilty of literal-mindedness. Poetry had been the one subject in which she had never excelled at school. Even when she brought the full weight of her intelligence to bear on certain poems, they had refused to give up their meaning. She remembered her English teacher telling her once, in exasperation, 'You want to extract the idea of the poem like a nut from its shell—to find out whether it is "right" or not—but if the poet had wanted to say something that could be summed up in a sentence like that, he wouldn't have written a poem, he would have written a slogan.' Perhaps believing was like poetry in this regard. It required a delicacy or subtlety of mind that she had yet to attain.

She looked down at herself. The long hairs on her ghostly white calves were swaying in the bath water like sea plants. Her toenails needed clipping. What was it Carol had said? She was uncomfortable with her femaleness? The smug little fool! She had as good as accused Rosa of being frigid. And why? Because Rosa did not conform to her twee, antique notions of femininity? Because Rosa had not jumped at the chance to have Mrs Levine forage through her pubic hair once a month? She leaned over the side of the bath to stub out her cigarette. No, Carol was crazy. And all that stuff about the chomer and tzuvah was a crock: a shabby attempt to justify treating women like crap. She sat up with a sudden, angry whoosh. It was actually a blessing that she had seen the mikvah today, before she had wasted any more time straining to defend the indefensible. Fuck Carol. Fuck them all. Let them spend their lives bowing and scraping before the cosmic class monitor they had invented for themselves. She, Rosa, would have to do without Him.

CHAPTER FIFTEEN

'Tanya's all for sending him to some retreat in Arizona,' Audrey said, flicking a speck of something from Joel's hospital blanket. 'For a thousand bucks a week, apparently, you get to meditate in the desert and have your shakti cleansed.' She arched her brows at Jean and Karla, who were sitting on the other side of Joel's bed. 'Can you imagine? So I said to her, I said, "That sounds lovely, Tanya, but will you really be able to afford it?"' She grinned at the memory of her own subtlety. 'She shut up after that, didn't she?'

'What *are* you going to do, do you think?' Jean asked.

Audrey's smile faded. 'Oh, I don't know, there's not much I can do, really.'

'Actually, Jean,' Karla said, 'there's a good outpatient programme in Queens that we might be able to get him into. I was telling Mom about it yesterday.'

Audrey smiled and cocked her head in Karla's

273

direction. 'She thinks she's going to get Lenny to schlep to Queens three times a week, bless her.'

'Have you considered an intervention?'

'Do me a favour, Jean! He's had twenty bloody interventions. If I have to read out another letter telling him how much I bloody care about him, I'll throw myself in a lake.'

'Well, what does Rosa say?' Jean asked.

'*Pfft*, you know Rosa. She wants me to throw him out of the house and not have him back until he's cleaned up.'

Jean considered this. 'There might be something in that, mightn't there?'

Audrey's jaw stiffened. She was about to retort when a nurse entered the room.

'Hiya! How you ladies doing?'

'We're doing fantastic, love,' Audrey said. 'What is it?'

'I have to drain Mr Litvinoff's trachea. You may want to step outside for a few minutes.'

To pass the time while they were waiting, the women strolled up and down the hallway, glancing through open doorways at the tableaux of other people's miseries: an old man flashing a vast, elephant-hide scrotum as he clambered out of bed; a teenaged boy in big, old-fashioned headphones like earmuffs, grimly watching cartoons; a hospital volunteer swaying with emotion as he serenaded a young woman on an electric organ.

'I've been thinking,' Jean said, after a while, 'I'm going down to Bucks County next week and I'll be there for the whole of August. Maybe Lenny should come and stay.'

'I don't think so,' Audrey said.

'Obviously, it isn't the long-term answer,' Jean

added. 'But it'd be good for him to be away from the city. And at least he'd be out of your hair for a bit.'

Audrey shook her head. She didn't *want* Lenny away from the city. She *liked* having him in her hair. 'Nah, it wouldn't work. Lenny doesn't do well when he's not at home. Do you remember that time he went to Turkey?'

'I think it's a good idea, Mom,' Karla said. 'Especially if we could get him back to the NA meetings.'

Audrey pretended not to hear. 'It'd play havoc with his allergies, being in the country,' she went on. 'He'd be miserable.'

'Oh, Audrey,' Jean said. '*Come on*. Allergies—'

'He won't want to go, I'm telling you. And I can't make him.'

'Yes you can. Just tell him you're going to stop giving him money if he doesn't.'

Audrey laughed. 'Bloody hell, he had one little relapse, Jean.'

Jean looked at her gravely. 'You've stopped taking these episodes of his seriously. But they are serious. One of these days, if you don't do something, he's going to kill himself.'

'You've been reading too many *Reader's Digest* articles—'

'The truth is, Audrey, he may end up killing himself whatever you do. But if you do nothing, he *definitely* will.'

'Oh, for God's sake.' Audrey began to fuss unhappily with the clasp on her handbag.

'Jean's right,' Karla said. 'I know how hard it would be for you to do this, Mom, but it would be a real act of love—'

'All right, all right,' Audrey interrupted. 'Spare me the fucking greetings card.'

They had stopped walking now. Next to where they stood in the hallway, an abandoned meal cart, piled high with used lunch trays, was giving off a sad, mass-catering smell of sour milk and instant gravy.

'I know you'd never forgive yourself,' Jean said, 'if you couldn't say you'd done everything in your power to—'

'All *right*!' Audrey exclaimed. 'I'll talk to him about it.'

*   *   *

Until the moment that she actually broached the subject with Lenny, it seemed just possible to Audrey that he would surprise her and decide, of his own capricious accord, that he *wanted* to go to Bucks County. But his first, long gale of laughter closed the lid on that fantasy.

'Oh, *Mom*, you know I hate it there,' he said. 'I'd go nuts living with Jean for a month.'

'She'll keep out of your way.'

'Yeah? Well, I guess if she moved out of the place, I'd consider it.'

'It's ever so pretty down there in the summer.'

'No it's not. It's depressing. And anyway, you know how I am with my allergies.'

When Audrey saw that she was making no inroads with the soft sell, she tried suggesting, gingerly, that he might go in order to please her. This only elicited a wounded look and a petulant 'Thanks, Mom. I didn't know you were so desperate to get rid of me.' At last, she got up the courage to present the ultimatum that Jean had suggested. If he didn't go, she would cut off his money. Lenny responded by denouncing her as a tight-fisted bitch and slamming out of the house, promising never to return.

When he reappeared, three hours later, he was weepy and repentant. He had not meant to lose his temper. He had only reacted like that because he was hurt and he couldn't bear the thought of being sent away. She wouldn't send him away, would she?

'Len, I have to,' she told him. 'I'm doing this for *you*.'

'Fuck!'

She stepped back with a wince as he kicked over a kitchen chair.

'Why are you doing this to me?' he screamed.

'Lenny, love—'

'Don't come near me! You heartless fucking *cunt*.'

It went on like this for the four days leading up to his departure. Every morning, he would start out wheedling and cajoling, then he would move on to pleading and crying. Finally he would explode in violent abuse, before starting over and going back to wheedling. In his presence, Audrey maintained a mask of immutable resolve. Away from him, she wept tears of despair. Jean phoned every day, trying to keep her morale up. And Karla dealt with all the practical arrangements that needed to be made—finding addresses for the Narcotics Anonymous chapters nearest to Jean's house, changing Lenny's cellphone number so that his dealers would be unable to reach him, and so on. But no one, Audrey felt, could *really* help her.

Her life was slowly and systematically being burgled of everything she held dear: Joel was gone, or as good as gone, trapped in the underworld of his coma. The integrity of her marriage—the nearest thing to an achievement she had ever been able to claim—had been snatched away by that harpy, Berenice. And now Lenny, her baby, was leaving her.

On the afternoon that Jean collected him, Karla left work early to come down to Perry Street and make sure that everything went off all right. Audrey was sitting on the stoop when she arrived, taking respite from the louring atmosphere of filial reproach within.

'Everything all right, Mom?' Karla asked anxiously as she came up the stairs. 'Where's Len?'

'On a plane to Rio,' Audrey said dully. She jerked her head towards the house. 'Inside, where d'you think?'

Lenny was curled up on the sofa with his back to them when they entered the living room. 'How're you doing, Len?' Karla asked.

There was a muzzy grunt from the sofa.

'He's not feeling well,' Audrey said. 'He's got a cold.'

'Oh dear. Have you taken something for it, Len?'

There was no reply.

'I gave him some DayQuil earlier,' Audrey said. 'I'm really not sure he's fit to travel in this state.'

Karla smiled. 'He'll be fine, Mom. Jean'll look after him.'

'I wouldn't think so. She'll probably have him mowing her lawn before the day's out.'

'Shall I make you a cup of tea?'

278

Audrey shrugged miserably. 'There's some coffee already made.'

When Karla had gone into the kitchen, Audrey went over and knelt down next to the sofa. On the side of Lenny's head that was pressed against the sofa, his left ear had become folded over on itself like a piece of origami. Audrey reached out cautiously to rearrange the ear, and then thought better of it. 'You ready to go then, love?' she asked. 'Jean says the weather is ever so nice down there at the moment.'

There was a brief silence.

'Fuck off,' Lenny muttered.

Audrey stood up and left the room.

In the kitchen, Karla handed her a cup of coffee. 'It's going to be okay, Mom. He'll cheer up when he gets there.'

Audrey shook her head. 'I don't think he will. He's in a terrible state. This is bringing up all his abandonment issues, I can tell.' She sat down at the table and looked wanly around the kitchen. 'Do you want to stay for dinner then?'

Karla bared her teeth in an expression of pained regret. 'I would, Mom . . . but Mike's expecting me back. We've got some stuff to do on our adoption application—'

'Oh. All right.'

'I could phone him if you like and tell him I'm going to be late.'

'Don't be silly. I was only thinking of you. I've got plenty to be getting on with, believe me.'

'Are you sure?'

'Do shut up, Karla, *yes*.'

Karla sat down at the table.

'So,' Audrey said, after a moment, 'how's this

adoption business going then?'

'Good, yeah.' Karla nodded vigorously. 'I mean, it's early days . . .'

'What are you getting, a boy or a girl?'

'We don't know, Mom,' Karla said. 'I mean, we're only at the beginning of this process. You're not allowed to specify the sex anyway—'

'I'd try and hold out for a boy if I were you. I bet that's what Mike wants. Men always say they don't mind what they get, but underneath, they all want boys.'

Karla wiped something from her eye.

'What's the matter?' Audrey asked.

'Nothing.'

'You're not *blubbing*, are you?'

'No.'

'Why are you blubbing?'

'Nothing . . . I'm just a bit emotional at the moment.'

Audrey studied her. 'You can't be crying about nothing. You're not *that* soppy.'

'Honestly, I'm fine.'

'What is it—do you not want to do this adoption?'

'*No*, of course I want to.'

'You don't seem too thrilled about it.'

'I am thrilled.'

'And Mike?'

'Mike's dying to be a father.'

'Is everything all right between the two of you?'

Karla gave a little sob. 'Yes. Of course.'

Audrey's eyes narrowed in speculation. There was a problem in the marriage, that was clear. If she had to bet, she'd say Mike was having an affair. 'I'm surprised you're doing this adoption now,' she said. 'It doesn't seem like you've been trying to get pregnant long enough.'

'Oh, we've given it a good shot, Mom.'

'It's only been eighteen months.'

'No, longer.'

'Really? How much longer?'

'Two years and a bit.'

'Blimey. Time flies.'

A tear ran down Karla's cheek. 'Anyway,' she said briskly, 'Mike wants us to get started sooner rather than later. He thinks it's important to have kids when you're still young enough to run around with them.'

Audrey's surmise now had all the conviction of scientific knowledge: Mike was having an affair. No doubt Karla was going through with this adoption in the hope that a baby would keep the marriage together. Audrey was not much moved by other women's marital difficulties, as a rule. Wives of straying husbands tended only to irritate her with their self-dramatizing unhappiness and their confident expectations of sympathy. *Big deal*, she always wanted to say to them: *Join the club*. Or, as her mother had told her when she got her first period at the age of thirteen: 'Well, now you know. Being a woman isn't fun.' Yet, something in Karla's misery stirred her—filled her with an outraged sympathy that she had not known she possessed. 'Who cares what Mike says,' she burst out. 'A man has nothing to say in matters of reproduction.'

Karla looked at her in surprise. 'But, Mom—'

'It's a woman's business.'

There was a silence. Audrey stood up, suddenly embarrassed, and took her mug to the sink. What was she trying to do? She couldn't save her

281

daughter from Mike's infidelity. Married life was hard: Karla would have to deal with it like everyone else. 'Forget it, I don't know what I'm saying,' she said. 'I'm going to see how Len's doing. Pour another coffee and bring it in for him, would you?'

*　　　*　　　*

On the long ride back to the Bronx, Karla thought about what her mother had said to her. It had been odd to hear her refer so dismissively to Mike's wishes. Audrey had never had a very high opinion of Mike, it was true, but she usually took his side. Most of her marital advice over the years seemed to have been based on the assumption that Mike had performed a remarkable act of charity in marrying Karla and ought to be rewarded for his kindness with complete obeisance.

At home, Karla found Mike lying on the floor in their bedroom, doing crunches.

'Well, he's gone,' she said, sitting down on the bed.

Mike was counting under his breath and did not reply.

'Jean's such a nice lady,' Karla mused. 'I really hope he's not going to screw this up.'

'One hundred . . .' Mike lay back on the floor and exhaled noisily. 'Of *course* he's going to screw it up, Karla.'

'Don't say that. We have to give him a chance.'

Mike sat up. 'Your essay is ready, right?'

'Oh God . . .' Karla covered her mouth with her hand.

'Don't tell me you haven't done it.'

282

'No, no, I have. I finished it during my lunch break today. It's in my case at work. I just forgot to bring it back with me.'

'*Jesus.*'

'Don't worry, I'll bring it tomorrow. One day won't matter.'

'I've been asking you for that essay for weeks. What's the matter with you?'

'I'm sorry, I really am. I've just been so busy—'

'And everything else takes priority, doesn't it? Sorry, Mike, my dad's ill. Sorry, Mike, I have to look after my fucked-up brother. Sorry, Mike, one of my patients is having a crisis . . .'

'What do you want me to do? Go back and get it now?'

'Yes, actually. I think you should.'

'You're kidding.'

'No, I'm not.' He assumed a prone position and started doing push-ups.

Karla sat watching, waiting for him to relent.

'Go on then,' he said, looking up after a moment. 'If you're going, go.'

*   *   *

Khaled's store was still open when Karla got to the hospital. Reluctant to have to explain her tear-stained face, she hurried past without stopping. Up in her cubicle, she turned on the computer and began to print out her essay. When the first page shuddered out on to the printing tray, she picked it up and read it over with an embarrassed frown.

My relationships with my parents and siblings have always been extremely good. We are a

283

close-knit family, with a shared interest in political activism and social justice. Some of my happiest childhood memories are of going as a family on peace marches and other similar events . . .

There was a knock at the door. Before she could reply, Khaled entered. 'I saw you downstairs just now,' he said. 'I called to you, but you didn't hear.'

'Sorry, I was in a hurry.'

'Are you okay?'

She turned back to the printer. 'Yup, I'm fine.'

'How come you came back to work?'

'I had to pick up some papers I left behind.' *Go on*, she told herself. *Why don't you just say it?* 'It's a document for an adoption agency, actually. My husband and I are trying to adopt a baby. I had to write an autobiographical essay for the application form.' She spoke in a great rush, babbling the words like a child in a school play.

'Wow,' Khaled said.

'Yeah.'

'You didn't tell me you were trying to adopt.'

'Well, it's a pretty recent thing.'

Khaled laced his hands together and placed them on the top of his head. 'This is big news.'

She gave a smiling half-shrug. 'I guess.'

'Congratulations.'

'Thanks.'

The printing had stopped.

'So what have you said about yourself?' Khaled asked.

'What?'

'In your essay. What have you said?'

'I don't know. Stupid stuff.'

284

'Like what?'

Karla picked up the papers from the printing tray. 'I don't want to tell you. It's too dopey.'

'Oh, come on, tell me.'

There was something vaguely hostile in his cajoling tone.

'Well, I said I'm caring and, you know, interested in social justice. I said I'm a cheerful and positive person—'

'Really?' he interrupted. '"Cheerful and positive"?'

'What?'

'I don't know. To me, you always seem a little sad.'

'I am not sad!'

'You have a sad face.'

'Thanks!'

'It's not an insult.'

'I'm not a sad person. I'm always smiling.'

'If you say so.'

Angrily, Karla shuffled the essay into order and slid it into an envelope. 'Right,' she said, 'I'm done.'

Khaled did not move. 'So when are you going to get this baby then?'

She sighed. 'It's not like that. There's no definite date. We have to be approved first. They have to do a home study. It takes a long time.'

They stood listening to the eerie susurration of the social-work offices after hours: the glub glub of the water cooler in the hall, the distant ping of an elevator, the whirr of a late-arriving fax in the next-door cubicle.

'I'm sorry,' Khaled said, at last. 'I'm sorry you're doing this.'

Karla nodded. 'I know you are.' The tears in her eyes were making the room wobble and shimmer. She looked down at the envelope in her hands. When she looked up again, Khaled was standing in front of her. *I don't care*, she thought, as he lowered his face to hers. *I don't care.*

His hands were dry and hot. He tasted of something spicy that he had eaten for lunch. When he put his mouth to her ear his breath roared like the sea in a shell. 'Is this okay?' he whispered. 'Do you want this? You must tell me.'

She felt a spasm of impatience. *For God's sake, don't make me say it.*

He drew back. 'Karla?'

She closed her eyes. 'Yes,' she said, her voice cracking with embarrassment. 'Yes, go on, yes.'

CHAPTER SIXTEEN

To lend some semblance of truth to the boast of 'a romantic garden' posted on the blackboard easel out front, the proprietor of the tiny Indian restaurant on Fifth Street had strung garlands of coloured lights across his concrete yard and placed tea-lights, bobbing in bowls of water, on each of the flimsy plastic tables. Overhead, in the branches of a gnarled crab apple tree, a speaker broadcast woozy instrumental medleys of easy-listening classics. In this urban oasis of music and light, Rosa and Chris Jackson were sitting one evening in late July, discussing Chris's latest documentary project about a family of methamphetamine addicts in rural Minnesota.

'The grandfather is my favourite character,' Chris was saying. 'He's this sweet-looking old guy with all this white hair and a big old moustache. You see him sitting around the house in his carpet slippers, watching NASCAR. You think, *Sweet guy.* Then he gets into his car with his fifteen-year-old granddaughter, looking like he's taking her to soccer practice or something, and it turns out he's driving her into town so she can turn tricks. He's his granddaughter's pimp!' He gave a little creaking laugh. 'You gotta love that.'

Rosa, whose attention had been momentarily hijacked by a mellow, saxophonic rendition of 'Tie a Yellow Ribbon', smiled and took a sip of red wine. 'You certainly have some rich material,' she said. It was a while since she had last spoken and she could tell by the exaggerated precision with which she was now forming her words that she had grown a little tipsy in the interim.

'Yeah,' Chris said contentedly, 'I'm excited about it.' He pointed at the plate of sweets in front of them. 'What do you think of the gulab jamon? Out of control, right?'

Rosa gave a queasy smile. The gulab jamon was quite revolting, she thought: a sort of rose-infused gummy bear.

'When I was in India,' Chris went on, 'I was totally addicted to this stuff. Most places in New York don't do it right, but the chef here is really amazing. He used to work for an Indian maharaja or something. He's a really interesting guy. We've hung out a couple of times and smoked bidis together. He's got some great stories . . .'

Rosa sat back, letting the drone of Chris's auto-conversation wash over her. There was a kind of genius to his dullness, she thought. There was nothing you could throw at him that he would not instantly transmute into something achingly uninteresting. Not that it mattered. Tonight, she was sloughing off her judgemental, perfectionist self and going with the flow of things. Chris was fine. She had already decided that she was going to sleep with him.

'This is fun,' he said. 'I'm really glad you agreed to come out tonight.'

'Me too.'

'I was kind of surprised, to be honest. You said no so many times. I figured you were still angry with me.'

'Angry?' Rosa smiled sceptically. Chris seemed far too insubstantial a figure to have ever inspired her wrath.

He gave her a coy look. 'You don't remember, do you?'

'What?'

'Ah well, if you don't remember, maybe we should just let it lie . . .'

'Tell me. When was I angry?'

'The last time we spoke at Bard, you were pissed with me because I'd lost your copy of *The Pedagogy of the Oppressed* and because I hadn't turned up to hand out pamphlets at something or other. You gave me this huge dressing down in the middle of the street.' He paused. 'You really don't remember any of this?'

Rosa shook her head.

'You called me "a complacent cretin".'

'You remember the exact phrase ten years later?'

'Sure. You don't forget something like that.'

'I'm sorry. I must have been extremely obnoxious.'

'No biggie,' Chris said with an unconvincing shrug. 'It's all water under the bridge.'

Rosa looked around the yard. The garlands of coloured lights overhead were beginning to blur and multiply. Partly out of a desire to make up for her past sins and partly out of boredom with the pre-coital preamble, she leaned across the table now and placed her hand lightly on top of Chris's. 'Shall we go somewhere and have sex?'

It took them fifteen minutes to walk to Chris's loft on Second Avenue. Having committed to the evening's denouement, Rosa was anxious to be done with it: Chris was still fiddling with his keys when she pressed him up against the building's heavy iron front door and thrust her tongue in his mouth.

'Take it easy,' he said, pushing her gently away.

Sheepishly, she withdrew and they climbed the six steep flights of stairs to his apartment without further physical contact.

Inside, Chris insisted on opening wine and turning on the stereo. Rosa watched hazily as he fussed over the choice of CD. At last, having settled on the songs of a depressive English folk singer, he turned to her with an amorous smirk. 'Let's get those clothes off you, shall we?'

She had worried that his conscientious mood-setting portended a tediously connoisseurial approach to sex, but this concern proved quite unfounded. Chris fucked with the speed and abstracted efficiency of a dog. The act was accomplished in just under ten minutes.

'Did you come?' he asked afterwards.

Rosa, ever the truth-teller, shook her head.

'Is there something you'd like me to do?'

'No, no,' she said quickly. 'It's fine. I mean . . . I don't have to, every time.'

'Yeah.' He nodded sagely. 'A lot of girls are like that.'

Rosa glanced at him in amusement. How fortunate to be so credulous.

'I had a girlfriend a while back who had an orgasm about once a year,' he said. 'It wasn't like the sex was bad or anything. The sex was amazing, actually. She just never came. So at first I was, like, "This is crazy, you need to go and see somebody." But she was, like, "No, orgasms just aren't that important to me . . ."'

Rosa watched him finger his tiny scribble of chest hair. He was never going to stop talking. The act of intercourse had been a mere caesura in the truly erotic business of listening to himself speak.

'Can I ask you something?' he asked.

'Sure.'

'Do you work out?'

'No.'

'I just wondered because you've got a great body, you know, but if you worked out, you could really tone it.'

'Ah, yes,' Rosa said. 'My room-mate tells me the same thing.'

'You have a room-mate?' Chris laughed in amazement. 'Man, that must be *rough*. I can't imagine having to share a bathroom at our age . . .' His laughter dwindled to a contemplative *Haaaaa*. 'It's funny the way things turn out, isn't it?' he said. 'I mean, I used to be so intimidated by you at Bard. You were so glamorous.'

Rosa registered the insult of the past tense without resentment. Fair was fair: ten years ago she had called him a cretin. He was entitled to some payback.

'I mean,' Chris said, 'if you'd asked me then what you were going to be doing when you were thirty, I would never have guessed that you'd be working in an after-school programme and living with a room-mate. I would have thought you'd be running an African country or something.'

Rosa looked up at the ceiling. What was the Talmudic phrase she had read in one of Rabbi Reinman's books? 'Accept the truth from whomever gives it.' Chris was right. She had not fulfilled her promise. She had lost her way. The proof of it was her presence in this bed.

A sudden nausea came upon her. She sat up and clambered out of bed.

'Have I offended you?' he asked, a little too eagerly.

She shook her head. 'No, not at all. I just need to pee.'

In the bathroom, she surprised a cockroach feasting on Chris's toothbrush. It scuttered across the sink and then froze, as if regretting its cowardice. Rosa had just enough time to kneel down at the toilet before unleashing a terrible, purple gush of tikka masala and red wine into the bowl.

'Hey,' Chris shouted from the other room. 'Do you want to hear some really amazing Ghanaian hip hop?'

'Sure,' she called out. She sat back and wiped her mouth on her forearm. The cockroach was perched on the sink faucet, waving its antennae good-naturedly at her. Through the window above Chris's bathtub, there came a distant drone of traffic and the plaintive *wap wap* of a tattered plastic bag trapped in a tree.

Please, God, she prayed, *if you exist, if you want something from me, give me a sign: tell me what I should do.*

She closed her eyes, waiting for a voice, a sudden gust of wind, the thud of a soap bar falling from its dish. But there was nothing, just the flapping of the plastic bag outside and the tinnitus of Chris's voice wafting down the hall. 'These guys are meant to be really amazing live . . .'

She stood up, disgusted with her own childish egotism. The God she believed in—or wanted to believe in—did not sit about in his cloudy house, waiting to help out drunken doubters with proof of his existence. He was not some whimsical dispenser of signs and special favours. He was *God*, for God's sake.

'Are you okay?' Chris asked when she returned to the bedroom.

'Yeah, fine.'

'I thought maybe you were going to be sick.'

'No, I'm good.'

She began to get dressed.

'What's up? What're you doing?' Chris asked.

'I need to get back.'

'Why?'

She hopped about, trying to force her foot through the twisted leg of her pants. 'I have stuff to do in the morning.'

'Are you mad at me?'

'No.'

'Is it what I said before about—'

'No, really. I just want to sleep in my own bed tonight.'

He watched her putting on her sandals. 'Are we going to get together again?'

She turned to him. He was not a bad person, she thought. A fool, certainly. But not a bad person. 'I don't think so,' she said. She smiled kindly. 'I appreciate your asking, though.'

CHAPTER SEVENTEEN

Karla woke up agitated, mystified. She turned off her alarm clock and looked around the room. 'Mike?'

She usually loved the mornings when Mike left for work early. Today, though, the stillness of the apartment felt ominous. She sat up, trying to locate the source of her unease, and abruptly, as the events of the previous evening came back to her, she lay down again. What had she done? *What had she done?* She pressed the heels of her palms against her eyes, until she saw dancing dots of phosphorescent blue. The weight of her sin lay on her like a rock, pinioning her against the bed. She could not go into work, that was clear. She could not possibly face Khaled. She would have to phone in and pretend to be sick.

In the bathroom, she caught sight of herself in the mirror and gave a little cry of anguish. Her chin was red and raw where Khaled had burned her with his bristle and there was a lurid, purple-and-green bruise on her hip where she had stumbled against the corner of her desk during their embrace. How would she possibly explain these marks to Mike?

The colleague who answered at the hospital was full of sympathetic concern when Karla said she was unwell. 'It's probably that stomach flu that everyone's been getting. Poor you, Karla.'

Karla grimaced in shame. This was the first time she had missed work in five years and the only time in her professional life that she had lied in order to do so. 'It's no big deal,' she said, 'I'll probably be fine by tomorrow.'

All day she lay on the sofa in her living room, flicking restlessly between daytime soap operas, trying to fend off the visions flitting through her head. It was a disgusting thing she'd done: disgusting and irresponsible and vile. She had not wanted to do it—not really. It had been a temporary madness. He had put his tongue in her belly button. He had even tried to lick—oh God. What a horrible, horrible man to do that. She was never going to speak to him again.

Mike was upset to come home in the evening and find Karla still in her nightgown. Karla rarely admitted to any sort of incapacity. To have her malingering about the place made him nervous and irritable.

'What's the matter? Are you depressed?' he asked accusingly.

'No,' Karla said, 'it's just a stomach bug, I told you.' This was the first time they had spoken since their row about her essay. He had already been asleep by the time she got back from the hospital last night. She was shocked to discover that her guilt did not altogether cancel out her lingering fury.

'Why didn't you go to the doctor today?' he demanded.

'There was no point. It's getting better. I'll be up for work tomorrow.'

He pointed at her face. 'What's that?'

'What?'

He came over and prodded roughly at her chin. 'That.'

'Ow.' She batted him away. 'Don't.'

'Well, what is it?'

'I don't know. I've been using a new moisturizer. I think it's given me an allergic reaction.'

He drew back in distaste. 'You should watch out it doesn't get infected.'

At work the next day, Karla found a note under her door.

Dear Karla,
I came to find you but you weren't here. I hope everything is all right. Please call me on my cellphone as soon as you get this.
Love, Khaled

She was still studying it when he walked in.

'You're back,' he said, closing the door behind him. 'I was worried. Are you okay?'

'Yes, of course.' *Look at him*, she thought. *He's nothing. A tubby man with a bald spot.*

Khaled smiled. 'I'm glad.' He stopped and pointed at her chin. 'Was that me?'

'Yes.'

He paused. 'I have done something and, if it is the wrong thing, you must tell me.'

'What?'

'I booked a hotel room.'

295

'Oh God.'

'I made it for tomorrow night. I thought, since you have yoga on Thursdays . . . It's a nice place, you know. Not sleazy.'

'Oh God, oh God.'

'I'm sorry. It's too soon, you're right.'

She looked at him, standing with his eyes to the floor and his arms dangling loosely at his side, like a reprimanded schoolboy. With a suddenness that made him flinch, she grasped his sleeve and pulled him towards her.

*   *   *

The Regency Suites was downtown, in Battery Park City, safely remote from both home and work. To get there, Karla had to take a 4 train, get off at Forty-second Street, take the shuttle from Grand Central to Times Square and then catch a 3 train to Chambers Street. She walked the rest of the way, using a map that Khaled had downloaded for her. It was a warm, pink-skied evening and the streets were crowded with people spilling out from restaurants and bars. On every block, it seemed, there was a different gaggle of tipsy women in miniskirts and strapless tops, screaming merry obscenities at one another.

She had always dreaded summer. It was the season of disclosure, of floaty fabrics and bare flesh and open toes, the time of year in which her exile from the world of carefree fun and sensual pleasures was driven home most painfully. In preparation for this evening, she had tussled in and out of several outfits including—madly—some items from her reliquary of 'skinny' clothes. She

296

had tried on a rubbery girdle that purported to Make You Lose Ten Pounds Instantly! but alas, the pounds had not been lost, only redistributed to either end of the rigid garment. Ultimately, she had opted for a tent-sized, calf-length black dress, which her mother had once told her made her look like the prow of a ship. She was, she thought, a comically implausible adulteress.

The hotel had an atrium lobby with a marble floor and several outsize chairs clad in candy-coloured velvet dotting its perimeter. Behind the front desk, there was an abstract mural—rough stripes of yellow and red and blue paint—and three clerks, all wearing black suits with mandarin collars. Karla wondered anxiously how much money Khaled had paid for a room in this frighteningly chic establishment. When she approached the desk and gave Khaled's name, she was amazed to receive a smile from the clerk and more astonished still to be given the room key without any questions or argument. Khaled had not yet arrived.

She rode the elevator to the eleventh floor, clutching her plastic key card. Room 1126 was at the far end of the corridor. She approached it slowly, as if the secret of her assignation were held in a bowl on her head and it was only by maintaining the most scrupulously even gait that she could keep it from sloshing on the carpet. At the door, she slid her card, now slippery with sweat, into its slot. A small green light flashed and she turned the handle.

She walked around the small beige room, breathing in its chill mustiness. Two tiles of chocolate had been laid on the bed pillows. She picked one up and ate it while considering the brown floral bedcover. She had seen a news programme once in which an investigative team had shone infra-red light on hotel bedspreads, revealing gruesome palimpsests of semen and blood stains. She decided to pull the cover off.

As soon as she had done so she regretted it. The bed looked horribly bare now, as if an operation were about to be performed on it. And what if Khaled interpreted her gesture as sexual impatience? Hurriedly she shook out the bedspread and put it back on the bed.

Feeling hot and a little breathless, she went to the window to see if it could be opened. When she pushed the curtains aside, she gave a small cry of surprise. The room faced directly on to the site where the World Trade Center had stood. She had never been to 'Ground Zero' before. The idea of making a special trip downtown to gawk at it from a viewing stand had always seemed to her in very bad taste. The terrible piles of twisted metal that she had seen in newspaper photographs had been cleared away now. In their place lay an enormous, antiseptic grey scar, surrounded by chickenwire fence and bathed in the surreal white glow of stadium lights.

She was still staring out at her view when she heard the door half opening behind her.

'Who is it?' she called out.

'Me.'

She went to the door and undid the chain. Khaled was standing in the corridor, looking eager and slightly harried, with a plastic bag in his hand. They smiled nervously at one another.

'It's a nice room,' she said, gesturing around her

like a realtor.

'Really?' he asked. 'It's okay? There wasn't a picture on the computer, so I had to take a chance.' He paused for a moment to survey the furnishings. 'Oh, yes . . . it's nice.'

He pulled out a bottle of wine from his plastic bag. 'It's French.'

'Nice.'

'The man in the store recommended it.'

She felt a pang of sadness, picturing him in the wine shop, earnestly canvassing the opinion of experts.

'I think I need to take a shower,' he said. 'Would you mind?'

'Go ahead.' Karla sat down on the bed and examined the tiger stripes on the carpet where the vacuum had rubbed the pile the wrong way. Everything was wrong. She had made a terrible mistake.

When Khaled returned, he was dressed in one of the hotel's white, waffle-weave robes, with a towel around his neck, like a boxer. 'That feels better,' he said. 'It's so hot outside . . .' He paused, registering her unhappy expression. 'What's the matter?'

She looked away. 'I have a bit of a headache.'

'Shall I give you a neck rub?'

'No, it's okay.'

He sat down heavily on the bed. 'You've changed your mind.'

She gave a little moan. 'I'm sorry.'

'It's okay.'

'No, it's *not* okay. I hate myself for doing this to you. It's just I've never . . . I'm not sure I can do something like this.'

He nodded. 'I understand.'

'I'll go halves with you on the room. I mean, I was going to anyway—'

'Please,' he said sharply. 'Don't insult me.' He picked up the bottle of wine that was sitting on the side table and examined it. 'It's my fault. I shouldn't have pushed you so fast.'

'You didn't push me, Khaled.'

He set the bottle carefully back on the table. 'I had a dream about you last night, you know.'

'Yes?'

'We were in a park together. We were lying on a blanket, eating a dessert—a dessert that we make in Egypt for special occasions, weddings. You liked it very much. You asked for more and more—'

Karla snorted. 'That figures.'

'And then, after a time,' Khaled said, 'I began to undress you.' He shot her a cautious, sidelong glance. 'It was very quiet. There was no one else around. You had a beautiful smile on your face.'

Karla took a deep breath.

'It went very slowly,' he went on. 'You were wearing many layers of clothing and every time I removed a garment, I had to stop to look at you. There was honeysuckle near by and the scent was very strong. I wanted . . .' He paused. 'Well, when I finally uncovered your . . .' He bowed his head. His hands were shaking.

Karla stood up and went towards the door.

'Don't!' he said. 'It's all right. I'll stop.'

She halted. 'No, it's not that. I just . . . if we're going to . . .' She smiled apologetically. 'I need the lights off.'

CHAPTER EIGHTEEN

'Thank you for coming in this afternoon,' Dr Krauss said, shutting his office door and gesturing for Audrey and Rosa to sit down. 'I hope the timing wasn't too inconvenient for you.' He perched on the side of his desk with one buttock on, one buttock off. 'I've asked for this meeting because—'

'Have you been away somewhere?' Audrey interrupted.

He paused, perplexed. 'Uh, yes, actually. I was just in Hawaii with my family.'

'I thought so. You look like you got some sun damage.'

'Ha, yes.' His hand rose defensively to his florid neck. 'You're right, I did get a bit burned, I'm afraid.'

'That's not good. I'd have thought, you being a doctor, you'd be extra careful about the sun.'

He chuckled good-humouredly. 'Well, we doctors aren't infallible, you know.'

'Tell me about it,' Audrey said unsmilingly.

He pulled himself up straight. '*Anyway*, as I—'

'Hawaii, did you say? That must have been nice. Pricey, though, I expect.'

The doctor's eyelashes fluttered. 'Well, we got a very good deal on the flights, so actually it wasn't too—'

Rosa scowled at the ceiling, infuriated by her mother's childish baiting of the doctor. 'You were saying, Dr Krauss?'

'Yes, right. Well, now . . .' His left foot began to

beat a tattoo against the side of the desk. 'In cases like Joel's, there often comes a moment—a very difficult moment for all concerned—when we have to take a long, hard look at the value of continuing the rehabilitation effort. Joel is, as you know, dealing with a number of health issues. The influenza is obviously the main concern at the moment, but there is also the infection around his trach site and the decubitus ulcers—'

'What are decubitus ulcers?' Rosa asked.

'Bedsores,' Audrey said. 'He means the bedsores. Which, by the way, Joel wouldn't have if he'd been getting proper care in this place—'

Dr Krauss made an odd, gargling sound somewhere in the back of his throat: a synecdoche of laughter. 'That's not *quite* fair, Mrs Litvinoff—'

'Yeah, yeah, whatever.'

Dr Krauss ploughed on. 'As you know, the most recent EEGs were not encouraging. On the basis of those results we have to conclude that Joel's chances of regaining a reasonable degree of mental function are very slim indeed at this point. If we then take into account his age and the length of time that he has been unconscious, and the various infections that he's fighting, there seems to me to be a strong case for reassessing his care plan.'

Rosa glanced at her mother. Audrey was sitting quite still, gazing at a vicious little bouquet of sharpened pencils on Dr Krauss's desk.

'What would that mean, exactly?' Rosa asked.

The doctor made a steeple with his hands. 'Well. There are several options you might want to think about. Joel has never had a DNR order, so that would be a place to start. Some families who find themselves in this situation will choose to withhold antibiotics, which is really a way of allowing nature to take its course. There is also the option of taking out the feeding tube—'

'Joel's got bedsores!' Audrey cried. 'My mum had bedsores. No one suggested killing her off because of them.'

'No, no, of course not. Perhaps I didn't make myself clear. The bedsores are just one of a raft of serious problems that Joel is confronting.'

'It was *you* who bloody gave him the bedsores and now you're using them as an excuse to exterminate him.'

'Okay,' Rosa said quickly. 'You've given us a lot to think about, Doctor. We appreciate your having been so straightforward. Perhaps the best thing now is for us to go away and discuss this with the rest of the family.'

* * *

'Joel's not making them enough money,' Audrey said, once they had left the doctor's office. 'That's what this is about, you know. They want to get rid of him so they can put someone more profitable in his bed.'

Rosa stared bleakly down the corridor. 'Let's not worry about what *they* want, Mom. The question is, what do *we* want? What would *Dad* want? I mean, if there's really no chance that he'll get better—'

'*Ohh*, I see where this is going. You agree with Ichabod Crane, do you? You think we should just kill him?'

'Would you stop it, Mom? You're not the only

303

one who loves him, you know. This is difficult for all of us. I'm just saying, if he has no quality of life—'

'How the fuck do you know if he has quality of life? You're not in his brain, are you? There's this book I read that says there's a lot of evidence to suggest coma patients have rich dream-lives. Who are you to say that's not worthwhile?'

'Oh, *Mom.*'

'What? This isn't bullshit. Read the book if you don't believe me.'

'He's in a vegetative state, Mom. Vegetables don't have rich dream-lives.'

'Well, thanks for the morale raiser. Thanks a fucking lot. That really makes me feel super.'

'I'm not trying to make you feel good. I'm trying to figure out what's best for Dad.'

'And I'm not? Is that what you're saying?' Audrey hitched up the strap of her handbag and began to stride away down the hall.

'Where are you going?'

Audrey waved her hand vaguely. 'I don't know. I'll be back in a bit.'

While she was waiting for Audrey to return, Rosa sat in her father's room, going through the pile of CDs in his bedside cabinet. During the early stages of Joel's coma, Audrey had demanded that music be played in his room at all times. But the hope that he might be triggered into consciousness by a familiar chord progression or lyric had long since faded: these days, the CDs were rarely brought out. Rosa gloomily inspected the titles: *Strauss's Last Songs, Louis and Ella, Aretha Franklin Sings Gospel*, the *St Matthew Passion*, the *Coronation Anthems* . . . She smiled. She and her father had once had a furious fight about the Coronation Anthems. She had attacked him for taking pleasure in 'reactionary' music that celebrated monarchy.

'But, sweetie,' he'd replied, 'this is some of the loveliest music ever composed.'

'There's no such thing as aesthetic "loveliness" independent of politics and ideology, Dad.'

'Isn't there? Well, then, you're just going to have to forgive your father his little weakness—'

'*Why?* Why should you be forgiven? Why shouldn't you be held to account for your contradictions?'

'Well, you know, Rosa, I've always said, self-contradiction is one of the occupational hazards of being an American progressive—'

'Bullshit. You just want to have your cake and eat it.'

'Listen, I respect your need to establish your independence from me. Challenging your parents is a necessary and valuable stage in your development. But right now, you're being a little bit of a pill—'

'You're such a hypocrite! You sit around congratulating yourself on how much you hate the system, how committed you are to the struggle. But the minute I object to one of your sacred pieces of classy art, you tell me to shut up.'

Joel finally lost his temper. 'How *dare* you talk to me that way! You little brat! You think you can lecture *me* on socialism? I've spent my life—'

'Yeah, I know. You've spent your life protecting the few pathetic rights that the ruling elite sees fit to grant its workers.'

Oh, what an abominable creep she had been!

305

All those years she had tortured him with her lectures—and for what? Not a single one of her precious principles had survived the test of time. Now her father was going to die and she would never have the chance to say she was sorry or to ask his forgiveness.

She took the disc out of its box and slipped it into the CD player. It would have suited her remorseful mood to be slain by the beauty of what she had once so arrogantly dismissed, but in truth, the music still sounded pretty silly to her. A bunch of snobby-sounding Englishmen tootling fruitily about king-worship. She was about to turn it off when a tall woman with long, silvery dreadlocks came into the room.

'I'm sorry,' the woman said, 'I was told there was no one with him. I'll come back later.'

'It's okay.' Rosa waved her in. 'You don't need to go.'

'Are you sure?'

'Sure.'

The woman studied her face. 'You must be Joel's daughter.'

'Yes, I'm Rosa.'

The woman did not introduce herself. And there was something grand in her manner that made Rosa hesitant to inquire her name. Perhaps she expected Rosa to know. She walked over to the foot of the bed now and considered Joel's waxen form.

'How is he doing?'

'Not too good,' Rosa said. 'He's got a bunch of different infections. They're pretty worried about him.'

The woman nodded. 'Right.'

306

Rosa glanced at her approvingly. A lot of Joel's visitors felt obliged to let you know their grief in tiresomely graphic ways. It was a relief not to have to cater to any showy misery.

'This is nice,' the woman said, gesturing at the CD player.

'Yes.'

They stood and listened.

Upon thy right hand did stand the queen in
   vesture of gold
And the king shall have pleasure!
Pleasure! Pleasure!
And the king shall have pleasure in thy
   be-au-ty.

'It's Handel,' Rosa said, after a moment.

The woman's brows arched in amusement. 'I know.'

'I'm sorry,' Rosa said, blushing. '*I* don't know anything about classical music, so I stupidly assume that other people don't.'

From behind them now, there came a cry—a piercing ululation of pain and surprise. They swung around to see Audrey standing wild-eyed on the threshold. 'Get out, you whore!' she screamed.

Rosa stared at her in horror. 'Mom, *please*, we have a visitor!'

'She's the one I'm talking to!' Audrey screamed. 'Go on! Get out! Get ooouut!' Her mouth was so wide open that Rosa could see the vaulted arch of her palate and the uvula waggling lewdly at the back of her throat.

The woman spoke with icy composure. 'Calm down, Audrey. I didn't come here to fight with

307

you.'

There was a moment's silence and then Audrey rushed forward, her arm held high in the air, ready to strike.

*   *   *

For a while, Karla feared disaster. She was graceless. Gargantuan. Her arms kept getting trapped in awkward positions. She did not know how to kiss properly. Khaled was sure to be disgusted by her. In a spirit of pre-emption, she grew cold and critical. His mouth was too wet. He was too heavy. His crowing enthusiasm was embarrassing and jejeune. Mike, in his poker-faced decorousness, had never shamed her by looking at her or making her look at him. He had certainly never *spoken* during the act.

At length, Khaled got up to fetch a condom from his jacket. Lying back on the pillows, Karla watched him as he moved across the room in a knock-kneed trot, his arms shielding his belly and his hands cupping his groin, like a man in a sex-farce.

'You're shy!' she exclaimed.

He turned round. 'A bit, yes.' He glanced down at himself. 'I am not a hunk, I'm afraid.'

The candour of the admission astonished her. How trustingly he laid himself bare! It was as if the possibility that they would be anything other than kind and forgiving of one another had not occurred to him. The tight little fist of tension in her stomach began to unfurl now. She felt giddy, freed, like a child who has finally escaped adult oversight. In this hotel room—in this bed—they

308

could do *anything*, she thought, and no one would stop them. 'Quick,' she whispered, holding out her arms to him. 'Quick, come here.' She was not making a discovery, it seemed to her, so much as retrieving a long-forgotten knowledge. For, once upon a time, before unhappy experience had inhibited her imagination, had she not *assumed* that adult love would be this way? Had she not, in her virginal innocence, had a presentiment of just this infinite sensual possibility?

Later, she slept. When she awoke, she found Khaled sitting on the edge of the bed, watching her. A thin shaft of blue light lay across the bedspread.

'What time is it?' she asked.

'Eight o'clock. Five minutes past. When do you have to leave?'

'Soon.' She paused. 'Not for a while.'

They smiled at one another. 'Did you look out of the window yet?' she asked.

'No.'

'Go look.'

She observed him tenderly as he went over to the window. His soft round torso and skinny legs reminded her of the figures that she and her siblings used to make with potatoes and cocktail sticks when they were children.

'Oh!' he said when he pulled back the curtains. He stood looking out for a moment or two. Then he drew the curtains and came back to bed.

'My cousin, he owns a deli in Yonkers,' he said as he lay down beside her. 'After 9/11, the police came to his home and took him away for questioning. They wanted'—he began to laugh softly—'they wanted to know why he had a picture of the Twin Towers on the wall of his restaurant.'

'You're kidding!' Karla said. 'How long did they keep him?'

'Oh, not very long. Maybe two days.'

'My God, that's terrible!'

'Well, he didn't like it, being put in jail like a common criminal. But there were people who had much worse.'

'There's American justice for you.'

Khaled shook his head. 'You're always saying bad things about America. This is a beautiful country. You don't know.'

Karla sat up. 'How can you say that after what you just told me?'

'My cousin wasn't beaten or tortured. He was set free after two days. In other places in the world, we would never have seen him again.'

'Khaled! America is bombing civilians in Afghanistan and, any minute now, we're going to invade Iraq. That's all okay with you?'

'Oh,' Khaled waved his hand. 'All countries are like this. All of them—they would do just the same if they had as much money and power as America. It's the way the world works, the way people are.'

'But, Khaled, nothing would ever change if everyone took that attitude.'

Khaled shrugged again. 'Things *don't* change.'

'Yes they do. You don't think people achieve things by fighting for their rights? Look at the union movement. It's transformed the lives of millions of American workers over the last century—'

Khaled sighed. 'You're probably right.' He began to stroke her back. 'Is this nice?'

'But wait a minute—'

'Let's not argue.'

'We're not arguing,' she said stubbornly. 'We were having a discussion.'

'Okay, let's not discuss it then,' Khaled said.

'Khaled, you really don't have any interest in politics, do you?'

'If I say no, will you be disappointed in me?'

'Yes.'

'Okay then, of course I am interested. Now, I would like to make love to you again.'

Karla looked down at him. His face was in shadow, so that only the whites of his eyes and the gleaming curve of his cheekbone were visible. When she was younger, boys had asked her to 'go to bed' with them, or sometimes to 'go all the way'. These days, she and Mike usually negotiated, in a businesslike way, about whether or not they were going to 'have sex'. But no one had ever proposed 'making love' to her.

Her cellphone began to ring. She rolled over to examine the caller ID screen. 'It's my sister.'

'Don't answer it,' he said.

'I have to. It might be about my dad.' She picked up the phone.

Rosa's voice was garbled and she was speaking very fast. 'Slow down,' Karla said, swatting Khaled away as he leaned in to kiss her. 'Tell me again.' She got out of bed and walked into the bathroom.

When she re-emerged, she had put on a robe.

'What is it?' Khaled asked. 'Is your father all right?'

'Yes. It's . . . I can't really work it out. My sister says my mom attacked someone at the hospital.'

Part Four

CHAPTER NINETEEN

A deer stood at the bottom of the long sloping garden, listening to the strange sounds that were floating down the lawn. Slowly, with an elegant, high-stepping gait, he moved forward in the direction of the noise. Just over the rise of the hill, he caught sight of Jean kneeling in a flower bed. She was wearing a boat captain's hat and singing as she dug holes for daffodil bulbs.

Early one morning, just as the sun was ri-ising,
I heard a maiden singing in the va-alley below.

All through the summer, the grounds of Jean's house in Bucks County had been noisy with the drone of dragonflies and the lascivious croaking of frogs, but it was quiet September now. The wild blackberries along the driveway had gone to seed. The croquet hoops had been put away. Jean's voice rang out through the chill air like a bell in a canyon.

Oh, don't deceive me, oh, never leave me
How could you use a poor maiden so?

She stopped abruptly and glanced up at the house, fearful that she might have woken Audrey. The poor thing needed her sleep. For the last five weeks, while Joel had been fighting pneumonia, Audrey had been constantly at his bedside, hectoring doctors and haranguing nurses, insisting that he not be allowed to die. Through the sheer force of her will, it seemed, she had got her wish and Joel had been officially pronounced out of danger. She, though, was a wreck: pouchy-eyed with exhaustion and savagely thin. She had arrived last night, planning to return to New York with Lenny first thing this morning, but Jean had taken one look at her and insisted that she stay a day or so to rest.

Jean heard something move behind her. She turned around and saw the deer loitering twenty feet away on the lawn. 'Hello, you handsome thing!' she murmured. 'How are you today?' The deer pawed at the grass and looked off into the middle distance, like a sulky child.

'Off you go then,' Jean said, raising her voice. 'You're not having any of my flowers today.' She waved her hands. 'Go on! Shoo!'

The deer gazed at her impassively for a moment, then turned away and, with two arching leaps, disappeared back into the woods.

* * *

Up on the top floor of the house Audrey lay in a frilly four-poster bed, listening to the throaty sounds of the mourning doves out on her windowsill. She was remembering a disastrous excursion to Kent that her family had taken one Bank Holiday weekend when she was ten. Her parents, who rarely ever ventured beyond Hackney, had approached the manicured Home Counties with all the trepidation of travellers entering an uncharted area of South American rainforest. Unwilling to broach the green silence of the countryside proper, they spent the first day of

316

their visit wandering about the drizzly precincts of the local village. (Audrey's mother, who was always hankering after some elusive notion of authentic Englishness, wanted to have tea in a teashop, but Mr Howard had vetoed this on grounds of expense.) On the Sunday, in one great stab at adventure, they hired bicycles and wobbled off on a ride. Shortly after setting out, however, Mr Howard developed a painful rash on his legs and, convinced that he had been bitten by a snake, he immediately retreated to the bed and breakfast to summon medical assistance. When the doctor arrived an hour later, slightly drunk and extremely ill-tempered at being called away from his Sunday lunch, he took one look at Mr Howard's shins and clapped his hand to his brow. 'Good God, man,' he exclaimed, 'have you never heard of stinging nettles?' Mute with shame, the family had returned to London that same afternoon.

Audrey was very sorry now that she had agreed to stay the weekend with Jean. She wondered how the two of them would fill the time. There would be a walk, she supposed—there was always a bloody walk—and perhaps, at some point, a game of cards. Then what? She stretched out her arms and surveyed the sea of rustic tchotchke that surrounded her bed. Jean's modestly sized guest room contained, among other things, a nineteenth-century commode, a sign for an English pub called the Crooked Billet, two milking stools, a rocking chair painted with daisies, ten framed embroidery samplers and a reproduction Welsh dresser. In the old days, when Jean's husband had been alive, Jean's passion for crap like this had been subject to some constraint. Max had insisted that most of her

317

flea-market acquisitions be consigned to the barn and the attic. But since his death twelve years ago, Jean's obsession had been liberated. The house now resembled a shrine to Mrs Tiggywinkle.

Audrey got up and dressed herself hurriedly in the clothes she had been wearing the night before. On her way downstairs, she passed Lenny's room. There was a sticker on the door, a souvenir from the days when Jean and Max played host to city children from the Fresh Air Fund. WARNING, it read, GIRLS HAVING FUN! Audrey knocked. When she received no answer she peeked inside. The room was very clean and orderly—eerily so, for a place being inhabited by Lenny. A folded towel and washcloth hung neatly on a rack in the corner. On the wall over the dresser, Lenny had pinned up the first verse of the Serenity Prayer:

> God grant me the SERENITY to
> accept the things I cannot change;
> COURAGE to change the things I can;
> and WISDOM to know the difference.

Audrey made a face and quickly closed the door before continuing on down to the kitchen. Here, on a table crowded with butter dishes shaped like cows and honeypots shaped like beehives and teapots shaped like English country cottages, she found a note from Jean: 'Am in the garden. Bagels and croissants in the cupboard.'

She poured herself a cup of coffee from the pot on the stove and went outside. It had rained the night before and the ground was soft beneath her Chinese slippers. Her breath formed wet, coffee-scented clouds.

At the sound of the screen door banging shut, Jean, who was now digging the flower beds at the foot of her barn, swivelled around. '*Hello*, dear! Did you sleep well?'

'Like a log. Where's Lenny?'

'Gone to a meeting in Doylestown.'

'*Another* meeting? Wasn't he at one last night?'

'He goes twice a day, one in the morning and one in the evening. He's very good about it.'

'How does he get there then?'

'I drive him mostly. One of his NA friends gave him a lift today.'

'Oh.' Audrey watched with a small grimace as Jean pulled a fat, pink worm from the soil and deposited it on one side. 'I had a look in at his room on the way down,' she said. 'It's ever so tidy in there. Have you been cleaning up after him?'

Jean shook her head. 'No, no, he keeps it that way himself.'

'Bloody hell. *I've* never been able to make him pick his clothes up off the floor. You must have some power over him that I don't.' She hesitated, waiting for Jean to contradict her, but Jean just shrugged and went on digging in the flower bed.

Audrey wandered down the lawn to the pond. Beneath the lacy-edged lily pads that matted its surface, a goldfish was creeping through the weed-silted murk. She smiled, recalling a winter evening years ago, when Joel had gone skinny-dipping in this pond. It had been a dare of some sort—or a forfeit—she wasn't sure. She and Jean and Max had stayed inside the house and watched from the window as Joel went streaking through the garden. His cries when he plunged into the icy water had sent all the birds on the hillside squawking into the

319

air. Later on, in bed, she had found a shred of pondweed still clinging to his pubic hair. Joel had never let the countryside intimidate him. He had simply filled its creepy stillness with his energy and noise; transformed it into another outpost of Joeldom.

'Isn't the garden looking lovely today?' Jean called. 'I do love this time of year. All the lovely fall *gunge*. I wish you could have been here this summer, though. The fireflies were *stupendous*.'

Audrey nodded absently. 'Yeah?'

'Oh yes. The garden just *teemed*. It was a real light show . . .'

Audrey looked around, wondering how long Jean was going to talk about nature. 'What's that over there?' she said, pointing to a freshly whitewashed shed at the back of the barn. 'That wasn't there the last time I came.'

'Oh no, it's always been there, I've just had it done up a bit. I've made it my writing nook.'

Audrey's eyebrows rose satirically. 'Your what?'

'I go in there to write my journal and poems and whatnot. I find it's the only place I can really concentrate.'

Audrey smiled. Jean really was a preposterous woman at times.

'Now look here,' Jean said, 'I've got hundreds of bulbs to plant. Would you like to give me a hand?'

'I don't think so, Jean. I don't know anything about gardening . . .'

'Don't be silly. Planting bulbs is as easy as pie. I'll show you.'

'Nah.' Audrey walked over to the porch step and began to roll a joint.

'I was thinking,' Jean said. 'You don't need to

leave tomorrow night. Lenny's in no hurry to get back. You could stay on a few extra days and really recuperate.'

'No,' Audrey said quickly. 'I have to go. I can't leave Joel for that long.'

'But the girls are there. Surely they can handle things for a bit?'

Audrey shook her head. 'They can't take care of him the way I can. They don't know how to deal with the doctors. I need to be there.'

Jean went on digging. 'How *are* things with the girls?' she asked.

'Oh, all right. Karla goes about looking like someone told her Santa Claus doesn't exist. Rosa's still busy being outraged and disgusted.'

'Well, I dare say she feels a lot of anger on your behalf, Audrey. Children always feel very protective towards the wronged parent—'

Audrey lit her joint and exhaled impatiently. 'Bollocks. Rosa's not worried about *me*. I don't even come into it. It's all about how betrayed *she* feels, how deeply, deeply disappointed she is with her daddy for not being the celibate saint she thought he was—' She stopped, having spotted Lenny coming up the gravel driveway. 'Hello, love,' she called out. 'Where's your lift then? Don't tell me you walked?'

Lenny shook his head. 'Nah, I got dropped off at the bottom of the drive.'

He had caught a bit of sun since Audrey had last seen him and put on some weight.

'Don't you look handsome?' she cooed. 'Come on'—she held out her arms—'come over here and give your old mum a hug.'

Lenny walked a little way towards the porch and

then halted. He gestured at her joint. 'It'd be really helpful if you didn't do that around me just now.'

Audrey looked at the joint and then back at Lenny. 'What—you mean—oh, right!'

Lenny waited until she had snuffed the joint out on the sole of her slipper and put the stub in her pocket before coming forward to embrace her.

'So how are you, sweetie?' Audrey whispered in his ear.

'Good,' Lenny said, stepping back. '*Really* good.'

Audrey nodded, obscurely put off by his aggressive assertion of well-being. 'I'm glad.' She patted her pockets. 'You got any fags on you?'

'No, I've been trying to cut down. I only smoke in the evenings now.'

'Ohhh! Aren't you being good!'

'Well, I've been trying to take care of myself—eat right and whatever.'

'Lenny goes for a run most mornings, don't you, Lenny?' Jean said.

Audrey laughed. 'My God, I can't imagine you as a *jogger*, Len.'

'It's the endorphins,' Lenny said earnestly. 'They really make you feel amazing. Dave—you know, my sponsor?—he turned me on to running.'

'Yeah?'

'Yeah. Dave's a really amazing guy, the best sponsor I ever had. He really kicks my ass, you know? Doesn't let me get away with any bullshit.'

'That's nice.'

'Actually, Dave's going to come by this afternoon. If that's okay with you?'

'Sure, why not?'

'Just to hang out and have a coffee. He wants to meet you.'

'Fine,' Audrey said, a little mystified. 'Whatever you like.'

'All right!' Lenny slapped his thigh resolutely. 'I'm going in to get changed now. I've got some work to do for Jean.'

'What work?'

'I've been stripping down this dining-room set for her. I need to get it varnished today.'

'Oh, go on! You can stop for five minutes to talk to your mum. It's not as if Jean's running a bloody labour camp, are you, Jean?'

'No,' Jean said. 'My goodness, of course not.'

'See? Jean doesn't mind if you take a break.'

Lenny shook his head. 'No. I promised I'd get the job finished before I went back. I want to keep my promise.' He stepped past Audrey and went into the house.

Audrey gave a little jump as the swing door slammed shut. She looked at Jean. 'Well, *he's* very full of piss and vinegar, isn't he?'

* * *

Dave turned up at four o'clock. He was a short, bearded man in his early forties—sinewy and handsome in a weathered, sea-captainy sort of way. He stood up when Audrey entered the kitchen and shook her hand with a lot of meaningful eye contact. 'It's great to meet you, Audrey. I've heard a lot about you.'

'Oh yeah?' Audrey said, disliking him already. 'All good, I hope?'

Dave laughed. 'All good.'

'So what do you do for a living when you're not looking after Lenny?'

'Actually, Audrey, I own my own carpentry business in Doylestown.'

'Oh, good for you.' There was something irritating about the way he kept using her first name. It was the sort of smarmy trick that politicians used when they were trying to be matey with old ladies at campaign stops.

'Dave's not just a carpenter, Mom,' Lenny added eagerly. 'He's more of an artisan. He does this really intricate carved work. You should see this stair rail he's just finished for some people in Frenchtown. It's got, like, faces and flowers and weird little designs all over it. Jean's thinking of commissioning one.'

'Is she now?'

'Lenny's been helping me out here and there in the workshop,' Dave said. 'He shows a lot of promise.'

'Uh-huh.'

'In fact, we've been talking about him coming to work for me.'

'I'd be like an apprentice, Mom,' Lenny broke in.

Audrey chuckled. 'Well, that's not going to work, is it, love? You can't commute down here from New York every day.'

Dave and Lenny exchanged quick glances. 'No, that's the thing,' Lenny said. 'I've been thinking that maybe I would come back and stay here for a while—get a place in Doylestown.'

'Oh, Len, forget it. You hate the country.'

'Well, Audrey.' Dave leaned across the table towards her. 'Lenny feels—and I agree—that going back to New York at this stage in his recovery might not be the best thing for him right

324

now.'

'How's that?'

'It's been so healthy for me being here, Mom,' Lenny said. 'I'm just beginning to feel really good about myself. If I go back to New York, all the work I've done on myself is going to be . . .'

'The trouble is, New York is the primary site of his addiction,' Dave said.

'All the people who enable me are there,' Lenny added.

'I've never noticed you needing anyone to enable you, Len. You've always seemed to be perfectly good at enabling yourself.'

'Yeah, but, Mom—'

'I would have thought being at home with your family was a lot better for you than hanging around in Bumfuck, Pennsylvania, with a lot of strangers.'

'They're not strangers,' Lenny said. 'I've got some really good friends here.'

'And, with all due respect, Audrey,' Dave said, 'family is often a big part of an addict's problem.'

'Excuse me?'

'Don't get me wrong. I know you love your son and you want the best for him, but I'm sure you're aware, family relationships can sometimes evolve into co-dependencies that are really unhelpful.'

'Oh, I see, *I'm* the problem, am I?'

'Don't take this the wrong way, Audrey. All we're saying is—'

'Crap. All you're saying is crap.'

Lenny blinked at her reproachfully. 'Dave's only trying to help, Mom.'

Audrey stood up and yawned loudly. 'You'll have to excuse me now. I have a crossword to do.'

Next door in Jean's sitting room, Audrey cleared a space among the sofa cushions and sat down, waiting for Lenny to pursue her. The motif on the toile de jouy cushion covers depicted an eighteenth-century lady and her admirer picnicking on the steps of a ruined summer house while a blank-faced rustic trudged past, leading a goat on a string. Audrey smiled bitterly. *Bloody country life*.

Several minutes went by and she was beginning to think that Lenny was not coming after all when at last he entered the room.

'Has Captain Sanctimonious buggered off then?' she asked.

'No, we're going to a meeting in a bit. I just wanted to talk to you before I went.'

'Oh.'

'You mustn't take this personally, Mom.'

'I don't take it personally.'

'Are you sure? Because it seems like—'

'What about Tanya?' Audrey interrupted. 'Is she going to move here too?'

'No.' Lenny said slowly. 'Tanya isn't a person I need in my life right now.'

'Is that what Chairman Dave says?'

'It's got nothing to do with Dave.'

'Of course not. So have you told her that you're dumping her?'

Lenny smacked his brow with the heel of his palm. 'Why are you so worried about *Tanya* all of a sudden? You don't even like her, Mom.'

'I like her better than that git in the kitchen. What's the story with him, anyway? Is he gay?'

326

Lenny shook his head sorrowfully. 'Why would you ask something like that?'

'I don't know. It just seems a bit odd to me, the way he's glommed on to you so quickly. It's all a bit intense, isn't it?'

'Dave is not gay. He has a girlfriend.'

'Yeah, well, that's not proof of anything, is it?'

'Why are you trying to make this into something bad? Dave's a really good guy. He knows a lot about recovery and he wants to help me—'

'Fuck it, Lenny!' Audrey shouted. 'You're so . . . you're so . . . suggestible! All it takes is one beardy arsehole telling you some shit about *co-dependence* and you're ready to shaft me.'

'I'm not shafting you, Mom. Jesus, I'm not married to you . . .'

Audrey clutched the arm of the sofa. 'You little *shit*.'

'No!' Lenny protested. 'I didn't mean . . . I wasn't talking about *Dad*. I just meant—'

'Forget it.' She looked away. 'I'm not going to argue with you. If you want to bugger off with a bunch of yokels, go ahead. I'm warning you, though, this is it. If you do this, I'm not having you back again. You're on your own.'

Lenny lowered his head. 'I wish it didn't have to be this way, Mom.'

'You'll wish it even more when you get tired of carving stair rails with old beardy-face. You'll come crawling back to New York and you won't have me to bail you out any more.' She paused, searching his face for any sign of hesitation, of second thoughts. 'Go on then, fuck off,' she said. 'Go complain about your wicked mother at your meeting.'

After he had gone, she sat for several minutes, considering the long, lavender shadows that the afternoon sun had cast across the floorboards. Presently she stood up and went outside to look for Jean.

She found her in the walled vegetable garden, tenderly examining her tomato plants. 'You're in luck!' Jean cried when she saw Audrey. 'We're having tomato salad for dinner tonight!'

'I assume,' Audrey said, 'that you knew about Lenny's plan to become a carpenter?'

'Ah.' Jean sat back on her haunches. 'I did, yes. I would have said something, but he really wanted to tell you himself.'

'And since when did we start going by Lenny's fricking agenda?' Audrey cried. 'He's a baby, Jean! And you were meant to be in loco whatsit! I only let him come down here in the first place because you made me. Now look what's happened.'

Jean shrugged. 'He's not a baby. He's thirty-four. And nothing so terrible has happened, as far as I can see. He's off drugs, he's attending meetings, he may even be going to learn a new trade.'

'Oh right,' Audrey said. '*Oh right*. He's a totally new fucking man, isn't he? Let me explain something to you, Jean. This born-again routine of his is going to last for a couple more weeks, tops, and then he'll be right back to scrounging money for dime bags.'

'Well, don't let's declare it a failure before he's had a chance to—'

'I see what this is. You're dying to show how much better a job you can do with Lenny, aren't you? Silly old Audrey made a mess of things for thirty years, and now, here comes Jean, the Flying Nun, to turn his life around in a month!'

Jean stuck out her bottom lip and exhaled a little puff of air, trying to remove the strands of hair that had fallen into her eyes. 'That's absolutely unfair, Audrey.'

'Well, that's me, isn't it? Nasty, unfair Audrey. I expect you and Lenny have had a lovely time together discussing my character flaws.'

'You're being ridiculous.'

Audrey stomped away. 'I'm going to bed,' she shouted as she disappeared through the door in the garden wall.

She did not go to bed, though. When she got back inside the house, the thought of returning to the junk-filled guest room and lying on that ridiculous four-poster bed, like the princess and the pea, was too unbearable. She retreated instead to the sitting room. She was still there, flipping disconsolately through a pile of holiday brochures, when Jean came in half an hour later.

'It's gotten quite chilly,' Jean said. 'Shall we have a fire?'

Audrey looked away haughtily. 'I don't mind.'

'Are we going to make up? Or are you going to mope all night?'

Audrey shrugged. 'Are those the only choices?'

Jean smiled and went over to the fireplace. 'I'm glad you're looking at those,' she said, pointing at the brochures. 'I was thinking there might be something in there for the two of us to do one of these days.'

'Oh sure,' Audrey said. 'Because I've got lots of free time and money for fancy holidays.'

Jean began rolling sheets of old newspaper into

balls and assembling them in the fireplace. 'Are you worried about money, Audrey?'

'Well, Joel's accountant did tell me the other day that I was facing a liquidity crisis . . .'

'Oh?'

'He thinks I should sell Perry Street, buy myself a granny flat and invest the leftover in a low something mutual something . . .'

'A low-risk mutual fund?'

'Yeah, maybe.'

'And what did you say?'

'I told him to bugger off, didn't I?' Audrey laughed. 'He was quite upset, the poor sod.'

Jean nodded gravely. 'Accountants can be beastly, I know. But it pays to listen to them, Audrey. They usually have sensible things to say—'

'Yes, well,' Audrey said, stretching her arms languorously, 'Joel and I have never been sensible about money, thank God.'

'No, quite. And it's wonderful, of course, not to care too much about that sort of thing. But money does tend to *become* important when you don't have enough of it.'

Audrey scowled. 'And how would you know?'

Jean looked down at the ball of paper in her hand and sighed. 'Well, in any case, I was thinking that our holiday would be my treat.'

Audrey held up a brochure for walking tours of Italy, opened to a photograph of an elderly man in knee socks and sandals, striding along the Via Appia. 'Just imagine having to face that fucker over your espresso every morning.'

'There are lots of other things there,' Jean said patiently. 'There's a Caribbean cruise that the *Nation* magazine organizes . . .'

330

'I'd rather stick a pin in my eye.'

'Oh? It looked quite fun to me.'

'What, floating around the islands with a bunch of old guys quarrelling over who gets to sit in the jacuzzi with Katrina van den Heuvel? You know, don't you, those boats are all riddled with legionnaire's disease?'

'Okay then, not the *Nation* cruise, but there's bound to be something in that lot that you'd find interesting—'

'Jean, what are you going on about? I have a husband lying in hospital. I can't be going off on pleasure trips with you.'

Jean gathered up a handful of kindling from a basket and began arranging it over the newspaper in the grate. 'I do think, Audrey, that at some point you're going to have to start facing up to certain things about Joel's condition.'

Audrey looked up. 'How do you mean?'

'I just think there's going to come a point when you have to, you know, let him go . . .'

Audrey clapped her hands. 'Ohhh! Here it comes—the "Let's Kill Joel" speech. Yeah, well, thanks for that.'

'Audrey, you know I don't—'

'Yes you do. You all do. Especially now he's turned out to have been shtupping that silly cow. You just want to get rid of him and wrap the whole thing up already. Well, let me tell you, I'm not letting that woman have the last word on my marriage—'

'Oh, for goodness' sake,' Jean cried, 'stop it!'

Audrey stared. 'Excuse me?'

Jean shook her head. 'Sorry. I didn't mean to snap. It's just—ever since this business with

Berenice came out, you've been angry with her, with me, with the children—with every one of us *except* Joel. I don't care if he's in a coma: he's behaved abominably. I think it would help you to acknowledge that.'

Audrey stood up slowly. 'You think I'm *not* angry with him?' she said. 'You think I don't hate him for what he's done to me? Of *course* I'm fucking angry, Jean! What am I, an idiot?'

Jean shrank back. 'I'm sorry, Audrey . . . you never said—'

'I've spent my *life* serving that man. I put up with his affairs for forty *years* and now, at the end of it all, I find out that he didn't love me at all. I find out that the great passion of his life was some fat fucking photographer!'

'Oh, you don't really think that. You *know* Joel adored you—'

'Please!' Audrey raised her hand. 'I know what my marriage was and wasn't.'

'But, Audrey—'

'He wrote that woman poems! Do you think he ever wrote poems for *me*?'

'I . . . I didn't realize you felt this way, Audrey.'

Audrey sat down again. 'Well, now you do.'

Jean laid a couple of logs on top of the kindling and struck a match. The two women watched as the flame caught the newspaper and crept upwards.

'Whatever your marriage was or wasn't,' Jean said, 'you can't change it now, Audrey. You have to let it go.'

Audrey shook her head. 'And what am I supposed to do when I've let it go? Arse about on cruises with you for the rest of my life?'

'Forget the cruises, okay? There are hundreds of other things you can do with your life. Productive, fulfilling things. You're only fifty-nine.'

'Thanks for reminding me.'

'That's young! You're still an attractive woman. Perhaps you'll meet someone else.'

Audrey moaned. It was terrifying, certainly, to think that her sex life was over for good, but marginally more terrifying to think that it was not. The idea of courtship at her age was grotesque. She did not want to become one of those hormone-replacement floozies bopping around in a leather skirt, boasting about her still-vibrant sexuality, trawling in the back of *The New York Review of Books* for someone to share her love of Pinter and Klee and rainy days in Montauk. No. It was ridiculous, it was so . . . *American*, all this talk of reinventing oneself and moving on. She had made her apple-pie bed and now she would have to lie in it.

'You could get more involved in politics,' Jean said. 'You could get a job. Or write a book. You might even decide you want to go back and live in England.'

Audrey covered her eyes with her hand. 'Are you *trying* to depress me?'

'All I'm saying is that your life is not over. You've given up a great deal to be Joel's wife—you've said so yourself, many times—and now you have a chance to do some of the things you've always wanted to do.'

Audrey shook her head forlornly. It was true: she had often spoken of the accomplishments that might have been hers had she not dedicated her life to Joel. But she had never really *believed* what

333

she was saying. Deep down, she had always known these aggrieved remarks for what they were—self-flattering delusions, face-saving fantasies. The truth was, Joel had held her back from nothing. He had saved her. Without Joel, she would still be typing in Camden Town, or living in some hellish suburb, married to a man like her sister's husband, Colin.

She looked down at the brochures splayed on the floor. 'No, Jean,' she murmured, 'it's no good. I'm done.'

CHAPTER TWENTY

'Welcome,' Berenice said, standing in the middle of her living room and extending her heavily braceleted arms towards Rosa and Karla. She was wearing a long scarlet dress—a robe, really—and golden sneakers, cloven at the toe, like camel's feet. 'This is wild, isn't it?'

Karla laughed nervously. None of her imaginings had prepared her for the exotic reality of her father's mistress. She wondered whether Berenice had dressed up for the occasion, or if she looked this extraordinary all the time.

'Wow,' Berenice said, shaking her head. 'It's pretty weird to meet you guys at last.'

Sensing that Berenice could not go on mining the theme of her amazement indefinitely, Karla struggled to think of something to say that might carry the conversation forward. She glanced at her sister, hoping for assistance, but Rosa, who appeared to have absented herself from all responsibility for this encounter, was staring glassily at the floor.

'You . . . have a lovely apartment,' Karla stuttered.

Berenice nodded serenely. 'Isn't it great?'

The three women looked around them. The walls of Berenice's living room were busy with framed black-and-white photographs and cryptic bits of text torn out from newspapers and magazines. 'We Are All Under Fire Now', one of the cuttings said; 'Locals Hate Us' said another. An old chair, upholstered in cracked pink vinyl, stood in one corner of the room, and a bookshelf, fashioned out of milk crates and planks, stood in another. The centre of the room was completely empty, as if in readiness for a performance of some kind.

'Joel was responsible for getting me this place, you know,' Berenice said.

Karla started at the mention of her father. 'Oh yes?'

'Yeah, these apartments are rent-controlled, so they're really tough to get into. Joel did a deal for me with the super.' She made a rubbing gesture with her thumb and forefinger. 'Gave him a little baksheesh.'

Karla's eyes widened.

'Hey, can I get you guys something to drink?' Berenice asked. 'I was going to make myself some peach tea. Would either of you like to try some?'

'Sure,' Karla said. 'That sounds very nice, thank you.'

Rosa shook her head. 'I'm good.'

Berenice disappeared into the kitchen and Rosa knelt down to examine the books on the bookshelf.

Karla watched her scanning the gerund-heavy, non-fiction titles: *Mindful Eating, Writing the Body, Understanding Gynocritical Theory, Reading Tarot.* After a while, she wandered over to the window. Berenice's apartment was on the fifteenth floor of a building overlooking the FDR Drive. In fine weather, you could probably have seen clear across to JFK Airport from here, but today it was overcast and drizzling. As Karla stood staring out at the ruined watercolour of slate sky and rain-dimpled river, a tear fattened in her eye and fell.

Ten days ago, at a noisy bar in Midtown (her cowardly choice of venue), with the evening news blasting from a television overhead, she had ended her affair with Khaled. 'I can't see you any more,' she had told him.

'What do you mean?' Khaled had asked. 'What are you saying?'

'I can't do this.' It was embarrassing and at the same time oddly thrilling, to find herself using the time-honoured locutions.

'What do you mean, "this"?'

'You know, *this*. Us.'

'I don't understand. Aren't you happy with me?'

She felt a stab of irritation at his guilelessness. 'This isn't what I *want* to do.'

'Why then?'

'Because—oh, you know why.'

He smacked his hand on the table. 'Christ!'

The two of them gazed miserably at the television over the bar. The president was on, giving a speech in Tennessee to rally support for the Citizen Corps: *My most important job is to keep our families safe. That's my most important job now. I want you to know that there's still an enemy out*

there that hates America. I'm sure your kids, they're
wondering, why would you hate America? We didn't
do anything to anybody. Well, they hate America
because we love freedom. We cherish our freedoms.
We value our freedoms. We love the fact that people
can worship an almighty God in a free land, any way
they choose to worship . . .

'When did you decide this?' Khaled asked.

'I don't know. A couple of days ago.'

'What happened?'

'Nothing happened. I've just been seeing what my mother is going through and I—you know, I just don't want to lie any more.'

'So don't lie! Tell your husband you love someone else and leave him.'

Karla lowered her head. 'I—I couldn't. I—'

'You're not brave enough.'

'It's not about being *brave*, Khaled. I'm trying to do what's right.'

'No you're not. *This* is the right thing. You know it. You're just scared.'

'Well, yes, okay, I am. I'm scared of hurting Mike—'

'No, you're scared of what he and everyone else will say about you if you do what you really want.'

Karla was astounded by the unfairness of this charge. And yet, she was glad of Khaled's anger. Now they were being equally unkind to one another.

'You don't love your husband,' Khaled said. 'He doesn't love you. You said so.'

'That's not . . . Why are you being like this?'

'How should I be then? You want me to smile, be nice, tell you it's all right? Okay, you are a great saint. You are going to spend the rest of your life

337

with your shitty little union man. Congratulations.'

It was hard to believe now, but when she left the bar that night, she had felt almost euphoric with relief. Her thrilling day at the fair was over, she told herself: now she was back on solid ground, ready to resume the plain, nutritious diet of real life. The high had not lasted long. By the time she arrived back in the Bronx, and found Mike ordering household fire extinguishers online in preparation for the adoption agency's home-study inspection, it had already begun to fade. Mike was in a foul mood. He wanted to know why he was doing all the work for the home study and she was contributing nothing. Pitying him his unknowing ingratitude, Karla did not attempt to defend herself. She endured the complaint in silence and retired to bed.

Depression, in Karla's experience, was a dull, inert thing—a toad that squatted wetly on your head until it finally gathered the energy to slither off. The unhappiness she had been living with for the last ten days was a quite different creature. It was frantic and aggressive. It had fists and fangs and hobnailed boots. It didn't sit, it assailed. It *hurt* her. In the mornings, it slapped her so hard in the face that she reeled as she walked to the bathroom. At night, as she lay next to Mike, with a filthy film loop of the things she and Khaled had done together running through her head, it bit her in the neck and kicked her in the groin.

She wiped her eyes now and turned around to face the room. Rosa had abandoned the bookshelf and was standing in front of one of Berenice's black-and-white photographs. Karla went over and joined her. Clasping her hands behind her in the

338

reverent manner of a museum visitor, she peered closely at the picture. It was a blurry, tenebrous close-up of something—what, exactly, she was unsure.

'Was this taken underwater?' she asked, pointing at a mass of coiled, springy-looking matter that looked as if it might be seaweed.

Rosa shook her head. 'Look at the title, Karla.'

Karla leaned in to examine the pale, pencilled cursive on the right-hand corner of the mount. *Black Cunt # 3*, she read.

'I see you're admiring my dirty picture,' Berenice said. She had returned, holding a tray. 'Here's your tea.'

'Thanks very much,' Karla said, taking a mug. 'Is . . . is that one of yours?' she asked, gesturing at the photograph.

Berenice smiled. 'Yes. My photograph, my vagina.'

Karla felt her face grow hot.

Berenice turned to Rosa. 'Are you sure you won't have anything?'

'No thanks,' Rosa said curtly.

Berenice put her tray down on the floor and sank down elegantly beside it in a cross-legged position. 'Please,' she said. 'Sit.'

After a moment's hesitation, Karla and Rosa joined her on the floor.

'Would you like to see a picture of Jamil?' Berenice asked them.

'Oh yes! Sure,' Karla said, still dizzy from her encounter with Berenice's genitalia.

Berenice stood up again and went out to the hallway. 'This was taken six months ago,' she said as she came back in. 'He's already changed a lot since then.'

Karla and Rosa looked at the gap-toothed, fluffy-haired little boy in the school photograph that Berenice held out. 'He's beautiful,' Karla said. 'Where is he now?'

'At a play-date.' Berenice sat down again. 'I wasn't sure what to expect from this meeting and I didn't want to risk exposing him to any, you know, bad energy . . .'

'Ah, right.' Karla nodded.

'I mean, I really hope that the two of you will want to have a relationship with Jamil. But things have gotten so ugly . . . I just felt like I needed to find out from you how you felt about all of this, before I . . .'

'Sure, no, we understand,' Karla said.

'How does your mom feel about your coming to see me?' Berenice asked.

Karla blushed. 'We didn't . . . She doesn't know we're here.'

'Oh.' Berenice smiled. 'Don't worry, I'll never tell.'

Karla looked away, offended by the idea of being in league with Berenice against her mother.

'Listen, you guys,' Berenice said, 'you mentioned on the phone that you had questions you wanted to ask me.'

Karla and Rosa looked at one another.

Berenice laughed. 'It's okay. You needn't be shy. I'm happy to talk about whatever. Just shoot.'

'How . . . how did you meet him?' Karla asked. 'Our father, I mean.'

Berenice cocked her head in sentimental recollection. 'I met him at a party in Chelsea. It was a book party for a poet friend of mine. Your

340

dad and I got into this funny argument because he was eating cocktail sausages and I told him he shouldn't eat meat. He teased me for that.'

'When was this?'

'Let me think. We met in '96. Do you know the Italian expression "rapporto di pelle"? It means, like, rapport of the skin? Well, that's kind of what me and your dad had. It was a very instant, chemical thing.'

'How long did it last?'

'Well, we stopped being romantically involved about three years ago. But, you know, we've stayed friends. I mean, I'll always love your dad.'

'And why did it end? If you don't mind saying.'

'I don't mind. It's just kind of a hard question to answer. I mean, it's always complicated, isn't it? Trying to figure out why something ends. I guess with your dad and me, there was a point when the joy of it went away for both of us. It got very hard to take, after a while—the sneaking around and everything. Joel always had a lot of guilt.'

'Did you . . . want him to leave my mother?'

Berenice wagged her head from side to side, musingly. 'No . . . no, I never really pushed for that. In the beginning we certainly talked about it. But I knew he really valued his life with you guys. And I'm not the kind of woman who's ever been, like, desperate for a husband or anything.'

'No,' Rosa said suddenly. They turned to look at her. 'Why would you bother with a full-time husband when you can borrow another woman's?'

Berenice gazed at her compassionately. 'May I say something, Rosa? I can see that you're in a lot of pain right now, but I'd like to give you some advice. Whatever anger you're feeling, you mustn't

341

let it harden your heart against your father.'

'Oh right—'

'Wait.' Berenice raised her hand. 'I haven't finished. Your dad was—is—an amazing person with a very, very special spirit. He is not a bad person. He didn't choose to fall in love with me, any more than I chose to fall in love with him. It was something that happened. The truth is, we all do some hurtful shit in our lives from time to time, but it doesn't, you know, make us evil. It's part of what makes us human.'

'Ah yes,' Rosa said, flashing a terrifying incisor-filled smile, 'I can see that must be a very convenient philosophy for you. Adultery as a humanist gesture.' She stood up now and turned to Karla. 'I'm going. Will you come, or do you want to stay?'

Karla hesitated. Rosa was behaving abominably, she thought. It was unforgivable to invite yourself into someone's home and then treat them like this. Still, family was family. She stood up. 'I'll come.'

At the front door, Berenice calmly handed them their coats and umbrellas. 'I know this was hard for you,' she said to Rosa. 'I want you to know that I value the honesty and passion you showed me today.' She turned to Karla and kissed her on the cheek. 'You're a special lady, Karla.' When they reached the elevator bank, Berenice was still standing at the door, watching them. She held up a palm. 'Peace.'

As soon as the elevator doors closed, Rosa's indignation began to pour forth.

'Can you believe it? The whole thing was even more squalid and pathetic than I thought. "Rapporto di pelle"! She was awful! Awful! Not a

342

bit of remorse! Not an apology! She actually tried to justify it . . . How could he? A ridiculous woman like that, with her revolting photographs and her . . . her *peach tea*.'

Karla listened uneasily. She could not say that she had liked Berenice, exactly. But she had not found her ridiculous. 'You didn't have to be so rude, you know, Rosa,' she said. 'It was a very awkward situation for her and she—'

'It was not awkward for her! She was having a *wonderful* time. She's one of the most self-satisfied, narcissistic people I've ever met. Did you take a look at her idiotic books?'

'No,' Karla lied.

'Oh God! It was all *How to Read Palms* and diet books.'

'Well, you don't love someone because of the books they read—'

'Don't you?'

Karla thought of Khaled and his astrology charts and enneagram tests. She shrugged.

In the street outside Berenice's apartment building, roadworks were under way. The sisters paused beneath their umbrellas to look. Behind a crude fence veiled in bright orange plastic netting and dotted with round orange hazard lights, two great holes, each fifty foot wide and a hundred and fifty foot long, had been gouged in the road, exposing ancient-looking, rust-barnacled pipes. In the middle of the site, a fat concrete funnel was steadily spewing bright white steam. The excavation had been hurriedly abandoned when it started to rain: a Coca-Cola can was standing on a carpenter's horse, and on the little rickety plywood bridges that spanned the gaping cavities, plastic

343

buckets attached to long pieces of string lay flung on their sides.

'Did you ever suspect before now that Dad was unfaithful?' Karla asked.

Rosa shook her head.

'Me neither. There used to be things in the papers that insinuated—'

'Oh yeah. I always assumed that was just the right-wing press making up stuff.'

Karla nodded. 'I guess I did too. I remember once when I was little, I read something in the paper that called him "a notorious ladies' man". I asked Mom about it and she said it meant that Dad always treated ladies like a perfect gentleman.' Karla laughed. 'I guess I was pretty naive.'

'No you weren't!' Rosa protested. 'It's not naive to trust your father—to expect him to be loyal to your mother. It's not your fault if Dad turned out to be a fraud.'

'He wasn't a *fraud*—'

'Excuse me? Did you not hear what she said about that apartment? Dad paid a *bribe* to get her in there. He paid off someone so his girlfriend could jump the line for a rent-controlled love nest!'

'We don't know that for sure.'

'Yes we do! She said it, Karla!'

'Well, I'm not defending it, but . . . I don't know, maybe they really did love each other.'

'Love!' Rosa made a disgusted face. 'People use that word to rubber-stamp anything they happen to feel like doing. Love isn't about submitting to your urges because "it feels right" and never mind who you hurt in the process. Love is about commitment, about caring for your family, your community, about recognizing something larger and more important than your own desires.'

Karla stared at a yellow hard hat that was bobbing about in the rainwater at the bottom of the pit. How lucky to be Rosa, she thought. Rosa would never be felled by her desires. Nothing Rosa had ever wanted to do had been significantly at odds with what she knew was right. Even as a little girl, she had been incorruptible. The anarchic spirit that had occasionally compelled Karla and her friends to throw their toys down the toilet, or to steal sprinkles from the kitchen cupboard, or to write FUCK very, very small in crayon on the living-room wall, had never once possessed Rosa. It wasn't that she had lacked the courage for mischief. She simply hadn't seen what fun there was to be had from being bad.

'I don't understand why you're trying to deny it,' Rosa said. 'He was a *liar*. He betrayed us, he *stole* from us. Every time he saw that woman, he was giving her attention and time that was rightfully *ours*.'

Karla considered this. Try as she might, she could not think of herself as a victim of her father's sin. Whatever energy her father had expended on Berenice, it had surely not been embezzled from a finite family supply. To the extent that Berenice had made Joel happy, it was perfectly possible that Karla and her sister—even her mother—had actually benefitted from the affair. She thought about the glowing good will she had felt towards her patients, towards strangers on the subway—towards even Mike—during the six weeks that she had been with Khaled. Never had she been filled with so much reckless magnanimity. It was one of the discomfiting paradoxes of her adultery: sin had made her a better person.

Rosa turned to her suddenly. 'I'm sorry, Karla,' she said. 'I don't know why I'm giving you such a hard time. You, of all people, don't need my lectures on being good.'

Karla blushed. 'Oh, I'm not so good.'

*   *   *

Mrs Mee was lying in wait when Karla got home. The way she leapt out from her front door just as Karla was getting off the elevator strongly suggested that she had been watching for her through the peephole. She wanted to discuss the latest developments in her war with the boss at her beauty salon. The letter that Karla had composed at the beginning of the summer had not succeeded in getting the old tipping system reinstated and the women had never carried through on their threat to report the boss to the Labor Department. Now, the boss was proposing to keep the salon open until ten o'clock every night. 'I told him,' Mrs Mee said, ' "I got a family, this is no good for me." And he just says to me, "You don't like it, you find another job"—'

Karla raised a hand like a pupil in a classroom. 'I'm so sorry, Mrs Mee, I really want to hear about this, but Mike is waiting for his dinner. Would you mind if we talked tomorrow?'

Mrs Mee smiled sympathetically. She knew how men were about their meals. 'Of course, Karla. We talk about it tomorrow.' Before Karla made it to her apartment, Mrs Mee called out to her again. 'Karla! You want to come play bingo with me on Friday night?'

346

Karla pressed her index finger to her chest. 'Me?'

'Yeah! You should come! Maybe you win!'

Karla shook her head. 'Thanks, but I'm going to be busy that night.'

'Okay,' Mrs Mee shrugged. 'Maybe next week.'

Mike was sitting in the kitchen, elbows on the table, knuckles at his temples, reading the paper. He had had his hair cut that afternoon and the kitchen smelled faintly of barber-shop cologne.

'Hey,' he said, looking up.

Karla dumped her shopping bags on the floor. 'Hey.'

'Did you see her then?'

'Yup.'

'How was it?'

Karla looked away, repelled by the vampiric excitement in his voice. Mike's official posture regarding Joel's infidelity was one of deep sadness and disappointment, but there was a part of him, she knew, that had exulted in the revelation—that was still exulting. The Litvinoff family's romance of itself had been dealt a mortal blow and he was happy.

'It was okay,' she said.

'What did she say then?'

'I don't know. A lot of things.'

'What was she like?'

Karla thought for a moment. 'Very . . . sophisticated.'

Mike made a derisive clucking sound. 'Ohhh.'

'No,' Karla corrected herself, 'I mean, unusual. Artistic.'

'Did she apologize?'

'No . . . not outright. She said she was very

347

concerned that this whole thing would harden our hearts against Dad.'

'Duh. So, did you meet the kid?'

'No, he was out.'

'And what was her apartment like?'

Karla paused. She did not want to provoke further sneering by telling Mike about the vagina picture or the baksheesh. 'Just a regular apartment,' she said. 'What do you want for dinner?'

Mike turned back to his paper. 'I'll have a shake.'

Karla began unpacking the groceries. 'I saw Mrs Mee in the hall just now and she asked me to go to bingo with her on Friday night. Can you believe it?'

Mike looked up. 'You can't go Friday. You've got canvassing that night.'

'I know, Mike. I wasn't thinking of going. I was just amazed that she asked me, that's all . . .'

Mike shook his head. 'That's what people like her waste their money on. Lottery tickets and bingo.' He dabbed his index finger against his tongue and turned the page of his newspaper.

'No, I meant, why would she think I would want to go with her?'

Mike shrugged. 'Why not? You're friends, aren't you?'

'Mrs Mee? And me? No we're not! We're neighbours.'

'Well, you're always talking to each other, sharing your little secrets.'

'That's not true! I never tell her anything about my life.'

'Whatever.' Mike bent his head closer to his

paper.

'I don't understand how you could think of Mrs Mee as my friend,' Karla said.

Mike did not reply.

The freezer door wasn't closing properly. Karla took a knife from the silverware drawer and began jabbing at the furry white ice that was jamming it. 'We have nothing in common,' she continued. 'She's almost as old as my mother—'

'All right, Karla, I get it!' Mike said. 'You don't have to make a federal case out of it!'

Karla turned around to look at him. The skin on the back of his neck was inflamed where the barber had shaved and there were tiny bits of shorn hair stuck to the inside of his shirt collar. She had gone to sleep and woken up with this man every day for the last five years. Now, she would go on doing so for—what, thirty, forty more? Sooner or later, the adoption would go through and she would become a mother. Her days would be taken up with washing baby clothes in special hypo-allergenic detergents and doling out Cheerios from plastic snack bags. She would go on working part time at the hospital, and doing yoga on Thursday nights and one day, no doubt, she would surrender and start going to bingo with Mrs Mee . . .

She resumed hacking at the ice around the freezer door.

'Don't do it like that,' Mike said irritably. 'You'll get water all over the floor. Put down some newspaper.'

Karla laid the knife on the counter and walked out of the room, leaving the freezer door swinging open.

In her bedroom, the furniture seemed to be

349

crouched in malign watchfulness, waiting for what she would do next. She lay down on the bed and stared at the bulge in the ceiling where water had come through from a leaking pipe in the upstairs apartment. Mike was right, she thought. She and Mrs Mee were well suited. They were both of them too cowardly, too wedded to their own misery, to grasp happiness when it was offered.

After a while, she heard Mike moving slowly around in the kitchen, opening and closing cupboards. A wave of remorse swept over her. *Poor Mike. He could have married a beauty. He could have married someone fertile. And yet he has endured me—my fatness, my barrenness—without complaint. He has chosen to spend his life with me, not because I am beautiful or sexy, but because he believes I am a good person who shares his values and commitments. And how have I—foolish, vain woman—repaid him? By going to bed with the first man to tell me that my ugly body is attractive.*

She got up and went back into the kitchen. Mike was standing at the sink, rinsing out the glass he had just been using.

'Mike,' she said, 'I'm sorry—'

He shook his head. 'Don't worry about it.'

'Mike—'

'I put away the groceries,' he said quickly. 'I didn't want them to go bad.'

CHAPTER TWENTY-ONE

Rabbi Reinman held up a pomegranate. 'Esther, can you tell me why we eat this fruit on Rosh

Hashanah?'

Twenty people were sitting around the Reinmans' dining table, grazing on the remains of the Rosh Hashanah feast. They paused now, to hear Esther's reply.

'Is it because they have crowns on their heads?'

The rabbi wagged his finger and turned to his elder daughter. 'Rebecca, what about you? Do you know?'

Rebecca twisted uncomfortably in her seat. 'I'm not sure, Daddy . . . I forgot.'

Rosa raised her hand. 'I know. It's because the pomegranate is said to have as many seeds as there are mitzvot.'

The rabbi blinked in humorous surprise. 'I can see you have been doing your homework, Rosa! Since you have grown so knowledgeable, I am sure you will be able to tell me how many mitzvot there are.'

Rosa nodded. 'Six hundred and thirteen.'

'Oh, Rosa, that wasn't kind,' Mrs Reinman said. 'Now you have deprived him of the pleasure of teaching you something.'

Everyone around the table laughed. Rosa blushed with pleasure. It was hard to believe that this was the same house in which she had dined so unhappily four months ago. When she looked back on that torturous occasion now, it was with the sort of smug pleasure that a man lying in a warm, dry bed recalls his cold walk home.

'Have you ever actually counted the seeds, Rabbi?' she asked.

The rabbi shook his head in benign reproof. 'Now, that is a mischievous question, Rosa.'

'Have you, Daddy?' Esther asked.

'I have not. But, you know, Esther, there are other explanations of the pomegranate's significance on Rosh Hashanah.' He glanced at Rosa slyly. 'Your grandfather used to say that the seeds in a pomegranate represent all the good deeds that exist within even the least observant Jew.'

Mrs Reinman and the other women began to clear the table. Rosa got up to help, but the rabbi motioned for her to follow him out on to the deck at the back of the house.

The day was cold and on the garden's withered lawn Esther's plastic Wendy house was tipping from side to side in the wind. Mrs Reinman ran out after them with a scarf for her husband.

'She always thinks I'm going to get a chill,' the rabbi said with a smile when she had gone inside. 'But I like some fresh air after a big meal. It clears my mind.' He sat down on the edge of a lounger and beckoned Rosa to take a chair. 'So. I gather you are going home this afternoon.'

Rosa sighed regretfully. 'Yes, I'm sorry. It's terrible timing, but the girls at my programme are performing in a special show and I have to attend. I hope you understand.'

The rabbi studied her thoughtfully.

'I know I'm not meant to travel today,' Rosa went on, 'it's just something I couldn't get out of.'

He cleared his throat. 'Tell me, Rosa, where do you think you are in terms of your religious progress? I know you had a little crisis in the summer that you felt you worked through. But now I get the sense that you've run into another roadblock. Am I right?'

'Not at all! I mean, my family's been going

352

through a lot lately—'

The rabbi nodded. Rosa had told him about her father's affair.

'So I guess I've been pretty tied up with that. But going to shul and talking to you has been an enormous help to me in getting through the whole thing. I've been feeling very positive about the religious part of my life.'

He nodded. 'Yes, I can see that you feel "positive". It's comforting for you to feel some ethnic connection, to go to shul, to eat a little cholent on Friday night. I understand. But I'm talking about something more than that.'

'Oh, I know—'

'Judaism is not a folkway, Rosa. It is a religion. You can't be a Jew just because you think we have some colourful holidays and some neat songs. If that's what you want—a dance and a song and a bagel with cream cheese—you should go join the Reform. They are very good at this sort of thing.'

Rosa sat back, startled by the severity in his tone. The rabbi had spoken often of his contempt for the intellectual sloppiness, 'the religion lite', of Reform Judaism. To steer her in this direction was an insult of the most pointed sort. 'But I don't want to join the Reform,' she said.

He cocked his head. 'Are you sure?'

'Yes, of course.'

'Because, you know, if you *are* serious, Rosa—if you are looking for a real relationship with your Creator—sooner or later you have to make some sort of commitment. You have to decide whether you really want to remain part of the secular world—a world in which men behave as your father has behaved—or whether you are willing to change.'

Rosa gave a little panting laugh of incredulity. 'I don't understand. Is this all because I'm going back to the city this evening?'

'No, no. It's not only about this evening—it's about your general approach as I have observed it over these last months.'

Rosa shook her head. It was hard not to feel that she was being dealt with unjustly. For weeks the rabbi had been wooing her with patience and sympathy—letting her believe that her earnest interest was virtue enough. And now, without warning, he had turned bad cop. No more Mister Nice Guy. It was time to shit or get off the pot. 'Rabbi, forgive me, but I don't think you're being fair. I've been doing this for such a short time—'

'I understand. I am not necessarily trying to speed up your process. I simply want to make sure that you are on the right track. God wants certain things from you and, right now, you are choosing not to give them to Him. I think, intellectually, you see that Yiddishkeit works, that it is coherent. But emotionally you are still resisting. You know that if you really commit, you will be obliged to totally change your life. And no one wants to change. It's hard.'

'No,' Rosa said. 'No, it's the other way around. Emotionally, I do get what the frum life is about. It's intellectually that I have problems with it. You said that I should just hang in there and try to live with my discomfort. And that's what I've been doing. I have really tried. I've read the books you've recommended and I've had all these very interesting theological discussions with you and I've enjoyed them tremendously but I'm still not sure that I am capable of living life as you do. I'm still not sure I can believe like you do.'

The rabbi shrugged. 'Faith is hard, Rosa. Non-believers often speak of faith as if it were something easy, a cop-out from the really tough business of confronting a meaningless universe, but it's not. It's doubt that's easy. The invisibility of Hashem, the fear we sometimes have that He is indifferent to earthly suffering, the explanations that science seems to offer for almost all the phenomena we once considered mysterious—these things make believing an enormous challenge. Especially for a person like you, who has no inheritance to draw upon. You know, it says in the Talmud, "In the place where ba'alei teshuvah stand, even those who were always righteous are not able to stand." That is a recognition of how especially difficult and trying the journey is that you have undertaken. But you will not advance simply by standing on the sidelines.'

'What am I meant to do? I can't join in before I'm completely sure.'

'You may never be sure *unless* you join in.'

Rosa was shocked. 'Surely you don't want me to go through the motions without really—'

The rabbi smiled. 'Do you remember what the Israelites said at Sinai? "We shall do and we shall hear." Their choice of syntax was meaningful, Rosa. They were expressing their willingness to do God's will before they really understood it. That is the crucial lesson of the Sinaitic revelation—God doesn't need our perfect understanding or even our perfect faith. What He wants is our commitment, our actions.'

355

*   *   *

It was raining by the time Rosa set off back to New
York. The Monsey bus line wasn't working because
of the holiday so she had to take a taxi to Naunset
three miles away and then catch a Greyhound.
When she got into New York, she did not have
enough money for another cab from the Port
Authority, so she walked ten blocks in the rain
to the GirlPower show, which was being held
on Thirty-second Street. Members from the
downtown and uptown divisions of the programme
were performing tonight and, in order to
accommodate all the families and friends who
were expected to attend, the programme's director
had hired a tatty auditorium on the fifth floor of a
commercial building. When Rosa arrived there,
the proceedings were already under way and a girl
was up on stage reading a poem.

> You want to tell me how I should be
> You always fussing and nagging at me
> But I am a human bean and I need to be free.
> To my heart, only I hold the key.
> So go away, fool, you ain't the boss of me.

Rosa's heart sank as she surveyed the room. Of
the seventy folding chairs that had been set out, no
more than twenty-five were occupied—at least
seven of them by programme-workers. Raphael
was in the front row, grinning madly at the girl on
stage. When she finished, Rosa spotted him trying
valiantly to fill out the thin applause by whooping
and stamping his foot.

The next act was a group of girls giggling their

356

way through a song about being true to themselves and following their dreams.

I am special, special, special, in my own way
I have so much to give and so much to say
If I try my best I know that I will win the
day . . .

The bleak setting could not, it seemed, have been better calculated to cast doubt on the song's sentiments. Here, in this draughty, ugly hall, the poor odds of any of these resolutely unspecial girls winning the day were cruelly manifest.

Now it was time for Rosa's group to perform their dance number. She watched approvingly as her girls filed on to the stage in T-shirts and sweatpants. (After a long struggle, she had finally succeeded in vetoing the low-necked tank tops and miniskirts for which Chianti had lobbied.) When the music started and the girls began to gyrate their pelvises, an expression of puzzlement appeared on Rosa's face. This was not the sugary pop anthem that had been agreed upon: it was a rap song. An obscene rap song. And every one of the more provocative moves that she had personally excised from the routine during rehearsals had been reinserted. She looked over at Raphael, who was standing up, clapping in time to the music. She felt a flash of anger, succeeded by a slow wave of tired resignation. It didn't matter. None of it really mattered. She closed her eyes as the girls bent over and wagged their buttocks at the audience.

Gimme your booty, cutie . . .

357

Shortly before the song ended, she slipped from the room. She was halfway down the stairs when she heard Raphael shouting after her.

'Where are you going, Rosa?'

'Home!' she shouted back.

'Wait!' He caught up with her on the ground floor. 'You can't go yet. You haven't even congratulated the girls! They'll be really bummed if you just disappear.'

Rosa pushed open the front door. 'I'm sure they'll understand if I don't congratulate them on *that* performance.'

'Oh, come on,' Raphael said, following her out into the rain. 'They just changed back a few things. Don't sulk about it.'

'I'm not sulking. I just—I'm not in the mood to pat them on the back.'

'It's not all about your *mood*, Rosa. They've achieved something that means a lot to them and they need to know that you're proud.'

'But I'm *not*. I'm not proud. They danced a nasty little pornographic dance not very well. What's to be proud of?'

Raphael uttered a low growl of exasperation. 'Would you get off your high horse for a second? It doesn't actually *matter* whether you liked their performance or not. The idea is to give these girls some self-esteem.'

'I understand. But don't they have to do something estimable first?'

People hurried past, glancing at them as they stood in the downpour. *They must think we're lovers*, Rosa thought. *Only lovers would be passionate enough to argue in the rain.* She felt a sudden urge to call an end to hostilities, to have Raphael hug her and laugh fondly at her seriousness. But there seemed no way to change tack now.

'I don't get you,' Raphael said. 'I really don't. You say you want to help these girls but the truth is you don't seem to actually *like* any of them. You go on about how crappy their lives are going to be— about their "class destiny"—but you never give them an inch. If they're not going to get scholarships to the Bronx School of Science, you consider them lost. Doesn't it wear you out, being so fucking judgemental all the time?'

She gave an odd, rueful laugh. 'Yes, it does a bit.'

'I'm glad you think this is funny.'

She shook her head. 'I don't. I'm sorry. It was just . . .' She looked down the rain-veiled street. 'Look, I wish I could be like you, Raphael. I wish I could feel confident that I was doing something useful with this work. But I don't. It frustrates me. It *depresses* me.' She sighed with the relief of saying it at last.

'Well, fuck off then, why don't you?' Raphael shouted. 'These girls deserve better. There are plenty of people who'd be thrilled to have your job and who wouldn't spend the whole time bringing everyone down with their shitty attitude. You're always dissing the way everybody else lives their life, but, hello? What's so great about yours?'

She nodded. 'You're right. I need to help myself before I can try to help others.'

He turned away, contemptuously. 'I mean it, Ro. Just fuck off. You don't belong here.'

She watched him walk back into the building

with a strange smile hovering about her lips. *Accept the truth from whomever gives it.* The wind had picked up now and was driving the rain along the sidewalk in strange, scalloped formations. Her toes were squelching inside her soaked sneakers. After a moment, she tucked the rat's tails of her wet hair behind her ears and set off up the shiny, black street.

CHAPTER TWENTY-TWO

One blue-skied morning in October, Susan Sarandon stood on a stage in Central Park's East Meadow, addressing a rally of twenty thousand anti-war protestors.

'We need to let the president of the United States know that we do not accept his phony rationale for this war. We are an intelligent citizenry! We question! We demand answers! We are not prepared to sacrifice our sons and daughters in a war for oil!'

A decent-sized roar rose up from the front of the crowd. Further back, by the entrance to the meadow, where Audrey was sitting under a tree with her mother-in-law and Jean, the response petered out to polite, golf-tournament applause.

Audrey looked up from burrowing in Jean's cooler. 'What's this, Jean?' she said, waving a plastic tub.

'Seafood salad,' Jean said. 'Try it, it's delicious.'

Audrey wrinkled her nose. 'Didn't you bring any sandwiches?'

A terrible squawk of feedback issued from the

giant speakers by the stage and all three women scowled in pain as they pressed their hands to their ears.

'No, dear,' Jean said, after a moment, 'but there's a baguette and some paté. You could make yourself a sandwich.'

Audrey shook her head. 'Doesn't matter. I'm not that hungry anyway.' She glanced over at Hannah, dozing in her wheelchair in a pair of horn-rimmed dark glasses. Hannah looked rather glamorous this morning, like a convalescent Joan Crawford. 'You all right, Nana?' Audrey inquired loudly.

Hannah sat up and pointed at the stage. 'Who is this woman speaking?'

'Susan Sarandon,' Jean said. 'She's an actress. Quite a good one.'

Hannah nodded approvingly. 'Attractive woman, isn't she?'

'Well, anyone can look good at this distance,' Audrey muttered. 'She's probably very wizened when you get up close.'

'Oh look,' Jean exclaimed, pointing across the crowd to a man stalking about on stilts in an Uncle Sam costume. 'Isn't he splendid?'

Audrey glanced at her irritably. Jean was dressed in what she cheerfully referred to as her 'demo gear'—an outsize painter's smock, black leggings and a preposterous woollen cap that someone had recently brought back for her from Jamaica. It was really too much. Audrey was going to have a stern word with her one of these days.

'I've never understood how people do that,' Hannah remarked, gazing at the man on stilts. 'It must be murder on your legs.'

361

'It looks fun, though, doesn't it?' Jean said. 'I'd love to give it a go sometime.'

'Oh, Jean, you're so young at heart, aren't you?' Audrey remarked scathingly.

Jean smiled at her absently and turned to Hannah. 'I must say, it's a pretty good turnout today, isn't it?'

The old woman nodded. 'Yes, marvellous!'

'Get out!' Audrey said. 'This is *pathetic*. You've got to have at least a hundred thousand at these things to have any chance of being on the news. This little get-together won't merit two lines in tomorrow's paper.'

Jean smiled fixedly. 'And we've been terribly lucky with the weather.'

'It probably won't even *be* in the paper,' Audrey added bleakly.

There was a pause.

'Right!' Jean stood up. 'I'm going to wander around for a bit and take some pictures, if that's okay with you two.'

'Be my guest!' Audrey said, managing rather brilliantly to give and take offence at the same time.

*   *   *

A few hundred yards from where the women were picnicking, Rosa and seven of her GirlPower charges were sitting on the grass, watching a group of female protestors, costumed in diapers and papier-mâché skull masks, perform a 'die-in'.

'What they *doing*, man?'

'They're crazy.'

'Why they wearing them ugly-ass masks?'

'Yo, they're protesting, stupid.'

'They got diapers on. What's that?'

'Maybe they shit themselves.'

'Oh my God! They shit themselves! They shit themselves!'

'Stop that!' Rosa said angrily. 'Stop that at once! You're being extremely rude.'

Today was the last time that Rosa would ever chaperone the girls on such an outing. Her two weeks' notice period at GirlPower did not end until the following Tuesday, but this event was her de facto farewell party, and it was proving—fittingly enough, she thought—a rather stressful occasion. Raphael, who was still barely speaking to her, had begged off from attending at the last minute with some shoddy excuse about a sore throat—and the girls, none of whom had ever attended a political rally before, were in a difficult, rambunctious mood. Already, she had been obliged to reprimand them three times for starting up their own, improvised anti-war chants while someone on the stage was speaking.

One of the girls tapped her on the shoulder now. 'Ro,' she said, 'don't be mad. I just wanna know why they doing that.'

'Well, why do you think, Malisha? What do their signs say? "No Dead Babies for Oil". What do you think that means?'

Malisha squinted. 'I don't know.'

'They're saying that the real reason our government wants to invade Iraq is to get hold of its oil reserves . . .' Rosa paused. 'Do you know what oil reserves are?'

Malisha was no longer listening. She and the other girls were pointing and giggling at an elderly white woman walking past in a Rasta cap.

'Oh my God—she's wearing a tam! She thinks she's a Rasta!'

'Rasta lady! You like Bob Marley?'

Rosa tried to duck her head, but it was too late. Jean had already spotted her.

'Hoo! Rosa!' she cried. 'Hello, Rosa! Over here!'

The revelation that Rosa *knew* this bizarre creature inspired such joyous mirth among the girls that several of them fell actually to the ground, convulsed with laughter, as Jean approached.

'Rosa, *darling*,' Jean said, kissing her on the cheek. 'How fantastic to see you!'

'Hi, Jean,' Rosa said. 'Girls, this is Jean. Jean, this is Malisha, Chantelle, Danielle, Chianti . . .'

Jean smiled with the special good will that middle-aged white liberals reserve for young people of colour. 'Hello! It's good to see you young ones at an event like this. We're depending on you lot, you know, to lead us out of the mess we've got ourselves into!'

The girls stared at her.

'Your mother is just over there with Hannah, you know,' Jean told Rosa. 'You must come and say hello.'

'Well . . . I shouldn't really leave the girls.'

'Don't be silly, Rosa, I meant all of you.'

'Yeah!' Chianti cried. 'We gonna see Rosa's momma!'

'No, really, Jean,' Rosa said, 'I don't think it's a good idea. Mom and I are not on great terms at the moment.'

Jean grasped Rosa's bicep. 'Rosa, dear, don't be

a stick-in-the-mud. Come with me.' Her papery hand had surprising strength.

The girls were dancing around in excitement now. 'Rosa's mama! Rosa's mama!'

Rosa sighed. 'All right. Come on then.'

Hannah was asleep and Audrey was reading a copy of *Mother Jones* when they walked up.

'Look who I've got here!' Jean said.

Audrey glanced at them over her reading spectacles. 'Oh, hello.'

'This is my mother,' Rosa told the girls, pointing stiffly at Audrey. 'And this'—she bent over and planted a kiss on Hannah's slumped head—'is my grandma.'

The girls leaned against one another, suddenly shy.

'Well now!' Jean said. 'Who wants to have a Coke?'

'Can we, Ro?'

'If you must.'

'Good!' Jean said. 'Why don't you stay here and take a breather, Rosa? I'm sure I can handle these ladies by myself.'

Left alone, Audrey and Rosa did not speak for some time. Audrey went back to reading her magazine. Rosa turned her attention to the stage and the old black minister who was thundering at the microphone.

'The presi-dent, in his wisdom, says, "You're either with us or against us." Now, you must forgive me because maybe I'm not so bright, but I have to ask: Who is this "us" he's talking about? And how does a man who *lost* the general election, who *lied* his way into power, have the *te-me-ri-ty* to talk so confidently about "us"?'

The crowd cheered and across the meadow yellow NO BLOOD FOR OIL placards bobbed up and down. Audrey looked up sourly. 'This is a very uninspiring event, I must say.'

Rosa smiled. For all her alleged dedication to collectivist principles, Audrey had never much enjoyed collective action. Her political opinions functioned for her much as arcane tastes in alternative music had once functioned for Rosa's eighth-grade friends: they were a badge of specialness; they served her temperamental need to be a member of a glamorously embattled minority. She proselytized constantly for her causes, but she did not really want to gather *adherents*, any more than Rosa's schoolfriends had wanted their beloved Indie bands to become chart-topping successes.

'I'm surprised you brought your girls to this,' Audrey said.

'What,' Rosa replied quickly, 'because now I'm such a religious freak I wouldn't be interested in world affairs any more?'

Audrey shrugged. 'Something like that.'

'Actually, this is my last outing with them.'

'What do you mean?'

'I've handed in my notice.'

'Oh yeah?' Audrey said, struggling to sound indifferent. 'What're you going to do instead?'

'You're not going to like it.'

'You've got a job at Morgan Stanley.'

'I think I'm going to go to a yeshiva in Jerusalem.'

Audrey gazed out at the park in silence. When at last she spoke, she sounded surprisingly calm.

'Why Judaism? That's what I want to know.

366

Why did you have to choose such a reactionary religion? You could have decided to be a Buddhist or, I don't know, a Hindu—'

'What is the reactionary part you're referring to?' Rosa demanded. 'Caring for the poor and the sick? Honouring your marriage vows? Trying to live honestly and decently?'

Audrey looked at her. 'Oh, go on, Rosa. If it was living honestly and decently you wanted, you could have stayed a socialist—'

'Really? Where did socialism ever get me? Where did Dad's socialist values get him in the end?'

'Your father's done more than you'll ever do to make the world a better place.'

'Including lying to his wife and family for the last six years?'

Audrey laughed. 'What do you think? That he had it off with that woman because of his politics?'

'Well, his politics certainly didn't stop him, did they?'

Audrey threw down her magazine. 'Oh, don't be such a baby, Rosa! There's no system in the world that can keep a man's dick in his pants. You think Jewish men don't fuck around on their wives? When you discover that one of your rabbis has been giving one to Mrs Feingold, are you going to feel "betrayed" by God too?'

Rosa screwed up her face in distaste.

'Do you have to talk like that, Mom?'

'Tell me this. Does the Jewish religion stop Jewish soldiers from shooting Palestinian children?'

Rosa was silent.

'What? Are you going to tell me Jewish soldiers

367

don't shoot Palestinian children?'

'I used to have a problem with Israel,' Rosa said. 'But I've been reading a lot on the subject and I've been talking to some very informed people and I see now, how much of the anti-Zionist argument is rooted in anti-Semitism.'

Audrey gaped at her. 'You're pro-Israel now?'

'I believe in Israel's right to exist. I believe in its right to defend itself against its enemies. If that's Zionism—'

'I don't know what to say to you any more, Rosa. Really, I don't.' Audrey buried her face in her hands. Several moments passed. At length, she raised her head. 'Are you going to go the whole hog with this thing? Follow all the rules, I mean?'

'Yes. Well, I'm going to try. I know a lot of the rules seem pretty out there, Mom—especially when you look at them out of context. They're not always easy for *me* to accept. I struggle with a lot of it, but—'

'Well, so,' Audrey broke in, 'perhaps it's not right for you. Just because it's right for them—you know, these friends you've met—it doesn't mean it's right for you.'

'But, Mom, if it's the truth, it has to be right for me, doesn't it? If you thought you'd found the truth about something, would you walk away from it just because it wasn't the truth you particularly wanted or expected to find?'

Audrey shrugged. 'I can't answer that. The truth would never reveal itself to me in that way.' She pointed into the crowd. 'Look, here they come.' Jean and the girls were slowly making their way back now. Each girl was carrying a can of Coke and a T-shirt printed with the slogan 'Agitated Agitator

Agitating'.

Rosa turned back to Audrey impatiently. 'But what if it did, Mom?' she asked. 'What if the truth *did* reveal itself to you in that way?'

Audrey continued to observe Jean's approach. 'Silly woman,' she muttered. 'She's gone and bought them all T-shirts!'

'Mom!' Rosa wriggled with impatience. Sometimes, as a little girl, she had been so desperate to catch her mother's wandering attention that she had actually placed a hand on Audrey's cheek and pushed her head around to face her. 'Mom! Are you listening to me?'

Audrey turned to her. 'You want to know what I'd do if the truth revealed itself to me and it wasn't the truth I wanted to find?'

'Yes.'

Audrey smiled. 'I'd reject it.'

CHAPTER TWENTY-THREE

When Karla woke at six, Mike was already up and creeping about the room in his underpants. Today was the day of the state and city elections; in an hour or so, the two of them would be setting off for one of the union's phone banks to help get out the vote. Mike was full of nervous tension, she could tell—rasping away at his hair with his military hairbrush, tapping into his Palm Pilot, opening and reopening his closet door to check if he'd laid out the right pair of pleated khakis the night before. She lay with her eyes closed, listening to the insect-like scritch-scratch of his pottering. At last, she heard the bedroom door close and from across the hall a faint squeaking of faucets, succeeded by the hiss of not quite adequate water pressure. She climbed stealthily out of bed and went to the window. Pulling back the curtains, she sighed. The sky over the sepia-toned city was a cold, unclouded blue. The meteorological disaster she'd been fantasizing about—the snow-storm or typhoon that would keep her from having to assist the governor in his widely predicted victory—was nowhere in sight. She was about to climb back into bed when the phone rang.

'It's me,' her mother said. 'I'm at the hospital. They want you and your brother and sister to come in. They seem to think your father is dying.'

Joel had had pneumonia for the last ten days. The antibiotics initially prescribed had failed to deal with the infection and further tests had since established that he was suffering from a drug-resistant 'super-bug'. Large doses of a costly super-antibiotic were now being administered, but the infection had not responded and the doctor on duty in the ICU this morning had just informed Audrey that he did not expect Joel to last the day.

Mike was still showering when Karla went into the bathroom. 'That was Mom,' she said. 'The doctors think Dad's at the end. They've told us to come in.'

'Oh shit.' Mike poked his head out from the curtain. 'Are they sure?'

'I don't know. I'm just going on what Mom said.'

'What are we going to do?'

Karla felt suddenly ashamed, as if she had willed her father to stage this crisis for her benefit. 'I have to go. I can't not, Mike.'

'No, of course not.'

She could see that he was horribly torn. He had been working towards election day for months. He didn't want to bail out now and miss the culmination of the campaign. She smiled forgivingly. 'You don't have to come this minute,' she said. 'No one'll hold it against you if you come by later, after the polls are closed.'

'Yeah . . . but what if I'm too late?'

Karla recoiled. There was something ghoulish about Mike's longing to be present at his famous father-in-law's death rattle. He spoke as if he were passing up ringside tickets at a Knicks game. 'Don't worry,' she said firmly. 'It'll be okay. You should go.'

'Really?'

'Really.'

* * *

Rosa was already at the hospital when Karla arrived. Audrey had spoken to Lenny in Pennsylvania and he was coming in by train that afternoon. Throughout the morning, the three women took turns sitting with Joel in his ICU room, wearing the regulation masks and flimsy plastic aprons provided by the hospital. It was received wisdom among the nurses with whom Karla worked that long illnesses were useful in preparing people for the eventual blow of their loved ones' deaths. A slow fade was said to be preferable to a bolt from the blue because it gave relatives the time to 'reconcile themselves to the loss' and because, when the patient did finally depart, a seminal part of the mourning process had

371

already been accomplished. Karla, who had cheerfully collaborated in the propagation of this verity for many years, was mildly outraged to discover what bullshit she had been spouting. It was perfectly clear to her now that the last eight months had done little or nothing to prepare the family for this moment. If anything, she thought, the length of Joel's illness had encouraged in them a bizarre sort of insouciance. Joel had survived for so long and returned from the brink so many times that they had come to think of death as a rather incompetent adversary—a bungling pantomime villain, wheeled out by the doctors from time to time to give them all a spooky thrill, but always safely vanquished.

The hours went slowly but the day went fast. Lenny turned up from the station just before three, weeping copiously and needing money to pay his cab. Soon afterwards, Hannah was brought in from Brooklyn by her home help. Audrey had tried to stop her from coming, insisting that she was too frail to be exposed to Joel's infection, but Hannah had refused to be put off. Lenny was sitting with Joel when she arrived. She unceremoniously turfed him out and proceeded to spend the next hour alone in the room. Eventually, Audrey delegated Karla to go in and see if she had fallen asleep in there.

When Karla entered, she found her grandmother sitting, without mask or apron, singing 'Rozhinkes mit Mandlen', an old Yiddish lullaby.

Unter yidele's vigele
Shteyt a klor vayse tzigele

372

Dos tzigele is geforn handlen
Doz vet zayn dayn baruf
Rozhinkes mit mandlen
Shlof zhe yidele, shlof

'Nana?' Karla whispered.

Hannah turned around. 'I want to kiss him before I leave,' she said. 'Could you help me?'

'I'm not sure that's a good idea, Nana. You really should be wearing the mask. You don't want to catch—'

Hannah closed her eyes. 'I'm ninety-three, Karla. It doesn't matter what I catch. Just do me a favour and help me up.'

Karla hesitated a moment. Then she walked over and carefully hoisted Hannah out of her wheelchair. The old woman leaned across her son's bed railing and placed a kiss on his forehead. 'Goodbye, my sweet boy.'

She glanced around at Karla, gesturing that she wished to be lowered back into her chair. 'Okay,' she said, 'you can take me home now.'

'Are you sure, Nana? This may be the last—'

'I know what it is,' Hannah said. 'I'm done here.'

*　　　*　　　*

After Karla had accompanied Hannah and the home help downstairs and put them in a cab back to Brooklyn, she returned to the ICU Rosa was standing in the hallway talking to a man in a dark suit. 'This is Rabbi Weiss,' Rosa said. Her eyes were shining. 'He's going to give Dad a berocha.'

Karla glanced suspiciously at the man. A laminated card hanging on a chain around his neck identified him as Officer of Rabbinical Services at NYU Medical Center.

'What do you mean, a "berocha"?' she asked.

'A blessing. He's going to say a blessing for Dad.'

Karla shook her head. 'No, Rosa, you mustn't. What will Mom say?'

'It'll only take a minute. It's really a beautiful blessing, Karla. Mom's not even going to know. She's down in the cafeteria with Jean and Mike.'

'Rosa, this is crazy.'

The rabbi raised a hand. 'If this is going to cause family problems—'

'No, no,' Rosa said quickly, 'it's not.' She handed him a mask.

'I don't understand. What's the point?' Karla said, suddenly infuriated. 'Dad was never religious. And he's in a coma. He's not even going to know it's happening.'

'God will hear the blessing, even if your father cannot,' the rabbi said.

Rosa grasped Karla's hand. 'Please, Karla, don't be upset. This is something that means a lot to me.'

'But this isn't about you, it's about *Dad*.'

Rosa let go of her hand. 'I'm sorry if you object, but I'm going to do it anyway, okay?'

Down in the cafeteria, Audrey and Jean were poring over that day's edition of the *New York Post*. Mike was at the counter getting tea for Audrey.

'Your mother's had a bit of a shock,' Jean explained when Karla sat down. 'There's this thing in the paper . . .' She pointed to a small item at the bottom of the Page Six column. Karla read it over Audrey's shoulder. It was headlined 'Too many Reds in the Bed?':

Which ailing lefty lawyer is having trouble keeping the peace between his wife and his mistress? It seems the two ladies ran into each other recently while visiting the legal lothario in hospital and the missis became so irate that she started throwing punches. (Some things even socialists don't like to share.) The young lovely at the receiving end is said to be so peeved about the attack that she's considering pressing charges.

Karla clutched her brow. 'I don't understand, Mom. How could they know about that?' Karla said.

'How do you think? That fucking Berenice planted it.'

'We can't be sure of that,' Jean said. 'It could have been a nurse, or—'

Audrey smacked the table. 'Of course it was her! Where else would they get that shit about pressing charges? And what fucking nurse is ever going to describe Berenice as a "young lovely"?'

Jean thought for a moment. '*No*, she just *couldn't* have, Audrey. It's such an awful, cheap thing to do . . .'

Audrey gazed up at the ceiling long-sufferingly. 'Oh, I know, and Berenice would never do anything awful or cheap, would she?'

Mike came to the table now, carrying a cup of tea. 'Have you heard?' he asked Karla eagerly. Karla gave a chilly nod.

'But why would she go to all that trouble to get a few lines printed in a silly gossip rag?' Jean asked. 'It's not as if anyone we know reads this stuff—'

'Are you kidding?' Audrey cried. '*Everyone* reads

375

this stuff! And, believe me, this isn't the end of it. This is just her warming up. She's probably selling her story to some paper as we speak.'

Mike tapped Karla's shoulder. 'I found it,' he whispered.

'Sorry?' she said.

'I was the one who found it—you know, the item.'

She stared at him. 'What . . . and you *showed* it to her?'

'Of course. She needed to know.'

Karla considered her mother's haggard face. For years, it seemed to her, she had been carrying within her a tiny bud of contempt for her husband and now, quite suddenly, it was blossoming. She could see it in her mind's eye—unfurling its terrible, scarlet petals, like a flower in time-lapse photography. 'You shouldn't have done that, Mike,' she said quietly.

He gave a nervous bark of laughter. 'Don't be silly, Karl. I was looking out for her. If there's something written about her in the paper, she has a right to see it.'

'No,' Karla said, shaking her head. 'It was a cruel thing to do.' She glanced at Jean and Audrey, who had fallen silent. 'Let's not discuss it now.'

'She was going to find out about it sometime,' Mike muttered.

Karla stood up. 'I'm going back upstairs now, Mom.'

Mike pursued her to the elevator. 'What's up with you?' he demanded. 'I was only trying—'

Karla shook her head. 'Not now, Mike. This isn't the time.'

'Well, I'm sorry. Don't blame the messenger.'

The doors of the elevator opened and they stepped in. 'Hey!' he said as they began to ascend. 'Have you seen the exit polls?'

Karla gazed stolidly at the floor numbers lighting up on the panel. 'No, Mike, I haven't seen the exit polls. I've been here all day.'

'Well, yeah, I know, but I thought you might have seen a TV . . .' He paused. 'Anyway, it looks like it's going to be a landslide.'

The elevator stopped at the ground floor. Karla stepped to one side. 'Mike, I think you should go home.'

'What are you talking about?'

Karla put her foot out to stop the elevator doors from closing. 'I think you should leave.'

'What's going on, Karla? Is this about the thing in the *Post*?'

'No. I don't know. I just don't want you here right now.'

The elevator doors kept sliding back and forth, slamming up against Karla's foot.

'You're nuts, Karla. I haven't even seen your dad yet.'

'*Please*, Mike.'

'I have a right to see him, you know. He is my father-in-law.'

Karla grabbed him by his sweater and pulled him to the door. 'Just go!'

A middle-aged couple and their teenaged daughter walked into the elevator. The daughter goggled at Karla and Mike, smelling the fury in the air and hungry to witness some adult discord.

With ostentatious dignity, Mike rearranged his mussed sweater. 'Fine!' he said in a low voice. 'I'm going.'

*　　　*　　　*

The family stayed at the hospital that night. Karla and Rosa and Lenny bedded down in the reception area. Audrey was given a cot in Joel's room. She lay awake for several hours, listening to the wheeze of Joel's respirator, trying to picture the events of the coming days. From time to time over the years she had daydreamed about Joel's funeral. Always, in these guilty fantasies, the event—a gorgeously solemn affair, held somewhere outrageous like Alice Tully Hall, or the old CP Headquarters on Twenty-sixth Street—had functioned as a thundering endorsement of her marital career, the apotheosis of her life as consort to a great man. She had envisaged herself wearing red, staggering the other mourners with her quiet dignity and the strength with which she bore the enormity of her loss. Now it was impossible to imagine the occasion as anything other than a ceremonial humiliation, an elaborate joke against her, hovered over by the presiding spirit of Berenice.

She did sleep, finally. But only briefly. Somewhere around two o'clock in the morning, she woke in a panic, convinced that Joel had died. She went over and put her ear to his chest. No—his heart was still booming away. That heart! Everything else was shutting down, but still it kept going, the last, tactless guest at the party, unwilling to accept that the revels were over. She looked at her husband's ravaged face. In recent days his colour had changed from a rather beautiful candle-white to the yellowish grey of weathered teak. He was so gaunt now that she could trace every jutting

378

line and curvature of the skull beneath his skin.

She got up and wandered out into the hall. In the waiting room, Lenny and Rosa, sprawled, top to toe, on the sofa, fast asleep. Over in a corner, Karla was sitting in a chair, rummaging blindly in a bag of tortilla chips.

'Midnight feast, is it?' Audrey said.

Karla jumped. 'God, Mom, you scared me.'

'What flavour are those chips?'

Karla stood up. 'Ssh. Wait, I'll come out.' She emerged blinking into the bright light of the corridor. 'They're lime.'

'Ooh, goody. Give us one then.' Audrey took the bag from Karla and sat down on the floor, leaning against the wall. 'What?' she said, registering Karla's shocked expression. 'I'm allowed to treat myself sometimes, you know.'

Karla sat down next to her. They both took large handfuls of chips from the bag.

'So, is Mike coming back tomorrow?' Audrey asked.

Karla shrugged. 'I guess.'

'Is something going on with you two? You seemed very snippy with each other, before.'

'No. Everything's okay.'

Audrey ate some more chips. 'These are delicious.'

Karla smiled. 'Eighty calories a serving, though.'

'Oh, that's not so bad . . . How much is a serving?'

'Ten chips.'

Audrey's eyes widened. 'Fuck that, take them away from me.'

Karla laughed.

'So, about you and Mike,' Audrey said.

'We're fine, Mom.'

'Good, good,' Audrey nodded. 'Because—'

'Excuse me, ladies,' a voice said. 'You're not allowed to sit here.'

They looked up to see a nurse coming down the corridor towards them.

'All right,' Audrey said, 'we'll get up in a sec.'

'I need you to get up now, if you don't mind,' the nurse persisted.

Karla made to stand up, but Audrey placed a restraining hand on her leg. 'I do mind, as it happens,' she said. 'I'm in the middle of a conversation with my daughter.'

The nurse shivered in affront. 'I'm sorry, ma'am, but it's a safety hazard to have people sitting in the corridor.'

Audrey cocked her head. 'I said I'd get up in a second. Now piss off, would you?'

Two bright patches of red appeared at the nurse's temples. She stared furiously at Audrey for a moment and then walked off quickly down the corridor.

'Stupid cow,' Audrey murmured. 'What's she going to do, call the police?'

'Perhaps we should get up, Mom,' Karla urged.

'No, I was going to say something.'

'What?'

'I was going to say, if things weren't good with you and Mike, I wouldn't want you to think you had to stick at it.'

'*What?*'

'I mean, if you were really unhappy.'

'I don't understand, Mom.'

Audrey tutted impatiently. 'Yes you do.'

There was a long silence. 'But *you* stayed,' Karla

said at last. 'You put up with—'

'That was completely different,' Audrey said quickly. 'I was happy.'

They looked up at the sound of footsteps coming down the corridor. The nurse was returning.

'All right, all right,' Audrey said. 'We're going.'

'Are you Mrs Litvinoff?' the nurse said.

'Yeah, why? You going to report me?'

'I'm sorry, Mrs Litvinoff.' The nurse clasped her hands piously. 'Your husband just passed.'

*   *   *

Audrey went directly to Joel's room. Karla stayed behind to wake up Lenny and Rosa. When the three children arrived in Joel's room a few minutes later, they found Audrey lying on the bed, rocking Joel in her arms. No one spoke. It was inconceivable that Audrey would accept their efforts to console her and there was no room here for their own grief. They stood for a few moments, watching their mother cry, and then, one by one, they silently crept away.

CHAPTER TWENTY-FOUR

'I'm not being funny or anything,' Audrey's sister, Julie, said for the third time that morning, 'but I do think it's very odd the way she's arranged things.'

Julie and Colin were sitting in the back of a cab on their way to Joel's memorial service. Jean, who had been delegated to chaperone them for the day, was sitting in the front passenger seat.

'I suppose you know, Jean,' Julie went on, 'that Col and I weren't even invited to the burial?'

'You did mention that, yes.'

'We went to all this trouble to get here as soon as we could and then we find out she's already had him done. That's not right, is it?'

'Well,' Jean said, 'it's this thing today that's the real event. This is the proper send-off.'

'Yeah, but it's still not the burial, is it?' Julie persisted. 'Close family should go to the burial. And why's she having this memorial whatsit in a cathedral anyway? Don't get me wrong, I haven't got anything against churches myself—Colin's a Christian, you know—but you'd have thought Audrey, with all her principles and whatnot . . .'

Jean glanced in the rearview mirror and smiled brightly. 'I think it was one of the few places she could find that was big enough. They're expecting a big turnout. And, you know, the people at this place—the priests—they're quite left-wing. They do a lot of work with the homeless and the poor and so on, so I think Audrey felt it wasn't an altogether inappropriate location.'

'I see,' Julie said, pursing her lips.

They saw the police barriers as soon as the taxi turned the corner on to Amsterdam Avenue. There looked to be at least a thousand people lining the block: rappers, actors, politicians, prostitutes, mullahs, community activists, university professors, congressmen, homeless people, even a silver-haired mafioso or two. (Joel had once caused a great scandal in the left-wing community by defending a New York don on charges of racketeering.)

382

'They're not all here for Joel, are they?' Julie asked, peering through the window.

'Oh yes,' Jean said, pleased by the shock in Julie's voice. She took her change from the cab driver and opened the door. 'Come on then.'

Julie hesitated. 'It's very . . . diverse, isn't it?' she murmured.

Inside the cathedral, another three thousand people were already seated. The front pews were filled and Julie was appalled to discover that the best seating option available was twenty rows back. While she fulminated over this insult, Jean scanned the crowd for any sign of Berenice. Audrey had expressed no concern about the possibility of Berenice attending but Jean harboured a nightmarish vision of the two of them running into one another on the cathedral steps. She was still gazing about her fretfully when twenty Native Americans in full ceremonial attire walked down the aisle to begin the obsequies with a drum circle.

Audrey had arranged an impressive array of speakers and musical tributes. After the Native Americans had performed, Charlie Rangel, the congressman from Harlem, made a speech. Then Lauren Bacall read a sonnet by John Donne and Patti Smith sang one of Joel's favourite songs, 'Horses'. ('Oh my God!' Julie giggled when Smith took the floor. 'Don't they sell hairbrushes round her way?') Next, there were a series of testimonials from Joel's pro bono clients. One woman spoke of how Joel had defended her on charges of panhandling. A homeless man described how Joel had visited him every day for six months, while working to overturn his conviction on charges of aggravated assault. Jean was moved. Joel had been a good man, she thought. An old scoundrel in many ways—but a good man who had done good things.

Towards the end of the service, Chuck D, whose former group, Public Enemy, Joel had defended against obscenity charges in the 1980s, performed the rap anthem 'Fight the Power'. Then Audrey, wearing a black dress that Karla had purchased for her the day before from Loehman's, stood up and announced that she was going to say a few words.

Jean glanced over to where Karla, Rosa and Lenny were sitting. She had been unaware that Audrey had any plans to speak and, from the looks on their faces, so had they. Audrey looked frail and very nervous as she climbed the little spiral of stairs to the pulpit, clutching a piece of paper in her hand. For one moment, both thrilling and terrifying, Jean wondered if she was going to make some sort of scene and publicly denounce Joel.

'Joel's chosen profession was the law,' Audrey began. 'He was a lawyer. But to me, he was and will always be a warrior—a warrior who fought unrelentingly, all his life, for equality and justice. Over the last forty years it has been my great privilege to fight alongside him and I can honestly say that there has not been a day in those forty years that Joel hasn't made me laugh, hasn't taught me something new, hasn't made me proud to be his comrade. As I stand here now, it is hard for me—as I know it is for many of you—to imagine going on without him. But I know that Joel would not want me to be mournful today. I know that he would want me—would want us—to be looking to the future, to be thinking, even now, about how we can best continue the struggle. That is why, today, my children and I would like to announce that we are starting a foundation in Joel's name. The Litvinoff Foundation. Through this foundation, we will build on Joel's legacy by giving grants to progressive political and community initiatives that further the cause of social justice. In this way, we hope to keep moving forward to the truly equal and fair society that was Joel's dream.'

'Viva the revolution!' someone shouted and the cathedral erupted in cheers.

Jean looked at her friend's pale face peering over the lectern. So this was Audrey's choice: to be the keeper of the flame, the guardian of the fable. Like the tired old priest who loses his faith but cannot bring himself to disavow the Church, Audrey would hide whatever sacrilegious sentiments lurked in her heart and carry on the official forms of worship regardless. From now on, until she died, she would burnish the myth of the Litvinoffs' perfect union; she would fundraise tirelessly for Joel's 'foundation' and attend conferences to accept posthumous awards on his behalf and oversee the archiving of his papers. At some point, she would no doubt hand-pick an appropriately pliable young person to write his authorized biography.

Jean stopped herself, aware of a priggish, censorious tone entering her thoughts. Who was she to say that Audrey was making the wrong choice? Or that this charade of reverent widowhood did not require its own sort of stoicism and courage?

The applause was dying down. Audrey continued:

'No one as uncompromising as Joel was in his fight for the poor, the disenfranchised, the victims of racism and inequity, could have lived his life without earning the hostility of the right-wing press. For many years, Joel has been one of the favourite bogeymen of the forces of reaction in this country. And I have no doubt, that in the days to come, those forces will do their best to taint his legacy in any way they can. The family that Joel and I made together was not a conventional family in many ways. Joel always used to say that he didn't really believe in families. He believed in tribes. But let me say for the record now, ours was a joyous tribe.'

She paused.

'I would like now to introduce you to a very special member of our tribe: my dear friend, Berenice Mason, who is here today with her son—Joel's son, *our* son—Jamil . . . Berenice? Where are you? Please stand up.'

A ripple of whispers ran through the cathedral. Jean, along with three thousand others, swivelled in her seat to see Berenice slowly rising from one of the back pews. She looked terrified. Out of the silence, a little boy's voice said, 'Why's everybody looking at us, Mommy?' There was a great roar of laughter and applause.

'What's she talking about?' Julie hissed in Jean's ear. 'What is going on?'

Audrey concluded her speech now by asking that everyone join her in singing 'The Internationale', the verses of which had been provided on the back of the programmes. As the organ struck up the opening notes, she remained standing in the pulpit, staring out across the crowd, like Boadicea in her chariot.

> Arise ye workers from your slumbers
> Arise ye prisoners of want
> For reason in revolt now thunders
> And at last ends the age of cant.
> Away with all your superstitions
> Servile masses arise, arise
> We'll change henceforth the old tradition
> And spurn the dust to win the prize.

The post-memorial reception at Perry Street had been planned as a select affair for Joel's closest friends and family, but by the time Jean arrived at the house there were at least two hundred people crammed into the living room. Perspiring young men in black ties were weaving their way through the dense crowd, bearing platters of canapes. At the bar, people were struggling to retain a semblance of funereal dignity as they elbowed their way towards the vodka. Audrey's revelation had energized the party, it seemed. There was an exhilaration in the air—a sense that something scandalous and possibly historic had just taken place. Berenice and Jamil, the event's surprise star turn, were standing, looking slightly dazed, by the fireplace, surrounded by people clamouring to introduce themselves.

Unable to spot Audrey anywhere, Jean wandered back out into the hall. Lenny, who was sitting on the stairs with Tanya, nodded at her sheepishly. Earlier in the week, he had announced his intention to stay on in New York for a while. The carpentry business had proven less interesting than he had hoped, it seemed. And, besides, he had told Jean, he wanted to be 'there' for his mother.

In the kitchen, a small team of caterers was preparing plates of smoked fish, and Rosa, looking fetchingly biblical in a black headscarf, was standing by the refrigerator being interrogated by Julie about Audrey's funeral oration. 'This "tribe" thing,' Jean heard Julie say, 'what's it about then? Is it free love and all that?'

'I really couldn't say,' Rosa replied. 'You'll have to ask Mom.'

It occurred to Jean now that Audrey might be lurking in Joel's office, sneaking a joint. But down in the basement she found only a couple of waiters taking a cigarette break and discussing the work of Stephen Sondheim. At the sight of Jean, they jerked into professional postures of doleful respect. 'Oh, sorry! We were—'

She raised her hand to silence their apologies. 'It's quite all right. Stay where you are. I was just looking for someone.'

She climbed back up the stairs and at last caught sight of Audrey. She was standing in the hall, by the living-room door, receiving the condolences of a white-haired man in jeans and rainbow suspenders. Jean waited at a tactful distance for the man to finish but as soon as Audrey noticed her she beckoned her over and curtly dismissed the speech-maker.

'Ex-Weatherman,' she said, gesturing at his back as he trotted off into the living room. 'Boring little git too. I thought I was never going to get rid of him . . .' She smiled at Jean expectantly. 'So? What did you think? It went off pretty well, no?'

Jean chuckled. 'You are a dark horse, Audrey. I

had no idea you were planning that.'

'I wasn't sure until the last minute if I was going through with it. I was convinced I'd lose my bottle.'

'It was certainly quite a coup de theatre you pulled off.'

Audrey's expression darkened. 'What's that supposed to mean? It wasn't a fucking Broadway show, you know. It was my husband's funeral.'

Jean opened her mouth and then closed it again. The time for confidences was over, it seemed. Henceforth, not even she was to be privy to what lay beneath Audrey's official pose of happy tribeswoman. 'No, of course,' she stuttered. 'I only meant . . . Public speaking is always a kind of performance, isn't it? What you said about Berenice was lovely.'

Audrey shrugged, grudgingly mollified. 'Yeah, I worked hard on that. I really wanted to get it right. For Joel's sake.'

Mike appeared behind Audrey now and tapped her on the shoulder. 'Sorry to bother you, Ma, but have you seen Karla? I can't find her anywhere.'

Audrey shrugged. 'I expect she's around.'

'I looked upstairs and outside. I just can't imagine where she's got to.'

'Well, not to worry—'

'But it's her father's funeral reception. She can't just have *gone off.*'

Audrey sighed. 'Do stop whining, Mike. She's probably gone off for a quiet little blub somewhere. Why don't you let her be?'

*   *   *

A quarter of a mile away, Karla was standing in the

389

Fourteenth Street subway station, waiting for the L train to take her to Brooklyn.

'Just tell me where you are,' Khaled had said when she had called him from the street. 'Wait right there and I will come and get you.'

But Karla needed to maintain momentum. She did not want to hang around. 'No,' she had told him, 'I'm coming to you.'

A rat was moving about on the tracks. Distractedly, she observed its jerky, rodent motion. What would Mike do, she wondered, when it finally dawned on him that she was gone? He would not leave the reception straight away, she was sure of that. For a while at least, he would skulk on the sidelines of the party, torn between despising the Litvinoffs' fancy friends and yearning to be accepted into their magic circle. Eventually, the desire to be acknowledged would override his animosity and he would accost a few of the more famous guests. But they would be unnerved by his strange, angry sycophancy and they would quickly move off, mumbling excuses about drink refills. Infuriated by these unaccountable rejections, he would give up and go. He would ride the 4 train all the way back to the Bronx, and an hour or so later, when he arrived home, vibrating with pent-up fury and carefully plotted rebukes, he would find the apartment empty.

The train roared into the station and Karla stepped forward, planting one foot on the yellow line at the edge of the platform. What if this was all a vast mistake? What if she surfaced from her romantic dream a few months from now and discovered that she had ruined her marriage for nothing? It was not too late. She could still go back and tell everyone that she had been out for a walk. Mike would reprimand her; life would go on.

Ding-dang, the doors slid shut. She was on the train.

Her car was filled with a group of wide-eyed, slack-jawed French boys. She sat down and closed her eyes, letting herself be lulled by their pretty-sounding, incomprehensible chatter. After a couple of stops, the door to the next car slid open with an ugly clang and a scruffy, middle-aged black man stumbled in. The tourist boys stirred anxiously. 'Hello, ladies and gentlemen,' the man said. 'My name is Floyd. I am homeless and I suffer from diabetes. Please don't be nervous. I ain't begging. I am here to entertain you.'

He closed his eyes and let out a long, wordless falsetto note. The song was 'The Lion Sleeps Tonight'—a silly novelty number that Karla had always associated with oldies radio stations and kitsch. But now, hearing it sung in this dingy subway car, she was struck by its beauty. How simple and true it seemed! How filled with the mystery and sadness of life!

The train suddenly emerged from the tunnel, and the car was filled with daylight. They were crossing the Williamsburg Bridge. From the window, Karla could see the Brooklyn waterfront spread out before her: the Williamsburg clock tower, the brownstones of Brooklyn Heights, the smoke stacks of the Navy Yard, the skyscraper cranes of Red Hook pointing yearningly out to sea. She thought of Khaled, waiting for her in his apartment, and she willed the train to go faster. If she didn't get there soon, he might disappear, or decide that he didn't want her after all.

Floyd finished his song and began walking up and down the aisle, holding out a crumpled paper bag. 'Ladies and gentlemen, if you enjoyed my musicality, please show your appreciation with a financial donation. Nothing is too little or too large. I take coins, bills, cheques, American Express...'

The train was pulling into the station by the time he reached Karla. 'Thank you, ma'am,' he said with a bow as he took her dollar bill. 'Thank you and God bless you.' The doors opened and he jumped off. As the train began to move again, Karla glimpsed him standing on the platform, sorting through the money in his bag. He looked up as she passed and she had just enough time to raise her hand in an awkward gesture of salute and farewell, before the train picked up speed and she was plunged into the darkness of the tunnel once more.

ACKNOWLEDGEMENTS

I am very grateful to Yaddo and the MacDowell Colony for allowing me to take two brief but highly productive holidays from domestic life in order to work on this book. I would also like to thank Jennifer Barth, Amanda Urban, Juliet Annan, Gill Coleridge, Sarah Coward, Norman Rosenthal, Melvin Konner, Scott Rudin, Patrick McGrath, Patrick Marber, Tshering Dolma, Marina O'Connor, Colin Robinson and Lucy Heller for all sorts of help, literary, technical and otherwise. Above all, I am thankful to my daughters, Frankie and Lula, who always ask when I'm going to be done writing, and to my husband, Larry, who never does.